PRAISE FOR **THE E**

'I absolutely LOVED this book ... was great as you really did fee. ... .ugh you were involved in the story'

Donna Maguire

'I love how much the story twisted. It lead you first one way, then another and another and another... And I just didn't know what to believe. There were so many suspects, so many mysteries.'

Tea Party Princess

'Kept me gripped from start to finish, what else could you ask for from a thriller?'

Bookworm Blogger

'The tension is there, but it creeps up on you and I found the investigation to be very cerebral, with the perpetrator's meticulous planning. Louth has obviously researched this part of the novel thoroughly and I found his explanations of how things had been done truly fascinating.'

Portable Magic

'This is a cracking book [and] has Number 1 bestseller written all over it.'

Nigel Adams

Nick Louth is a best-selling thriller writer and an award-winning financial journalist. A 1979 graduate of the London School of Economics, he went on to become a Reuters foreign correspondent in 1987. He was for many years a *Financial Times* columnist, and a regular contributor to *Investors Chronicle, Money Observer,* and *MSN Money.* It was an experience at a medical conference in Amsterdam in 1992, while working for Reuters, that gave him the inspiration for *Bite,* which was published in paperback in 2007 and in 2014 went on to become a UK No. 1 ebook bestseller. *The Body in the Marsh* is his fourth thriller. Nick Louth is married and lives in Lincolnshire.

www.nicklouth.com

ALSO BY NICK LOUTH

THRILLERS

Bite

Heartbreaker

Mirror Mirror

Crocodile Tears (short story)

FINANCIAL

Multiply Your Money

Funny Money

Bernard Jones and the Temple of Mammon

Dunces with Wolves

*How to Double Your Money Every Ten Years
(Without Really Trying)* (eBook)

The Body
in the Marsh

NICK LOUTH

LUDENSIAN BOOKS

Paperback edition first published in Great Britain in 2017
by Ludensian Books

www.ludensianbooks.co.uk
www.nicklouth.com

eBook first published in Great Britain in 2017 by Canelo

Paperback ISBN: 978-0-9554939-5-9
eBook ISBN: 9781911591771

British Library Cataloguing in Publication Data
A CIP catalogue record for this book can be obtained
from the British Library

For Louise, as always

She hated confined spaces and had always been terrified of the dark. But the tiny pantry was still the best place to hide from him. Somewhere he'd never think to look. She had crouched in this cubbyhole as a child playing hide-and-seek on seaside holidays. Empty shelves, lined still with parchment-stiff newspaper, rustling even as she breathed. Once, they had been stocked with her grandmother's home-made jams, with Be-Ro flour, Atora suet and tin after tin of Fray Bentos. Translucent spiders, all stilted legs and no body, had tiptoed like glass ghosts on the high shelf, among her grandfather's bottles of Bass and the tin of Rover biscuits. There had been seaside picnics, the scream of gulls and Wall's ice cream in blocks like butter that fitted in oblong cornets. Memories steadied her breathing and stilled her fear like the grasp of a parental hand.

She remembered the day when, aged seven, she had hidden for hours with a torch and read all the newspaper on the shelves. One article stood out: *Daily Express*, 23 June 1954. Grisly discovery. Detectives baffled. A young woman's body in the marsh. Romney Marsh, just a mile away. A dismembered body. Dismembered. In pieces! She'd had to look the word up, and it gave her a frisson of fear and excitement. She'd read the article again and again. For two days she couldn't sleep. Was the murderer still around? Would he come to get her too, she had asked her grandmother.

The slow scrunch of tyres on pebbles, a gritty sound like the slow beating of butter and sugar with a wooden spoon, dragged her back to the here and now. The slam of a car door. Her heart was hammering as she heard the key turn in the rusted lock and the door squeak open just a few feet from where she crouched. He must not find her, or it would all end now.

The prophetic shriek of gulls again: death, death, death. The body in the marsh.

Dismembered.

Chapter One

Scafell, Lake District. Friday, 14 October 2016

Three o'clock on a Friday afternoon. Freezing rain was driving in horizontally, the gunmetal rock face glossy. Craig Gillard gritted his teeth and risked a glance below. Two pitches up Botterill's Slab on Scafell's Central Buttress, one of Britain's toughest rock climbs. Rags and banners of cloud cavorted beneath, masking the harsh fans of scree hundreds of feet below and the serpentine path further out towards Mickledore and Wasdale Head car park.

A long weekend in the Lake District, 300 miles north of his Surrey base, was the way to forget about being a detective. Here he wasn't a chief inspector, and there was no respect, just one 48-year-old man, a few slings and some slender bits of steel against the elements and the insistent pull of gravity. He was scared. But getting gripped here, on the hardest solo climb he'd ever done, was more intense than the flecks of fear that peppered police work. Over the years he'd faced down knife-wielding drug dealers, been wounded in a shotgun blast and felt the gnawing in the pit of his stomach before a drugs raid. This was different. More than the cold and the wind, it was him against himself. Pushing out to his own unknown limits. Mastering fear. Fighting fatigue.

The next rain blast brought icy fingernails trickling down his neck and between his tensed shoulder blades. The weather had been okay when he started: overcast and a light south-westerly, but the strengthening westerly and rain had come earlier than predicted. His left hand was getting chilled from where he'd dug out the choss, bits of soil and rubble, stuck in one of the cracks lower down. He'd got a skin flapper from a graze, which was bleeding slightly, and he wanted to take a breather to tape the wound closed. Two of those left-hand fingers – third and little – were numb, which wasn't a great sign as he wasn't quite halfway up. He let go of the crimp, clipped his sling to the nearest bolt with a karabiner, and fished a roll of medical tape from an external pocket.

A heavy squall blasted in, rocking Gillard on his precarious perch. Heavy cloud filtered only a sallow light, and rivulets of water ran down the rock face. As he wound the tape over the graze he glanced down, drawn by movement on the ground. There was a dog running around something by a boulder in the bracken. He reached around to his rucksack, undid the clips and rooted through for binoculars. He looped the Zeiss Terra's strap around his neck, insurance against clumsy fingers, and pressed the freezing lenses to his eyes. A woman, lying on her side. She was wearing an olive-green cagoule, dark-blue hat and pink leggings. She was a good few hundred metres above

4

the path and out of view of it. The hurrying walkers below, hoods up, faces to the path, had their backs to the driving sleet, everyone going in one direction. Down, away from her. No one could see her.

A twisted knee or ankle, up here on a day like this. Potentially fatal.

He bellowed down to the woman, but she was upwind. Hopeless. The howling gusts tore his words away. In return came a shower of polystyrene-like pellets of ice which bounced off every surface and stung his face. The temperature had dropped several degrees in just the last minute, and a slate-grey wedge of snow cloud was building to the west. The woman would need help. He reached into his jacket, slid out his iPhone.

And dropped it.

The plastic casing smacked once against the granite face and cartwheeled into the void, lost to sight in a second. He allowed himself two seconds' inventive cursing, then returned methodically to the task in hand: rearranging his gear, and beginning a series of careful but rapid belay descents, wishing he'd brought a rope to be able to move faster. The wind was sometimes horizontal, sometimes from below, every gust laden with icy, lashing fragments. It felt like an hour, but he was down on the top edge of the scree in less than 20 minutes.

He forced his unfeeling digits to unclip his rucksack, extracting mountain boots, gaiters and mittens. It was as hard as dressing with chopsticks. Then he hunted for heat pads, fumbling to tear the wrapping with his teeth. In the rucksack he had chocolate, water, an exposure bag, an orienteering compass, first aid kit and a powerful LED torch. Once finished, he turned back into the blinding sleet and threw himself diagonally across one scree gully after another, towards where he'd seen her. Long, sliding strides, each bringing a mini-avalanche of rocks and pebbles around his ankles. As he crested a ridge he saw her, now sitting with her back to a house-sized rock in the lee of the snow. She waved frantically at him, and he loped over.

'Thank God,' she said, her face pink with cold and framed by fronds of dark wet hair. She was shivering, and her fingers bone-white. 'I've hurt my leg chasing the bloody dog,' she said. The young black Labrador wagged his tail and leaned against her winsomely.

'I guessed as much. We need to get you off this mountain quickly.'

She had on cheap-looking trainers – soaked, muddy and worn out. A thin cagoule, a soaking hat. No proper boots, no exposure bag, no gloves, no compass or map, no whistle. No idea, clearly. She looked 30 or so, old enough to know better. A lecture was playing in Craig's head, but he had other priorities.

'Put these on,' Craig said, sliding off his mittens.

'What about you?' she said, putting them on anyway. 'Your hands look frozen too.'

'I have a thinner pair of gloves in my bag,' he lied. 'So what's your name?'

'Sam.'

'I'm Craig.'

'Very pleased to meet you, Craig.' She blew a sigh and squinted into the snow. 'My God, how am I going to get down? It's my sodding knee. I can't put weight on it.'

'Let me see.'

She lifted the hem of her cagoule. The leggings were ripped, and her knee, already swollen, had bled a fair way down her calf.

'I'm going to press gently; let me know if it hurts.' He carefully pressed around the edges.

'Ow! *Jesus*, you said *gently*.' He then tried to flex the joint, and she raised her complaints by an octave. The dog began to bark wildly. 'It's all right, Boris, he's trying to help.'

Craig smiled and ruffled the dog behind his warm velvety ears, earning a slow wag of acquiescence. 'I don't think it's broken, but it's a bad sprain. Have you called the mountain rescue?'

'There's no juice on my phone.' He must have given her a look, because she then retorted: 'Look. I didn't think I was coming all the way up here, did I? I was up to see my parents in Keswick for the weekend and they said Boris needed a good long walk, but then he got away from me and went piling up the fell.'

'There's a dead sheep just over there, he could probably smell it.'

'Another couple of hours and I'd probably have been in the same condition,' she said, and laughed. She had a lovely smile. 'So are you going to phone them?'

'Ah. I dropped my phone.'

'You dropped your phone?' She looked incredulously at him, and then began to smile. 'Is it broken, then?'

'I was up there,' he said, pointing into the crags that were just visible through the cloud. 'So I expect so, yes. I had got it out to call the mountain rescue…'

'For me?'

'Yes.'

'Sorry! I suppose I owe you a new phone, then.'

'No. It was my butter fingers. Still, it was an iPhone.'

'Ouch.'

'One of the old ones.'

'Still ouch. So how are we going to get help?'

'Can you stand?'

'Just about.' With his help, she clambered to her good leg, but couldn't put any weight on the other one. She tried to hobble a few steps with her arm around his shoulder, but he was too tall for her and the surface too uneven. After a few steps he stopped. 'We'll both die of cold this way,' he said, letting her lean against the rock. 'How much do you weigh?'

She stared at him open-mouthed. 'Well, I'm not exactly Kate Moss, in case you hadn't noticed. You won't be able to carry me.'

'Well, if you prefer, we can always build the self-assembly helicopter I keep in my rucksack and fly out of here.'

'Don't be sarky.' She let out a yell of frustration. 'Christ, I take the dog for a walk and end up needing Superman to rescue me.'

Craig laughed and packed Sam's small rucksack inside his own, and strapped it on his chest. He crouched down with his back to her.

'Have you done much elephant-lifting before?' she said, as she put her arms around his neck. Despite her protestations, she wasn't heavy, and slim enough for him to give her a piggyback and join his hands under her bottom. The heat was an unexpected bonus. He gradually began to pick his way down the slope.

'Giddy-up,' she said, sniggering in his ear. 'I'll get you a nice bale of hay in Wasdale.'

He gave a little whinny in response.

The first half-hour was the worst, the rough rocks hidden in the bracken and the uneven tussocks of grass sending jolts which made her cry out. 'Sorry about squawking in your ear,' she said. The sleet turned to unremitting snow, and suddenly there was nothing to see more than five yards ahead. Craig made a decision.

'Change of plan. This will hurt, but we'll be on the path in five minutes.' He bucked her higher on his back, urged her to hang on, and began to run a long, steep scree trail. The dog bounded ahead, almost lost to the white-out. Craig was barely able to keep his footing with the extra weight, each giant stride a calculated but exhilarating risk. As he reached the path, breathless, a euphoric heat rose in his torso, perspiration gathered warm along his back and armpits, beating out the cold and finally reaching his aching hands. He set Sam down against a rock and shared his chocolate with her.

'God, it's even fair trade,' she said. 'You're well equipped for rescuing modern women, aren't you?'

'I rescued an entire group of women on Ben Nevis one January,' he said. 'They were on the first-ever attempt to reach the summit with ice axes and tampons.'

Sam groaned. It was an hour later when they finally descended into a snowy Wasdale. The lake was a brooding grey-green, flecked by pewter ripples. The car park was within sight, and beyond it the beckoning vision of a warm and welcoming pub.

Sitting steaming in the crowded stone-flagged inn with an obedient and sleepy Boris between her knees, Sam watched Craig ordering coffees at the bar. His tousled pepper-and-salt hair and rugged man-of-the-mountains face looked good on him, and for his age – perhaps mid-40s – he was clearly in great shape. He had carried her without complaint for several miles, stopping only twice. Her vile ex, Gary, for all his Parachute Regiment training, could not have done better. In fact, he would probably have made her crawl. Craig had bandaged her knee, dressed her cuts and slipped these amazing heat pads into her sodden trainers. He had thought ahead too. While she had refused his offer of a trip to hospital, he had borrowed a phone from a fellow walker so she could ring her parents. He had offered to drive her the 90-minute trip all the way back to Keswick to pick up her father and bring him here to retrieve her car which, because of her knee, she couldn't now drive. Craig might be a decade older than Gary, but quite a catch. For someone of the right age, she reminded herself.

In the meantime, she hobbled to the Ladies to make herself look human. The image in the mirror was a shock: her shoulder-length raven hair was wild and witch-like, her face bright red and her lips pale and chapped. A little lippy, a touch of eyeliner and a good brush made her feel a lot better. Self-respect restored, she emerged to find Craig waiting to help her thread her way back among the seats and tables to their space in the corner by the fire.

'So you've warmed up now?' Craig said, his eyes flicking to the heaped cagoule on the adjacent chair.

'Yes, thank you. But my leg's going to be a problem for work. I'm supposed to spend half my day on a bicycle.' She had decided to trust him with what she did for a living, something she rarely did until she knew what the reaction would be.

'Oh yes?'

'I'm a hobby bobby. You know, Police Community Support…'

He laughed and looked at the ceiling. 'That is hilarious,' he said.

Maybe she had misjudged him. She had found that almost everyone had a fixed view on the police, one way or another.

'Excuse me, we do a good job, for much less money…' her voice was strident, and she found she was pointing at him.

'I know you do.' He held up his hands in surrender. 'So where are you based?' he asked. *When had he found time to comb his hair?*

'At Caterham, in Surrey.' She watched his jaw drop. 'I just started last month. They're going to think I'm such an idiot.'

'No, they won't. They'll be happy to put you on the phones until your leg is better.' He really grinned this time, like warm sunshine. His eyes looked grey-green in the light. 'I'm in the Surrey force too, based in Guildford, but I live in Banstead. Not too far from your area.'

'You're kidding me. What do you do?'

He took out his wallet and slipped her his business card. She held it up and started to read in a mock American drawl: 'Detective Chief Inspector Craig Gillard. Hero and Rescuer. Prepared for every weather. Piggybacks a speciality.'

Half an hour later, with the darkness gathering, they were in Craig's car heading on the A66 to Keswick. He asked her lots of questions, and she confided in him about Gary. How when she had broken up with him, he refused to accept it. How he had called her day and night, making threats, coming round to see her, especially at night. Even when he had broken into her house, the police had been reluctant to take action. So she had borrowed money from her dad to get a court order, which was due to be heard in a month's time. Craig listened in silence.

'So are you married, then?' she asked suddenly, realizing she knew nothing about him.

'Was once.' His eyes narrowed, as if something on the road ahead could no longer be clearly discerned. 'It was quite short. It didn't work out. I suppose I'm quite difficult. That's what Valerie told me anyway.' He turned to Sam with a shrug. 'But it's partly the job, as you will discover.'

Sam had already noticed that Craig's car, a grey Nissan, was unusually tidy for someone who was a keen walker. No mud in the footwell, no discarded clothing on the back seat or parcel shelf, no sweet papers or other junk in the pockets, no stains on the seats or greasy marks on the steering wheel. Evidence of an ordered mind. But perhaps one entirely without passion. When they got to her parents' street of stone-built terraced houses she said: 'I'm so grateful for everything you did today, Craig. I don't know what would have happened to me if you hadn't seen me up there. You've probably saved my life, and wouldn't even let me buy you a coffee.'

'Maybe there'll be another opportunity,' he said. 'For the coffee. And good luck with your career.'

He got out to help her with her gear from the boot, and before she let him guide her down the path, she turned her face to him and stretched up to give him a kiss. Quick, but on the lips, and briefly reciprocated with an added touch of stubble. 'Thank you, Craig.' As she turned away she felt his eyes on her. She wanted to walk tall and swing her hips a little, but on the first step she staggered straight into the gate post.

Chapter Two

The tragic and unnecessary death of Girl F is a staggering indictment of the bigotry, myopia and indolence of the British police mentality. This young girl, in a desperate cry for help, begged for justice. But because she didn't fit the victim stereotype, what she got instead was prejudice, procrastination, and – even now, years after her death – platitudes.

(LSE criminologist Professor Martin Knight, interviewed on BBC *Newsnight*, September 2013)

Tuesday, 18 October, 8 a.m.

Gillard drove back to Surrey Police HQ in Guildford, feeling restless. What had been sleet in Cumbria was just rain in Surrey, but there was plenty of it. There hadn't been a decent gap in the weather for the rest of the weekend, and though he'd tramped a good 60 miles in all – around Wastwater, up Kirk Fell and amid teeming parties of schoolkids to the top of Great Gable – he'd given up his last chance for a really demanding rock climb. With a sinking feeling he remembered that another report was coming out soon about Girl F, a case that had for years been the bane of Surrey Police. A girl of 13 threw herself in front of a train back in 2009 after reporting repeated abuse by older men. The case, mishandled from the outset and still without a suspect, was now in the hands of the hindsight experts: highly paid barristers, child psychologists and criminologists deciding at their leisure what procedure should have been followed. One officer in the crosshairs was Detective Superintendent Paddy Kincaid, Gillard's own boss. Back in 2009 Kincaid was a DCI investigating Girl F's suicide, but had made little progress in finding out who had abused her. After criticisms from the family's legal team he had eventually been removed from the case.

The atmosphere at HQ would probably be foul, Gillard decided. To cheer himself up, he slid a CD of '80s hits into the player, and let his thoughts turn to Sam Phillips, the ill-prepared but shapely PCSO.

As he passed the security barrier, the imposing edifice of Mount Browne loomed. The former home of the Marquis of Sligo, the Gothic-style red-brick building boasted mullioned windows and high gables in extensive grounds. Behind it squatted the cramped and crowded car park and a hideous 1960s office block, Gillard's base for the last five years.

His deputy, DS Claire Mulholland, was already there in the incident room, gripping her chipped mug emblazoned with wobbly glaze: *Mum – world's best detective*. Her son Collum had made the mug at school when he was eight, and even though the handle had come off in the intervening seven years, few would take issue with the boast. If not the best, she was certainly pretty damn good. Claire's solid physique belied her former career as dance teacher and tae kwon do instructor. The day after finishing training as a WPC, the five-foot-five blonde mother of three had been put on a drugs raid, with instructions to stand at the back and keep out of the way. But when the gang's six-foot-three enforcer tried to stab a fellow officer, Claire had famously taken him down with a single kick to the stomach.

After greeting her, Gillard asked: 'So what's the latest on Girl F?'

'Coldrick has asked Alison Rigby to restart the cold case review,' she said. Assistant Chief Constable Rigby was a high-flyer, appointed by Chief Constable Graham Coldrick three months ago. She'd come from the National Crime Agency, with a reputation as a control freak.

'Kincaid will not be a happy bunny,' Gillard said, unable to control the smile on his face.

Caterham police station could be mistaken for a neglected suburban library were it not for the solitary patrol car outside. It was built for a full complement of officers, but now it was only intermittently staffed. Three civilian PCSOs and a desk sergeant, in theory. Today was more typical. PCSO Samantha Phillips was the only officer in the building, answering calls, logging incidents, the full desk-bound tedium.

It was late morning when the main Surrey call centre put through a report of a missing person in her neighbourhood.

'Oh, hello. My name's Katherine Parkinson, and I'd like to report a missing person. Liz Knight. She's a close friend of mine, and she's not turned up for work for two days. That's really not done if you are deputy head of a secondary school. Her husband's away at a conference in York and when I rang him he said he hasn't seen her since Friday. I'm really quite worried. It's so unlike her.'

Sam made detailed notes. Female, 48, missing at least two days. Not answering emails, her mobile seemingly switched off, and not returning calls to her landline. No answer at the doorbell. The address was Chaldon Rise, a crescent of beautiful houses in Old Coulsdon, where the southern fringes of London's suburban sprawl washed up against the chalky hills of the North Downs. A place Sam would love to live, if she won the lottery.

Thinking back to her missing persons training, Sam asked: 'Would you describe Mrs Knight as a vulnerable adult?'

'You mean easily led, or mentally impaired, something like that?' The caller laughed softly. 'No. I would classify Liz as anything but vulnerable. She's a dynamic, busy, confident and highly intelligent individual quite able to look after herself.'

'Are there any children?'

'Yes, two. Well, not children any more, and not at home. Oliver is a solicitor, 20-something, doing very well for himself, and Chloe has just gone up to Cambridge, her mother's Alma Mater. There's only Liz and her husband at home, though he travels a lot.

'Do you work with her, Ms Parkinson?'

'No, but I've known her for, gosh, 30 years. We're also in amateur dramatics together. Just a small village production, you know, but she failed to show up for a rehearsal for *The Mikado* last night, which is absolutely not her at all.'

'When did you speak to her husband?'

'Just an hour or so ago. He's breaking off the conference to come home, though he's not happy about it.'

'Why is that?'

'He thinks I'm being overly dramatic. And overly amateur with it, probably. He didn't want me to report her missing to you.'

'Did he say why not?'

'Well, he says he thinks he knows where she might be.'

'So why didn't you say this before?' Sam said, turning her pen over and over between her fingers.

'He thinks she has gone to Great Wickings. That's their holiday cottage, down on the Kent coast. It's a funny little wooden place, more like an overgrown shack really, close to that monstrosity of a nuclear power station at Dungeness. Anyway, it's where she goes when she needs to think or when they've had a tiff. She's got a little studio there, and likes to paint.'

'So don't you think it is possible that is where she is?' Sam asked.

'Well, perhaps. I have rung and left messages. But it's strange. You see, it's quite possible that she wouldn't want to speak to *him* if she was down there after they'd had a row. Completely possible. But she would certainly pick up the phone to me. I mean, I'm her closest friend. Have been for years. She certainly hasn't had a tiff with *me*. And she is such a stickler for courtesy and reliability. So I just cannot believe she wouldn't call in sick to the school or for the rehearsal.'

Sam concurred.

'Look,' Kathy said. 'It's possible this may turn out to be just some domestic crisis, but I would hate it if something had happened to her and nobody had tipped you off. I mean, you hear such terrible things now, don't you?'

'Of course.'

'One final thing,' she added. 'When you speak to Martin, don't say that I reported her missing. He's a bit fiery, and he might think I'm interfering. Can you just say it was the school?'

'I won't mention your name,' Sam said, and after thanking her, hung up.

Over the next three hours Sam Phillips spoke to the headmaster at Liz Knight's school, her friend Helen Jennings, and Bruce Cornwell, director of *The Mikado*. All backed up Kathy Parkinson's story. Liz Knight seemed to have vanished, and no one had heard from her since last week. She then made her fourth attempt to get through to the husband, Martin Knight.

'Knight.' The word was barked like an impatient goodbye.

'My name is Sam Phillips from Surrey Police. Am I speaking to Martin Knight?' The PCSO could hear a train conductor making announcements in the background.

'Professor Martin Knight, yes.'

'Of number 16 Chaldon Rise, Old Coulsdon, Surrey? Can I just ask you to confirm your postcode, sir?'

'Oh for God's sake. I think I'd better have yours first, young lady. How do I know this isn't some joker?'

After a few minutes' jousting over identity, Knight made his point and the PCSO gave him confirmation of the station's own address.

'Now if we can return to the main point, Mr Knight—'

'Professor…'

'We've had a report that your wife, Elizabeth, is missing—'

'I know very well what my wife is called, PC Phillips. You are a PC, I take it?'

'I'm a PCSO actually. Now, about your wife—'

'Shouldn't you be out on the beat? Cycling around in high-vis or something, searching for symptoms of anti-social behaviour? I've just come out of a meeting with the Home Secretary, and she was very receptive to my opinion that at well over £100,000 per crime detected, spending on the PCSO programme would be better targeted elsewhere.' He paused for a moment, and the tone of his voice softened. 'Look, I'm very sorry that you have been disturbed with this. I'm pretty certain that I know where Liz is, and I'm going to go there this evening.' Good cop, bad cop, Sam thought. And he isn't even a cop.

She persisted. 'When did you last see her?'

'At breakfast on Friday morning. She mentioned she was going down to Kent for the weekend to paint, which is where I'm sure she still is.'

'I've just rung your holiday home. There was no reply…'

There was a short silence. 'Look, I'd appreciate you not ringing our children about this. Chloe's only just gone up to

Cambridge, and it would worry her silly. At least not until I've had a chance to check out Great Wickings for myself. I'll ring you around six or so. If Liz isn't there, you have my full permission to dig up the garden and burrow under the patio,' he chuckled.

Sam took down the address of Great Wickings. Finally, she asked: 'Would you ring this number as soon as you get down to the house. Quote incident number 459.'

'I'll do better than that. I'll put her on the phone to talk to you herself, to put your mind at rest,' he said. 'And I'd like to apologize on my wife's behalf for putting you all to so much trouble.' The line went dead.

'I think I'd bloody vanish to get away from him,' Sam muttered as she reached for her notepad.

Sam Phillips had been due off at six, and it was now nearly seven. It had been a busy afternoon. A toddler had been rushed to hospital after an accident riding a supermarket trolley in Purley, and there were reports of vandalism at Coulsdon South railway station. She was just turning off her computer when she remembered Professor Knight. She checked the incident log, and then spoke to one of the control room staff. No call.

Just then she saw DCI Craig Gillard walk in wearing cycling gear. The full figure-hugging works, helmet with camera, plus soft green pointy shoes that clacked as he walked.

'Hello, stranger,' she said, catching her breath and thinking: *this cannot be coincidence.*

'Hello, Sam. How's the knee?'

'Not too bad so long as I sit with a bag of ice on it. I still need crutches for stairs. Naturally, I've had no end of grief about the incident from the rest of the team.' *He's come to see me!*

He smiled. 'I was just passing but thought I'd pick up the evidence for the Jackson case.'

A likely story. Sam wasn't familiar with the case, but looked it up. 'Is that the briefcase handed in yesterday?'

'Yes. It's not been checked for fingerprints or drug residues, has it?'

'No. It's still here.' She unlocked the evidence room, little more than a large stationery cupboard, and showed Craig in. 'It's on the top shelf if you wouldn't mind reaching.'

Craig leaned up and pulled down a huge brown paper evidence bag, while Sam glanced at his firm muscular legs and nice tight bum. Decidedly easy on the eye.

He hefted the bag and hesitated for a moment before starting to make his way out. 'Thank you, Sam. I'll be seeing you.'

Sam felt a small ripple of panic. He was *shy*, oh God. Come on, Craig, come on. Say something. 'Before you go, can I ask you a favour?' she blurted out.

'Of course.' He turned back to her and smiled.

She felt herself blush. 'I've had a missing person report this morning.' She described the bare bones of the case. 'The husband's gone off to find her and promised he would call either way an hour ago. He didn't, and didn't reply to the last message I left, so I went round to the house. No one answered the door, and neighbours say neither of their cars is there. So I was just wondering if you'd mind phoning him for me. He was quite rude to me last time. Reckons he's best pal with the Home Secretary.'

Gillard laughed. 'I've heard that one a few times.' That smile again. Sam slid the form across. 'It's *Professor* Knight,' she emphasized. 'He's quite up himself, to be honest. If someone senior like you rings him, at least you might get a bit of respect.'

Gillard rang the number, and when it clicked into voicemail he left a brief message and hung up. 'I'll try a bit later,' he said. 'You know, Sam, in this case he actually does know the Home Secretary,' Gillard said, still looking down at the inquiry notes.

Sam watched his expression freeze then soften, as if trying to contain something powerful. She'd seen the same struggle for control when she'd gone with a PC to tell a mother her son had been knocked off his motorbike and killed.

'So Liz Knight is missing.' He pursed his lips.

'Mrs Elizabeth Knight, yes. Do you know her?'

He glanced at Sam with narrowed grey-green eyes. 'Yes, vaguely.'

Sam had only been out of PCSO training for a month. But she knew a whopping lie when she heard one.

Chapter Three

Craig Gillard had known Liz Knight for almost exactly 30 years. Or, to be more exact, for a few short but blissful weeks 30 years ago. He and Roger Carlton were sixth formers at Beechcroft Technical College in Purley, and at Roger's instigation they had gatecrashed the sixth form summer barn dance at the Wallington High School for Girls. They had one objective in mind and one only: as Roger put it, to each find some high-class bit of stuff from the snob school and shag them senseless. Free tickets had been issued to a few of the fee-paying boys' schools in the area, but not to the nearby working-class schools in Purley. Roger's older brother Clive was employed as a lab assistant at one of the boys' schools and had pilfered a handful of tickets.

Roger, six feet tall and a rugby player, was by his own account the more experienced. 'I'll have first pick, obviously. You can have the flat-chested one,' he had laughed. Craig didn't much care so long as he finally got his end away. Roger had a *Miami Vice* T-shirt underneath a white jacket, Levi 501s, cowboy boots and sunglasses. Craig had a black long-sleeved shirt and trousers, an Adam Ant waistcoat with silvery buttons, and a pair of winkle-pickers he'd found in a charity shop. He'd slapped on rather too much Brut, hoping it would draw attention away from his acne. Roger had accused him of stinking like a cut-price Moroccan rent boy, as if he had any knowledge of that subject. After each having three pints of Stella, they rolled up at a quarter to eleven, unaware that they were almost at the end of festivities. 'Oh, will you look at that,' said Roger, watching a dazzlingly pretty girl laughing with two friends. 'I've got a hard-on already.' Craig felt intimidated by these confident leggy girls in their elegant dresses, their glossy hair and clear eyes. They made him feel inferior and unworthy. The other boys – well, men in many cases – looked sophisticated and moneyed in their expensive suits. It was the first time he'd ever felt what his father would have called class envy.

Craig and Roger armed themselves with a glass each of Buck's Fizz, which Roger complained was mostly orange juice, and picked among the stragglers. Roger, despite the firm pact to act as a team, was soon dancing with a tall girl with a long nose and glasses, but who sported what he would have called a 'rather fine pair'. Craig walked towards the remains of the food, which was laid out on a trestle table.

As he did so, he caught the eye of a pretty and petite chestnut-haired girl with shapely legs, who was with a mixed group of what Roger would have called 'retreads': less than top-notch crumpet, with glasses, straight hair, flat shoes and longer skirts with pleats or, in one case, corduroy. The boys around them were skinny, jug-eared and gawky. Tomorrow's mathematicians and programmers. Faced by these less overwhelming odds, Craig walked over to the group with a plate of pineapple and cheese in hand.

'Anyone for a chunk?' he said, perhaps the oddest opening line he'd ever tried.

'All right, I'll have a "chunk", said the pretty girl, smiling at him with soft brown eyes.

'I wouldn't, it'll give you zits,' said one of the taller boys, flicking his eyes towards Craig.

'Don't be silly, Tim,' said the girl, turning away from him. 'Which school are you from?' she asked Craig.

'Eton,' he said. The one word brought a huge guffaw from the group, who clearly thought it the funniest thing they'd ever heard. The girl stared sharply at them. 'Come on, Eton pineapple, let's get a drink. Pay no attention to the sneerers.' She steered him by his elbow, her fingers warm and pleasant on his skin. When they were a little distance away, she let go and said: 'You're brave, aren't you?'

'What do you mean?'

'Sneaking up here, into the posh school. Enemy territory, so to speak.' She smiled and tucked a piece of hair behind one ear. 'So what's your name?'

'Craig. And I've got a ticket, cost me a fiver.'

'Aha, a black marketeer too. Well *carpe diem*! She clinked her plastic cup of Buck's Fizz against his. I'm Liz. So where are you planning to go?'

Craig looked around, as if there was somewhere else to go. The band was packing up its instruments, and expensive parental cars were beginning to swarm at the drive at the bottom of the hill. 'Er, nowhere. But we could go to The Bell if you like. They serve after hours.' He was astounded at his own nerve.

Liz roared with laughter, a much deeper and more infectious laugh than he had expected. 'No, silly. After the summer. Which university?'

'Oh, I haven't decided.' In truth, he was far from sure he'd get the grades. 'What about you?'

'I'm going up to Cambridge. It's a bit of a family tradition. I'd thought about choosing music, but it's so hard to earn a crust, isn't it? So I've decided to study history and modern languages at Corpus Christi. But I might switch to economics for my master's and doctorate.' She took a sip of her drink, and eyed him to assess his reaction.

'And where have you chosen for your funeral?'

'Oh, what a wit. Come on, let's ring in at The Bell.' With that she hooked her arm through his and led him down the long sweeping drive, lined with rhododendrons and roses, that led to Cressington Road. In truth, the gentle descent of that hill, with a woman on his arm and the scent of roses in his nostrils was the first shaft of pure sunlight through the grey clouds of his youth. He could never recall the next two hours' conversation in detail, except that he couldn't fathom half the things she said. The way she peppered strange, presumably Latin, phrases into her conversation, and the way she seemed to show a genuine interest in what he thought: about politics, about religion and books. Her mind seemed like a library, packed with books he had never read but wanted to. She was able to extract quotes from them without effort.

When the pub finally closed, and the back bar frequented by underage drinkers was finally cleared of its throng by a world-weary landlord, loudly wondering if any of them had homes to go to, Craig spotted Roger. He was standing in the car park with his brother and a group of mates. Their only partners were cans of lager. A wolf whistle pierced the air as they spotted Craig with a pretty girl. Roger's expression was of unguarded envy. It was a moment Craig had dreamed about.

Liz turned to him and asked: 'Friends of yours?'

'Yeah. Well, I know them. Don't pay them any attention.'

'Well, let's give them something to talk about.' She reached up to him and kissed him gently on the mouth. It was the softest, warmest and most slickly exciting sensation he could recall. 'That should send your stock soaring when you next see them,' she whispered.

Liz allowed him to walk her to the end of her road. She pointed out her home, which was a large 1930s mock-Tudor detached house in a secluded street with views across the valley towards Farthing Downs, a local beauty spot. They kissed for a few blissful minutes, until she reminded him that it was past one o'clock. She took his number, promised to call, and then pointed him home. Craig floated the whole three miles back to South Croydon, drunk on dreams.

Chapter Four

Being in the hospital isn't so bad. It's the dawn of a new millennium, and the staff don't treat you like you're mad. The food is grim and institutional – not so much the taste, but the nursery room context: unbreakable melamine plates, no-spill beakers, flimsy plastic knives barely able to injure linguine, let alone wrists. All we need now is a ball pit and a bouncy castle. But some of the other patients are, well, frightful. As a prognosis for those who can't haul themselves out of the dark depths, these shadow residents are mutely articulate. The most terrifying thing came from outside these forbidding walls. It was the look on my children's faces when they came to visit. Chloe goggled at me and eventually asked: 'Is this a loony bin, Mummy?' Martin told her off, but she'd picked the phrase up from somewhere.

Oliver couldn't look me in the eyes at all. He kept fiddling with his Game Boy, and when I put my arms on his shoulders to cuddle him, he squirmed away as if I was that creature from Alien, erupting from someone's stomach. And all the time, my *precious husband, the man whose behaviour put me here, is smiling indulgently, an arm around each child as if they've come on a trip to the zoo, to see this, the scariest but most endangered animal in the place.*

Liz Knight, letter to Kathy Parkinson, February 2000

Tuesday evening

Craig got home just after 7.30 p.m. He was the on-call DCI from eight until midnight. Before he logged in to what would inevitably be a torrent of minor cases, he decided to have a second crack at ringing Professor Knight. He'd surely have arrived at Dungeness by now. Knight's mobile again went to voicemail, so Craig dialled the holiday home landline. It barely rang before it was picked up.

'Knight.'

'Professor Knight, it's Chief Inspector Gillard of Surrey Police. We were expecting a call from you, as you seem now to be at the house.'

'Good God, man, I've only just this second got here. Literally walked into the house and taken my coat off. I really was going to ring.'

'So I take it Mrs Knight is there.'

'Actually no, I think not. Her car's not here, so she must still be out somewhere. Much too dark for painting now, I would have thought. Bear with me, and I'll check her studio. That'll give a clear answer.'

'I'll stay on the line, sir,' Gillard said.

The buzz indicated a cordless handset on the move. 'Liz, darling, are you here?' Gillard heard footsteps and the squeak of a door. 'Liz?' Knight's voice then came back on the line. 'It doesn't look like she's been using the studio. She was intending to be here over the weekend. But the art stuff has been packed up. This is most mysterious. I do apologize for not taking it seriously when the PCSO called. Now, I must confess, I am a tad worried.'

'Well, take a good look around and call me either way. I'm off duty from midnight, so if it's later just leave a message with the duty officer. I'm sure she will turn up.'

'Yes indeed. Goodbye.' The line went dead.

Gillard was relieved that Knight hadn't realized that they had met, a couple of times, decades ago. The very first time, Knight would have had no idea, perhaps not even been aware of his existence. But for Gillard the first glance at his rival was seared into memory. Christmas Eve, 1986. He was just 19, and was riding his Kawasaki 250. It was a fearsomely fast bike, bought, on credit, mainly to impress his friends. He had pulled up at red traffic lights at the bottom of Marlpit Lane. There was one car in front, a racing green MGB 1.8 Roadster, a gorgeous vehicle beyond his wildest dreams. Through the back window Gillard could see a woman passenger turn to the right and speak to the male driver. She had wavy brown hair, which she swept back with a hand, and a gentle nose. He would know that profile anywhere. The two profiles, male and female, merged and kissed even as the lights turned to green. Pressing the Kawasaki's tinny horn for all he was worth, Craig gunned the bike and sped past. As he crossed onto the A23 he pulled a somewhat risky wheelie, roaring south towards Gatwick at 85mph with tears of rage and agony fogging his vision.

Gillard went to the fridge and took out three different M&S ready meals. Taking a moment to decide, he plumped for the Thai green curry, pricked the lid with a knife, and placed it in the microwave. To accompany it he took out a nicely chilled Cobra beer, and sat down to watch TV. Once again he thought about the bubbly young PCSO Sam Phillips, who had literally fallen into his life. She had nice dark wavy hair, and a rather lovely mouth, almost Brazilian in its kissable pout. But he'd bottled his chance to ask her out. Well, there was a reason for that. As soon as he realized Liz was missing, it just seemed wrong somehow. It wasn't a time to be thinking about anyone else.

The noise downstairs was subtle but Sam woke with a start. A click and a squeak, as if a door was being opened. She grabbed for her phone, which she now always kept by the side of the bed. She flipped on the bedside light and listened. Since the last time, the bedroom door had two huge bolts fitted on the inside, and there was a state-of-the-art window lock. When the fitters came, she had used the excuse that burglaries in this part of Croydon were quite common. But really it was all about Gary. When she'd moved house again, and started her new job, she thought she would feel safer. But that didn't last long. He'd found her within a month, smashed up her car and sprayed 'whore' on her front door. He would never give up. He'd always said that. She was his forever, he had said. If the threat of a court order hadn't stopped him, nothing would. He just didn't care. For a long minute she heard nothing, and began to relax, but then she heard the stair creak.

She had been going to ring 999, but hesitated. Gary had managed to trash her reputation with the Met Police, in whose patch she lived. The first two occasions she had called, after loud noises downstairs at three in the morning, the cops had come screaming in, sirens blaring, but by the time they arrived there was no one there. No sign of forced entry. The look she'd got from the male PCs when they asked her what she did for a living spoke volumes too. Her new neighbours had complained about the row the next day. The third emergency call, just last week, they'd taken an hour to come. No sirens. And they treated her like *she* was the criminal. Gary was clever. It was a campaign to undermine her in the eyes of friends, neighbours and colleagues. He was saying to her: you'll only ever have me, because everyone else knows you're worthless.

She scrolled to recently added contacts, which showed Craig's work mobile. It was half four in the morning. Could she dare to ring him, to ask for yet another favour? The bedroom door handle began to turn, slowly and stealthily. Her heart in her mouth, she watched it reach the maximum point and the door shift just inwards a millimetre until it ran up against the bolts. The hissed words carried clearly from the landing: 'Samantha. It's *me*, your beloved but *neglected* boyfriend. Let me in.'

She hit the 'call' button, and for the second time in a week, began to shiver uncontrollably.

The unfamiliar ringtone of his new iPhone cut straight through Gillard's dreams, and he grabbed it to still the noise. He had somehow expected it to be Martin Knight. When he heard the state of Sam's voice he was out of bed in a second, dressed in a minute and, pausing only to grab a stab vest, into his unmarked police Ford Focus in two. She'd begged him not to alert the Met, but had agreed to keep the line open while he punched her address into the satnav. It quoted him 20 minutes. At this time of night he reckoned he could be there in half that. He slid the phone into the cradle on the dashboard, put it on speaker, and was doing 60 down Winkworth Road when he heard Sam's screams as the door to her room burst open. There was a man's voice, a bang, some whimpering and the line went dead ten seconds later. It wasn't answered on recall.

The rest of the drive was an agony of not knowing. It was only as he was pulling into Sam's cul-de-sac that she called him back on a Surrey Police mobile. Between sobs, she said her ex had just left.

'Are you okay?'

'He punched me a couple of times, but yes.'

Just as she spoke, a white Audi A3 shot past Craig in the other direction. Craig pulled a discreet U-turn and followed the car on a right-hand turn towards the main road. He asked Sam to describe her ex. The details weren't encouraging. Gary Harrison was six foot three, a paratrooper who'd served in Afghanistan and now worked as a chef. Knives. Violent temper. The stab vest had been a good move.

'Don't tangle with him, Craig, I don't want you to get hurt.'

'It's okay. I'll be careful.'

'He's stolen my phone again. He'll be going through it to see if I have a boyfriend.'

'Do you?'

'I did until a month ago, until Gary threatened him. He'll see your name and number too.'

'I can handle that.' Craig pulled up behind the car at traffic lights. The street lamp glare stopped him seeing the driver, but he memorized the number plate. The Audi had slowed, and he could hear the bass hammering of rap resonating through the chassis. There were no signs the driver was aware of being followed. That would undoubtedly change at some point, given how little traffic there was. Craig fell back 100 metres, intending to trail Harrison to his home, an address in New Addington that Sam had just given him. But then the Audi pulled into a large all-night petrol station on the Purley Way. Craig slid the Ford Focus into the space by the car wash, slipped on a pair of thin black gloves, and watched. The man who emerged was every bit as big as Sam had said, crop-haired, wearing a brown bomber jacket, jeans and high-top trainers. He walked with a gym-user's swagger, as if carrying an invisible roll of carpet under each arm. He tossed his car keys in his hand, and seemed to be humming. There was no orange flash of locking.

Craig realized that Gary Harrison was probably quite pleased with himself.

Bastard.

While Harrison was approaching the shop, Craig slid his vehicle up right behind the Audi as if to refuel, and then looked through his door pocket looking for useful tools. There wasn't much. A phone charger and cable, a roll of gaffer tape and a heavy-duty Tesco plastic carrier bag. He stuffed them in his pockets, got out of the car and slipped forward three metres and into the Audi through a rear door. He lay sideways, as much into the rear footwell as possible, his concealment aided by charcoal-grey upholstery which matched his stab vest. There were non-standard sports seats in there, and Craig had a quick look for the recline lever. Harrison was back in a minute, tossed a crackling bag of some kind of snack onto the passenger seat, gunned the engine, then drowned them both in music. The Audi left the forecourt, turned hard right back onto the Purley Way, then took a left after a short while. Craig could only see the street lamps and the tops of houses, still enough to distinguish a residential street from a major road. He waited to make his move until the sound of passing traffic diminished and the car had slowed.

He swung up between the front seats and pulled the plastic bag over Harrison's head, twisting it tight around his neck and yanking it back. There was a shocked gasp, and the car screeched to a halt in the middle of the road and then stalled. Craig tied the phone cable around the neck of the bag, then twisted it around the base of the headrest assembly. As Harrison's hands shot up to scrabble at the cable, Craig triggered the seat recline and pulled Harrison back so he could really get at him. A massive punch to the solar plexus, followed by two in the face, and Harrison was helpless. There was blood running down the inside of the bag, and the inhuman sound of choking.

Gillard reached forward and killed the music, the phone cable still firmly cinched to the headrest. Then he leaned close to the bag and in his best south London gangster patois whispered: 'Listen careful, you miserable facking piece of shit.'

Harrison's hands still flapped towards the bag, which was now pressed close to his nose and mouth as he ran out of air. Behind the supermarket's slogan 'Every little helps' Craig could make out Harrison's eyes, wide with terror, unable to see anything beyond the blue-striped, blood-smeared logo.

Gillard whacked him in the face with an elbow. 'Oi, still it and listen when I'm talking.'

The hands stopped moving.

'Gary, you are a nasty little bully. But you are now officially out of your league. Leave Sam alone. If you so much as breathe within ten miles of her, I'm going to come round to yours and douse your body with petrol and burn you alive. I've done it before, and believe me it hurts. No one will mourn your passing, and your ashes will be used as cat litter. Understand?'

The bag nodded, and more wheezing sounds emerged. 'Don't try to be clever with me, owight? Your flat is being watched – I know who you call, where you work, and I know everywhere you go. Do you understand?'

The bag nodded again. Craig released the wire a little and unwound it from the headrest to allow some air in. There was a great shuddering whoosh of inhalation, after which Craig tightened the wire again with his hand. He turned Harrison over, gaffer taped his wrists together and bundled him onto the back seat. 'Now lie on the seat and stick your feet in the air over the headrests. If you move those feet in the next ten minutes I will know.' He removed the wire from the neck of the bag, replaced it with gaffer tape and made a small nick in the bag so air could get in. He searched Harrison's bomber jacket and found Sam's phone and Harrison's own, which he took, along with the Audi's keys.

Detective Chief Inspector Craig Gillard then got out of the car, slightly shocked at his own behaviour. There was no one around. As he walked back to his own vehicle, he dropped the Audi keys into a drain. There was only a slight chance that Harrison would be stupid enough to call the police. Just as well. As a serving officer, what he had just done, on a whim, could get him thrown out of the force. But he also recognized something that his own boss Paddy Kincaid had confided to him years ago: just occasionally, heat-of-the-moment justice not only feels good, it works a treat.

Craig set the hands-free to call Sam back, and when she tentatively picked up he said, 'It's sorted. I don't think you'll have any more trouble from our Mr Harrison.'

'Oh, Craig, thank you.' She paused for a moment, then asked tentatively: 'What did you do?'

'Don't worry, nothing dramatic. I gave him a warning he won't forget. I'll be with you shortly.'

When Gillard pulled the Ford into her cul-de-sac he recognized her house immediately. It was the only one with all the lights on. It was a basic 1990s new-build terrace mostly made of uPVC and plastic cladding with a garage tucked into the ground floor, a small patch of weeds as an apology for a garden, and a front lean-to for dustbins, gas and electric meters. He rang the bell, and waited for a good couple of minutes: first for the slow bump-click tympani of a woman descending stairs on crutches, and then for the opening of a seemingly endless series of locks. When she opened the door, wearing just a long T-shirt, slippers and a self-conscious smile, he was shocked by how small, pale and vulnerable she looked, especially compared to the size of the black eye Harrison had given her. It made him want to go back and thump the bloke a few more times. But he was equally stirred that she had applied lipstick and a little eyeliner on the good eye, and what smelled like arnica cream on the bad one. Dignity in the face of mayhem. He wanted to compliment her, to say she looked nice. But many years ago he'd learned words weren't really his thing, especially compared to Liz who really knew how to use them. Looking at Sam now he couldn't think how to phrase what he wanted to say without it sounding silly or a lie. So instead he smiled, and after he had closed and double-locked the door behind him, gave her a hug. Her body began to shake silently against his.

'It's all right, it's all right,' he said as he rubbed her back. Again, he felt the need to use words without it sounding like he was trying it on. 'Do you want me to kip down on the sofa, if you're feeling nervous?'

'Would you?' she said. 'There's a divan in the spare room already made up.'

He looked at his watch. He'd be lucky to get two hours' sleep before having to get up.

Whether it was minutes or hours later, he couldn't say. A sound on the landing had him instantly awake. It was still dark. He'd not yet figured out how Harrison had got in before, past all the locks. If it was him again…

But it wasn't. The bedroom door cracked open, and a faint silhouette showed a feminine figure in T-shirt and shorts, wavy hair down to her shoulders. Sam eased her way quietly into the room. He pretended to be asleep, not sure otherwise what to do. She lifted the edge of the duvet and eased into the bed. She was very warm. Her arm snaked around his chest, her head resting on his shoulder and her sprained leg sticking out of the side of the bed. Within five minutes her heavier breathing indicated she was asleep. He lay awake for some time, his arm going dead where she was lying on it, wondering how his orderly life, his refuge, was going to survive the avalanche of chaos and responsibility that had arrived with this woman.

Chapter Five

Disastrous dinner party. Martin, losing an argument, mentioned my depression and stay in a psychiatric hospital. Helen loyally waded in on my side, before the shouting began. What's happened to him? The night I first met Martin was the most wonderful of my life. The man was a force of nature, buzzing with ideas, and happy to share, listen and discuss with anyone, even a forthright woman like me. Now he's well known and respected in the wider world, those private moments which were for listening are gone, just brief bursts of static in the Knightly broadcast. Conversation becomes one-versation.

Liz's diary, November 2003

Gillard always gave DS Claire Mulholland a lift into work on a Wednesday morning. It was some unfathomable domestic algorithm of childcare, cars and school: a husband who often worked nights; three teenage kids, one of whom was working but had her own one-year-old daughter; two dogs and a neurotic rabbit. Claire's family life was as complex as his was simple. Give him a VAT fraud any day over a life like that.

Most mornings Craig had plenty of time to get there at 7.45 a.m., but not today. He had woken up in an unfamiliar room to the sound of Sam moving around downstairs, and to the smell of toast and coffee. But he had barely had a chance to sample them before racing off, doing a quick change of clothes at home then leaping back in the car. As he queued his way through the Cobham rush hour, already 20 minutes late for Claire, he regretted not having had the good grace to patiently wait through Sam's extended thank you. 'I'll never forget your kindness to me,' she had said.

He finally pulled into the street where Claire lived. The front yard of her 1960s semi had been paved over, and once he'd pulled into the kerb and emerged from the car there was, as usual, a van and two cars on the pavement to squeeze past to get to the side door. Husband Baz was still there, judging by the presence of the plasterer's van. Gillard rang the doorbell which, as always, unleashed an avalanche of dogs against the door's glass panels, and a cacophony of barking and shouting. Claire, a cross between zoo-keeper and jailer, finally emerged with a volley of instructions back into the house about homework, shopping and granddaughter Kyra. In the past Claire had invited him in, but Gillard now knew it was better to wait outside. Most crime scenes were tidier than her lounge, and he'd more than once been pinned against the wall by their Irish wolfhound, Dexter, who had once left a jowl full of saliva on the crotch of his charcoal-grey trousers.

Claire followed him to the car, and as they pulled away into traffic she exhaled deeply. 'Bad traffic today, was it?'

'Yeah, and a bad night's sleep,' he said. He wasn't ready to tell the real story. He didn't even know yet what the story was. It was far from straight in his head, though he was sure that Claire of all people would understand. She was a handsome woman, with smiling eyes that belied her steely character.

She turned to him with a smile. 'I found some new graffiti about you yesterday,' she said.

Gillard couldn't suppress a grin. One cubicle in the Ladies toilet in the portakabin outside the detective block at Surrey Police HQ had a whole conversation about Gillard's sex appeal biroed into the grouting between the tiles. 'What did it say this time?'

Mulholland raised her eyebrows. 'It was of the "I'd like him to do me" variety, just a bit more graphic. She wanted to be handcuffed first, too.'

Gillard chuckled.

'Maybe we should get forensics to find the culprit,' Claire said, examining her nails.

'I expect office services will rush to paint it over again before Alison Rigby sees it.'

'Who knows, maybe she wrote it,' Mulholland said.

Gillard's yelp of laughter caused the car to twitch, sufficient for Mulholland to put a hand out to steady herself on the dashboard. 'Steady, tiger,' she said. She turned to him and then said: 'Of course if it was Alison, it would be you who'd be in handcuffs, right?'

Gillard kept the wheel steady this time, even as he howled with laughter. The assistant chief constable was a formidable woman. Over six feet tall, firm-jawed, with short spiky hair dyed jet black and ice-blue eyes. Paddy Kincaid had nicknamed her The Dominatrix.

Traffic for once wasn't bad, and they arrived at Mount Browne on time. Gillard greeted the civilian receptionist and made his way quickly through to the main incident room. After checking with the call handlers, he discovered that Professor Knight had not called back. This was too much. He checked through his notes, and methodically rang each of the numbers they now had for the Knights: two landlines and two mobiles. He also left a message with Caterham to get an officer to visit the Coulsdon house.

Gillard went straight in to see his senior officer. Kincaid, a balding stocky figure in short-sleeved white shirt and skewed purple tie, was leaning over at least 30 box files which he had arranged like a mini Stonehenge on his desk. Horizontal files bridged a dozen others standing on end.

'Best use for the Girl F inquiry paperwork,' Kincaid said, spreading his arms to display his creation. 'A judicial fucking monument to last ten thousand years, and to be looked at in wonder by future generations who will wonder: "What the fuck was it *for*?"' He looked up. 'Jock McKinnon's here this afternoon to second-guess my part in the investigation.' The notoriously ferocious chief constable of Police Scotland was conducting the latest probe into Girl F, and would report to the broader Home Office inquiry under Lord Justice Cunliffe.

'I'm not looking forward to it,' he said gloomily, slapping at one end of his box file creation so it tumbled with a clatter across his desk, spilling two or three boxes onto the floor.

They both stared at the stationery carnage until finally Kincaid broke out of his reverie. 'So what can I do for you, Craig?'

'It's a missing person's case, sir.' Gillard sketched out some details, partly to see if he could persuade himself: an absence of five days, completely out of character, a husband who seemed, at least initially, to be less-than-normally concerned, and now seems to be refusing to return calls. 'I want to go public, appeal for him to get in contact, call in some CSI resources.'

Kincaid cleared his throat with impatient scepticism. 'Couldn't this just be some marital tiff, Craig? You've no idea, you're a single man—'

'Divorced, sir.'

'Oh yes, I'd forgotten about *her*.' He said it with more disdain than his two brief meetings with Valerie five years ago seemed to justify. The marriage had disintegrated within six months, and there followed a few months when Craig was sufficiently lonely to agree to go out for long drunken evenings with Kincaid. Paddy's idea of cheering him up was to try to rope him in on persistent but hopeless attempts at picking up young women in the pub.

'Whatever.' Kincaid's face tightened into an uglier knot than his tie. 'Christ, I wish I had a pound for every time Muriel flounced off to see her bloody mother and wouldn't return my calls.'

'It's not just the husband. Nobody has heard from her. Not her employer, not her friends, and she's missed several critical meetings. It's extremely out of character, sir. She's a stickler for reliability.'

'Really? Oh, well. I expect we'll find her swinging gently from some beam in the house above some poetic note culled from Sylvia Plath.'

Craig winced at the image. 'This is potentially very high profile, sir. We have to go by the book. The husband is Professor Martin Knight of the LSE…'

'Him? The one who shoots his mouth off on the TV? Christ almighty.' He rubbed his eyes with a hand that showed the tell-tale nicotine habit he had never quite been able to quit. Kincaid's throat emitted a deep growl of irritation. 'That fucker wrote the initial report on Girl F. "Twenty-first century police technology but eighteenth-century attitudes." That's his opinion of us, Craig. Never met him, but Coldrick has. A bumptious prick, was how he described him.' He drummed his fingers on the desk.

'Well, Gillard, it's right up your street. As you say, it'll have to go absolutely by the book, which I have just reread as part of my corrective re-education.' He sighed. 'She's probably not a vulnerable person, but we'll need a risk assessment anyway. If you think he's bumped her off, you'll be aware of the additional procedures that need to be followed. Knight will undoubtedly have influential friends in Whitehall.'

'Yes, sir.'

'I'll certainly be able to dig up any resources you need.'

'We will need a CSI in Kent, at the Knights' holiday home.'

'Okay, I'll liaise with Kent, but you remain SIO.' Kincaid bent to one of the open files, revealing a freckled pate around which sparse coppery hair nestled, surplus wiring to an overtaxed brain.

'One final thing, sir.'

'Yes?' He looked up sharply.

'I used to date the missing woman…'

'For God's sake, Gillard!' Kincaid looked heavenwards, and took a deep breath.

'It was 30 years ago. For about six weeks.'

Kincaid stared at him, drumming his fingers on a box file. 'Ah, that's a bit different. No recent contact?'

'Not for a quarter of a century.'

Kincaid shrugged. 'That's okay, I suppose. Might give you extra insight too.'

'Sir.' Gillard nodded. 'Can that just be between us? I don't want anyone else knowing.'

'Okay, now bugger off. I've got half an hour to prepare for that kilted lunatic McKinnon. And Gillard?'

'Sir?'

'The professor is a very influential man. So find her alive, for Christ's sake.'

And for mine, Gillard thought as he turned to leave. He paused at the door, wanting to say something about Liz Knight. Something along the lines of: if she's dead, I'll not rest until the villain that did for her is caught. But when he looked at Paddy Kincaid he saw that the detective superintendent looked like a

47

dog that was about to be taken out and shot, by a ferocious Scot no less. He decided to keep his mouth shut.

Craig hadn't mentioned a subsequent time he'd met Liz in recent years. He'd been called to reports of a burglary at a house on Chaldon Rise back in 2011. It was 10 p.m. The householder, an elderly woman, was in shock at the mess her home had been left in and was being looked after by neighbours three doors up. When he knocked at the neighbours' to take the woman's statement, he found himself staring at Liz Knight. Subtly changed by the intervening years, a little filled out, but with the same warm brown eyes and delightful smile framed by the subtlest of creases. Her hair, still wavy, was pulled back into a ponytail.

She seemed not to recognize him until he introduced himself, and added: 'Hello, Liz. It's been a long time.'

'Well, well,' she said, her smile broadening. 'So now you're Detective Chief Inspector Craig Gillard. Come on in.' She brought him into a large lounge where a frail and rather tearful lady in her 80s was sitting on a large leather sofa, surrounded by balled tissues.

'Mrs Edwards,' Liz said. The woman looked up. 'They've sent the best detective brain in Surrey to solve the case. I can personally vouch for his dedication, so I think everything is going to be all right.'

Craig smiled. 'We're going to do our very best to catch him.' After taking a statement, Craig joined Liz in their large family room for a biscuit and a cup of tea.

'You seem to be doing just as well as I knew you would,' Craig said, taking in the large house and peering out into the long, tree-fringed garden behind.

'Yes.' She let out a brief sigh as she too scanned the garden. 'Martin's done very well. I've just started as the deputy head of King Edward's in Oxted. Oliver is at Oxford and Chloe's doing very well too. Aiming for Cambridge, we think.'

'So you're happy, then.' A question buried within a statement, and Liz shot back a look which indicated troubles of some kind. Craig was surprised to detect his own cruel pleasure at this fissure in her perfect existence, as if he could somehow, after all these years, slip through and snare her for himself. He was self-aware enough to wonder at his own stupidity.

'So Craig, what about you? Wife, kids, a settled family life now?' Liz asked, holding her cup to her mouth and eyeing him closely.

'Well, not exactly. I only married last year, but it didn't work out. We're separated. No kids.'

'I'm sorry to hear that.' Her stare seemed to look right into his head. 'You deserve to be happy.'

Further discussion was interrupted by the back door opening and the entry of a bear of a man, bearded and with unkempt hair, dressed in worn corduroys and a lumberjack shirt. 'Bloody broadband's gone again,' he announced, as he kicked off a pair of mud-spattered Crocs. 'Any tea on the go?' He picked up a copy of the *Guardian* lying on the kitchen table and glared into it.

'Martin, Detective Inspector Gillard's here to see Mrs Edwards,' Liz said.

'Mm?' His head remained buried in the paper.

'The burglary, you know.' Getting no response from her husband, Liz glanced at Craig and rolled her eyes. 'Martin, I think Mrs Edwards would like it if you went in there and expressed some sympathy,' she added.

Martin looked up, quizzically.

'She's in the lounge. Go and say hello. She's quite upset. And you had said you'd mend that fence for her last year. The one that the burglar got in through.'

'Oh, Christ, I did.' Martin gave Craig a nod of acknowledgement before shambling off.

'Academics,' she said, with a conspiratorial chuckle, the same surprisingly deep and infectious peal he recalled. A call from the control room called him away and he went to the car for some privacy. Fifteen minutes later, when he'd hung up, he looked back at the huge house, reflecting on the woman's life that just once he had thought he might have shared. Now he might as well have been staring at the moon.

With backing from the DCS, Gillard called a meeting in the force control room with Detective Sergeant Claire Mulholland, Response Intelligence Officer DC Rob Townsend and Family Liaison Officer Gabby Underwood, plus the four detective constables who were going to make up the team.

He briefed them on Mrs Knight's disappearance and appointed DS Mulholland to be the investigating officer, who would ensure that the missing person's details were circulated on the Police National Computer. The incident room would be set up at Caterham police station, just 15 minutes' drive from the Knights' home. As RIO, Rob Townsend would liaise with all the specialists – the Hi-Tech Crime Unit for seized computer equipment and phone tracing, the CSI unit and forensic labs – leaving Gillard and Claire Mulholland free to question family and friends. It would save the hour-long drive from Mount Browne every time they had a piece of evidence.

'With any luck, this will be a short operation but let's make it utterly professional. Professor Knight is a public figure, a long-time critic of the police, so I assume the refusal to ring back is part of some petty point-scoring exercise. We mustn't get drawn into it. I hope he'll make his whereabouts known pretty quickly. Any sign of her car, Rob?'

'Nothing on ANPR. The PCSOs have searched a half-mile radius. Her mobile's been switched off since late last Thursday, so that doesn't help either. But we'll keep monitoring.'

Rob was an expert on the automatic number plate recognition database, which drew on a national network of digital cameras on major roads and in patrol cars.

'Good. Do the same for Professor Knight. If we haven't heard from him this evening I want to know every mast he's pinged in the last week, every text sent and every number called.

'CSI is going in for a quick look at their home this morning. I don't want to go public on the missing person's case before we've done that, because the press will be down there, getting in the way. I've pencilled in a five o'clock news conference for tomorrow afternoon, but with luck both Knights will turn up and we won't need it. The tech boys will have a press briefing room set up for us at Caterham. In the meantime, it's likely we'll get calls from journalists, and I want you to refer them all to the press office, who are going to take a hard line. No off-the-record briefings, whatever your relationship with reporters for other cases, understand? We're going to keep an entirely open mind on this case.'

They all nodded in agreement. Gillard went on. 'I'm meeting Oliver Knight, the son, at their home in Chaldon Rise in Old Coulsdon this afternoon. The daughter is coming down later. Mrs Knight's elderly parents live just a half-mile away, and Claire is seeing them this morning. At the moment, as per the regs, the Knights are absent rather than missing persons. Any questions?'

There were no questions, just an array of folded arms and smug grins. Professor Martin Knight, a previously lofty enemy, seemed to have fallen at their feet.

Wednesday afternoon

The London School of Economics squats on a cramped site in Houghton Street just off the Aldwych in central London, and is one of the most understated homes of educational excellence. The buildings are a mishmash of architectural styles, and the internal structure a warren of never-quite-finished renovation. To a casual passer-by the only evidence it even is a university is the preponderance of youngsters gathered on the steps of the two principal buildings. In the 1970s and early '80s, when most of Britain's dailies were based in Fleet Street, only a five-minute drunken stagger away, the LSE was always a good place for a lazy journalist to find evidence of student political mischief. Craig Gillard's first experience of the place was as a youthful PC on public order duty, trying to contain a demonstration against student fees that threatened to spill out into one of London's busiest thoroughfares.

Martin Knight's academic secretary, Zakira Oglu, was a very tall and disarmingly friendly African-looking man wearing jeans, a linen jacket and – surprisingly, considering the warmth of the room – a colourful outdoor scarf. Craig Gillard was offered a coffee and a Hobnob. Mr Oglu closed the door and posted a whole biscuit into his own mouth, where it disappeared, apparently without a single chew.

'We're all a bit surprised by this,' Oglu said, not betraying a whisper of a foreign accent. 'Martin works from home a lot, but also at the Home Office where I believe they have given him a perch.'

He smiled at Gillard as he lifted up piles of files and located his own laptop. 'Right. As I said in my email, I can certainly send you a log of his academic emails, his appointments and so on.'

'What about his phone calls?'

'The system records incoming and outgoing numbers.'

'Did he just have the one mobile phone?'

'Yes, I think so. Look, we have recordings only of conference calls, would you want those?'

'Not for the moment. How soon can you get the emails?'

'Technically, within a few hours via our IT department. Once we have permission from the director. That may take a few hours more.'

Gillard shrugged. He didn't yet have the manpower to go through thousands of emails, and hoped it was never required. But getting early permissions in place always speeded an inquiry.

'How long have you worked for Professor Knight?'

'I've worked *with* him for three years,' Oglu said. 'But I report to someone else, the departmental manager. Still, it's enough time at least to have got to know a little about him.'

'So how would you describe him?'

'I'm sure you know of his academic career already. As a colleague, it wouldn't be unfair to say he's brisk and demanding; focused without being monomaniacal. He can be irascible and abrasive, but he's also kind. He cancelled a meeting to give me a lift home, all the way to Walthamstow, the day I got knocked off my scooter, and helped me with the insurance claims. He doesn't suffer fools, period. But he cares, very deeply, about justice. You'll discover that when you finally meet him.'

'I hope I do,' Gillard said, letting the ambiguity lie between them. 'When was the last time you saw or spoke to him?'

'Yesterday afternoon, when he was on the train from York. He wanted me to draft a letter of apology to the committee for him missing the last two days. He was furious that this report of his wife going missing had caused him to have to return home. I can't recall his exact words, but he was angry with her for going off in a huff.'

'Has he ever expressed his anger with her to you before?'

'Not that I recall. He rarely mentions her.'

Gillard chewed back a gristle of irritation. 'She may only have been reported missing yesterday, but no one has seen her since last Thursday. So I'd really like you to cast your mind back to all the conversations you had with Professor Knight over that period.'

'I saw him on Friday afternoon, when he was here. He sent me an email over the weekend, about arrangements for the conference in York. And he must have spoken to me a half-dozen times, either in person or by voicemail, during and after the conference. I've not heard from him since yesterday.'

'And you're sure that he didn't give any hint that he was going away on a business trip, or for some family event or anything that would interrupt his working schedule?'

Oglu shook his head. 'No.'

The door opened and an athletic man of Mediterranean mien with a shaven head and a burgundy-coloured leather jacket came in. His arms were filled with papers and books which he dumped wearily on the desk next to Oglu's.

'Ah, this is Vuk Panić, a senior lecturer in criminology at our Mannheim Centre,' Oglu said. 'He's worked closely with Martin for a number of years. Vuk, this is Detective Chief Inspector Gillard. He's going to help us find him.'

'And his wife, who has been missing for six days now,' Gillard said, shaking hands with the lecturer. The man had an iron grip, and an intense gaze. With his coffee-coloured head and dense, dark stubble he looked more like an upmarket security man than an academic. 'If you know him well, perhaps I can ask you a few questions,' Gillard said.

'Sure, come to my office,' Panić said, in a gravelly, heavily accented voice. The office was on a lower mezzanine floor reached from a narrow staircase, and was little more than a cubbyhole crammed with books and journals. 'Sorry it's so cramped. Can I get you a tea? Almond or camomile is all I have here, but if you want builder's tea, there's a machine in the hall.'

Gillard declined the offer, but accepted a chair and was given one more piece of information. 'My name is pronounced pan-itch, not panic. Of course I appreciate your best efforts not to mispronounce my first name either. Vuk as in book.' He smiled briefly, betraying efforts to deal with what must have been years of jokes at his expense.

Formalities completed, Gillard waded in: 'So when did you first meet the professor?'

'At Oxford when I was a graduate student about ten years ago. I had come over from Serbia after the war, and he was very supportive of my studies. I was at Strathclyde University and then in the US for a number of years, but we kept up email contact. I did quite a lot of work towards the Rossingdale Inquiry and later on the Girl F report, so we had a lot of contact over that.'

'Did you ever meet his wife?'

'Yes, Liz and I got on very well. Their parties at Oxford were always quite fun. She's very bright and entertaining.'

Gillard had to restrain himself from agreeing. 'Can you offer any insight into why either of them might have gone missing?'

Panić looked up to the ceiling and breathed heavily, as if scenting the question for traps. 'I have no idea, actually.' Gillard watched as the Serb rubbed an eyebrow with his thumb. 'I can't think of anything.'

Gillard locked eyes with the lecturer, crossed his arms and waited. The empty seconds expanded, until Panić blinked and looked away. Gillard had telegraphed his disbelief effectively. He stood, picked up his briefcase and overcoat and shook the lecturer's hand. 'I would ask you to think carefully about what we've discussed. If anything comes to mind, this is my number.' He gave Panić a business card on which he had written in ballpoint the new incident room direct line. 'We all hope of course that both Professor and Mrs Knight reappear safe and well, but if there is any doubt about it you will be hearing from me again.'

Panić pointed him along the corridor towards the lift. As Gillard left the room, the Serb called him back. 'There's a name you should know, but please don't say I told you.'

Gillard looked back expectantly.

'It's Krugman. Dr Natalie Krugman.'

The detective wrote down the name and looked up, ready to ask who she was and where she fitted in. But Panić had closed the door.

Gillard walked to the lift, pressed the call button and in two minutes was standing outside on Houghton Street. It was just beginning to rain, and as he stood on the steps of the university, he took in the groups of students chattering, smoking and laughing. They were just the right age to be his sons or daughters, if things had turned out differently. Young lives to live, aspirations to fulfil, love affairs to begin. And to end.

Love or its absence explains a lot. If your wife disappeared, wouldn't you call the police? Not just once to report it, but again and again to find out what might have been discovered about her absence? Of course, anybody would. Yet no one had heard from Martin Knight. He hadn't responded to any of the dozen phone messages and emails sent by the police since yesterday. To Gillard that silence was beginning to look more and more suspicious. The idea of the Knights as a normal, untroubled family was already feeling false.

Chapter Six

Professor Martin Knight is Prince Khalifa ul Haq Professor of Criminology at the Mannheim Centre of the London School of Economics and Political Science, and visiting Hiram Wacke fellow at the University of California, Berkeley. He chaired the British Society of Criminology in 1995–8 and 2002–4. He was born in 1961, educated at the Parkdean School, Manchester and then at Jesus College, Cambridge. At St Peter's College, Oxford he won the 1988 Horniman Prize for his M.Sc. dissertation Thinking Crime, Doing Time, which later became the basis for the young offender rehabilitation programme adopted by the Danish government. He has been an adviser on youth justice to the Home Office since 1997, is a frequent commentator on criminality and the justice system on television and radio, and has a weekly column in the Guardian, as well as regularly contributing articles to The Times, the Washington Post and numerous other leading publications. Among his many works, which have been translated into more than 60 languages, are Crime and Double Punishment, Consigned to Criminality and Lessons in Failure: A History of British Incarceration 1920–97, as well as Condemned from Birth: Essays in Class, Crime and Offending, which was the winner of the Howard Speake Award for popular sociology in 2008. His Reith Lecture on 'The Civil Society' in 2012 was voted the most accessible critique of British justice by the Barrister magazine. He is a fellow of the British Academy and was awarded Finland's Paremmuusjärjestyksessä (Order of Merit) for his role in redesigning that country's youth justice system in 2009. He is married and lives in Surrey.

(Foreword to the 2014 edition of *Consigned to Criminality*)

Gillard's train back from Waterloo to Guildford had been late, so he flicked through some of the pile of Knight's work that Oglu had given him. Inevitably he drifted into looking again at Knight's report on Girl F. The full story was awful.

Francine Cole was a 13-year-old of mixed race who had been in care since she was two. A one-girl whirlwind of shoplifting, antisocial behaviour and absconding from social services' care in Purley, she was known to treat Surrey Police as a taxi service, ringing up to demand a lift back to the home when she had run out of stolen cash or felt like some food. On one such trip in February 2009 she mentioned that an older man was in the habit of picking her up in a silver car, giving her drink and drugs and then taking her back to his flat, where one or two other men had sex with her. The last time had been four days previously, or possibly three. She wasn't sure. A day later she retracted the allegations during formal interview, then two weeks later reinstated them to her social worker. Surrey Police, having initially failed to gather DNA evidence from her clothing, then began a belated and rudimentary investigation. The girl was driven around the part of Croydon where she said the incident took place, but was unable to identify the actual address. The man they were looking for she knew as Barry. He had a strong Scottish accent, but was otherwise made for invisibility: average build, medium height, late 40s to perhaps as much as 60, tidily dressed, metal-framed spectacles. Always sucking mints. That peppermint breath was the clearest impression she retained.

Surrey Social Services were sceptical. Their report said that while Girl F was vulnerable because of her near-adult appearance and sexual precocity, she was a fantasist and had 'long-established issues around honesty and truthfulness'. Surrey Police concurred, handing the matter back to social services. The informal police conclusion, found in one officer's notebook during the IPCC inquiry, was simpler: Girl F was a lying little scrubber, and her allegations a waste of time and resources.

Two months later she threw herself in front of the Gatwick Express as it hurtled through East Croydon station. She had left a suicide video on her phone, which she had emailed to a friend just before she killed herself. The friend then posted it on YouTube, where it went viral. The video's tearful tirade against social services and police for failing to believe her hit the news, and suddenly Surrey Police and Surrey Social Services were side by side in the court of public opinion.

The initial failure to take her allegation seriously was then compounded. In the seven years since, no one had been arrested. The silver car she had been driven away in had never been found. The house where she'd claimed the abuse took place had never been identified. There was not a scrap of DNA evidence to support her case, and most inconveniently of all, the only witness was dead.

Scottish Barry might never have existed. The trouble was that the lawyers, the media, Her Majesty's Inspectors of Constabulary and the judiciary believed he did exist.

So now, whether he existed or not, he had to be found.

Chaldon Rise is a quiet crescent of large 1930s mock-Tudor homes set into the lower slopes of Farthing Downs. The Knights' house, like most on the Downs' side, was set back and shielded from view by large and well-tended box hedges. A tarmac drive and paved front path, both now cordoned off by blue police tape, led up through the hedges and revealed long and well-tended lawns to the bay windows and double front door. While Tyvek-suited crime scene investigators walked in and out, a uniformed PC stood by the door, talking to another man: Oliver Knight. Gillard parked the unmarked Ford and, with DS Claire Mulholland at his side, opened the gate and climbed the path. Knight greeted them confidently, every inch the solicitor: dark suit, polished black shoes and a paisley-patterned mauve silk tie. He looked like a man who had already spent too long sitting on a chair. Stocky, thick-necked and with the beginnings of jowls. The thick-framed spectacles added to the impression of a man who had hit his 40s, even though Gillard knew he was just 24.

'This is only precautionary,' Gillard said, nodding towards the CSI activity. 'But if anything has happened to your parents, early clues are vital.'

Oliver nodded. 'In the meantime I hope they won't make a mess.'

'No, everything will be restored to how it was found,' he said. 'You mentioned rental properties. How many are there?'

'A house divided into two flats in Thornton Heath, and a terraced house in Purley. Mum runs them really. I just do the legals.'

Gillard was itching to take a look inside Liz's home, to see how she lived now, but he didn't want to get under the feet of the CSI team. They had quickly established that Liz wasn't there. The front door opened, and Yaz Quoroshi, senior CSI for the forensic service now shared between Surrey and Sussex police forces, emerged with a plastic bag in each hand.

'Plenty of computer kit in there,' he said to Gillard. 'There's a big wooden shed, more like a chalet really, in the garden, which seems to be an office.'

'That's where dad works,' Oliver Knight said. 'I hope you didn't damage anything.'

Gillard walked with Quoroshi down towards the large CSI van, and out of Oliver Knight's earshot. 'Have you seen the size of that bloody garden?' Yaz muttered. 'It's 100 metres by 30, and full of mature trees. If we have to dig it up looking for a body it'll take months. And then just behind are the Downs.

Hundreds of acres of protected chalk grassland. The excavation required would be like the Valley of the Kings.'

'Let's hope it doesn't come to that,' Gillard replied.

Quoroshi loaded the two bags into the van. He then pulled down his hood, revealing trickles of sweat on his shaven, nut-brown forehead. 'Analysis of this lot is going to take some time. As well as the desktop PC there is a tablet computer and an old laptop. From Mrs Knight's office there's a desktop and laptop. Debby did a quick scoot around upstairs, but everything looks in order.' Yaz pulled down his glove to look at his watch. 'We've got a kebab shop stabbing scene to examine in Woking today, so we're not doing dabs or blood searches here at this stage, if that's okay.' He pointed to the van. 'We've bagged up and labelled hairbrushes, combs and toothbrushes for DNA should they be needed. And we've got the household financial paperwork you asked for.'

'Good. Any sign of Mrs Knight's diary? She supposedly keeps it in her office.'

'No. Nothing there.'

DS Mulholland had joined them at the van. 'Craig, the LSE has called. Professor Knight has taken compassionate leave for five days, apparently.'

'When?'

'Sent an email to the departmental secretary's number just a few minutes ago. The secretary says he has a regular Wednesday afternoon departmental meeting. He sounded well miffed that Knight hadn't called to apologize for dropping them in it.'

Gillard sighed. The professor wouldn't return official police calls, but had the nerve to message his employer. He turned to Quoroshi. 'Did you find his passport?'

'Hers, yes. Not his.'

'Well, we've got ports and airports looking out for him and his car.' In truth, this was Gillard's biggest worry. That Professor Knight was doing a runner.

'I want to know where he was when he sent that email, Claire. There's every reason why he might want compassionate leave, but I smell a rat. I hope we can get CSI to finish off here tomorrow. We'll need Oliver's and the daughter's swabs for elimination, of course. Check the local crime database for any previous incidents linked to this address. I'm taking the son up to Croydon to look at the rental houses. Get on to Rob Townsend to make sure we get every cell tower Knight's phone has pinged, plus verbatim texts and all the ANPR. I also want to know exactly where his car is.'

Gillard left Claire talking to Quoroshi and returned to the doorway, where Oliver was showing something to the PC on the doorstep. 'These are the family photographs Detective Sergeant Mulholland asked for,' he said to Gillard. Professor Knight looked every bit the patrician: firm-featured, with a good head of salt-and-pepper hair, a solid nose and piercing eyes. The beard was light and not quite well-trimmed enough to be trendy. But there was a presence, to be sure. Something of Hemingway about him: a solidity and a swagger. Oliver said his father was about five ten and weighed just under 15 stone. The pictures of Liz were taken at her birthday party in August and were something of a shock to Gillard. The smile he remembered so well was still there, falteringly, but the dimples were lost in a fleshier face. Her neck looked thicker, and the cheeky little chin he recalled was now a double. Liz's brown eyes, so alive in his memory, looked less sure, less confident, and were partially obscured by large thick-framed spectacles that made her look even older. Did she somehow fear she was going to be killed, or was it just him projecting that fear onto her?

Oliver Knight seemed anxious to excuse his mother's physical deterioration. 'Things went a bit downhill for her in the last 12 months,' he said. 'She never had to wear glasses before, and she's been diagnosed with arthritis in her leg, and the drug she was taking caused her to put on weight. I've got some better pictures you might prefer.'

As Claire rejoined them, Oliver brought out two, showing a much slimmer, more attractive, and self-assured Liz, sitting at a sunny table near a beach. It was more the woman that Craig had expected she would become in middle age. 'How old are these?' Claire asked.

'Two or three years,' Oliver said. 'These are the ones Mum would have chosen if she was here. Do you want to use them?'

Craig, still mesmerized by the pictures in his hands, hesitated, but Mulholland jumped straight in. 'No, we can't. It's important we use the most recent pictures that reflect what she looks like now, whether they are unflattering or not.'

Craig knew she was right. In the age of social media it happened all the time. Relatives of the missing seemed to think they were assembling a model portfolio, when what you needed to do was stand a chance of recognizing the person as she was now. Poor Liz, thought Gillard. He never would have guessed that, 30 years on, he would now be thinking about where her lifeless body might be buried.

It was gone five when DS Claire Mulholland parked in Marlpit Close and surveyed the 1930s semi-detached houses which made up the secluded and leafy street. Just a mile from the Knights' own home, these were well-to-do, solid middle-class homes where you could imagine the soft chimes of a grandfather clock and the clink of bone china cups. The front gardens were well-tended and extensive: no tendency here to pave them over to provide off-street parking.

Claire climbed the granite steps to the wooden front door and rang the bell. She heard no ring, but a small dog began barking. A white West Highland terrier ran to the door, where she could see through the lead-lighted panel that its tail was wagging.

A few moments later a tall figure in mustard-yellow corduroys and a brick-red shirt opened the door.

'Mr Bishopsford? I'm Detective Sergeant Claire Mulholland. We spoke on the phone.'

'Do come in. Geraldine is just making tea.' Tom Bishopsford was a tall but slightly stooped fellow of perhaps 80, with snowy hair. As she followed him in, the dog fussing around her ankles, she noticed how the careful combing of the front third of his hair did not extend to the back, where baby-soft white strands stood out at wild angles, like the stuffing from an old settee.

'Do take a seat in the parlour.' He showed her through to a rather untidy lounge, overshadowed by dark sideboards and glass-fronted cabinets. He pointed to an old-fashioned three-piece suite, one chair of which was clearly claimed by the dog, whose hair-flecked bed occupied it. Half the settee was buried under newspapers and periodicals and some knitting. The final, heavily used, chair looked like it had collapsed. There was no TV in the room, but she heard from another room the faint sound of posh vowels from a radio.

Mrs Bishopsford came in with a tea tray and set it down on a magazine-cluttered coffee table. 'Make yourself at home, dear,' she said. She was a rounded, matronly woman in twinset and pearls, with long dyed brown hair, held in places by seemingly random oriental wooden pins, bows and clips. She poured a cup of strong tea into a large slightly chipped mug which bore the face of a West Highland terrier. 'I've given you Westie because it holds more. You're probably gagging after the day you've had.'

Claire sat down on the sofa, setting off an avalanche of copies of the *Daily Telegraph* and *Radio Times*. The dog tried to jump on her lap, and after she pushed it off, Tom chided it with a wagging finger. 'Naughty boy, Aristotle. She doesn't want to talk to you.'

'Have you found our daughter yet?' Geraldine asked, smiling. 'I'm afraid not.'

'Oh dear. She always has been such a headstrong girl. She's bound to be down at Great Wickings. She's always loved it there,' she said.

'They told us she wasn't there, dear,' Tom said gently. 'This morning, remember?'

'Oh yes. You've spoken to Oliver, I hear. And Chloe rang this morning.'

'When did you last see your daughter?' Claire asked.

'A week last Sunday,' Geraldine said. 'She normally comes around for tea. Last Sunday of course, she was down in Great Wickings, painting.'

'You should know,' Tom said gently. 'That Elizabeth has always had her "moments", times when things get a little too much for her.'

'It started when she was a teenager. After BBC Young Musician of the Year. She was runner-up, but had worked so hard to do better,' Geraldine said. 'But then the piano is so competitive.'

'We do know that she had depression on a number of occasions, and I believe was a voluntary in-patient at a psychiatric hospital,' Mulholland said. 'We've got a request in for her medical records.'

'Yes, well my guess would be that she's just gone off somewhere to get away from everybody. That would be why she isn't returning telephone calls.'

Claire could now hear discordant classical music drifting in from the kitchen.

'Not a fan of Hindemith, then?' Tom asked, seeing the expression on Claire's face.

She smiled it away. 'Has Elizabeth ever threatened to kill herself, do you know? Has she ever confided in you that she was unhappy enough to do that?'

'No,' said Tom firmly. 'She's a very private and a very resourceful person. If she has a problem she just works it out. Do you know that she represented England's women at a chess Olympiad in 1983?'

'It was 1984, in Budapest, actually,' Geraldine corrected. 'And since she gave that up she has become an extraordinarily good bridge player.'

'She and her friend Helen have a rubber or two with the humans most Sundays,' added Geraldine. Catching the look of confusion on Claire's face, she grinned. 'Moira and Simon Hewman,' she said, spelling the surname.

'Does Martin play too?'

'Gosh, no. He's much too important!' laughed Geraldine. 'All that work for the Home Office. No, he doesn't play games. In fact he hated it when Elizabeth beat him blindfold in chess all those years ago. He used to play chess for Middlesex when he was a boy, but he never played *her* again.'

'It sounds like they had some rivalry, then?'

'No,' said Geraldine, inclining her head. 'No, it wasn't quite like that. They were both very busy with their academic lives in the early years, and like all families they had to make decisions, compromises. Of course Elizabeth gave a little ground because she was going to be a mother. That's natural, isn't it?'

Claire suppressed the urge to disagree. 'Did they ever have violent arguments or rows?'

'I wouldn't have thought so,' Tom said. 'Elizabeth wasn't the kind to shout or make a scene. Never.'

'Decorum,' intoned Geraldine. 'It's very important, you know.

Of course today, nobody gives a hoot about it. But we always brought her up to be a good girl.'

'Did her husband ever assault her, do you know?'

'My goodness, what a question!' retorted Geraldine. 'Martin's a professor. At the London School of Economics. For goodness' sake!' she turned to her husband, as if to say: Where *do* they get these policewomen?

'Martin is a man of words and ideas,' Tom said. 'If you want to see his pugilistic side, read what he writes. His pen is definitely mightier than any sword. He would never have laid a hand on our daughter, we're confident of that.'

It was late afternoon by the time Gillard had completed his tour of the rental properties. Oliver told Gillard that his mother had bought the first one about six or seven years ago, and seemed to be quite astute in her choice of property. 'It always takes me by surprise how many things she's been good at,' Oliver said.

The terraced Victorian house in Purley was occupied by a Carl and Leanne Dawkins, a young couple with two kids. Leanne, a short woman with pink hair and studs up one ear said none of them had seen Mrs Knight for a month. It wasn't usual to see her unless there was a problem, and the rent was paid by standing order. At the converted house in Thornton Heath, less than five miles north, Oliver Knight showed Gillard into the hall and stairway. The tenant of the upper flat was Aleksander Horvat. 'He's an electrician, and is always out early. I can let you into the flat if you want – I do have a key, as did Mum,' Oliver said.

'I think we can leave that. I'd prefer to have his permission at this stage.'

Oliver then let Gillard into the empty downstairs flat. The detective donned a fresh pair of latex gloves and shoe covers and asked Oliver to wait while he looked around. It was a one-bedroom place, reasonably light and airy. It smelled of air-freshener and stale cooking, which went well with the scuffed woodwork and white, not-quite-woodchip wallpaper.

'How long has this been empty?'

'About three months. The last tenant stayed 18 months. She was a middle-aged divorcee who worked at Sainsbury's at night, and as a cleaner in the mornings. A real hard grafter. She was from Guyana originally, but I think she now lives somewhere in north-west London.'

Gillard picked up a big pile of mail, mostly bills and official brown envelopes, some addressed to Horvat, some to a Mrs Aruna Edun, and a couple to a Mrs P.M. Jones. 'Was Mrs Edun the most recent tenant?'

'Yes. Pam was a bit more trouble. A widow from the Midlands and a bit fond of the bottle, apparently. Mum was always on to her about rent arrears. She gave her notice in the end.'

Oliver nodded and held out his hand. Gillard passed the post across and then said, 'I'm going to ask you to give me your keys to this flat, and to the rental house, just for now. With luck it will only be for a few days.'

Gillard drove Oliver the short distance back to his legal office, Barker Caynes Tipping, part of a national conveyancing and family law chain. The office was closed, but Oliver let him in and ushered him to an interview room while he searched for the tenancy paperwork. He returned with a couple of thin files and pulled up a chair. 'Okay, fire away.'

'We're just interested in basic background at the moment. Were you aware of anyone who might want to harm either of your parents?'

'No. Absolutely not.'

'What about debts? Did either of them have any financial problems?'

'Quite the reverse. Dad inherited quite a bit of money when his mother died. They've invested it in Spanish holiday property.'

'But no disputes? Nothing like that?'

'I would have known if there had been. I do a lot of the legal work.' Oliver radiated a certain annoying smugness. Gillard decided to change tack.

'Perhaps you can help fill in a bit of family history. Were either of them married or in a partnership before?'

'No. It was first love for both of them. I've heard endless stories about it.'

First love. Gillard felt a stab as he wrote it down. 'Did either of them have any affairs, to your knowledge?'

Oliver Knight's right hand rubbed across his mouth. 'Well.' He looked out of the window and sighed. 'My mother accused Dad of having an affair several years ago. I had just come down from Oxford, and there was an almighty row that evening. Chloe was really upset, and actually ran away from home for three days.'

'Was it true?'

'I have no idea. We never talked about it, I mean afterwards. Mum is very good. Loyalty is a great strength. She never tried to get me or Chloe onside, so to speak, by talking about her suspicions. For good or ill, I think she compartmentalizes her life. However, I think it was instrumental in Mum's depression, which came back with a vengeance. That's when she spent time in hospital in Epsom.'

'A psychiatric hospital?'

'Yes. It was voluntary. She was never sectioned or anything.'

'She'd had previous occurrences?'

'Yes. You'd have to look at her medical records. Have you spoken to Kathy?'

Gillard consulted his notes. 'Kathy Parkinson?'

'Yes. She's Mum's best friend and confidante. She can give you chapter and verse, I'm sure.'

'We'll interview Ms Parkinson tomorrow.'

'Have you seen Mum's parents yet?' Oliver asked.

'DS Mulholland saw them earlier.'

'I rang them this morning, and they are terribly shocked,' Oliver said. 'If anything should happen to Mum they would be finished off. I mean it would be the end.'

'Claire Mulholland is very diplomatic, I assure you.'

'It's not that. Mum had a little brother who died when he was less than a year old. Andrew was hit by a car, right in front of her. She was only five.'

'I never knew that.' The words slipped out before Gillard could control them.

'Well, of course,' Oliver said, opening his hands. 'There's no reason why you would have done. Anyway, my grandparents have basically tried to wrap her up in cotton wool ever since. They were overprotective, I suppose, but one could understand why.'

Gillard said nothing. He recalled how reluctant Liz had been to introduce him to her father, particularly. He had always had to say goodbye to her at the end of the road.

'But you can't keep someone in cotton wool their whole life can you?' Oliver asked. 'Life is out there and has to be lived.'

Gillard was just walking down the stairs when his phone went. It was the RIO, Rob Townsend, and he said he'd got Knight's mobile phone records. 'Go ahead, Rob.'

'The professor's phone's been switched off since Tuesday night when you spoke to him, except for the email to LSE which was sent from Dungeness. There are plenty of incoming texts and call records held on the server, but no outgoing. The cell site analysis up until that point confirms his own story. Tuesday afternoon, down on the train from York to King's Cross, Victoria Line, then Victoria to Coulsdon South. Half an hour later, he was driving down on the A23 while making a long call. The ANPR camera cross-references his BMW at roughly the right time.'

'Hmm. Any criminal record?' Gillard asked.

'He's got a public order offence in Oxford from student days. Drunk and disorderly. She's got a driving without due care and attention from 2007. Nothing else.'

'Okay. Would you do the same for their kids? I think we've got details on file. Claire will be bringing in details of Mrs Knight's tenants. I suppose we should check the cleaner too, just to be exhaustive. She comes on a Thursday morning, and might have seen Mrs Knight last Thursday.' Gillard paused. 'Rob, I've just been told that there was some substantial money changing hands in the family in the last year, from an inheritance. Given that both parents are missing, I think we have to take a closer look at Oliver Knight. Can you arrange for a warrant for the removal and analysis of his computers and phones from his home and office?'

'Certainly.'

'He won't be happy about it, but at least it eliminates the possibility that a clever and greedy young solicitor may have bumped his parents off.'

There was one important family interview remaining. News of her mother's disappearance had brought a distraught Chloe Knight back from Cambridge University just a few weeks after starting her first term. With the family home in Chaldon Rise taped off for crime scene investigation, she was staying three doors down at number ten with the family of a friend. Family liaison officer Gabby Underwood was already there, preparing the ground for a formal statement.

It was just after six when DCI Gillard and DS Mulholland arrived. Gillard had his own reasons for wanting a reliable number two for this interview. Chloe Knight was 18 years old, exactly the same age Liz had been when he dated her all those years ago. He had expected some unsettling resemblances, but was relieved when he saw the girl. She was dressed in ripped jeans and sweatshirt, sitting cross-legged on a settee, surrounded by half-eaten biscuits, cups of coffee and evidence of a chaotic arrival. She was blonde, unlike her mother, and when she stood up to greet them it was clear she was around six inches taller than Liz's petite five three. Her complexion was ashen. But some of the other family features were there: high cheekbones, a strong jaw and those soft brown eyes he remembered so well.

Gillard began by thanking her for making herself available so quickly, and stressed that despite the large police presence and formality, everyone was of course still hoping for good news.

'Yeah, but where is my dad?' Chloe asked.

'We're hoping he will call in today sometime. He spoke to us 24 hours ago from your family place in Dungeness,' he said. 'He said that is where your mother would go if she was upset about something.'

'She goes there to paint, so that makes sense. But if she isn't there why doesn't he call?'

'We can't answer that. We don't know where he is. We already have your father's mobile phone details, so we're going to be able to find him pretty quickly.'

'So what can I do?' she said, chewing a nail on a long delicate finger.

'Well, we just need to get some idea of how things were between them at home,' Gillard said. 'If they had arguments, that kind of thing.'

Chloe blew a long sigh. 'They coexisted well, but didn't spend a whole lot of time actually together by choice. Dad travels a lot, to conferences, up in London, all that stuff. Mum, well,' she sighed again. 'There's school, of course, WI on Tuesday, coffee mornings at the weekend and charity work for refugees on Wednesday evenings, and so on.' She waved a dismissive hand. 'To be honest I lost track of it years ago. Oh, there was the am-dram group as well, two rehearsals a week.'

'We know your mother had a history of depression, and she had health problems recently. She would have had every excuse for feeling a bit down. Had she complained of being depressed in recent weeks?' asked Claire.

'No, quite the reverse,' Chloe said. 'She seemed to be going through a good patch. It was her birthday in August, and even though the drugs she was on made her swell up—'

'Which drugs?'

'I don't know the names, but they're for the arthritis in her leg after the accident. They made her face puffy.'

'That was after the RTA in 2007?' asked Gillard, looking down at his notes.

'What's an RTA?'

'Sorry, car crash. Road traffic accident,' Gillard added.

'Yeah. She drove into a skip coming back from a dinner party in Guildford.'

'Have you ever heard your mother threaten suicide?' Claire asked.

'Only jokingly. It was along the lines of: "If my leg and teeth get any worse I think you're going to have to take me to the vet and get me put down."'

'Teeth problems too?'

Chloe nodded. 'From the accident. She needed some dental work done after she banged her head in the crash. I tried not to hear about the details, it's a bit gross.'

'Can we talk about your father now?' Gillard asked. 'Were you close to him?'

'I'm closer to Mum. Dad is a bit distant. He's got so important now, he spends half the time away, and when he's here he's always in his office. That pretty much suits the rest of us, because he isn't always walking around the house like a bear with sore balls,' she giggled. 'I remember when he had his office in the house we always had to tiptoe everywhere because he was working. He'd, like, shout at me and Oliver.' She rolled her eyes. 'I thought it was pretty ironic, frankly, when I read my dad's report on youth justice, which was basically, some hippy-shit "deal with it in the community, not prison" idea because he's way more strict at home than any of my friends' dads. When I was ten he made me stay in my room for two whole days without any toys or music, just books.'

'Did he ever punish you, physically?' Claire said gently.

'No. And he never touched me up, either, in case you're wondering.' Her face challenged them to disbelieve her. Not close to her father, but fiercely loyal. It was a trait that Gillard approved of, perhaps one she had inherited from her mother.

'Sometimes we do have to ask distressing questions,' Gillard said softly.

Underwood and Mulholland exchanged a glance. 'Now Chloe,' Claire said slowly. 'Do you think your father could have harmed your mother?'

She shook her head. 'No way.'

'Did you ever witness violent rows?' Gabby Underwood added.

'Yeah, I mean, I remember the rows, especially during her dark days. Dad didn't get it. Tried to shake her out of the depression, maybe literally on a couple of occasions.'

'Did he ever strike her?' Claire asked.

'No way, absolutely no way.' Chloe shook her head. 'Dad wouldn't harm a fly. He's an ivory tower guy. He has a loud voice and a commanding presence, so when he shouts, that is scary enough, but I don't think he'd know what to do with his fists beyond banging them on a table.'

'You're quite sure?' Gillard asked.

'Yes. If you ask Oliver, you'll get the same answer.'

'We did,' Gillard said. 'I understand your parents came into a lot of money recently. Did they ever argue about that?'

'Not really. I'd have preferred if we'd given more of it to the refugee charities Mum worked with than spending it on property abroad, but it's really Dad's, so he limited that.'

'What kind of charity work is your mum involved with?' Claire asked.

'She got really involved over the Syrian refugee crisis. She didn't just give money. She and Helen Jennings got some sponsorship from the local church, and in March went down through Macedonia and Greece in a big lorry loaded with supplies, and then to some island where the refugees were coming in by boat.'

'How long was she gone for?' Claire asked.

'Six weeks or so, I think,' Chloe said, perking up. 'Mum got special leave from the school, and when she came back she was all fired up about it. It was great, actually. She'd got the Women's Institute to raise money for them too. They bought 100 tents and 500 blankets. I'm sure they saved lots of lives. She's got some amazing pictures on her computer, which I'm sure she'll happily show you when she…'

No one said anything for a minute, and Chloe's head sagged. 'It's my birthday next week,' she said, her voice thick and choked. 'I just know you're going to tell me that my Dad killed my Mum and then ran away somewhere. But I can't believe it. It's impossible. He's a gruff old bear, but he loves her, I know that he loves her.' She lifted her head, and tears were already tracking down her sweet, youthful face.

'We're still hoping for good news, Chloe,' said Claire. 'The fact that your mum had endured some depression makes it a bit more likely that she's just run off somewhere for a while to be on her own.'

Or committed suicide, Gillard thought.

'All right, Chloe,' Claire said brightly. 'We're nearly done for today. I just need to take a cheek swab so we can eliminate your DNA when we test the house.'

'What are you doing in the house?' Chloe looked alarmed.

'It's just a precaution – we need to know if anyone beyond family has been there.'

'Okay.' Chloe sagged visibly, and started to chew her nails again.

'Gabby will stay with you for another hour or so, and will be available on the end of a phone for as long as you need her. If

81

you remember anything call her first, or even if you are just a bit worried and want a chat. We understand it's a very trying time. Try to get some rest. We'll let you know the latest as soon as we can.'

She reached out and held Chloe's hand. 'Fingers crossed, eh?'

Chloe nodded mutely, her beautiful eyes brimming. As Gillard walked out with Claire, he realized just how good at this she was.

It was nearly seven when Craig dropped Claire off at Caterham Police Station. She was buzzing with energy over the Knight case, and was going to look more closely into Oliver Knight. Craig, by contrast, was exhausted. Broken sleep last night, a tough day today, and now he needed to be in good form for a date with Sam in less than two hours at a bistro in West Croydon. She had rung him earlier to thank him for the flowers he had sent her, and offered to take him out to dinner. Part of him would have preferred to crawl into bed and sleep, but he didn't want to defer because with the way the Knight case was going he'd be working every hour for weeks. So he said yes. He had no idea whether he'd have time to get home and change first. Probably not. He had always kept an unopened new white M&S shirt in his desk, but that was back at Mount Browne, two hours away through rush hour traffic.

Before that he had a job to do. Craig got out of the car and opened the boot. In it was the ACESO kiosk, a briefcase-sized computer designed specifically to grab all the data from a mobile phone without having to send it away to a lab. He'd signed out one of the precious machines earlier, saying he wanted to teach himself how to use it. Actually, it was useless for the Knight case because they didn't possess the phones, but one phone he did have was Gary Harrison's, Sam's troublesome ex. Craig drove into the secure car park, put the device on his lap and followed the instructions. Five minutes later the information that tumbled out about Gary Harrison lowered him even further in Craig's estimation.

Craig was only ten minutes late, and had called ahead to let Sam know. She was already sitting there, at a candlelit table, in a stunning lacy black blouse and with her hair up in some kind of sophisticated arrangement that reminded him of the girl in *Breakfast at Tiffany's*. By contrast he was wearing an M&S polyester suit and a tie that had been strangling him all day.

'Sam, you look beautiful.' Her dark eyes looked huge in the candlelight, and there was barely a trace of the bruise.

'Well, you've only seen me as a mountain scarecrow, a hobby bobby in that ridiculous uniform, or as a stalker's punchbag. I thought it was time you saw the other me.'

'Tell me about this other me.'

Over the next few minutes Sam disclosed some of the highlights of her life that she'd been too embarrassed to boast about when he was carrying her out of the mountains. The fact she had been a catalogue model in her late teens, was a fully qualified windsurfing instructor and had run a couple of marathons for charity, the second time dressed as a rabbit. 'Don't ask,' she said. 'I fainted from the heat at 17 miles.'

When there was a pause in the conversation, Craig asked: 'How did you meet Gary Harrison?'

She groaned, and twisted her wine glass in her fingers. 'Through a dating website. He was absolutely charming at first. He told me about the life of a top chef in a restaurant on Park Lane. Working with Gordon Ramsay, meeting celebrities. So I was swept off my feet at first. But then he started getting possessive. Didn't like me seeing my female friends, let alone my male ones. He used to edit the contacts on my phone. It was more than two years ago when I dumped him, and I'd already lost a few friends. But it was only then it started to get really scary.'

Craig sighed. 'I've been looking into our Mr Harrison. He's told you some massive porky pies. First off, he's a catering manager at some college in Bromley. I can find no evidence he ever worked in a big West End restaurant. He was never in the Parachute Regiment either. He was in the catering part of the Royal Logistics Corp but I couldn't find any trace of him serving overseas. Biggest lie of all: he probably told you he was divorced, but he's not. He's married with two kids, but they're not at the address he gave you.'

Sam Phillips shook her head slowly. 'I feel sorry for her, whoever she is.'

'So do I. But I sincerely hope none of this is going to be your problem any more.'

Sam leaned across the table and kissed him, slowly and with feeling. 'Thank you, Craig.'

While Craig was sipping wine in the bistro, DS Claire Mulholland was tangling with an officious young solicitor.

'You are making me feel like a criminal,' said Oliver Knight, standing impotently at his front door just after nine in the evening as two burly detectives carried out large clear plastic bags containing computers, laptops and mobile phones to a police Transit van. 'And that's completely unnecessary. I have cooperated completely, and now I have to watch you ransack my home,' he said, staring at the house opposite where two elderly people were staring at him from the window. In the quiet suburb of Whyteleafe this was clearly a rare and exciting event.

'This is only a precaution at this stage,' Claire said, putting the warrant back in its envelope. 'The next stage might make you feel even more uncomfortable. Officers are currently with a keyholder at the offices of Barker Caynes Tipping and will be taking your computer there. We also need to take a DNA swab to eliminate you from any markers we find in your parents' house,' she said. 'Perhaps you could lead me to the kitchen and we can do it there.'

Oliver sat down at the kitchen table as requested, while his girlfriend Sophie watched from the doorway. Mulholland donned a pair of blue latex evidence gloves and took out a cotton bud. She held his chin and asked him to open wide, while she stroked the inside of his cheek with the swab. Oliver had closed his eyes, and she tried hard to suppress a snigger as she thought how like a fat schoolboy he looked, awaiting a sweet. She inserted the cotton bud into the plastic tube, sealed the lid and slid it into a pre-labelled evidence bag. She also reminded herself to check that the medical and dental records for the Knights had arrived.

Preparations for news of a death. She hoped they would not be needed, but something told her otherwise.

It was half past eleven when they left the bistro. The meal had gone well, and Craig had offered to drive Sam home. He was halfway there when she murmured to him: 'I've got a spare toothbrush if you'd like to stay.'

It was times like this when Craig hated his job. He had a very early start tomorrow, to drive to Dungeness and look over the Knights' holiday home, something that couldn't be deferred. He tried to explain: Tired. No more spare clothing. She looked offended at this litany of trivia, until he blurted out: 'But you could come and stay with me, if you don't mind letting yourself out in the morning.'

They stopped and kissed for a few minutes, then he turned the car round, and cut back through Purley's sweeping tree-lined suburbs to get back on the road to Banstead. Adele's 'Rolling in the Deep' was on the radio, and Sam was lightly resting her hand on his thigh when Craig suddenly gasped and braked hard in the middle of the road. He jumped out of the car, door open, leaving her wondering if he had just hit a cat. He was looking at a parked car, a Nissan Qashqai, and crouched to take a picture of its number plate with his phone. When he got back in he was smiling.

'What on earth was that about?' she asked.

'By sheer luck we've just found Liz Knight's car.' He looked along the avenue, topped with substantial semi-detached homes and extensive gardens turned over to lawn and shrubs.

'Does that mean I've got to go home now?' she asked. He watched a pout form.

'No, Sam, I'm all yours.' He kissed her cheek. 'I'll phone it in for some poor uniformed bugger to check up on.'

'Do you think she's staying in one of these houses?'

Craig sighed. 'I hope so, Sam. But somehow I doubt it. I think it was dumped here in the hope that it wouldn't be discovered for a while.'

After he'd made the call, Craig drove off. Could Liz Knight be in one of those big posh houses? Not willingly, surely. Not when she's failed to ring even her closest friends, or attend her play rehearsal, or gone to work.

Chapter Seven

I feel an aching void at the centre of myself where love used to be. He used to look at me with hunger, now his eyes roll over me with less interest than for a pizza delivery flyer. But then pizza has the upper hand. Freshly baked, delivered to your door, always a new topping to try.

Liz's diary, April 2009

Thursday, 20 October

PCSO Sam Phillips awoke in a strange bed, with the caress of a stranger's hand on her face, a stranger's whisper in her ear. 'I've got to get up now, Sam,' Craig said.

She groaned and stretched. 'What time is it?' Her body ached pleasantly, tingling in hidden places. The bed was warm with the musk of a man.

'Ten to five, just gone. Sorry.' She felt rather than saw his smile.

'God. I'm not on until eleven.' She blew a sigh.

'Don't worry. You can stay as long as you like. Let yourself out,' he said. 'There are some croissants, or there's cereal. Skimmed or semi-skimmed milk. I defrosted a wholemeal loaf in case you wanted toast. There's a tenner for a taxi.' He put the cash on the bedside table.

She murmured an acknowledgement as she felt the hand withdraw, and the other one that had been caressing her thigh slide away. The cash, particularly, made her feel cheap, though that obviously wasn't his intention. But it still felt transactional, as if she had given him something in exchange for the favours he had done her, on the mountain and dealing with Gary. Through sleepy eyes she watched Craig ease out of bed. In the silhouette of the bathroom light, the well-muscled back and tight bum drew her eye. She wondered whether it was the rock climbing or the cycling that kept him in such good shape. She'd not been idle in the days since they'd met. She'd made her own inquiries, from a friend who worked at Surrey Police HQ. Craig was an enigma, much-fancied, known to have had the odd fling. But who his long-term girlfriends were, nobody knew. All this had excited her and troubled her in equal measure.

What had happened last night she had wanted to happen. At one level the sex was great. Craig had extraordinary self-control; each crest of pleasure was wonderful. But it seemed somehow less than personal, like her father's pride in tickling a tricky carburettor into life on his old Triumph motorcycle. She craved passion for *her*, even if it were amateurishly delivered, rather than this detached focus on performance.

An hour after Craig's departure, Sam was padding around his flat eating toast, wearing the same white shirt she had enthusiastically torn from his back last night. A naughty part of her was dying to delve into drawers and cupboards, to find out if the cool detective chief inspector had any past. She excused her own curiosity. There was little to see otherwise. He clearly lived alone now, five years after the brief marriage. Apart from the large bedroom where they had slept, the flat had a tidy, somewhat understocked kitchen; a spare bedroom full of neatly arranged mountaineering gear, with an expensive lightweight bike hanging on the wall. There were no family photographs anywhere, though she found a wedding picture in a drawer of a younger Craig with a dark-haired woman. Neither of them looked as happy as you should on your wedding day. Maybe they already knew it was doomed even before they got hitched. It's amazing how many people do, but are trapped in marital momentum.

She carefully slid back the picture, closed the drawer and turned to the few shelves of heavyweight books: Shakespeare, Dickens, John Donne, Robert Graves. Gillard the intellectual: this was something that nobody knew about. She flicked through the volumes. They were mostly old cheap paperbacks, bar one. This was the hardback edition of the selected letters of Rainer Maria Rilke, in a dust protector. She picked it up, and inside on the flyleaf saw a dedication, written in fountain pen and dated 18 September 1986.

Dearest Craig,

As the great man said: We need in love to practise only the act of letting each other go. For holding on comes easily; we do not need to learn it. When I go to Cambridge next week, I will slip the moorings of your love. But one day, who knows, I may seek out your harbour. In the meantime, take this, my favourite book. Keep it close and look to the bold, blue horizon. There are many fine ships there, seeking havens as sheltered and welcoming as yours.

Farewell.

L. xx

Sam stared in amazement, before guilt made her slip the book back. This couldn't be his wife, it was far too old. She walked away, then found herself pacing backwards and forwards across the lounge. A decision made, she returned to the shelf, slid out the book and took it into the kitchen. She grabbed a sheet of kitchen roll, dabbed some diluted washing-up liquid on it and then wiped the plastic dust protector. No fingerprints now. With a tea towel she then picked it up and returned it carefully to its slot, as if it were radioactive. Craig was a detective, after all, by reputation a very good one, and she had committed a crime. She had slipped between sheaves of precious memory and burgled his heart.

Six thirty on a grey and windy Thursday morning found Gillard on the A23 heading out of London towards Brighton and the south coast. The car ate up the miles as he turned off onto the anticlockwise carriageway of the M25, the truck traffic already heavy on the inside lane and the early commuters yawning their way to work. He thought about the pretty woman probably still snoozing in his bed. It made him smile. He jabbed through the radio stations and settled for some retro 1980s hits as he headed east towards the M20. Berlin's 'Take My Breath Away', Simply Red's 'Holding Back the Years', Chris de Burgh and 'Lady in Red'. Older memories washed over the new.

He almost overshot the M20 junction and had to cross the between-lane hatching, an offence. That wouldn't do. Having examined the map, Gillard was surprised to be reminded how far away Dungeness really was. The elbow of Kent stuck out east below London for 60 miles, looking to dig Europe in the ribs. Hanging beneath it, between Hastings and Folkestone, was a little fin of marsh and shingle sticking out south into the English Channel. At its furthest point, Dungeness.

At Ashford, Gillard turned off the motorway and headed down into Romney Marsh, a densely hedged and pastoral land of sheep and pretty villages. Gradually the dirty white chalk hills toward Hastings came into view on his right and the landscape became more open, dotted with wind farms and pylons. After the small towns of New Romney and Lydd the grey boxy bulk of Dungeness 'B' nuclear power station rose in the distance.

It was 30 years since his previous and only trip down here, with Liz, a five-foot-three-inch bundle of affection, tucked behind him on the Kawasaki. Every time he'd accelerated hard, he had felt her arms tighten around his waist and the lower edge of the visor on her helmet dig into his back. As he lowered the bike into sharp corners he had relished her little squeals of fear and excitement. The anticipation had been almost unbearable. She had promised to make love with him, but only if they had a proper bed and no chance of interruption. For weeks he'd been unable to think of a way to arrange it. Craig knew that her parents wouldn't let her stay away overnight, not even with close friends like Kathy. Then one night in the pub, she had waved the key to Great Wickings at him. 'But we have to be there and back in a day,' she teased. 'Can your motorbike manage that?' Craig just grinned. He would have pushed the bike to Dungeness if that was what was required.

The Ford swept past the gravelly wetlands, a huge expanse of Romney Marsh famous for its birdlife, and took a right turn into the village of Dungeness. Great Wickings, as he well remembered, was a sprawling single-storey wooden house, more like a fishing shack on the coast of Newfoundland or Labrador than a holiday cottage in the Garden of England. There had originally been an external staircase to a dormer room in the roof, which had been used for drying fishing nets but had been turned into bedrooms by Liz's father. The sky-blue painted door and window frames were as he remembered, but the front garden which he recalled being full of forget-me-nots and wallflowers was now going native. Rosebay willowherb and numerous long-stalked weeds whose names he didn't know had spread across the finer shingles and the shallow, gravelly soil. A police patrol car sat outside the property, and a single strand of police tape stretched across the door. He got out of the Ford and walked up to the patrol car. An officer in high-vis sat in a reclined seat with the radio on low, his arms folded across his chest. Asleep.

Gillard rapped on the window with his phone, and the officer jerked. He looked up, slid the window down and scrutinized the ID card that Gillard held in his face.

'Apologies, sir,' the PC said.

'Any visitors?' Gillard asked, looking back at the house.

'No, sir. A few locals have popped past, but there's nothing I can tell them.'

'Okay. I'm going in to take a quick look myself. I've got the full Noddy suit, so you won't have to worry about contamination. I believe my office has contacted your CSI chief to tell them.'

'Righto.'

Gillard returned to the Ford, opened the boot, and from a plastic bag slipped on a crackly white Tyvek overall, plastic overshoes and blue latex gloves. He slipped a compact camera into his pocket. He walked over to the drive, which was of very coarse beach-type shingle, leading up to a car port which adjoined the house's left-hand side. He walked up carefully, and noticed signs of disturbance among the stones where smaller, damper shingle from underneath had been uncovered. He walked into the car port, which was a concrete slab just big enough for a typical saloon car. There were no recent signs of oil spillage on the concrete, but there were some vague tyre marks of indeterminate age.

Gillard took Oliver's key from his pocket. It was an old and rather simple iron mortise key, somewhat corroded in the shank, with a paper label dangling from it on a piece of string. It wouldn't fit the front door; he'd already seen there was a more modern Yale lock on that. He tried the door that faced the car port. The key fitted, turned, and he was in. He was immediately hit by the bottled-gas cooking smell that reminded him of caravan holidays in his youth, and of a rather special day here with Liz in 1986.

They had arrived at Great Wickings one Tuesday in September at half past nine, and Craig had almost leapt on her the moment she had opened the front door. She, the more experienced, made him wait, and had slowly undressed and caressed him. Only then did she show him by guiding his virgin hands how to gently and unhurriedly arouse her. His first view of her naked body straddling him, his hands on the hard little nipples on her apple-sized breasts, his first experience of the grasping, sweet joy of entry had remained with him for ever. But there was more. He remembered still the green whorl patterns of the loose-weave curtains of her parents' bedroom, the insanely squeaky bed, the curling roses on the wallpaper he stared at as he surrendered to the inevitability of post-coital sleep, and the stupid little porcelain dog figures which stared down at him from the shelf. He lost himself in five or six hours of endless pleasure in Liz's embrace, her heat, her delightful energy. And then, while it was still light and with the rain just beginning to sweep across the shingles, she nudged him awake. They had to return. The bittersweet memory – of a chilly journey back, of a perfect day that somehow he knew would never be repeated – ate into his heart even more than the cold and the rain.

As Gillard trod carefully further into the house he scented something else – an unsavoury odour, a combination of bad drains and rancid meat.

He stepped into the storage room. There was a chest freezer there. He lifted the lid. The smell didn't come from there. It was barely a quarter full, mainly of branded frozen veg, and items wrapped in silver foil. It looked like a normal collection of household food, something for CSI to investigate.

The corridor behind the storage area took him through to a dining room, in which there was a big La-Z-Boy-type recliner. To the left was an old-fashioned looking kitchen with side-by-side butler sinks designed for doing laundry. The taps had the old-fashioned rubber nozzles on he hadn't seen for decades. The kitchen windows gave out onto the sun lounge. Nothing seemed out of place. He opened the refrigerator, an old-fashioned waist-high job with an open icebox. There was a bottle of white wine with a vacuum stopper in it, and a couple of cans of beer. Next to it was a pantry, its shelves still lined with newspapers. There was no fresh food. Strange, if Liz had been down here for a painting weekend.

He went up the two steps into the lounge and turned on the light. The room seemed clean and tidy. He could no longer detect the bad smell that had assailed him. He took the staircase and peered into the two upstairs dormer rooms. The rose wallpaper was still there, but the curtains were different. He pressed the modern bed. Not a squeak. Not really a surprise after 30 years. Having satisfied himself there were no bodies in any of the rooms he made his way downstairs, took a quick glance into the kitchen, and then let himself out the way he'd come in. At the back of the house, the plot just ran away to the distance where marshes and reeds began. In the far distance were old fishing boats, up on repair frames, abandoned long ago to the rain, the salt air and the wind. This was the strange thing about Dungeness. There were a couple of rough roads, but few fences or boundary marks, and the hundred or so homes, fishing sheds, abandoned boats and shipping containers that were randomly scattered across the shingle looked like they had been washed ashore by some giant tsunami. The only mark of human planning was the narrow-gauge railway whose track ran along behind the shoreline and ended with a loop just by the power station.

Craig turned his gaze back to the immediate area. At what looked to be the end of the plot, marked by a line of scraggly bushes, were a couple of wooden sheds, side by side and weathered to the shade of parchment. In front of them was a blackened and dented oil drum in which fires had been lit. It still smelled of old bonfires, or even barbecues. He'd leave that one for the Kent CSI boys. He peered into the sheds through mildewed windows, but could see nothing more than a few old tools. Gillard peered down the hand-width gap between the two sheds and spotted something at the far end, partially hidden under the remains of a toddler's plastic beach set, its bucket cracked and bleached by the elements. It was a garden spade, the varnish on the wooden shaft still intact, not salt-paled like most of the wood here. He took several pictures, then carefully walked around to the back of the shed, where he could reach it. Lifting it up and away, he saw the blade in the space beneath. At the base of the handle, where the wood fitted into the metal sleeve, was a tiny smear, like a squashed midge, a couple of tiny legs stuck in the air. He knelt down on the unforgiving shingle to take a closer look. He removed a folding magnifying glass from his pocket, popped it out of its sleeve and leaned as close as he could. It confirmed his initial suspicion: there were a couple of folded human-looking hairs in a sticky fleck of blood, trapped in the metal sleeve of the spade. At least one had the root intact, so there could be DNA. He would normally be reluctant to move any evidence before the CSI people arrived, but he didn't want to leave it at the mercy of the weather until tomorrow, so he took two large evidence bags from his pocket. The first he slid over the handle, where any fingerprints might be recovered, and the second he carefully eased over the blade, then taped it well up the shaft and above the hairs.

Something unsavoury had happened within the Knight family, he was increasingly certain. He was used to terrible discoveries in lock-up garages, tragedies in cramped, untidy rooms in worn-out council estates, to the twist of the knife in families whose lives were at the best of times a maelstrom of chaos. The strangest thing about this case was not what might have happened but the fact that it had happened to the Knights: a gilded family, the kind of family who never experience horrific events.

Could there be any innocent explanation for what he had found? Or was this evidence of an ignominious end to Liz's life, crushed beneath a spade wielded in all probability by her husband? As he looked to the horizon, and the line of cliffs to the west, a gust of wind came. It wasn't particularly cold, but he shuddered and turned his back on it, his mind as dark as the gathering clouds.

While DCI Gillard was just approaching Dungeness, DS Claire Mulholland was showing Kathy Parkinson into the interview suite at Caterham Police Station. Ms Parkinson was an elegant woman in her mid-40s in a royal blue trouser suit and black court shoes.

'Mrs Knight is still missing, I'm afraid,' Claire said.

'Oh God. What's Martin got to say about it?'

Claire paused, unsure how much to reveal. 'We spoke to Professor Knight just after he arrived at the holiday home on Tuesday evening. But he's been avoiding us since then.'

'I just don't understand it,' Kathy said. 'If something had gone wrong between her and Martin, I'd be the first person she'd call. But there's been nothing.'

'Perhaps we can go back to the beginning. How long have you known Mrs Knight?'

'Liz and I went to school together from the age of 11. She went up to Cambridge, and I went to Bristol. We spent occasional weekends with each other, when Martin wasn't around or was busy. I was one of her bridesmaids when she got married in, oh…'

'1991?' Claire said, looking down at her notes.

'That's it, yes. We lost contact for a while, and then I got married too, and it was down to cards at Christmas and the odd phone call for a few years. When she first got depression she came to stay with Keith and me at La Porcherie and then—'

'La Porcherie?'

'The pigsty. It's the holiday home that Keith, my ex-husband, stupidly bought for us to do up in Normandy. It actually used to *be* a pigsty, and needs masses and masses spending on it. Now he's gone, and I'm single, I can't see me ever doing the work to get it up to scratch. I got it in the divorce settlement in exchange for the Merc and caravan, but I'm beginning to think he got the better end of the deal. It's not even in a saleable condition...'

Claire cleared her throat to steer the conversation away from the woes of DIY and divorce. 'What about in recent years?'

'Well, Liz and I ended up living back in the same area. When Martin got the LSE post and left Oxford, Liz managed to persuade him that they should move back near her parents in Old Coulsdon, as they were getting elderly, and I'm not so far away in Warlingham. There was a bit of argy-bargy apparently, but he eventually agreed when they found this beautiful house with a long garden on the edge of the Downs. Martin quite fancied slowing down a bit, getting a chocolate Labrador and going for long rambles on the Downs. But of course he hasn't. The Home Office consultation and report work started in earnest then, so he's been nose to the grindstone ever since. And of course Liz was stuck with having to do the garden as well as working as a deputy head and bringing up the kids.'

Claire capped her fountain pen and set it aside. 'Can I ask you if everything seemed all right in Liz and Martin's marriage?'

'Well, where to start?' Kathy said with a groan. 'Liz has given everything up for him. She had a fantastic career just waiting for her, but he always managed to get his own way. When she was at Cambridge she researched and wrote some amazing paper about the Spanish Civil War. She'd gone off to Spain under her own steam, managed to interview some of the surviving Republican prisoners who had only just been released after the death of Franco. It won the 1988 A. J. P. Taylor prize for undergraduate history, and on the back of that she was offered an Eleanor Roosevelt bursary and research fellowship at Harvard. I mean, it's a quarter of a million dollars, there's only one offered every five years, and it's a huge honour. She was only 20! Now Martin, who was doing pretty well himself, had just got his MA at St Peter's College in Oxford, and been offered a funded research fellowship there, though tiny compared with the Harvard one. He didn't want to lose Liz, so he pulled out his ace in the hole and proposed. Liz was head over heels with him anyway, so she foolishly gave up the bursary and, after she graduated, followed him to Oxford. But I actually don't think she ever forgave him, quite, in later years when she realized that she wasn't ever going to have a second chance. Once the children arrived, and then she was ill, she never quite fulfilled the initial promise.'

'And in recent years?'

'Things had definitely got worse. She got very down... actually I mean it was more than that, it was clinical depression. Then she was in a car accident when Martin drove into a skip in Abinger Hammer.'

'Martin was driving?' Claire asked, recalling that Chloe's version of events had her mother in the driver's seat.

'Yes, silly drunken bugger. He was all right because of the air bag, but her face hit the dashboard and she got a badly broken ankle too, and the ambulance took ages to get there. All this meant endless bloody hospital appointments, pins being fitted and God knows what. Now there's arthritis in it. She has good days and bad, but when it's bad, she needs a stick to walk. The poor woman's only 48, for God's sake.'

'So there is a lot of resentment. Anything else?'

Kathy took a deep breath. 'I suppose I should tell you about the affairs. Martin had an affair with a doctoral student in the late 1990s. This was pretty hateful, because Liz had Oliver who was eight, and Chloe, just two. What chance has a mother run ragged by two young kids, clearing up vomit and used nappies against a honey-skinned Brazilian with big tits? I mean, it's just not fair, is it?'

Claire, divorced once herself, could feel the divorcee solidarity neurons working on her just as it had on Kathy, a woman who had by the sound of it been in a similar situation.

'That one only lasted a few weeks. The major affair began in 2010. Dr Natalie Krugman, *the* Dr Natalie Krugman.'

'Sorry, I don't know her.'

Kathy seemed slightly surprised. 'The bestselling author of *Menstruation and Martyrdom*. Ring any bells? She's quite famous in feminist circles.'

'Sorry.' Claire shrugged. 'I don't even have time to read *Family Circle*.'

'She's quite glamorous, I suppose. Anyway, Martin apparently chased after her like a dog that had scented a truckload of Winalot. It was pretty shameless. I told Liz she should divorce him.'

'So Martin isn't your favourite person?'

'No, but I'm pretty good at hiding my feelings. I see them both a lot, they have a wide group of very faithful friends, so I keep my counsel. I don't think he's got the faintest idea how much I know about their marriage. There are some things that I know that no one else does.'

'Such as?'

'He hit her! I dropped in one Monday evening when Martin was away, and she had a humdinger of a black eye. I asked what happened and she responded: "The official version or the real one?" The official version was that she'd fallen off the mountain bike Martin had given her for Christmas. She'd been practising to get fit, because he wanted her to go with him on weekends away in the Peak District, puffing up muddy paths in some hopeless quest for fitness. What had really happened is that he'd punched her. Can you believe it! She wouldn't give me the details, and swore me to secrecy. I think she was too ashamed. She abhors violence, and it was entirely new to her to be on the receiving end.

'When was this?'

'January, I suppose. I pleaded with her to divorce him, and she said maybe she would once Chloe left university. I told her she could do a Helen Jennings...'

'A who?'

'Helen Jennings. A delightful friend of ours who's actually made it work. She got the dream divorce deal. A villa in the Algarve, a Saab turbo, half his huge pension. She's still got the looks, lucky thing, and has been dating a succession of charming younger men.'

'And what did Liz say?'

'She looked at me very soberly, and said: "Not everyone can be like Helen. The probability is that I would end up in the majority: one of those lonely middle-aged women, radiating desperation and disappointment from every pore, stuck in a one-bedroom flat while her ex marries a woman a dozen years her junior." Kathy shrugged and rolled her eyes.

'Was that a dig at you?'

'I felt it was an observation. Not particularly kind, but unfortunately rather accurate. If Keith could get away with it, and sad to say he has, then Martin certainly could. Keith is a balding and increasingly rotund middle manager in a car component business. Even his best friends would be hard-pressed to describe him as a catch. Yet he's now married to a 26-year old marketing manager in Bracknell that he met on a dating website. I have absolutely no idea what she sees in him. Of course, he had secretly been stashing away money for this for years. And Keith has neither the brains nor the attractiveness of Martin.'

She looked away and shrugged. 'Anyway, as Liz observed, wedding day dreams die a slow and painful death in most marriages. Nothing in the cold bitter daylight of divorce brings them back.'

Claire mulled the sentiment. 'Perhaps it's just growing older. You can't live in daydreams.'

'That's true, but it's the realization that men give less consideration to the fabric of the marital relationship than they do to the garage which contains their precious toys.' She smiled. 'Look, don't get me wrong. I have a lot of fun, and I'm not bitter. I've got my career, which is as good as Liz's. Well, as good as Liz's is *now*. But I don't have kids, and now I'm too old to have any. She, by contrast, never wanted them, really, and has two. If she divorced Martin, she predicted that he'd probably want to keep the house, and the grown-up children would get to know a new woman, who would undoubtedly be younger and more fun than a mum who's put on loads of weight, lives on her own, looks ten years older than she is and walks with a stick. I do see what she means.'

'We have no record of her reporting an assault. Do you know if she went to see the doctor about it?'

'If she did, it would have been reported as a bike accident. Look, I have to go pretty soon. But if you've got any questions, please call or email.' She passed across a business card: senior lecturer in psychology, King's College London. 'By the way, I've been told that the officer in charge of the investigation is one Craig Gillard.'

'Yes, he's my boss.'

'Interesting. Is he by any chance the same Craig Gillard who used to go out with Liz back in the 1980s?'

Mulholland tried to glaze her shock with a smile. 'He didn't say anything to me about it.'

'I'm not surprised. She broke his heart, you know. The man was in pieces after she dumped him for Martin. If anyone has the motive to bear enmity towards the eminent professor, it's your detective chief inspector.'

Chapter Eight

The night that Chloe was born, that fearful pain, like turning myself inside out, his hand was there for me to hold. I held it so tightly I could feel every bone. 'I'll always be there for you,' he said. 'You can squeeze my fingers until the blood seeps out, but I'll never pull my hand away.' I saw that hand yesterday, almost a decade and a half later. It was scratching at the back of his neck while he read some journal. I once knew every inch of that hand. It steadied my heart, and its pulse matched every cadence of my life's breath. Does it now only explore another woman's breasts, divide another's thighs?

Liz's diary, January 2011

King Edward VII's School in Oxted was everything Gillard had expected. As the detective's Ford slid between the wrought iron gates with their stone lion posts, he spotted the half-timbered Jacobean hall at the centre of extensive lawns and the magnificent cedars that cloaked the rest of the school from view. Gillard had been due to meet the headmaster at noon, and as it was now nearly 12.40 p.m., he was slightly nervous. Mr P. W. J. Cordingley had been the devil's own job to track down on the phone, and a rather steely secretary had offered him half an hour, notwithstanding the official nature of his inquiries. 'It's all I can manage, because we're in the middle of Ofsted. Please be punctual. Philip is a very busy man.'

The detective found the gravelled car park, and as he emerged he realized it must be lunchtime. The faint sound of handbells stirred neat pupils in magenta and grey uniforms to brisk but unhurried movements from one red-brick building to another. Asking for directions to the headmaster's office, he was addressed as sir and accompanied by a boy the entire way along a glass corridor built between an ivy-covered chapel and a modern library. The child then directed him up hushed stairs where gilded portraits of educationalists for the last two centuries stared sternly down at him.

'I'm terribly sorry that we've not been able to show you appropriate flexibility,' Cordingley said as he invited Gillard into his spacious study. 'Ofsted inspectors are like the Spanish inquisition...'

'Nobody expects them,' Gillard said.

'Exactly,' Cordingley said. 'Chief weapons: fear, surprise and a fanatical devotion to the national curriculum.' He was a tall and upright fellow with sparse white hair and a soft voice. 'Now, I have to tell you we are all quite horrified that Elizabeth has gone missing. It is absolutely out of character, and we are bereft without her. Not only as my deputy and head of history, but the Christmas play, the school orchestra, the Chess Society, and her wonderful charitable endeavours.'

Gillard was happy to let Cordingley document Liz's activities, and to show him to her office, which was small and modern. He agreed to keep it locked until officers could come to take away her computer for examination, and to provide passwords as required. 'It's just a precaution,' Gillard said. 'Her school email record could give us some leads as to where she might be.'

Chapter Nine

Getting the kids up, dressed and breakfasted; heading off to a school whose headmaster genuinely believes it runs itself; smiling at staff, listening to children, glad-handing parents. Shopping, preparing food, talking to my friends. Every day I do my marital origami. Folding each exterior leaf of my life carefully inward, the crisp creases covering the jagged hole in the centre of my soul. A last flap of self-esteem, sealed carefully, so that no one can see the void or guess its existence.

Liz Knight, email to Kathy Parkinson, June 2011

Thursday, 4 p.m.

Gillard was at Caterham police station making final preparations for the news conference in an hour. Paddy Kincaid and Alison Rigby had just arrived, so he could now begin briefing the full investigative team on what to look for once the public's calls began to flow in.

'Okay, let's run through what we've got,' said Gillard. 'Rob, off you go.'

'Right, Mrs Elizabeth Knight, nee Bishopsford, reported missing on Tuesday morning at 10.45. No one has actually seen her since last Thursday at 1 p.m., except her husband who said he saw her on Friday morning. Setting his account aside, that's six whole days. She's missed several important events, quite apart from work. Last Thursday evening she was supposed to attend a birthday drink for a friend, at a pub in Carshalton, and texted her apologies just half an hour before she was due to arrive. The mobile operator confirmed this as the last outgoing text or call on her missing phone. It has been switched off since then.'

'Do we have cell site analysis on that text?' Gillard asked.

'Yes. Old Coulsdon. As far as we can work out, she was at home.'

'Okay, next,' Gillard said.

'Professor Martin Knight, missing person.' There were a few chuckles around the room, which Gillard silenced with a glare. 'LSE academic, missing since 8 p.m. on Tuesday, so less than 48 hours. However, given that he was speaking to us, from a landline at Dungeness in Kent, just a few minutes before, we can be quite clear that was a firm last contact. There was also an email yesterday, sent to the departmental secretary at LSE, which pinged a cell site in Dungeness. So he's still about, but evading us.'

'What about his car? Presumably gone?' Kincaid asked.

'Yes,' Townsend said. 'Last ANPR contact for that vehicle was on the M20, prior to the phone call. We've got it on nationwide alert. The vehicle's not been booked in at ports, airport car parks or the Chunnel. Kent Police have secured the Dungeness address, but they've had their work cut out since yesterday with two bodies discovered in an emergency refuge inside the Channel Tunnel. Consequently they won't have the resource for a full CSI until Friday morning…'

Gillard groaned, and someone muttered: 'Why can't the French deal with it?'

'…but they can confirm his car isn't at the address in Dungeness,' Townsend said. 'No other vehicles there either. There are no neighbours nearby, but Kent Police are doing house to house. Many of the homes are unoccupied in the low season, so we shouldn't expect anything much.'

'What about her car?' Kincaid asked. 'Why did that turn up where it did, more than two miles from her home?'

'Uniform are doing house to house in that street too,' Gillard said. 'Doesn't seem that anyone there knows her, or him. Forensics are crawling all over the car, but results will take a day or two.' He turned to Townsend. 'Tell us what you know about his mobile, Rob.'

The research information officer repeated what he had earlier told Gillard, and added: 'He rang his wife's mobile at least 16 times between Sunday and Tuesday evening. We've got messages for the first recorded few, but by Monday evening her mailbox was full. He's clearly been going through the motions of the distraught husband.'

'Did anyone interview the cleaner?' Alison Rigby asked.

Claire Mulholland held up her hand. 'I did, ma'am. Her name is Doreen Henderson, age 57, part time lollipop lady too, clean as a whistle on the PNC. I'd trust her account.'

'May I interrupt? asked Rigby, walking up to the whiteboard. 'Let's step back a little and do a little speculating. There are two reasons we might not have heard from Professor Knight: one, he killed his wife, by accident or design, and is in a panic. Or two, they are both dead, killed by someone else.'

She stepped away. 'Let's invert the logic. As I see it, if Mrs Knight is alive, there should be no reason for Martin Knight not to return our call.' She stared at each of those present in turn, her blue-eyed gaze intense. 'Come on, someone fault my reasoning. I won't bite.'

There was an uneasy silence. Gillard looked at Kincaid, who made an almost imperceptible shake of the head: she does bite, and how.

A hand went up at the far end of the room. 'Ma'am,' said a young, newly qualified DC, Aaron Gibson. He looked so young that he could have been answering a question at school. 'What if she's been kidnapped, and Knight has received a ransom demand, which tells him not to call the police.'

Rigby inclined her head in consideration of this. 'That would explain Knight's repeated calls to her phone which then ceased after the time of the last contact with us.' She looked to Gillard. 'Craig, what do you think?'

'It's unlikely for many reasons, ma'am,' Gillard said. 'There was no sign of disturbance at the house which you might expect from an intruder. More importantly, if she went out after the cleaner saw her, then the kidnapper came back into the vicinity later to send a text about missing a birthday meal, which is implausible. But if that text was genuine, then

Elizabeth Knight *was* in or near the house. Above all, I just don't think the Knights have the kind of resources to attract kidnappers this professional.'

'In other words, this is Surrey, not bloody Beirut,' muttered Kincaid.

At that moment the duty sergeant poked her head in the door. 'The Knight family are here for the press conference.'

'Show them into room C, would you?' Gillard said. He looked at his watch. A quarter to five. Fifteen minutes before everyone in the country would know that Liz and Martin Knight were missing.

'The family just gave us some video of Mrs Knight,' the sergeant said, handing across a disc.

'Let's have a quick look,' Gillard said. Townsend inserted the disc into his laptop, and as the officers crowded round, ran the video that Oliver Knight had given them. It showed Liz at her birthday party in August. The party was in the family room of their house, packed with about 30 middle-class, middle-aged friends making polite conversation, slightly embarrassed by Martin Knight wandering around with a camcorder. Towards the end he homed in on Liz, walking around with a tray of nibbles. Her face was swollen and a little florid, she was wearing the awful glasses and her gait seemed stiff and restricted. Even from the back, it was obvious that Martin's running commentary was irritating her. After he had followed her around for a minute or two, she turned to the camera and said: 'Martin, I think that's quite enough.' The recording stopped.

'Poor old cow,' Kincaid muttered. 'How old did you say she was, Craig?'

'It was her 48th birthday party. It's written on the balloons,' Gillard replied, trying to keep the sarcasm from his voice. His opinion of Kincaid's detective abilities had never been high.

'Use it,' said Alison Rigby. 'Newspapers like to run clips of this kind of thing on their websites, and it's a natural for TV.'

'We can get it on our Facebook page too,' Townsend added. 'It not only shows the missing woman, but the character of the family she came from—'

Gillard interrupted. 'My only misgiving is that we don't have any video of Professor Knight. I want people to have a clear picture of him, because if we find him, we'll find her.'

'Because only he knows where the body is?' Alison Rigby suggested.

Gillard could only nod. 'That's my gut feeling, yes.'

The assistant chief constable scanned the rest of the officers. Her pale-blue eyes, powerful even through her tortoiseshell glasses, scanned each of them there. 'Can I emphasize to everyone that we are not going to give even a hint of these suspicions. This is a missing persons' inquiry, nothing more, until we get clear and unequivocal information. Is that clear?' There was a murmur of approval. 'Good. Then at least we're all on the same page.'

'Thank you for joining us at such short notice,' said Assistant Chief Constable Alison Rigby. The press conference room was pretty full, with several national newspapers in attendance, all the Surrey regionals plus the BBC, Press Association and local radio. Sitting with her behind the table were Craig Gillard, DS Mulholland, Surrey Police press officer Christina McCafferty, Liz's parents Tom and Geraldine Bishopsford, and Oliver and Chloe Knight.

'Before I hand you over to Detective Chief Inspector Gillard, I'd just like to say that a recording of this briefing will be available as a webcast. Now over to you, Craig.'

'Thank you. Surrey Police yesterday launched a missing person's investigation into Mrs Elizabeth Knight of Chaldon Rise, Old Coulsdon, who has not been seen for eight days. Today, we would like to ask for the public's help in finding her. The last public sighting was at 4 p.m. on Wednesday 12 October in the car park of the school where she is deputy head. She was wearing a charcoal-grey trouser suit and carrying a shoulder bag. She may be walking with a stick. Given the number of days she has been missing, we are extremely concerned for her safety. We are also urgently trying to contact her husband, Professor Martin Knight, who has been missing for 48 hours. We are keeping an open mind at this stage about what has happened, but it is completely out of character for either of these two busy, professional people to fail to turn up for important appointments or to return calls from friends and family. We believe these two incidents are connected, and we appeal to Mr Knight to come forward.'

Gillard looked at Oliver Knight, and moved the microphone towards him. 'My mother is a strong, independent, career woman with an ordered life. For her to just disappear without letting anyone know is unprecedented.' The image of the consummate professional lasted until the last word, when his voice broke. He rubbed a hand across his face and paused before continuing. 'Dad, if you are watching this, please, please get in contact.'

The conference was turned over to questions, none of which spared the sensibilities of the family, and which Gillard handled as best he could:

'Is this a murder inquiry?'

'No, it's a missing person's case. As I said, we're keeping an open mind at this stage.'

'Is this the same professor who lambasted your force over its handling of youth justice?'

'It is, but obviously that does not affect the way we run the case.'

'We noticed the crime scene people at the house. Are you digging up the garden to look for a body?'

'Not at this stage. The involvement of CSI is a precaution. This is still, as I said, a missing person's inquiry.'

After shielding the family from questions on whether the Knights had a violent relationship, or whether either had a criminal record, Gillard drew the conference to a close.

Rigby shepherded the family into a side room and, with Gillard there, closed the door. 'I would like to assure you,' she said, meeting the eyes of each of them in turn, 'that Surrey Police will allocate the fullest resources to solving this case as rapidly and effectively as possible. Professor Knight may have criticized this force, among others, in the past, but we will continue to treat this case just like any other. If any of you have any misgivings about the way the case is being handled, at any stage, I encourage you to ring me on my direct line.' She handed out a business card to each member of the family.

Gillard had plenty of respect for Rigby. She had made her name in the drug squad in Hull, almost the toughest posting she could have been given. She managed a clever sting operation which netted a Pakistani 'Mr Big' in 2002. He and his associates had been pushing half a ton a month of heroin into Britain sealed in sheets of rubber which were secured above false metal ceilings in shipping containers. The rubber's scent-absorbing powers had fooled the sniffer dogs, and it was only when a crane operator at Immingham damaged a container that the heroin was discovered. Alison had the container repaired, the drugs replaced with talcum powder and a GPS transmitter embedded in the rubber, before letting it continue on its way. The drug squad finally swooped on a freight yard in Birmingham, netting 18 members of the gang and drugs with a street value of £400 million.

Once the family had departed, Alison Rigby took Gillard aside and asked: 'What's next?'

'We've got two dedicated phone lines staffed here, four officers available until midnight, and two through the night. I'll be on call this evening in case the TV appeal tweaks any recollections. Tomorrow I'm hoping we're going to get something substantive from analysis of the Knights' computers, and Kent CID will be starting CSI on the holiday home. We've got a few statements to take from family and friends. By late tomorrow we should know everything about the family's finances, and we'll be able to watch where his bank card transactions pop up.'

'Have we got a full CSI report in the works on the Coulsdon house?' she asked sharply.

'No. They didn't have time to do dabs or a full search. It's pencilled in for tomorrow.' You couldn't get anything past her, Craig had to admit.

Rigby gave him the full blue gaze of death, one eyebrow slightly raised.

'You think I should go there now?' he asked

She nodded curtly. 'Good decision. Use your initiative.'

Craig certainly wanted to have a look around Liz's home. But having spent 40 of the last 48 hours at work, leaving eight hours in bed and less than half that asleep, he had hoped it would wait until tomorrow. Fat chance.

Gillard drove to the Knights' Coulsdon home for 7 p.m. The house was dark, with only the faint bluish light of a phone illuminating the duty PC standing by the porch. Probably checking Facebook, Gillard thought. Still, at least this one is awake.

Gillard reread Quoroshi's notes on his iPad, then got out and walked to the boot. Once he was fully Tyveked, he hefted the box of tricks he had earlier signed out from the newly installed Caterham CSI cupboard. Crackling his way up to the PC he was greeted courteously and checked in on the clipboard. 'Anyone else been here since Quoroshi left?' Gillard asked.

'CSI technician came to do dabs at 3.25 p.m., left at 5 p.m. He said to tell everyone it's all right to touch door handles, light switches, banister, taps and so on now. At 4.17 p.m. Oliver Knight arrived and wanted to go in "just for a minute", but I wouldn't let him. Lots of press, of course. Politely told 'em to bugger off, sir.'

'Quite right too.' Gillard took the keys the PC offered him, let himself in and flicked on the lights. The hall was short and wide. On the right was a small study-cum-library with a desk, typist's chair and floor-to-ceiling bookshelves, groaning with academic titles. The whiter patch on the faded melamine desk showed where the computer had been. Using a single gloved finger he carefully opened the drawers beneath. A locked drawer had been forced, as referenced in the CSI notes, and was empty. He returned to the hall and glanced into the lounge where five years ago he had taken Mrs Edwards' burglary statement. Tidy, classic 1990s. But no TV.

Straight on from the front door was a very large family room, hardwood-floored, with dining table, kitchen and breakfast room. Its large windows gave onto a patio and a garden that rose steeply in slightly overgrown terraces to a wooded slope on the bottom edge of Farthing Downs. There were a few dishes stacked in the sink, a few papers on the kitchen table, but no signs of an obvious hurry to leave.

Gillard climbed the open-plan staircase to the first floor. His nose caught the tang of cleaning products or perhaps air freshener. The master bedroom was at front left over the lounge, with a king-size bed, fitted wardrobes with sliding doors, and a mirrored dressing table standing on a small green rug. Yaz's notes said two hairbrushes from this dressing table had been booked in for evidence, and toothbrushes from the en-suite bathroom. They also referenced a wine stain on the carpet now covered by the green rug. Gillard flipped the rug over, the taint of bleach invaded his nostrils. The rug had been put in place to cover a big bleach stain on the oatmeal carpet, and the smell indicated it was fairly recent. Tiny splashes of what appeared to be red wine were still visible beyond it. Craig reset the rug, and looked at the bedside table. It was heavy with brain food. *Eternal Golden Braid*, by Douglas R. Hofstadter; a biography of Simone de Beauvoir; Homer's *Odyssey* in classical Greek, a bookmark three-quarters of the way through; and a tatty, well-thumbed classical Greek–English dictionary. He ached to remove his gloves and caress those books, as if it was somehow possible to absorb through his fingertips the mature woman that his Liz had become.

Gillard made his way to the larger of the back bedrooms. A little untidy, with the bed unmade and a man's jacket and grey trousers lying on top. A white crumpled shirt was on the carpet near the linen basket, a pair of socks balled nearby. It seemed that Martin Knight no longer slept in the marital bedroom.

The untidiness struck Gillard as evidence of a quick turnaround when Knight had come back from the conference and before he headed off to Dungeness. A pile of criminology periodicals were haphazardly stacked on the bedside table, next to a letter, faded and creased. The sight of her handwriting made him catch his breath, though the target was not his heart but another's.

The heat of You

That first embrace in Cambridge, I remember so clearly. The wind from the frozen fens, with its breath of Siberia. Your warm arms around me in the pub doorway. The hearth you built around me, somewhere to bury myself in embraces on every darkling February day. Inside that huge old coat, a tepee of wet dogs, you were a crow with all your wild ideas, sparking in every direction, and flying up to the stars like bonfire motes. I remember when we squeezed, giggling, into the phone box on Sidney Street, you intending to ring your parents and proclaim: 'I've found the One,' even though it was two in the morning and we were both drunk. The gum-jammed box wouldn't take coins, remember? Then reversing the charges, and they wouldn't accept the call. Martin, I feel like I have been tipsy on you for all our happy years, but do accept this call. You saw, I think, an independent woman as sturdy as you, but I'm not that strong any more, you know, and today I feel corroded by anger.

There is a woman down the hall here, wiry as a coat hanger, who shrieks all night, jangling like an empty wardrobe. It fills the place with madness, and I fear I may tip over too, one day. The nurses are kind, and there is one elderly man here from Lahore who plays a fabulous King's Gambit. But I miss your warmth.

I can fight my way out again, you know, but I don't want it to be forged in anger. I need the loving heat of you, Martin. I still need the proximity of your hot, beating heart to fire my happiness. I need to know that you won't see her again. Don't leave me with cold grey ashes; don't leave me with two teenagers and only the *memory of your smile, and the fading echo of your laughter. You always said I was the One. Make me the One, again.*

One.

Just One.

Gillard took a deep and ragged breath, and pocketed the letter, intending to find an evidence bag later.

The other back bedroom was clearly Chloe's room. There were posters of boy bands on the wall, neatly folded clothes in a chest of drawers, and a mostly empty shoe organizer in the back of an open wardrobe. There were books too: Shakespeare, Dickens, some Beat Generation novels that Gillard had read, and plenty of French and German classics that he hadn't. Like mother, like daughter, it seemed. Gillard had seen plenty of teenagers' bedrooms, not normally in happy circumstances. This was easily the most orderly.

The smallest bedroom, front right, was given over to linen and box storage. Gillard poked his head into the main bathroom, between the two back bedrooms. Nothing looked particularly out of place. There was a stack of *Private Eye* magazines in a basket plus a few copies of the *Times Literary Supplement*. Reluctantly, he repressed his fascination with the minutiae of Liz Knight's life. He walked down the stairs and had his hand on the door handle ready to go out when he glanced up.

There was a slight brownish stain around the plastic rose on the hall light fitting. The light was too dazzling to tell more, so he switched it off. He grabbed a dining chair to stand on, and used his torch to take a closer look. The hand-sized stain was where plaster had bubbled, indicative of a water leak -- what builders call 'blown'. Water from a rusting tank, perhaps. Gillard unscrewed the rose and let it slide down on the cable. The plaster beneath was badly damaged. Was this an old leak? Something inside him was nagging, wouldn't let it go.

Craig got a small electrical screwdriver from his bag of tricks and climbed back on the chair. He prodded the blade up alongside the white electrical cable and into the plaster. It was soft as marzipan. As he pulled the blade out, a little rusty snow flurry dusted his Tyveked head. He dug in again and dislodged something that – *plop!* – landed on his bottom lip. He wiped with a finger and lifted it into his vision. A fingernail-sized white plaster wedge topping a glistening gem of blackcurrant jam, like some doll's house dessert with a special filling.

Congealed blood.

Chapter Ten

Gillard was trembling so much it took five attempts to get a good photo of the area around the rose. He deposited the lump of dried blood in a cheek swab tube and then got back off the chair. Sweat was sliding down his back and he was breathing hard. A grim suspicion was crystallizing inside him, and he had trouble keeping it in check, forcing it to the back of his mind. He climbed the stairs again, back up to Liz's bedroom, with his CSI toolbox. They seemed like huge steps, dragged by his tiredness and a sense of foreboding. On his hands and knees by the side of the bed, Craig once again flipped up the green rug. He brought out a Stanley knife and cut a cross in the middle of the bleach stain. Then he pulled up the corners of the carpet until the underlay was exposed. Where the carpet lifted there were several incisions now visible through the fabric. Beneath was a glossy, sticky mess like a spilled pot of jam, but the metallic taint gave it away. The spongy rubber underlay was drenched in it. With his screwdriver he found a join between underlay sections and he pulled them up too, exposing more blood on the floorboards. A few more minutes and he had removed a section of underlay, then used a hammer to extract the nails on one short board. Levering it up, he rested it to one side, and shone his torch within, into the space between the hall ceiling below and the bedroom floorboards.

Blood everywhere. Almost black, it had run under the joists, soaked into the insulation material, and run in rivulets right across the plasterboard ceiling. Swinging his torch in each direction he reckoned the stain was the size of a double bed sheet. He fought hard, again and again, to suppress the inevitable conclusion.

Breathing hard, he got back into a standing position. He jumped as he caught his own reflection in the dressing table mirror. A white Michelin man, smeared with blood to his elbows, sweat coursing down his forehead, bubbles of saliva at the corner of his mouth. Then all attempts at professionalism finally gave way. His shoulders trembled, then shook, his face dissolved, and he fell to his knees sobbing her name, again and again and again.

Chapter Eleven

Gillard emerged unsteadily from the front door, and one glance from the startled PC said it all. 'Bad news, sir, by the looks of it?'

He nodded as he waddled down the path to the car in his blood-flecked Tyvek. It was 20 minutes before he was composed enough to ring Yaz Quoroshi. He described what he had seen, and then said: 'There were cuts in the carpet. As if the bastard stabbed her while she was down. It was those cuts that allowed so much of the blood to seep right down beneath the floorboards. The wine spillage and the bleach was a cover-up. '

'Can you estimate how much blood?' Yaz asked.

Gillard paused. 'You're the expert, Yaz. But it was like a paddling pool, honestly. Unsurvivable.'

After the call had finished, Craig looked at his watch. He'd never sleep after this, and he had plenty to get out of his system. By tomorrow he would be running a murder investigation, so tonight might be his last free evening for weeks. He dropped off his evidence at Caterham, told the civilian staffer to get it sent off for analysis, and headed off to the leisure centre.

Craig normally went to the local swimming pool at eight o'clock – between the over-50s club and the aqua-aerobics. The 30-metre pool had only a single lane for fast swimmers, and he often had it to himself as he whizzed past the grannies splashing along side by side in the main section. He'd normally do a couple of kilometres, front crawl with tumble turns, then finish off with 20 lengths of breaststroke. This time he counted 90 fast lengths of crawl by the time the lifeguard started dismantling his lane rope just before 9.30 p.m. He pulled himself out, arms shaking, and took a long, hot shower.

Despite his best efforts at sublimation, ten minutes later he found himself sitting in his own Nissan Note with a greasy takeaway burger in a box on his lap, at the entrance to Marlpit Close, staring at the house where Liz had grown up. This was exactly where he used to sit on the Kawasaki all those years ago, revving idly, watching; for what? Something to give him hope. And in 30 years, Liz had grown up, glimpsed a fabulous career, got married, had kids, lost the best part of her happiness, and then in all probability been killed by her husband. He, meanwhile, was still sitting at the end of her street eating junk food, listening to Simply Red and mooning about what might have been.

Once the burger was finished, and all the effort of those watery laps offset in cholesterol and grease, he drove home the slow way, which just happened to go past The Bell. He slid the car into one of the few slots available in its massive new car park, got out and looked the place over. When he and Liz used to go there, it was a quiet rural pub in a forgotten fold of the Surrey hills. They had found a favourite garden seat, a rustic wooden bench overlooking a pond, him with a pint and her with wine, and maybe sharing a bag of salt and vinegar Twists. That was all gone now. The pub was now part of a well-known chain, and the old country lane was a commuter rat run. A children's play area with climbing frame and slide, all safety-conscious and built on chipped rubber fragments, had consumed half the garden and swallowed the pond. Behind it and adjoining the pub, where the rustic garden benches had once been, stood an enormous conservatory dining room full of well-to-do pensioners eating, by the look of the blackboard, caesar salad and goat's cheese filo pastry parcels. A past destroyed, bit by bit.

Gillard strolled into the bar, the oldest part of the pub, looking in vain for the equivalent of the green whorled curtains, the rose wallpaper, or some other nostalgic hook on which to hang his engulfing melancholia. 'What can I get you?' asked a short barmaid with wavy chestnut hair and a lip-ring that almost spoiled her smile.

Caught unawares in his reverie, he scanned the pump clips and bought a pint of IPA. As the barmaid turned away he glimpsed a tattoo of a curling red rose on her shoulder. 'Four twenty-five,' she said impatiently, apparently for the second or even third time, swinging her shoulder away from his stare and substituting into the line of his gaze a small, pale open hand into which for one stupid second he thought of placing his own.

'I'm sorry,' he said, fumbling for money, and finally finding a fiver.

'Are you all right?' she asked, as he retreated from the bar, slopping half the pint over his shoe. He took one quick gulp, jingled the paltry change in his hand and abandoned the drink on the pub windowsill. He then headed for the safety of the car, as purposefully as he could manage for a man who had suddenly forgotten how to walk.

Chapter Twelve

My Dearest Craig,

This is a very hard letter for me to write. When I met you at the school dance just those few weeks ago, I never realized how far and how fast things would go, and how it would take us in such dangerously differing directions. I already knew I was going up to Cambridge, and that my life would be transformed. I suppose now I was just trying to have a last little tryst in the protected vale of bucolic memories in which I grew up, before taking on the Tripos and then the wider world. That, I suppose, was selfish of me. Though I have gloried in your utter devotion and puppyish affection, I didn't realize at first how much all this was going to mean to you. For that I am utterly sorry. I have never meant to hurt you, though I suppose I must. I won't blame you if you hate me. All I can say is that it was never meant to be. I shall always think kindly of you, and hope that in some far future, when you have a lovely wife and two (three?) delightful children, you will *still find room in your heart to think without regret of our loving time together.*

Yours
Liz xxxx

Detective Chief Inspector Craig Gillard carefully folded the precious letter and returned it to the shoebox under his bed. He remembered like yesterday the agony of receiving the letter, tearing it to shreds in a fury, then days later retrieving every scrap from the family dustbin and laboriously taping it all back together.

Aged 18, his first forensic act.

He put the box aside and scanned his bachelor flat: two tidy bedrooms, a lounge-diner, no kids and one quite unpleasant divorce to his name. And then he thought about a bloodstain under an oatmeal carpet where Liz in all probability lost her life.

He tried to displace the image with thoughts of Sam. Last night he'd suggested they go to see a film, and he'd offered to cook her a meal. He'd given all the signals that he'd like to spend more time with her, and at one level he did. Even now, after all these years, was he not able to stop making the comparison, vainly seeking to match the unmatchable?

He went into the second bedroom-cum-office, fired up his computer and logged onto a dating website that he had last perused four or five months ago. His subscription hadn't yet expired, and he trawled through his message box. There were several 'winks' on his profile, some now quite old, and just two messages. One was from a bespectacled Essex '50-ish' saleswoman with red hair who enjoyed walks by the sea and horse riding, and another from a 'separated and adventurous' Hampshire hairdresser of 41 who liked shopping and techno music. He then looked on his 'saved' folder. There were 15 profiles there, all in the 'petite' and 'five-foot-to-five-four' height categories. Every one of them had wavy hair, either brown or black, and their eyes were generally brown. They were all highly educated – indeed he had specified that in his search – and one or two were academics. He'd messaged a few, and got mostly positive responses, but for some reason he had shied away from meeting any.

Right now, Gillard felt that he'd prefer to be on a wind-buffeted rock face in Wales or the Lakes, lashed by the elements, with only a belay and a few cleats to secure him. At least he'd feel alive. Instead of what he felt like now. The complete opposite. He picked up his mobile, checked a number, and rang it.

Sam Phillips was eating a bowl of pasta and watching *Strictly* when Craig called. She'd spent all day hoping for a call or even a text to show that he appreciated or at least recalled that they had spent the night together yesterday. 'Hello, Sam, how's it going?'

She muted the TV and replied: 'Fine, Craig, how are you? You had a busy day, I imagine. I saw you on the TV news.'

'Yeah, it's been crazy busy. But things have moved on since then. Looks like we've got a murder on our hands.' He told what he had discovered in the Knight house. 'And there could be more in the holiday home.'

'Is it her blood?' Phillips asked, setting her pasta down on the table as her stomach began to curdle.

'We'll know by morning, but it doesn't look good. So that means I'm going to be busy. Lots of overtime, late nights. Could last months. I know I said we should see the film...'

Sam said nothing for a moment. 'I know how it is, Craig. You know that. I won't make demands. We'll just see each other when we can, a quiet meal out. Keep it flexible.' She thought: why the hell am I already in *this* conversation?

'Well, it's just that I've been thinking more generally...'

He said no more for a moment, so she said 'Are you trying to tell me something, Craig?

Another pause, then he said: 'You seem to be quite keen, and I don't want to hurt you. I like you but... I'll be devoting...'

Devoting all his time to Elizabeth Knight. And no time for me. Of course. Sam suddenly recalled seeing Craig, days ago, looking shocked when she showed him the missing person report form, when he first realized that Mrs Knight was missing. Liz, he'd called her. There was emotional baggage there, Sam had been sure of that right away. But when she'd stayed at Craig's flat in Banstead she'd been slow to make the next connection. Of course! It would be the same woman who'd dedicated the book to him. L was for Liz.

'So you're not that keen on me, Craig?'

'Oh, I think you're great, Sam. You came crashing into my life like a crazy rhino, sending everything flying. You've knocked me off my feet, but I don't know, I just can't—'

'Can't what, Craig?' *Did he just call me a rhinoceros?* 'I've just slept with you yesterday, remember?' He didn't reply. 'It wasn't to say thank you. It was because I like you. Craig, do you remember that?' Her voice was hard because she knew. It was over, before it had even begun. The die was cast.

'Of course I remember,' said Craig.

'I don't sleep with just anyone. I hope you know that.' He didn't reply. 'Craig? I'm a bit upset and I have to go now. And you know what? I think you should go back to your precious Liz.' She slammed the phone down. Sam had lost out to other women before, once or twice.

But never to a corpse.

Sam slipped on her coat, went out to the car. She felt like a drive to clear her head. She didn't know where she was going, and she didn't care. Just out. She had Beyoncé on loud. She'd save Adele for when she got sad, as she knew she would be. Bloody men. Useless. Every last one.

She drove around aimlessly for half an hour, then stopped at the huge Tesco in Purley. Swamped with exhausted mothers and their noisy offspring in the day, at night it wasn't so busy. It was nearly half eleven. The alien lighting, the cavernous hangar of consumer glitz and the sheer anonymity of being there were a welcome distraction. As she parked her old green Renault she noticed a middle-aged man squatting behind his car, mending something. At her approach he stood up hurriedly, and set off ahead of her to go into the store. She walked past, waited until the man was inside, then she went back to look at his car. There was something wrong with the number plate. She realized that there was a strip of black tape, turning a five into a six. It was starting to come off. She knelt, used the camera on her phone to zoom in, and flashed a picture. She then walked away to examine it. There wasn't just one alteration. More tape had been used to turn an F into a P.

False plates. She'd remembered the training course. Illegally altering a plate wasn't just an offence, it was indication of a criminal trying to cover his tracks for something more serious. See an identical car to your own make and colour, clone their plate and you can drive around pretending to be them. Every parking ticket, toll fine or worse goes to another address.

She'd report it tomorrow.

Inside the store she saw him again. No gangster, that's for sure: average height, slim, pale thinning hair, beige fleece top and grey trousers. Could be 60, but probably less. He was utterly forgettable apart from the grey shiny slip-on shoes. She glided past with her hand basket and got a waft of minty breath. She glanced into his trolley. Blank DVDs, cable ties, disinfectant, hair dye, a bumper bag of extra-strong mints, man-sized tissues, lots of cling film and a few big bottles of Coke. Something she'd read on one of the police bulletins was niggling her mind. Cable ties, tissues: abduction? This couldn't wait until tomorrow. She thought about calling Craig, but dismissed the idea. He was bound to think she was seeking attention. Yet again. No, this she would do herself, at least for now.

At the self-service till, she checked out her own purchases: ready meals, breakfast cereal and milk, and hurried back to her car, three bays down from his. He was back two minutes later. After loading his groceries, he reversed out his silver VW Polo. She followed. The man was driving slowly and cautiously, indicating well ahead of each turn. That made it easy. Sam's knowledge of tailing was gleaned from films. She didn't have the confidence to let any vehicle come between them, instead hoping the darkness would provide cover. After ten minutes she followed the Polo down a parking-choked street of terraced houses in Croydon, and saw it stop in a residents' bay, the only available space. She drove past, then circled the block again, spotting him unloading groceries into a house. She parked around the corner on double yellows, then walked back to where she could see down the street. The man was gone, but the car was there. She approached the house. It was as average as he was: Victorian pebble-dashed, three-storey, end-terrace. The door was still ajar.

She looked around the empty street, took a deep breath and walked up to the door. She could hear TV or radio, and peering in saw a long maroon-carpeted hallway, covered with carpet protectors. The place was gloomy, despite the dangling, shadeless bulb, and now she noticed that the magnolia walls, which had just looked glossy, were in fact lined with something like cling film. The place smelled too, mainly of plastic, but stale, as if the windows were never opened. That was enough. She got out her phone to take a photo before withdrawing, but heard a slight noise behind her on the street. Before she could turn around she was pushed hard, and tumbled into the hallway. The man followed in a gust of peppermint, and slammed the door shut behind them.

Chapter Thirteen

Gillard slipped into the incident room at Caterham at 6.15 a.m. with three hot, strong coffees carefully balanced in his hands. He tiptoed carefully up behind Carl Hoskins and Colin Hodges, the two detective constables who had been there overnight. Both nondescript pudgy mid-30s geezers with similarly shaven-heads, they were known as Tweedledum and Tweedledee because of their resemblance to each other. Hoskins, still on the phone but slumped in his chair, spun round when he heard the DCI approach. Hodges, sprawled over his keyboard and desk, struggled to get back to vertical.

'You two look like roadkill,' Gillard said, placing the paper cups on the desk between them. 'Pasty, unappetizing and more than a little flat.'

'Thank you, sir. Been preparing that line, have we?' Hodges asked. 'But thanks for the coffee.' DC Hoskins nodded his thanks while he finished making notes, thanked the caller, and hung up.

'What have you got?' Gillard asked.

'Nothing much,' Hoskins sighed. 'Lots of enthusiastic schoolkids who saw Mrs Knight leaving school on the day of her disappearance. A few wild card sightings that need checking out.'

Gillard looked at the log. There had been sightings reported by the public of each of them, everywhere from the library at Trinity College, Dublin to a Morrisons car park in Aberdeen and a Catholic church in Canterbury. No sightings claimed they were together. Corroborating any of these with CCTV would take time.

'Plenty of time-wasters happy to call at three in the morning, as usual,' Hodges said.

The two detectives had well-known strengths and weaknesses. On the minus side, two years ago they had been unable to catch a 12-year-old girl caught in the act of shoplifting. She had sprinted away and cleverly led them on an eight-floor chase up a council tower block where the lift didn't work. She crossed on a walkway to an adjacent block, then took the lift down into the street and escaped. Hodges spent two days under observation in Croydon University Hospital after collapsing on the walkway with chest pains.

On the plus side, they would work all hours, albeit slowly and without imagination, grinding out with reasonable proficiency the boring tasks which are the bulk of detective work. They'd racked up hundreds of hours of overtime on the Girl F case watching CCTV footage from Croydon town centre. Long evenings passed on fast-forward, 'Like a gazillion silent comedies back to back, without the laughs,' as Hoskins had described it. In the end they had Girl F with a middle-aged man on just two seconds of footage, the proverbial needle in a haystack. In all the years since he hadn't been identified. In that trawl they had also found evidence of 16 other crimes, which had been passed back to the Met, in whose patch Croydon fell. No thanks received for that, either. Still, Gillard was happy to have Tweedledee and Tweedledum on the team. Detective work is a game where you need far more tortoises than hares. A thick shell to hide in can come in handy too. Ask Kincaid, the original tortoise king.

Surrey and Sussex CSI had promised a call by nine. The lab had been working overnight on the blood sample from the spade recovered in Dungeness, plus samples from the blood spillage in the Knights' master bedroom. When Yaz Quoroshi rang, Gillard was almost dizzy with anticipation and dread.

'It's Mrs Knight's blood,' Quoroshi said. 'I'll give you the full details when I get there.'

'Okay, thanks.' Gillard gritted his teeth to stem the tide of images of Liz that were flooding his mind. He made small talk with Quoroshi for a minute while folding away his pain and sliding it into a dark, hidden place.

The incident room was packed by the time Quoroshi arrived, a dapper figure with a neat beard, cropped hair and a nice line in silk ties. There were four full-time detectives working with DS Claire Mulholland and RIO Rob Townsend, plus ten uniformed officers manning the phones next door. Paddy

Kincaid, having apparently survived Wednesday's mauling by Jock McKinnon, was leaning against a table, happy to see some real-time detective work in action, while Quoroshi set up his laptop, projector and screen.

Gillard, in crisp white shirt, dark-blue tie, polished brogues and black trousers, paced between the various whiteboards where evidence was listed. 'All right, you all know the basics. Mrs Knight has now been missing for eight days, her husband for just over two. We've been treating this as a missing person's inquiry, but that has all changed now. I'll hand over to Yaz to fill you in.'

'Hello, everybody.' He started with an overview of the case, with pictures of each of the main rooms in the Knights' house and the items recovered. 'We've got some very clear results.' His next slide showed a wide-handled woman's hairbrush on a dressing table. 'There was a lot of hair, all from one person, and many intact follicles. These gave a very good match with the blood DCI Gillard found.' There was a collective gasp when he clicked onto a slide which showed the huge extent of the bloodstains in the ceiling cavity.

'The DNA's identical.' He then showed a slide of the spade. 'This spade was recovered outdoors in the holiday home in Dungeness. Here we've had a little more difficulty, because the blood sample was tiny and had been out in the elements, but it is human blood, and it's probably the same person, with an 85 per cent chance. There's a partial match too on the follicle root of the hair on the spade with the hairs in the brush.'

'Anything on timings?'

'Yes,' said Yaz. 'Some of you will have heard of Tryptophan fluorescence. It allows us to measure the decay of a certain element within blood. So we can be sure, to within a day either way, that the ceiling blood is a week old. We weren't able to corroborate that with the tiny sample on the spade.'

'What about the rest of the house?'

'There are traces of DNA from six people in the house, from toothbrushes and from hair recovered from bedding, clothes and traps beneath shower drains. Two, recovered from spare bedrooms and the kitchen-diner, match the elimination samples given by the son and daughter, while prints on the oven and vacuum cleaner match those of the cleaner. Prints in those rooms corroborate the kids' elimination prints. Hairs recovered from discarded clothing in the second bedroom we presume to be that of Professor Knight. We also have fingerprints and DNA on a glass, and prints on several surfaces which we presume to be his too, because they match the comb and one toothbrush. These prints will be matched with those from his workplace and home computers, which are all in our possession, but we may not get all the results until later.'

'I make that five,' Gillard said. 'Who was the sixth trace?'

'Oh, there was a dirty glass in the dishwasher. Lipstick marks and a good DNA sample on the rim. We've got no match for that as yet. It's not the cleaner. But it may not be significant.'

'So, to summarize,' Gillard said. 'Mrs Knight was seen nine days ago, a Wednesday. She was seen leaving school by dozens of witnesses; she was also seen having a drink with her friend Helen Jennings at a wine bar later on that evening. She was at home on Thursday and the cleaner saw her before she left at 1 p.m. That is the last independent sighting. According to the blood fluorescence, time of death is from late Wednesday last week at the earliest, to perhaps Friday morning at the latest. However, assuming we trust the cleaner, we can eliminate up until Thursday at 1 p.m.' He wrote down the key points on the whiteboard. 'Rob, would you care to dovetail this with what we know of Professor Knight's movements during that time?'

'Certainly. Knight's phone records have given us a pretty comprehensive idea of his movements during the crucial 36 hours, most of his working day well corroborated. Cell site analysis shows he took his usual 16.08 Blackfriars to Coulsdon South train. That would get him to Coulsdon South at 16.44 and home by just after five. Then there is about five hours at home, until a Skype conference call, from his home computer, with colleagues from the United States at 10 p.m. But during that time his mobile was on, and he took some calls. The next phone trace is half past eight on the Friday morning, and with witness corroboration we can get him into town for scheduled meetings in London with the Ministry of Justice from 10 a.m. to 1 p.m.'

'Clearly he's going to struggle to get an alibi for this,' Gillard said, with satisfaction.

'He's pretty ballsy though, our Professor Knight, isn't he?' asked Kincaid. 'I mean he kills her, let's say, last thing on Thursday. Lots of blood. Cleans up, then off to the Ministry of Justice of all places, for a meeting next day. Like nothing's happened.'

There was some nodding around the room.

'So where is he, Craig?' Kincaid asked. 'Where's our fiendish professor hiding?'

'We've no idea. There has only been one single ping on his phone since I spoke to him on the landline to Dungeness on Tuesday, and that was when he emailed the LSE on Wednesday asking for compassionate leave. He was in Dungeness at that time. Apart from that, the phone's been switched off.'

'He could have bought another phone,' Kincaid said.

'Naturally,' Gillard said. 'We assume he will have. Rob Townsend has been working on that.' He turned to Rob.

'Yes, sir,' Rob said. 'We've got two pieces of call analysis software working at the service providers. First, we're monitoring every number on his contact list from the original phone. If any of those numbers is called by a number that's new to them, we'll get a copy of the metadata.'

'Metadata?' Kincaid asked.

'Yes, who called the number, when, from where and for how long,' Townsend said. 'Not the content. Obviously we don't know what is said or emailed. We'd need a warrant specific to the recipient for that. Likewise, we're getting a copy of all the calls that pinged the Dungeness cell site from the time we last heard from Professor Knight. If any of these calls connects with a number on Knight's original contact list, we reckon that'll be Knight's new number.'

'Excellent thinking,' Kincaid said. 'Okay, everybody, good work. We'll probably need another meeting at 4 p.m. before the big news conference at 5.' His phone buzzed, and he stopped to take the call. As Gillard watched, his face changed shape, almost melting into a look of amazement.

'What is it?' Gillard asked.

Kincaid lifted the phone away from his head. 'That was a mate of mine in the Met. A female Surrey PCSO has been attacked in Croydon. But you are never going to believe this…'

Twelve hours earlier

Sam Phillips banged her head on the wall on the way down, and landed on her side. The man dived onto her, a leg either side of her hips, his arms reaching down and grabbing her wrists. 'Why were you following me, lassie?' he said, breathing peppermint into her face, the Scottish burr soft despite the power in his arms. 'Come on then, ye tasty wee thing, I can see you want some.'

She didn't answer, but tried desperately to free her legs. Gary had held her down like this, many times. It was his idea of foreplay. He had been far too big and strong to shift. But this man? He wasn't big, or heavy, and he was much older.

Maybe, just maybe, she could take him.

The police self-defence training sessions of two months ago were still fresh in her head. The man was using his weight and superior position to force her wrists backwards either side of her head, to insert a knee between her thighs and force her legs apart. She kept the pressure on with her left arm, but shot her right arm wide. This unbalanced him enough so she could buck up her left hip, and with her good leg braced beneath rotate them both to the right. As she did so he yelled 'bitch', let go of the left wrist and punched her in the side of the head.

Something snapped in her, and she lashed out. The heel of her left hand caught him a hard crack on the underside of the nose, sending his glasses flying. He yelled and rolled further towards the wall. She was up on one knee and gave him a flurry of stinging slaps as he tried to drag her down. But it was seeing him in a kneeling position that gave her the true opportunity. It was no longer this faceless middle-aged stranger in front of her, but a more recent, more intimate enemy. She grabbed him by the ears and smashed her good knee hard into his face. 'You bastard, I hate you! I hate you. I hate you!' What happened in the next blurred seconds – her wildness, her rage, her unanticipated strength, her animal growls of fury – she didn't recognize in herself at all. But when it was over she was breathing hard, standing up, looking down at the vanquished man curled up on the floor. He looked up at her, his eyes wide in shock, glasses smashed, his hands raised, trembling in surrender, trying to protect his bloody nose and mouth. There was blood flecked on the wallpaper, on the carpet protector, on her hands, on the knee of her yellow leggings.

And, for once, finally, not a single drop was hers.

She had wanted to say: *That's for every woman who was ever attacked, bullied, stalked or raped.* But seeing him, she actually felt pity. 'I'm so sorry,' she gasped, on the verge of tears. 'That was meant for someone else.' She opened the front door and fled, hobbling away as best as her bruised leg would allow. Only when she reached her car, and was clearly not being pursued, did she ring 999.

'Which PCSO?' Gillard asked, as soon as Kincaid finished taking the call.

Kincaid looked down at his notes. 'Samantha Phillips, she works here, apparently.'

Gillard leaped to his feet, grabbed his mobile and left. 'I'll be back in a mo,' he said.

As the door closed, Kincaid chuckled. 'Another of his girlfriends?' Once the laughter subsided, he returned to regaling the incident room with the rest of story: the plucky newbie PCSO who had spotted a false number plate while at the supermarket, followed the vehicle in her own car, and then fought off the attacker who ambushed her. 'It seems he'd been hiding in his car, and left his own front door open to entice her in. The Met are holding the guy, by the name of Harry Smith. He's clean on the PNC, but given that the car is a silver VW Polo, they are going to pass him to us to see if there is a Girl F connection.'

'Could Scottish Harry be Scottish Barry?' Mulholland asked.

'Maybe,' Kincaid replied.

Gillard walked back in two minutes later, fresh from leaving a consoling message on Sam's mobile.

'I shouldn't worry about her, Craig,' Kincaid said. 'She made mincemeat of him, apparently. Broke his nose, fractured a cheekbone, knocked out a couple of teeth. God, she must be built like a tank.'

'Not at all, in fact she's very attractive,' Gillard said. The eyes of every woman in the room suddenly settled on him for this uncharacteristic comment. Whether he would be judged gallant or merely sexist, he couldn't tell. But judged he certainly would be. Kincaid's look was different, a kind of astonished envy: *She's not been in the force five minutes and you've actually had her already, haven't you?*

'Anyway, the ACC will be delighted, given the cold case review,' Gillard added.

'Yes, won't she?' Kincaid smiled. 'You can leave me to pass on the good news.'

As soon as the meeting broke up, DS Mulholland called Gillard over to a stack of files on her desk. 'I dug out the details of Mrs Knight's RTA in 2007. The attending officer definitely recorded her as the driver.' She passed a single sheet of rather yellowed paper to Gillard. In typical neutered police language it recorded the collision of a Renault Laguna with a skip owned by Aardvark Equipment Hire (Dorking) Ltd at approximately 12.15 a.m. One injured female treated at the scene, broken ankle, facial injuries. Breathalysed, negative. Male passenger, unhurt but rather vociferous, possibly 'in drink', claimed the skip was unlit. Broken plastic fragments at scene indicated skip light fell off during collision. Returned to scene at daylight and recovered skip lighting unit from woodland approximately 40 metres from scene. Mrs Elizabeth Margaret Knight charged with driving without due care and attention and pleaded guilty by post. Fined £150, and a £75 victim surcharge for the skip company to buy new lights. Three points on her licence.

'Assuming Ms Parkinson got the real version of events, Martin Knight was driving but persuaded his wife to take the blame,' Gillard said.

'And then tried to claim the skip was unlit by throwing the lights into the undergrowth,' Mulholland said.

'They should have done him for perverting the course of justice, as well as due care,' Gillard said. 'In a single air bag vehicle it should be obvious the driver was the one without facial injuries.'

'Yes, but the officer was late on the scene. The paramedics called the police only when they realized that there was another party involved, i.e. the skip hire firm. From the docket it looks like 40 minutes after the crash.'

'So drunken Martin Knight made sober Liz agree to take the rap for driving before he'd agree to call an ambulance. And he never called the police at all.'

'I think that is jumping to conclusions, Craig. Besides, she might have had her own phone.'

'What a bastard, a first-class bastard,' Gillard muttered.

'I bet you wish she'd stayed with you, eh?' Claire said, looking up at him.

When Gillard said nothing, she added. 'Come on, Craig. Kathy Parkinson told me. Made me feel a complete prat. It would have helped if you'd told me first.'

'It was a long time ago. A lot of water under the bridge, and all that.'

'But a pretty important bridge, right?' She was looking at the paperwork when she said it, but he still felt almost naked.

'So let's make sure we've got all the paperwork in order,' he said.

'Does Paddy Kincaid know?'

'About me and Liz? Yes. I told him, right at the start.'

'Did he laugh?'

'Yep.'

'Let me see, did he ask if you'd shagged the murder victim?' Mulholland rested her chin on her hand and looked up at him.

'Not initially. But later on, yes. Rogered was the term he used.'

'And did you?'

Gillard permitted himself a small smile. 'The DNA technique's not been devised yet that could prove *that* after all those decades, one way or the other.'

Claire Mulholland shook her head. 'We won't need that if Kathy Parkinson goes to the papers, will we? It'll be assumed.'

'She wouldn't do that.'

Mulholland snorted with derision. 'Don't be naive, Craig.'

'I'll have a word with her.'

'If she wants to, she's got you by the short and curlies. Fortunately for you, it wasn't she who supplied the mystery DNA on the wine glass in the dishwasher. There's no match. Still, if she ends up a suspect, you really would be compromised.'

'Look, I'm sorry, Claire. I really should have told you.'

'Yes, you should.' She paused for a moment, then asked more gently: 'So what was she like then, your beloved Liz?'

'She was lovely. Bloody lovely. And I can't believe that bastard killed her.'

'If it *was* him, Craig. It could have been someone else.' She looked up and gave him a frosty glare. 'Though not in your mind, obviously. He's already convicted up there.' She tapped the side of her head, then stood up and walked away, anger radiating from her stride and the door that slammed behind her.

It was Friday afternoon. Sam had been invited to the Met's Croydon police station to give a detailed statement. A huge uniformed black officer, Sergeant Winstanley, met her there, and laughed in amazement at what she had done as he wrote it all down in a huge looping longhand. 'There's no knowing what he would have done to you if you hadn't fought back,' he said.

'I know exactly what he would have done,' Sam replied. 'Has he said anything?'

'Two DCs from Surrey came to talk to him first thing, about Girl F. But he didn't say a word, apparently. Surrey CSI is looking over his house and car. But he's already been charged with the assault on you.'

The desk sergeant, a barrel-chested Ulsterman called Connolly, brought them each a cup of his trademark milky coffee. 'We've got to take yer man to the doctor again this afternoon, then he's off to Surrey Police. He's on painkillers for that cheek, poor wee mite.'

Winstanley giggled again, a high but infectious sound for such a big man.

'Do ye want to take a look at him?' Connolly asked Sam conspiratorially. 'He's in the suicide cell because of the medication so we've got a CCTV feed.' Winstanley put a finger to his lips as he ushered Sam through to the monitoring station, where a female civilian was watching a bank of screens. After Connolly had made the introductions, and praised Sam's heroism, he leaned over the woman and tapped a pudgy finger on a screen where a bruised-looking Smith was shown sitting on a mattress staring at the opposite wall.

'God, he's a mess,' Sam said.

'Nothing the evil wee bastard didn't deserve,' Connolly said. 'I clocked him for a nonce just by the shoes. Never trust a fella who wears grey slip-ons.'

'Long white socks too,' said Winstanley. 'Very dodgy.'

'He's not moved an inch for hours,' Connolly said. 'As if he's sure he'll get off.'

After swearing everyone to secrecy about the illicit visit, they let Sam go on her way. On the way out she checked her phone to see that Craig had left her a voicemail. It was cumbersome but heartfelt, hoping she was okay, and fairly heavy on the apologies. It made her smile, nonetheless, as she thought about snowstorms and piggybacks, and Craig's heroic intervention to warn off Gary. She'd reply, in her own time. Just not yet. Let him sweat.

Chapter Fourteen

'Have you arranged the flights?' Martin asked casually, an untidy sandwich halfway to his lips as I walked in laden with shopping. I'd just finished a two-hour departmental meeting with the impossible Sarah Hodgkins, spent 40 minutes with dear Mrs Thomas from the refectory whose granddaughter has just been diagnosed with leukaemia, and then took the bus to Addiscombe to get Martin's car back from its service. My reply was more direct than I intended. He sniggered, a greasy smear of mayonnaise on his cheek, and all I could think was: what on earth did Natalie Krugman see in him? I struggle to recall what I saw in him. No, that's not true, but how the acid years of acrimony have corroded us. Only the wire struts of habit are left, and then what?

Liz's diary, May 2012

Helen Jennings confirmed that she and Liz Knight had shared a quick after-work drink at a wine bar on Wednesday, 12 October. Helen had been pushed for time, and it was a glass of Perrier for her and a small glass of red for Liz. 'If I'd had the faintest inkling it was going to be the last time I'd ever see her we would have had champagne,' Jennings said, as she brought in ice-cold highball glasses brimming with home-made lemonade for Gillard and Mulholland.

The two detectives were perched on a low-slung tubular sofa in Jennings's large and sunny seventh-floor flat, with the afternoon light filtering in. Jennings said she had chosen it because it was just two minutes' walk from East Croydon station. She was, she said, 'always on the go'.

Gillard could see why. Jennings was a slender five foot ten with an extraordinary figure for a woman of 54. She wore a tight white blouse and a short denim skirt, and padded around on the thick carpet with tanned and beautiful bare feet as she talked of her friendship with Liz Knight.

'I met her through schools chess in the 1980s,' Jennings said, as she seized a handful of nuts from a bowl, which she then passed to Gillard. 'Of course, she was so much stronger than me, always was, but we girls had to stick together against hundreds of pushy and patronizing grammar school boys. I thought she was spunky and clever, and I admired her.'

'And did you keep up the friendship throughout all those years?' asked Mulholland.

'No, not at all. I didn't stick with chess for long. I came up to see her at Cambridge for a weekend and well, I suppose it doesn't matter to mention it now. We had a bit of a fling. Just experimental for both of us, actually, though there was a great deal more exploration done, and vastly more pleasure had, than either of us had really expected.' Jennings laughed at the reminiscence, her hazel eyes bright in the saffron afternoon light from the balcony. 'For her I think it was a last chance to taste another world, seeing as Martin had just asked her to marry him. I think we both knew that it wouldn't happen again, at least with each other. For me, though, it was an eye-opener. I had a bit of a crush on her. She, I think, became a bit embarrassed about it, and for ten years we didn't really have any contact.'

'Let's fast-forward to the last couple of years,' said Mulholland.

Part of Gillard was transfixed by this revelation, another side of Liz he knew nothing about, but he could sense Claire's impatience. She bristled at this showy woman with her carefully and expensively layered hair, and her overweening self-confidence.

'Well I already knew Kathy, I think you must have spoken to her, and we were going to arrange a drink in Covent Garden one Friday with Liz, but it kept not happening. But I ran into Liz on the train about three years ago; I'd just got divorced and we got on like a house on fire.'

'Did you get any sense of her relationship with Professor Knight?' Gillard asked.

'Yes. She wasn't happy, that was clear.'

At that moment, a ringtone sounded and Helen scampered over to pick up her mobile. There was an exchange of gushing endearments, and a final whisper: 'They'll be gone in half an hour, dear. Hold your horses.' She hung up and turned to the detectives. 'Anyway, I'd been divorced from miserable Mike for three years, been given the villa in the Algarve in exchange for the house, and half his rather considerable pension. With that and my lovely flat, I was set fair. So naturally she was envious.'

'Did she ever say that Martin had struck her?' Gillard asked.

'Gosh, no. Did he?' She paused. 'I wouldn't have assumed he had that level of passion, unless it was on the subject of government policies and policing, of course. Still, he did have all those affairs.'

'Recently?' Mulholland asked.

'Well, I don't know. She didn't spill, dear loyal Liz. She had no intention of divorcing, I don't think. In some ways it was rather old fashioned. It was a marriage and she wanted to make it work. I suppose that's out of the window now, one way or another.'

'So she didn't mention any recent affairs?'

'Well, I hope I'm not talking out of turn here. But during one of our lunches over the summer she did mention that Martin seemed to be up to his old tricks. The name Natalie Krugman had emerged again. I tried to tease out some more details, but she wouldn't say anything except that she had given Martin what she called a final warning back in 2012.'

Mulholland nodded. She had emailed Krugman twice already asking for a statement, and had left a message at her university office in New York, but had yet to receive a reply. 'What did you take that to mean?'

'Divorce, I presume. What other lever did she have?' Helen's elegant face showed the conceit of a person who had passed that predicament long ago. Craig wondered whether she really understood what difficulties someone as loyal as Liz might face in accepting that her marriage was ending.

The beep of a text made Helen Jennings jump. She looked at her phone.

'Actually it's mine,' said Craig, fishing his phone out of his pocket. Rob Townsend had asked him to call, urgently.

Craig walked out to the bathroom and closed the door before returning the call. The room was lined with mirrors, and as he inspected his rather patchy shave in the brilliant light he couldn't help noticing in the reflection some lacy black lingerie drying on a rack over the bath.

'What have you got, Rob?'

'Bit of a breakthrough by the tech boys. I'm in Redhill forensic computing lab at the moment. We've just stumbled on evidence that Professor Knight has spent weeks planning to kill his wife.'

'I'll be passing Redhill on my way to Dungeness. I'd like to see this for myself.' After he hung up, Gillard smiled grimly to himself. So Professor Knight's act was not one of temper or a moment of madness. It was cold-hearted premeditation.

Forty minutes later Gillard had dropped Mulholland off at Caterham, and was sitting around a large computer monitor with DC Townsend in a spacious open-plan office near Redhill railway station. A young tech whizz called Paul Armstrong with a goatee beard and an earring was sitting at an adjacent terminal, telling them what he'd discovered on Knight's computers.

'We recovered three computers from his office. A modern desktop – Windows Ten – an old Acer laptop running Windows XP, and a Samsung tablet. We got the ISP to send us three-month search histories for each of these, and there was nothing that stood out. A little porn, seemingly legal, that was it.' He looked across at the two officers. 'So just as a back-up I got into the hardware log file on his router to look at the household's Wi-Fi activity.' He tapped a few keys, and both screens filled with a list of codes, each six sets of two characters separated by colons. 'This is the list of the machines that have used this hub in recent weeks.'

Gillard peered at the screen. 'There are seven codes, four more than he had.'

'Very good,' Armstrong said. 'This one is Mrs Knight's ancient desktop. They all share the same network.' A cursor appeared on both screens halfway down. 'Her Hewlett-Packard laptop is immediately beneath.' The cursor flicked to the bottom. 'This is Chloe Knight's MacBook Pro.'

'What about this one?' Gillard pointed at the one line that had not been referenced.

'Exactly,' said Armstrong. 'Another machine. Not one we have in our possession. However, these codes are MAC codes, part of it assigned by the Internet service provider to each machine, and part intrinsic to the hardware. Now we saw from Knight's own webmail account that he bought a new laptop about six weeks ago from Amazon using his credit card. We think it was this machine, because the manufacturer code buried within the MAC matches the make shown on the receipt. Last use…' –

the cursor flicked to the time stamp code – '…corresponds to a time when we know he was at home.'

Townsend leaned conspiratorially towards Gillard: 'Good detective work, yes?' Gillard nodded.

'Using the assigned MAC code we were able to get the ISP to send us the device's entire search history since activation.' He tapped a few keys and the screen filled with references and search terms. Gillard's jaw dropped as he read the terms: 'Body disposal, quicklime, John Haigh…'

'That's the 1940s acid bath murderer,' Townsend muttered.

'I know,' Gillard responded. 'The 1954 body in the marsh murder, that's there too. Of course, he is a criminologist, but he'd searched for nothing like this on his main computers.' He pointed to the screen. 'There's a whole list of murders where dismemberment took place: Jeffrey Dahmer, Jimmy Bartram, Stephen Marshall. There are searches for fake ID, false passport, power tools. Bloody hell!'

'Knight was probably unaware that broadband routers log the unique codes of the devices they connect with,' Armstrong said. 'If he'd done this search in a library or a café, we'd not know of the device's existence. He's definitely slipped up.'

'So we can track him as he uses it?' Gillard asked.

'Ah, that depends. It's fairly technical, but the MAC code will partly change depending on which Wi-Fi hub it is using. There are various IP address/location databases which can help.'

'Has he been using it since this last search?' Gillard tapped the screen.

'Unfortunately not, so far.'

'Maybe he's not so stupid,' Gillard said. 'He's either ditched it or he has another device. A new smartphone would do both jobs, wouldn't it?'

'It would,' Armstrong said.

The enormity of Knight's guilt seemed to expand hour by hour. Before he could take in the full implications of what he'd heard, Gillard's mobile rang. It was Nigel Cropper, head of CSI at Kent CID. 'We've made a major discovery in the house at Dungeness which you should see,' he said.

'I'm on my way,' Gillard said. 'You've found her body, right?'

There was a slight pause. 'Well, yes and no.'

Gillard's throat went dry. Yes and no? That could only mean one thing.

It took Gillard the best part of an hour and a half to drive to Dungeness from Redhill. All the time the mysterious 'yes and no' comment stuck in his head, like a dire but catchy song. All he could think of was that it meant dismemberment. Poor Liz!

There were four white Kent Police vans parked outside Great Wickings, and a large plastic CSI tent shrouding the front of the wooden house. Two uniformed women PCs stood by the front gate talking to a knot of members of the public. He went to the boot, pulled out his own white coveralls and polythene shoe covers.

As he did so a couple of scruffy-looking reporters with faces suitable for radio approached. One pressed a microphone towards him just as he had one foot on the back bumper, putting on his second shoe cover.

'Kieran Todd, Channel Coast 93.2 News,' he said, a straggly apology for a moustache failing to add any gravitas to his thin, inquisitive face. 'Seems to be something of a breakthrough this morning, Chief Inspector Gillard. Got anything to tell the listeners?'

'We've no comment as yet,' said Gillard, irritated that the press already seemed to have wind of what the Kent lads had found.

Once he'd donned his gloves, Gillard brushed past the reporters, flashed his credentials to the PCs and disappeared inside the flap of the tent. Adjusting his eyes to the peculiar space-station light of the crime scene tent, Gillard approached two figures in white overalls who were hunched over a laptop which sat on a plastic table. CSI officers always looked to Gillard like escaped Jelly Babies of some uninteresting flavour, like vanilla or mint or pot noodle. When they looked up, the image was barely dispelled. A short, prematurely balding man in his 30s with purple-framed spectacles introduced himself as Nigel Cropper, the man he'd spoken to on the phone. His number two, if anything even shorter and wider, was Diane Cooke.

After introductions, Cropper pointed to the laptop and said. 'We've got a DNA positive for Elizabeth Knight on the spade, and a nice clear thumbprint on the handle which matches one from Martin Knight's LSE phone. We separately tested the blood and hair, fortunately a couple of full follicles, and they're definitely hers. We haven't got the results for our other findings, though. That will take a couple of hours.'

Cropper led Gillard through a polythene tunnel built on metal plates to the car port and into the house, which looked like a scene from *Invasion of the Alien Teletubbies*. Two were leaning over the butler sink in the kitchen, and two crouching down on the inside of the sun lounge.

'We got some fingerprints on the taps which match those of Martin Knight, which may or may not be significant. However, after what we read about the bloodstains in the other house, we were expecting to find a body, or body parts somewhere here. We sprayed the house pretty thoroughly with Bluestar, concentrating on the kitchen and bathroom,' Cropper said. 'But the killer was pretty thorough, I have to say. All over the sink and work surfaces, the taps, the hall. Lots and lots of clean-up happened here, and I think quite recently. In the old days with Luminol we would have struggled because we got loads of hydrogen peroxide flare-up, it was almost dazzling. The killer knew what to use. It was really quite hard to spot any blood, until...' He led Gillard to the sink, and with a plastic-shanked scraper pointed to the sink splashback. 'Here he had cleaned the tiles very thoroughly. But the grout lines are recessed, and if he was scrubbing back and forth, he wouldn't have got them all. We wouldn't have noticed with Luminol, but Bluestar gives off slightly different colours for blood and for oxygen bleach. So we got five tiny residual blood spots, mostly smaller than a full stop. We have carved two out on a fragment of grout here' – he pointed to a chip missing from the grout – 'and that is currently being tested.'

'The other benefit of Bluestar,' Cropper said, 'is that unlike Luminol it doesn't damage the DNA in the blood. They are small samples, so we shouldn't hold out any hope for a resounding DNA match, but you never know.'

'Good work, Nigel, very impressed.' Gillard tried desperately not to imagine the grisly scenario that Cropper seemed to be hinting at.

'That's not all. We disconnected the U-bend, and made a rather interesting discovery. I'll show you the picture, but essentially it's a tooth with some attached metal wings, probably a piece of dental bridgework. There was a substantial amount of what for the moment we'll call organic residue in the U-bend, which prompted us to remove the plastic pipe down to the trap. There we made another interesting discovery, which we are currently testing.'

'Are you hinting at something?'

'Well, yes. The pipe hasn't been properly cleaned for some time, apart from the pouring down of some household cleaner which was presumably done in the last few days. As is common with domestic pipes, there is effectively an internal sleeve of organic matter deposited over a period of years. We cut the pipe lengthways and were able to remove it whole. It's here if you want to take a peek.' Cropper gave a grim little smile and led Gillard out through the kitchen door into the sun lounge. Two technicians were looking at something wet and viscid lying on a polythene sheet. It was a four-feet-long tube of residue, glossy with grease and ball-bearing sized bubbles of fat.

Gillard crouched down with Cropper to take a closer look. 'There's a lot of hair,' he said.

'Yes, that in itself may not be indicative of anything,' Cropper responded. 'Many people wash their hair at the sink.' Cropper pointed to clearly discernible tea leaf and coffee grounds, slender pin-like bones which could be fish or chicken, and then something else. 'This,' he said, pointing to something shiny in the column of grease, is far more interesting.'

'What is it?' Gillard said.

'It's a very small, specialist stainless steel screw. We recovered another two from the sump. I can't be absolutely sure, but the consensus here is that it is a surgical fastening used in limb repair.'

'Liz Knight had a road accident in 2007, and her medical records show she had pins inserted in her leg,' Gillard said.

'I know, we saw the scanned documents late yesterday. We also found a couple of human lower incisors in the trap, and a molar. So all the evidence we have seen so far indicates that the killer spent several hours here, working on separating and perhaps even rendering the body, or parts of it, at this sink. Subject to DNA confirmation, of course.'

'I presume this house has a septic tank?'

'Yes. But crucially, this sink didn't connect to it. It's simply a soakaway out in the shingle. We're going to excavate it, but I don't think we'll find much more.'

'So what are you saying?' Gillard asked.

'Well, we think the kitchen was largely used to dissect Mrs Knight. The body parts will have been hidden elsewhere.' Cropper gestured with his chin out of the sun lounge window, north to the vast expanse of Romney Marsh. Gillard followed his gaze. Of course, it's so bloody obvious. If you want to dispose of body parts, here is a vast expanse of brackish, muddy water to conceal them.

'Have you got the divers booked?'

'Yes. There's a double-sized team coming this afternoon. Arc lamps, more tents, you name it,' Cropper said.

'So in the meantime, all we have left of the woman is this sleeve of jelly from inside a pipe?' Gillard said.

'Effectively, yes. But it would be enough for a conviction even if nothing else turns up.'

Gillard nodded. 'From the Internet searches we retrieved from Knight's laptop, he certainly spent a good deal of time investigating how to dissect and dispose of a human body. But until you showed me this, I really wouldn't have thought he had the stomach for it.'

'Agreed. I just can't see it,' Cropper said. 'I've done a couple of dismemberment cases, and as part of that read up on most of the rest in recent UK history. They're normally either organized crime jobs, or if it's a domestic murder the suspect almost always had training as a butcher, or on a farm or abattoir, something like that. But a middle-class academic? It's not easy to cut a body up. They'd run a mile faced with the sheer amount of residual blood, the fat, the gristle and the stink.'

'Martin Knight had some outdated forensic textbooks on his shelves, presumably from his university studies. He might have done some practical forensic study, I suppose, we'll have to check. But his work was policy and always had been,' Gillard said.

Cropper looked across at the selection of forensic evidence now laid out across plastic-covered tables inside the house. 'I know it's not my job to theorize on what happened. But the somewhat brutal modus operandi here would normally suggest to me that we are more likely to find that the perpetrator was a third person, someone habituated to what inevitably would have been a gory process.'

'That doesn't quite square with Knight doing the research, unless it was a conspiracy to murder that went wrong,' Gillard said.

'Did they have any enemies?' Cropper asked. 'I presume you have checked for debt?'

'Yes. There's no hint that either of them had enemies, certainly not the type who would be prepared to do this,' Gillard said.

'Well, whether it's Professor Knight or someone else, whoever did this was determined, quite careful and forensically aware. Apart from the waste pipe oversight, he tied it up pretty well here.'

'Yeah, the crime scene in Surrey was much messier,' Gillard said.

'Not surprising,' Cropper said, with a grim smile. 'A live person is much harder to deal with than a dead one.'

When a body is discovered a missing person case becomes something else: an accident, a suicide or a murder investigation. The timing of breaking the grim news of the death of a loved one to a family is usually clearly determined by events. But in a few cases, where there isn't a complete body, merely evidence of one, there is a grey line. This was just one of those cases. Detective Chief Inspector Gillard was pretty sure he knew what had happened to Liz Knight the moment he'd found the spade. But that's not enough for a family. Families need closure, they need certainties, not probabilities. They need answers, not more scope for questions. The discovery of human teeth didn't eliminate those questions, merely narrowed down the range of possibilities. Though getting the identification might take a while, Oliver and Chloe Knight should be told to prepare themselves for bad news. Gillard put in a call to DS Claire Mulholland and briefed her on the discovery. She and liaison officer Gabby Underwood would arrange to go and visit the family at Oliver's home. The part of the job every copper hates.

Mulholland and Underwood arrived in an unmarked car, but the door of Oliver's home was opened to them before they had knocked. He and Chloe were standing together in the hall. Their faces were ashen, and the fact that Claire had refused to give details over the phone confirmed all their worst fears. 'You've found Mum, haven't you?' Chloe said.

That was not a question that could be answered yes or no, so Claire ignored it. She stepped inside, wiped her feet, and Gabby carefully closed the door behind them as they made small talk about the weather. Only when they were all sitting down in the lounge did Claire say: 'I'm sorry to have to say we've found human remains at the house in Dungeness. Only part has been tested so far, but we have a DNA match with your mother.'

Chloe buried her face in her hands and began to silently shudder. Oliver put an arm around her and then turned his face accusingly to the policewomen. 'I don't understand what you mean. You've either found her or you haven't.'

Gabby's thin-lipped smile of sympathy broadened even further, until it looked like her face would slip off her jaw.

'We're really so sorry,' she said. 'Why don't you let me make you a cuppa? I'll be able to find where everything is.'

Oliver nodded, and patted his sister on the back. She continued to make a low wailing sound.

'The details, I'm afraid are not very pleasant,' Claire said. 'But all I can really say at the moment is that there is evidence that a dismemberment took place in the kitchen of that house.'

Oliver's face froze in horror, but tears welled up and rolled down his face. Then a moment later he began to emit huge whooshing sounds, and his solid solicitor's face crumpled into that of a distraught teenager.

Chloe looked up, her make-up streaked and her eyes moist. 'Where's my dad? We need him. Why isn't he here for us?'

'I'm sorry. We just don't know,' Claire said, as Gabby came in with two mugs of strong tea. 'But based on what I've just told you, this is now going to be a murder inquiry. And your father is someone we urgently want to speak to in connection with that.'

After tea and biscuits, and the gradual regaining of composure, Claire began a new subject. 'There is going to be a news conference this afternoon. This isn't like the missing person's conference. We don't need you there, unless you think appealing to your father to give himself up would help. It usually doesn't in cases like this, and I can see that it would add a lot of stress while you are still upset. But what you have to prepare yourself for is the attention of the press. This is going to get a lot worse and more intrusive from now on. They'll be peddling their own theories, and will try anything to dig up details of the history of your family, talking to neighbours, old school friends, that kind of thing. Gabby will be here to help, and you can call her at any time. But I would strongly advise you not to talk to the press, at least not yet. You might find it's easier to unplug the landline, and buy a new mobile to call friends and family. Always use the withheld number facility. Gabby can fill you in on the details.'

Claire finally eased herself away from this pit of misery, grateful that Gabby, with her ever-present smile and bottomless well of sympathy, would be there to take the strain.

On his return, Gillard gathered his investigative team together to brief them on the day's discoveries. Claire Mulholland, Rob Townsend, Hoskins and Hodges were joined by the final two detective constables, Shireen Corey-Williams, a 40-year-old qualified accountant and financial specialist, and newly qualified DC Michelle Tsu. Liaison officer Gabby Underwood was there, along with Surrey Police's press officer Christina McCafferty, a brunette with prominent teeth, whose phone seemed to vibrate every minute or so.

Hodges, who was known to adore Christina, offered her a home-made chocolate brownie. The giant plastic box he brought contained dozens. He, at least, was never put off his appetite by crime scene pictures. Unfortunately that was also true of Carl Hoskins, who could detect a chocolate brownie at 50 paces. Christina was the only person in the room who declined Hodges's culinary gambit.

'Let's get on, shall we?' Gillard said. The room was buzzing with the excitement that a flow of fresh evidence always brings.

There was plenty to tell, and Gillard went through it carefully: the discovery of human remains in Dungeness, the match of the blood from the spade with Liz's DNA, the recovered search history from Professor Knight's absent laptop.

'So it's got to be him, then,' said Carl Hoskins, while munching his second brownie. 'It can't be anyone else, can it?'

'I wouldn't put it quite that strongly, but it's powerful evidence that he was planning the crime, even if someone else committed it,' Gillard replied. 'But let me emphasize this. We're not going public with any of this at the moment. The news conference will be confined to the bare minimum: that following the discovery of human remains at two addresses, this is now a murder investigation and we are urgently seeking the professor.'

'We've had enough calls already,' said Christina, waving her phone. 'Once this gets out it's going to be insane…'

The door swung open and Paddy Kincaid stood there, looking pleased with himself. 'Sorry to interrupt.' He looked anything but. 'I'm delighted to say we got some more resources. Five more call handlers at Mount Browne, who will screen the calls before passing them on here. Plus some more specialist resources as and when required.'

There was a general murmur of approval as Kincaid hauled himself onto the desk behind which Christina McCafferty had been sitting. 'Carry on, don't mind me,' he announced, kicking his feet backwards and forwards.

'Back to fundamentals,' said Gillard. 'The one thing we have no clear idea about is motive. Michelle, I know you've made a start on the LSE emails. I'm going to need you to dig further back too. Knight was appointed to the LSE in 2012, and was at Oxford for the previous five years. We're going to need warrants to get those, I suspect. The legal department can get you the correct applications. We need to do this by the book. Full warrants, not production orders. I don't want anything that will come back and bite us on the bum.'

'Yes, especially if he turns out to be innocent,' Michelle said.

Kincaid chuckled heartily. 'I've had 30 years' experience, darling,' he said tapping the side of his nose. 'If it turns out he didn't kill her, I'll eat my desk. And we're talking best MFI do-it-yourself assembly chipboard.'

The wave of laughter swept past a stony-faced Michelle. Gillard gave her a slight nod in recognition of Kincaid's patronizing comment. 'Well, while the boss chews the furniture, there's a chance that money played a part. Shireen, what have you found?'

'I've just spent most of the last day with Oliver Knight to make sense of the family's finances. There are certainly some surprises,' she said, standing up and walking to the whiteboard. 'The Knights are a wealthy family. Martin Knight's father bought a fourth-floor flat in a bomb-damaged London house in 1947 for £1,400. After Martin's mother died in 2013 it was sold for just under five million.' She wrote the sum on the board.

Jaws dropped around the room. 'Five million, for a two-bedroom flat?' Kincaid gasped.

'It's in Grosvenor Crescent, Belgravia,' Shireen said.

'I think it's safe to say that was a good investment,' said Gillard.

'Well, five million is a good motive for a murder,' Kincaid said, then turned round to his left where Christina McCafferty was struggling to see past him. 'I'd bump off my missus for that,' he whispered, with a wink. Everyone who had worked with Kincaid was familiar with his frequent disparaging comments about Muriel, his wife of 25 years and mother of his three children.

Shireen raised one delicate dark eyebrow, then continued. 'Martin is an only child, and had been gifted the flat ten years previously, so didn't pay any inheritance tax when his mother died. Liz Knight had been a small-scale landlord around Croydon for a few years, and the next step was when she and Martin jointly purchased a large villa near Marbella in June, which has several hectares of development land attached. The whole family went to see it in May, and according to Oliver were very excited by it. She and Martin were due to go over to start renovation work.'

'How much did they spend?' Kincaid asked.

'Five and a half million euros, so just over four million pounds. It's got a huge pool, a spa, various mod cons.' She flicked through a glossy brochure, before handing it to Kincaid. 'It does seems legit. The deal was notarized in Spain, and Oliver said his mother went to the Spanish land registry in person to get it verified. She speaks fluent Spanish.'

'Looks tasty, might go there myself,' said Kincaid, flicking through the brochure.

'And the rest of the inheritance?' Gillard asked.

'Still there. Over a million spread between three accounts, one of them joint.'

'No debts, then?' Gillard asked. 'No reason to disappear?'

'Not that we can see. There are no bank or credit card debts. They seem to have about £300,000 in stocks, bonds, National Savings and private pensions, in addition to the occupational pensions they have accumulated. They both have life insurance, but it's not big in the context of their assets, certainly no motive for murder there. Professor Knight has just one current and one savings account. We had Martin Knight's banks run their suspicious transaction software over them and nothing got flagged up, apart from the property deal, which is of course because of its size. Otherwise a normal pattern. Oliver has copies of their wills, and is registered as the executor. Each has the other as prime beneficiary, then the two kids. It's all very conventional. The bottom line is that most of what the Knights have is in bricks and mortar, either here or abroad, and that is hard to steal.'

'Doesn't that give the son a strong motive to kill them both?' asked Michelle Tsu. 'He's the executor, first in line to inherit?'

'That's why I had his computers and phones seized yesterday,' Gillard said. 'He didn't like it. Did you find anything on them, Rob?'

'The messages and emails are just what you would expect,' said Townsend. 'He's tried hard to reach his father by phone and email, on the same addresses and numbers that we have. I passed on the financial data to Shireen.' He turned to her.

'I only had the chance for a cursory look,' she added. 'No significant sums have come into any of his accounts in the past three months. If we do suspect him, it's going to be worth taking a deeper look, of course.'

'Well, I'd like you to make that your project over the weekend, Shireen. Can you put up a motive, means and opportunity for Oliver Knight to kill one or both of his parents? We'll then meet on Monday morning and see if we can knock it down.'

'Okay.' She returned to her notebook. 'Mrs Knight's own finances are straightforward. She has current accounts with Barclays and RBS, plus a savings account with the Nationwide, pretty much all run online. She runs her local property rental business, two flats and a terraced house from the RBS account. Oliver does the legal work.

'Could someone have been threatening the Knights?' asked Carl Hoskins. 'If they disappear here, they could go and stay at the Spanish villa and start a new life.'

'It's a line of inquiry,' Gillard said, simultaneously managing to convey that he didn't think it likely. 'We've got her passport, so it would only be Professor Knight. If Knight was a scrap metal dealer from Bermondsey, Marbella would be the first place I'd expect him to pop up. I don't buy the idea of them being threatened. I think they would have told somebody, even if not us. Neither Oliver nor Kathy Parkinson mentioned anything like that. As they don't appear to owe money that's the biggest potential source of trouble removed. Besides, if you want to escape some villain and start a new life the last place you would choose is somewhere just half a day's drive from the Costa Crime.' He looked to Shireen Corey-Williams and she continued.

'So to sum up, I can't find an obvious financial motive either for the husband to kill the wife, or for anyone else to kill them both.'

Gillard shrugged and said. 'Okay. We've actually got lots more witnesses to interview. We're going to go back into the history of Mr and Mrs Knight. Their interests, their friends, their enemies, and their lovers...' He caught Claire Mulholland's arched and quizzical eyebrow at this point. 'We're going to dig down until we find out exactly what happened here. Why a wealthy, privileged, well-educated and well-thought-of couple could have ended up embroiled in death and dismemberment.'

Chapter Fifteen

Going through Martin's trousers prior to the wash, I found a credit card receipt. Lunch for two, with wine. A business lunch? Or a meal with 'her', whoever she may be this time. It could of course be perfectly innocent. I promised myself I would learn to trust again, and I will, as I must - otherwise why bother with reconciliation? But if this is Natalie Krugman again, I won't stand for it.

Liz's diary, July 2013

Just as Gillard had predicted, the news conference was rough: rough on the family, rough on the police, and riding roughshod over the facts. Fortunately, Alison Rigby was there, and totally unflappable.

'So let's get this straight,' said a reporter from the *Daily Mirror*. 'You've found traces of Mrs Knight's body, but no traces of the husband's. This couldn't be someone having killed them both?'

'We've not actually ruled anything out,' Rigby said. 'I don't want to speculate at this point, but we are trying to be helpful when we say that we are looking at this in a domestic context. That's our current line of inquiry.'

A grubby-looking man with a leather jacket put his hand up. 'Jez Collins, the *Sun*. How come it took Surrey Police more than a week to realize this was murder? Wasn't it all really a refusal to believe that anything could go so wrong in such a prominent, successful family?'

'No, not correct,' Rigby said. 'We took this very seriously from the first report. We followed our missing person's policy to the letter. You have to realize that adults go missing all the time. Many more are notified missing than ever are the subject of press conferences like this. The majority turn up again at some point. As you know, and as our policy makes clear, we have to prioritize cases where vulnerability is a key issue: children, confused adults, suicidal teenagers...'

A man standing at the back held up his pencil. 'Mrs Knight had been a mental patient. Why wasn't she classed as vulnerable, then?'

Over the next 15 minutes, ACC Rigby made a firm but embattled defence of the decision to wait for forensic evidence before increasing the size of the team involved in the case. Then she left, leaving Craig Gillard to deal with the remaining questions. He was soon surrounded by a scrum of jostling reporters, wanting to know about every aspect of the case. Right at the back, a young female reporter shouted for attention: 'Excuse me, Detective Chief Inspector!' Gillard saw her, a petite brunette, little more than a schoolgirl, with her badge on upside down.

'Emily Tye, *Dungeness and Lydd Observer*. Can I just double-check the make and type of the car you are looking for?' she said, trying to make herself heard above the babble.

'Silly cow.' Jez Collins, standing at the front, rolled his eyes at Gillard conspiratorially, but the detective refused to acknowledge the jibe.

'It's like the one in the picture in your press pack. The registration number is in there too.'

'Then I've seen that car. I know where it's parked,' she said.

There was immediate silence. A burly *Daily Mail* reporter who had been pressing himself against Gillard's desk for the last five minutes did an about-face. 'I've got my Merc outside, darling,' he said. 'You show me where it is, and we'll share the credits, oright?'

'Hold on a moment,' Gillard yelled. 'If you have any evidence to offer, would you come this way?' He shepherded the young reporter into a back room, leaving press officer Christina McCafferty to deal with a now distinctly unhappy press pack.

Emily Tye was a cub reporter on an obscure regional paper with a circulation of less than three thousand. It limped along as a weekly in an era when eBay and the Internet in general had sucked the lifeblood out of the classified ads that used to provide these papers with sustenance. But for all that she was only just 20, Emily had the instincts of a professional. She quickly traded her discovery into an exclusive but informal interview with the lead detective on the case. Craig Gillard, having established that she'd been given a lift by a colleague to the conference, was happy to drive her the 70 miles from Caterham back to Dungeness. But as the darkness of evening deepened across the dull carriageway of the M25, he detected some frustration from the young reporter that so few of her questions were eliciting a straight answer. He didn't want to let her know anything that hadn't already been disclosed at the press conference.

Finally, she got a little snappy. 'Aren't you supposed to stick to the speed limit?' she asked, as they roared through dazzlingly lit but unmanned roadworks at 75. The 50-mile-per-hour limit was backed up by signs for speed cameras.

'No.' Gillard accelerated further to get past a lumbering group of lorries.

'Why not?'

'We have an exemption for emergencies. This number plate will come up on the ANPR as being a police vehicle.'

'Oh.' She was quiet for a moment. 'So what's so urgent about finding the car?'

'Plenty. If the car's been dumped, we might find a body, hers or even his, nearby. Even if not, he may have switched vehicles. There could be witnesses. I've already called in Kent Police to secure it as a potential crime scene, just in case he came back to take it away.'

'Oh. Wow.'

'My turn to ask a question,' Gillard said. 'What made you photograph the BMW's number plate?'

'From where it was parked, I'd assumed it belonged to the owner of Cherry Farm Properties. I'd been trying to get an interview with him and he wouldn't return my calls. I was going to follow him. His name is Michael A. Knowles, and of course there was MAK in the personalized number plate.'

'Whereas it actually belongs to Martin Knight, or Martin Alaric Hildebrand Knight to give him his full name,' Gillard said, with a smile. 'You'd make quite a good detective, Emily. I'm impressed.' As he grinned at her, he noticed a rosy bloom climb up her long slender neck to her cheeks. She looked up at him shyly through a fringe the colour of freshly fallen conkers. Her dark eyes were large and doe-like. He turned back to the road. *Too young, Craig, and probably trouble.* His inner emotional caution kicked in, but it was usually right. Maybe he'd been talking too much.

'If you've finished all your questions, we can have some music,' Gillard said, indicating the glove box. Emily opened it, and removed the stack of CDs. After a minute shuffling through them with a look of glazed horror, she slid them back and closed the compartment. For a few seconds she held her hand against it, as if Simply Red, Celine Dion or Jennifer Rush might otherwise escape that '80s tomb. 'We could listen to the radio?' she suggested. He shrugged his assent.

Half an hour later, following her directions, Gillard found himself on a new housing development, or more accurately a building site, which occupied the grounds of an old hospital near Hamstreet, a village a few miles from Dungeness. The access road wound up a slight hill, along the crest of which huge sentinel windmills threw their giant rotors in lazy circles. Shiny new aluminium street lights tossed pools of light onto pavements and fences which hemmed in shadowy muddy fields scattered with construction equipment and Portakabins. There were trenches aplenty, some concrete foundations set, but not a single line of bricks had yet been laid. Trenches. Concrete. A good place to dispose of body parts.

'This whole development is by Cherry Farm Properties,' she said. 'They've got outline permission for over two thousand homes. Phase one, which is right over on the far side, is going ahead, but phase two, here, needs the green light from the archaeologists from the University of Kent before they can start. It's been hugely controversial.'

'And a really quiet place at night,' Gillard whispered, as they rounded a final corner. A patrol car from Kent Police was already there. Gillard got out, greeted the two PCs, then went up to the BMW parked beyond, next to an unoccupied Portakabin. He walked around it. There was nothing visible on the plush white leather interior. There were no scratches, no dents, and no obvious fingermarks along the boot edge.

Gillard had to give Martin Knight some credit. Hiding a car isn't as simple as it used to be. Until ten years or so ago, it was easy to park a vehicle in long-stay car parks at any UK airport, and then make your way out on foot. Unless you actually went into an airport building you would be unlikely to be caught on CCTV. There had been a couple of gangland cases of well-sealed bodies being left in the boot of vehicles that were not discovered for more than a year. But ANPR machines ended that. Every car going into a major airport car park is identified by registration number which connects to the name and a credit card that made the booking.

Multi-storey car parks had been favoured too, until worries over the safety of women in their frighteningly blank landings, hallways and lifts led to a campaign to increase CCTV coverage. Those with connections to organized crime could still hide cars – in shipping containers, in lock-up garages, underneath railway arches – and not have them found for years. But for academics, even clever criminologists like Professor Martin Knight, there were problems. Where to park a rather smart, not-very-old BMW where it wouldn't be noticed, yet wouldn't be stolen or vandalized and thus notified to the police. Somewhere where there wouldn't be anyone to notice him walk away. Somewhere where neither a CCTV camera nor ANPR would trace him. Somewhere that he could get to and from the Great Wickings house in Dungeness, and then onward, to wherever he was hiding, and with whoever was giving him cover.

'Are there bus routes that run anywhere near here?' Gillard asked.

'There's the 553 from Maidstone to Ashford airport, but the nearest stop is a good hour's walk I reckon. I'd get a taxi.'

Gillard harrumphed. He wasn't going to share his thinking with this enterprising young reporter, but Martin Knight, with a face now plastered across national TV, wasn't going to risk taking a taxi, or even a bus. That left two options. He had either placed a second car here, much earlier before Liz had gone missing, or – and this was the tantalizing and increasingly likely possibility – he had someone who was helping him. That would presumably take a little coordination. Knight's own phone had not been used at all after he disappeared, but he could easily have been using a disposable. There had been no hits so far on Knight's old contact list, according to Rob Townsend. Still, early days.

Gillard gave Emily a lift home, delighted with her scoop, and then returned to Knight's car on Orchard Way. Kent CSI were due in 15 minutes to look at the BMW, but having obtained the spare car keys from the house at Chaldon Rise, Gillard couldn't resist. He half expected to find Liz's remains. It was a prospect that filled him with dread. He pressed the fob and unlocked the vehicle. Donning a pair of latex gloves and with torch in hand he gently lifted the boot lid.

The distinctive metallic taint of blood hit him immediately.

Chapter Sixteen

Week in, week out my bookshelves reproach me with what might have been. The textbooks, box files and papers on the Spanish Civil War, the early accolades, the A. J. P. Taylor prize certificate, the Eleanor Roosevelt bursary award letter, the Harvard invitation, all those glowing peer reviews, the academic correspondence. All these stare out at me from my shelves: 'Come on, Liz,' they whisper. 'You've still got what it takes. Forget this misplaced loyalty and start again without him. Be strong!'

This morning I dumped the whole lot in a box and put it out for recycling. I watched the binmen scoop up my life and toss it away. Then I cried, and cried and cried.

Liz's diary, March 2014

Gillard shone his torch inside the boot. It was largely empty and there was no blood to be seen, but right at the back was a black bin bag, a metre long and knotted at the neck. It contained something bulky and seemingly cylindrical, not bulky enough for a body. At least not for a whole body.

That was enough for him. The detailed search and opening of the bag was a CSI job, and he'd leave them to it. He closed the lid and, returning to his own car, peeled off the gloves. He found an evidence bag and popped them inside, writing a label for the date and location. He then sealed it and tossed it in the Ford's boot. His mobile rang, and he answered.

'Good evening. My name is Cunliffe,' said a soft but steely voice. 'I apologize for being rather insistent about speaking to you. I have just heard the news about Martin Knight and thought you would appreciate my input.'

'Do you know where Professor Knight is, sir?'

'Good grief, no. But I was with him on Saturday, we played a vigorous game of squash and I found him in rather good form that day.'

'I'm sure this is going to be very useful information,' Gillard said as he noticed the Kent CSI car arrive. 'I'm outside at the moment. Could I call you back in a little while?'

'Of course. I'd be delighted to help. But I just wanted to say that I've known Martin and Liz for more than 30 years, and I am horribly shocked at this turn of events.'

'It's a widely held view,' said Gillard, and then asked for call back details.

'Gerald Cunliffe,' he said, and gave the phone number.

'Sir Gerald Cunliffe?' Gillard realized that he was talking to one of England's most senior Appeal Court judges, the one who was writing the latest report on Girl F.

'The very same. Look, I'm available on Sunday morning if you want to come and take a statement. You can come over to me, I presume? It's terribly tedious to go into an interview suite. I spend too much time drinking dire institutional coffee as it is.'

'Yes, I can certainly do that. How about 11.30?'

'Yes, good.' He gave Gillard the address, in the picturesque village of Woldingham, nestling in the North Downs not far from Caterham. 'This is a very bad business, Detective Chief Inspector. I expect the press will have a field day.'

'No doubt, sir,' Gillard responded.

Saturday, 22 October

Gillard managed a lie-in until eight before reaching for his iPad to see how yesterday's news conference had been reported. The coverage was just as lurid as he had feared. The *Daily Mail* had its front page dominated by a close-up picture of an angry-looking Martin Knight, under the headline: 'The Evil Professor: Home Office Criminologist who cut his wife to pieces'. The *Sun*'s headline was similar: 'Knightfall: from top prof to evil murderer'. On the inside pages it showed a picture of Liz as she had looked in her 30s, more glamorous and less tired than she had looked in the pictures the police had circulated. The *Daily Express* had 'Knight of the Dead'. The *Star* simply said 'Knightmare'. The broadsheets ran detailed pieces, covering every aspect of the investigation, including profiles of the 'quiet but dignified beach village of Dungeness'. The *Guardian* looked in detail at the various spats with senior policemen Knight had instigated in recent years, undiplomatic quotes from his reports including: 'If all the top policeman in Britain were laid end to end, you still wouldn't reach a solid conviction.' Another was 'Justice to me is about opening doors for the young, not locking them,' and 'You can't punish youngsters into reaching their potential.' That went side by side with the likely sentence he might get, according to a leading barrister: 'Given the aggravating circumstances, the failure to turn himself in, and without mitigating circumstances, he'd be looking at 20 years.'

The vibration of his mobile broke Gillard's concentration. He finished the last mouthful of toast and marmalade, tipped the crumbs off his iPad and reached for the phone. It was a brief email from Nigel Cropper at Kent CSI about what was found in Martin Knight's car last night. The bin bag contained a blood-soaked rug. The rug was also contaminated with human hair, mucus and what appeared to be a torn fingernail. Samples had been sent for analysis. Cropper was too professional to jump to conclusions, but Gillard knew where the evidence was drawing him. The rug, probably the original one from Liz's bedroom, was used to partially wrap her body for transport to Dungeness. It was all falling into place. Now it was high time to visit the place where in all likelihood her dismembered body had been dumped.

Walland Marsh is a 24-square-mile blank on a typical British road atlas. Bordered by the medieval town of Rye to the west and the town of New Romney to the north, this part of Romney Marsh is for naturalists, birdwatchers and environmentalists a unique site for migrating birds, rare marsh species and shingle-loving plants. Two or three minor roads cross the marsh, plus the famous Romney Hythe and Dymchurch miniature railway line, whose steam locomotives haul thousands of holidaymakers back and forth across this unusual, and for the most part unspoiled, landscape.

For all its beauty and tranquillity, Walland Marsh is a perfect place to dispose of a body, or parts of one: vast, lonely, deep in places, but for the most part too shallow to permit easy diving. There are few vehicle access points or boat ramps, which would limit the ease of disposal of a whole corpse. But body parts, distributed at night, could easily be placed by an individual in waders or even by someone in a kayak. To search it all would simply be impossible.

Gillard stood at the edge of Dungeness Road, watching a group of 15 wellingtoned volunteers giving up their Saturday to prod through a chest-high thicket of reeds and rushes. With him was Geoff Coker, chief ranger for the local wildlife trust. Coker was a giant oak of a man, all beard and spectacles with an enormous pair of binoculars dangling round his neck. 'Quite a good chance of unearthing an unexploded Jerry bomb, of course,' he said. 'Lydd airport's three miles over there,' he said, pointing vaguely north-east. 'It's just a little airport now, despite the silly new name of London Ashford. It's mostly light aircraft. But of course in the war it was a key front-line airfield in the Battle of Britain. Got a real pasting from the Krauts.'

While Coker was talking, Gillard's phone went off. It was Kent's chief CSI, Nigel Cropper. Gillard excused himself and walked out of earshot. 'Go ahead, Nigel.'

'Craig, we've got preliminary results from hair and blood samples around the sink and in the U-bend and pipe. Most of the hair belongs to Liz Knight, though we have another DNA profile there too. That's not too surprising – occasional hairs from hair-washing over the years would be expected to accumulate in the grease sleeve of the pipework. However, with blood we're on stronger ground. There is a positive match for the blood specks on the grouting, and in the pipe. There are other DNA markers too, which will take a little longer to clarify, particularly from the pipe. Small bone fragments, for example. They could conceivably be animal residues.'

'Animal?'

'Well, yes. From food preparation. It was in the kitchen, after all. I wouldn't be surprised to pick up poultry or porcine markers, for example.'

'Sounds reasonable. What about the teeth?'

'Our dental specialist obtained Mrs Knight's dental records yesterday afternoon, and has managed to get a confirming ID. The bridgework was the giveaway. Her dentist fitted a tooth with a couple of metal flanges that exactly match this back in 2007.'

'It might have been related to an RTA she had that year.'

'Yes. The dentist is positive it's hers. We'll have to wait a little longer for the DNA because they have to extract it from the core of each tooth. I wanted to get the dental records finished first in case of damage to the teeth.'

'Is that it?'

'Not quite. We're waiting for the full NHS records on her leg pins, which I presume are also from the RTA. We've chased a couple of times, but the consultant involved doesn't work there any more, and they are still trying to find the paper records.'

'That's great, Nigel, thanks. I'm assuming you're almost done on-site?'

'Well, it depends if we want to locate the rest of the body. It's quite possible that parts of her are buried on-site, and it would be a big job. The shingle is very hard to excavate, and of course it might be a wild-goose chase.'

'We've got better hopes with the marshes, to be honest,' Gillard said, gesturing to the expanse of reeds and water in front of him, even though Cropper wasn't able to see it. 'I'll get my detective super, Patrick Kincaid, to ring his opposite number in Maidstone. Harpinder Singh? Did I pronounce that correctly?'

'Yes, she goes by Harpy. Very sharp brain. You'd like her.'

On Saturday morning DS Claire Mulholland and DC Colin Hodges were in Croydon, their third attempt to catch up with the remaining uninterviewed tenant from Liz Knight's little property empire. Three notes through the door and two phone calls hadn't done the trick. Finally, arriving in person did.

Aleksander Horvat was a lean and bespectacled man in his 40s, with an anxious face. He looked like he needed a square meal or two. The flat behind exuded an aroma of the sickly-sweet air fresheners used in taxis. Once they explained what they wanted, he rubbed a bony hand over his face, nodded, and begrudgingly let them in.

'It's mess,' he said unnecessarily, pointing to the lounge which was heaped high with clothing, and where two or three old pizza boxes were stacked next to the large TV and DVD system. While the two officers exchanged expressions of distaste, he cleared room for them on the faux-leather settee, which had been repaired in several places with insulation tape.

'So how long have you lived here?' Mulholland asked.

'Two years, more or less.'

'Your nationality is Slovenian, is that right?' He nodded. 'Can I see ID, please?'

He went into a bedroom and came back with his driving licence.

'I'd prefer your passport,' Mulholland said.

Horvat slouched slowly back into the bedroom and, when he emerged, tossed the document onto the coffee table. 'EU citizen, see,' he said. It gave his date of birth as March 1971 in Ljubljana. The picture was washed out, but it was probably him. Then she looked at the name. It wasn't quite the name he'd given.

'This says Timon A. Horvat.'

'Yes, is my birth name. But I use Aleksander, my middle name.'

'When did you first come to the UK, Mr Horvat?'

'September 2006.'

'And you are an electrician, is that right?'

He nodded. 'Fully qualified Registered Competent Person Electrical register. BS 7671, the doggie's bollocks. The full safety. Want to see document?'

'No, we're not here about that. It's about your landlord, Mrs Knight. She's gone missing.'

'I have always pay rent. I have book.' His worried face became even more hangdog.

'I'm sure you have, Mr Horvat,' Mulholland said. 'But when did you last see her?'

'Long time. When wash clothes machine upstairs leak was last time.'

'When was that?' PC Hodges asked.

'Winter. January, maybe?' Horvat haltingly explained that he'd only ever seen Mrs Knight about three times. Mulholland asked if it would be okay to bring in a couple of technicians for an hour or two to sample for her fingerprints and DNA.

Horvat froze as if accused. 'Why? She's not here.'

'It's just a precaution, nothing to worry about,' Hodges said. 'We can do it while you're at work.'

'We're also going to need to take a DNA sample from you,' Claire said.

At that he looked really horrified. 'I have done nothing. I promise. I don't want trouble.'

It took several minutes of careful persuasion before Horvat was content to sit on a breakfast bar stool in the kitchen and let Mulholland take a cheek swab. He still wasn't happy about it, and muttered to himself even as he let them out of the door.

The two officers waited until they were outside on the street before talking. 'He's a jumpy thing, isn't he?' asked the PC.

'Must have had some problem with the authorities to be that nervy.' Mulholland smiled. 'He's not on the Police National Computer under the name on the lease – I tried yesterday. But having seen the passport I'm going to try some variations of his name on the PNC. And I'm going to get his dabs done, just in case.'

Once CSI had withdrawn from the Knights' home and had restored everything as far as possible to how they had found it, DS Claire Mulholland and liaison officer Gabby Underwood arranged to show Oliver and Chloe Knight around, to see if they noticed anything unusual. As the two police officers pulled up in an unmarked car, they noticed a group of three teenage girls tying some flowers to the lamp post outside. The girls turned around hurriedly, as if what they were doing was wrong. Gabby, who was in uniform, called out to them. The girls – blonde, skinny and fashionably dressed – appeared to be about 14. They muttered inaudible replies and looked at their feet. One had tears running down her face.

'Are you pupils at Mrs Knight's school?' Gabby asked. They nodded in reply, looking at each other for reassurance. 'Did Mrs Knight teach you?'

'She took me for history,' the shortest of the three said. 'We can't believe what's happened.' The other two nodded in agreement. 'She was really nice. Much better than most of them. She gave me a lift home the day my dad died.'

'She ran the school chess club,' said the tearful girl. 'She let me beat her in the first game.'

'She coached my sister in Spanish vocab in the sixth form,' said the tallest. 'She got into Oxford.'

As the girls drifted away, Claire looked at the neatly written note on the post with the flowers, which after various endearments ended with one large word in crayon:

Why?

Claire Mulholland couldn't but agree. That question went to the heart of the case. Something that would inevitably come up now that Oliver and his sister had arrived. CSI had restored everything as closely as possible to match the pictures they had taken upon entry. Little was said as they walked around downstairs, into all the various bedrooms except Liz's, where the door was kept shut. They confirmed the discarded clothing in the second bedroom as their father's and Chloe confirmed that her room was unchanged. Mulholland then led them into the garden and Martin Knight's garden office. 'Did you come into here much?'

'Well, we've both been in,' Oliver said. 'It was my father's bolthole, so as youngsters we weren't encouraged. He kept it locked in later years after there had been an intruder one night. I suppose I must have come in a few times a year.'

'Similarly for me,' Chloe said. 'If the intercom was broken, which it was most of the time, I'd go and call him in for dinner, stuff like that.' Neither of them was able to say whether the office looked any different from usual.

'Now there's just one more room I'd like to take you to,' Claire said. She took them back into the house, and upstairs into the main bedroom. The room smelled musty, and metallic. They both looked around, then Chloe said: 'This is different.'

'How is it different?' Gillard asked. Neither Mulholland nor Gillard had mentioned to the Knight family where they suspected their mother was killed. Chloe stared at the green rug, recently returned from the lab.

'There's a Moroccan rug here, normally, not this old thing,' Chloe said. 'Isn't there, Olly?'

Oliver shrugged. 'I don't remember.'

Chloe looked again, lifted up the rug and then saw the bleached carpet underneath. Then her eyes widened and she dropped the rug. Her hands slid up to cover her mouth. 'Oh God, oh God, oh God. This is the place, isn't it? Where it happened?' Gillard watched her beautiful soft brown eyes fill with tears.

'Let's get you downstairs now,' Gabby Underwood said, sliding an arm around Chloe's waist. 'And get you a cup of tea.' She led a sobbing Chloe out of the room.

Oliver looked at the carpet. 'So the bleach means it was cleaned of bloodstains?' he asked.

'Yes, we think so,' Gillard said. He looked at Mulholland, who was scanning the son's face for signs of guilt or recognition. But all either of the detectives could see was a growing realization that this was the place where his mother had died. Oliver shuddered and said: 'I think I'd like a tea as well, please.'

It was after seven, and the last of the slanting Saturday evening light was gilding the operations room blinds. It was suddenly quiet enough for Gillard to hear the murmur of voices manning the phones at the far end. He looked up from his files and saw the printer was flashing a light. It needed paper, again, or maybe toner. Gillard got up, stuffed another ream into the big old Hewlett-Packard and set it going again. It went back to clattering out the last three months of Professor Martin Knight's work emails that LSE's Zakira Oglu had emailed him earlier.

This was only going to be a tip of the information iceberg. Gillard had already asked DC Michelle Tsu to read all the emails separately recovered from Martin's absent smartphone, and to pursue Oxford University for his emails going back to the start of his 2010–2012 affair with Natalie Krugman. That would take weeks, but it was in the last three months that Gillard expected to find some clue or hint as to why he might kill his wife. Finally, at nine o'clock, with all but the overnight crew gone, Gillard turned to the task he had been saving for himself: examining Knight's enigmatic email correspondence with Dr Natalie Krugman. The American academic and feminist had finally agreed to Claire's request for an interview, which coincided with a brief visit to London on Monday. Gillard wanted to know everything about her before then.

There were plenty of conventional academic emails between the two, though all gave a hint of affection. But then, in April, there was a single thread over one evening which showed something that could be construed as conspiracy.

From: Dr Natalie Krugman (natalie@krugmanunlimited.com)

Received: 14 April 2016 15:01:17

To: Martin Knight (KnightMProf@lse.ac.uk)

Hey Marty,

Great to speak last week. Things haven't been great for me since. Thibault is getting v. clingy, and will fight to retain the LA house. So I'm back in NY again. It's not ideal. Looking forward to better times. Spain! How I dream...

Always yours

Nel

From: Martin Knight (KnightMProf@lse.ac.uk)

Sent: 14 April 2016 15:08:22

To: Dr Natalie Krugman (natalie@krugmanunlimited.com)

Dearest Nel,

Not so long to endure. I just have to deal with Liz, finally(!)

Mxxxx

From: Dr Natalie Krugman (natalie@krugmanunlimited.com)

Received: 14 April 2016 15:13:19

To: Martin Knight (KnightMProf@lse.ac.uk)

Marty, seriously, the sooner the better for both of us.

From: Martin Knight (KnightMProf@lse.ac.uk)

Sent: 14 April 2016 15:13:54

To: Dr Natalie Krugman (natalie@krugmanunlimited.com)

Ah Nel. It's not so simple, believe me. She is so smart.

Mxxxx

From: Dr Natalie Krugman (natalie@krugmanunlimited.com)

Received: 14 April 2016 15:22:09

To: Martin Knight (KnightMProf@lse.ac.uk)

Not smarter than me, nor as horny: I'll screw every last drop out of you. Remember Leeds? You'll beg for mercy!

Gillard made some notes: to cross-check the professor's diary for trips to Leeds, and to get Shireen to more closely check the holiday home transaction. That enigmatic reference to 'dealing with Liz'. It could be anything or nothing. If Martin Knight had been intending to kill her, it was a little foolish to make this reference in an email. It could just as easily be referring to asking for a divorce. Whatever it was, a few months later something got out of hand. There was a huge bloodstain under the carpet in Liz's own bedroom to testify to that. Perhaps if Liz had discovered Martin's rekindled affair with Krugman, that could have been the trigger for a final, brutal row. If so, there were three people he knew were involved: Liz, who was dead; Martin Knight, presumably on the run; and Natalie Krugman herself.

Chapter Seventeen

Sunday, 23 October

Sir Gerald Cunliffe's home was tucked away amid a mature beech wood on a minor road that ran along the scarp slope of the North Downs. It was a Grade I listed Tudor thatched house with flint walls and a sweeping gravel drive. Gillard had looked it up as part of his research on Cunliffe. The man's steps from Cambridge undergraduate lawyer to the highest echelons of the establishment were unfaltering: called to the Bar (Middle Temple) in 1988, Recorder by 1996, a Queen's Counsel by 1998, High Court Queen's Bench, Presiding Judge of the South-Eastern Circuit 2009–2012, and joined the Appeal Court in 2013, the same year as his knighthood.

Gillard parked in front of the house, but got no reply when he used the brass door knocker. He wandered around the side and found the judge in a Victorian-style conservatory surrounded by stacks of legal files. A balding, ruddy-faced man with small, dark eyes that roved above half-moon spectacles, Cunliffe was dressed in a Led Zeppelin T-shirt and jeans. A can of Red Bull sat on the walnut-topped table. 'Take a pew,' he said, glancing up.

Gillard sat down on a wicker chair, then took a tape recorder and notepad from his briefcase and placed them on the table. On the wall behind Cunliffe there was a framed photograph of a much younger man, electric guitar held on high in some crowded gig. Watching his gaze, the judge said: 'Youthful aspirations, circa 1983. Sadly never fulfilled. Filing cabinets are the only heavy metal in my life now.' The twitch of disappointment pulled Cunliffe's mouth for barely a second. He took a stack of files from the table and slid them into one of three huge legal document cases that sat on the floor. 'Just to be clear, I can't talk to you about Girl F,' he said, nodding at the tape recorder.

'I'm not involved in the case.'

'Be that as it may, don't tell me anything and don't ask me anything. Saves complications. My report's coming out soon anyway.'

'That's fine. I just want you to tell me about Martin Knight, and about last Saturday.'

'Pretty straightforward really. We'd had this long-running arrangement for fortnightly squash, and it was my turn to host. We went to the club near the village. He was there just at 11.30 a.m. We played for roughly half an hour, then had lunch in the clubhouse. I think he left at around 2.40 p.m.'

'Did anything about him seem different?'

'Not really, except his energy. He was playing better than usual. He also seemed happier than I'd seen him for a while.'

'How do you mean?'

'Well,' Cunliffe leaned back with his arms behind his head, 'I've known Martin for a long time. We went up to Jesus together.' Seeing the look of bewilderment on Gillard's face, he clarified. 'Don't worry I'm not religious, thank God.' He permitted himself a self-congratulatory nod. 'Jesus College, Cambridge. And I was there on the evening that he and Liz met.'

'So you knew her too?'

'Oh God, yes. Martin rather fancied himself as a Ted Hughes figure, and affected this hurried gait with an enormous second-hand coat flapping around like some wild, windswept crow. He was neither tall enough nor handsome enough to carry it off in quite the way Hughes did, and his poems…well frankly they were execrable, but he grew his hair long, and held fort at, Christ, can't remember what the pub is called now. Can you believe it? I must have spent several undergraduate months lying semi-conscious on its floor in the sawdust, and can't remember the bloody name.'

The judge leaned forward with a glint in his eye, and gestured conspiratorially to Gillard. 'Anyway, Martin was trying to avoid buying his round by telling some long ghost tale about this bombed-out house his parents had bought in London, when in walks this extraordinarily pretty girl with wavy dark hair, with a whole gang of comely friends, and Martin spies her and said: "And the ghost took the form of an angel with dimpled cheeks and… My God! There she is!" and leapt to his feet pointing his empty glass at Liz.'

Gillard caught his own smile. Oh yes, he could see her.

'Quick as a flash she held up her arms and declaimed: "And sir, I have come from the very pit of hell, the kitchen of Corpus Christi, to visit upon ye drunken rogues the pox of the never-filled pint." She hammed it up a bit, but it was very quick, and there was a round of applause. Martin bought the round, and a glass of wine for her, and at her insistence some particular packet of crisps she liked. God, what are they called? You can't get them any more…'

'Twists?' supplied Gillard.

'Yes! That's it, well done. Anyway, they were always a couple after that. So anytime anyone wanted to chat her up, and there were quite a few, believe you me… I mean, she was quite something in those days…'

'I can imagine,' Gillard said. He could.

'… they would always begin by offering her a bag of…what was it again?'

'Twists.'

'Right. Wonderful days, honestly.' Sir Gerald beamed at the reminiscence, then looked up. 'Anyway, Martin and Liz were the golden couple. She was quite the cleverest woman I ever met,' he said, leaning forward. 'I am mortified that she is dead. If I could be forgiven some inadmissible hearsay, I have to say I find it impossible, just impossible, to believe that my friend Martin Knight could have done anything remotely like this.'

'You were saying he looked happier than he had for a long time.'

'Yes, well. He'd hinted at unhappiness in his marriage in recent years, which I thought was sad—'

'Did he talk about any of his affairs?' Gillard interrupted.

'Well he wouldn't have done with me because of my loyalty to Liz.'

'*Your* loyalty?'

'Yes. He knew I'd been in love with her all through college. Ever since she played the Moonlight Sonata on the college piano for me on my birthday.' He paused, and Gillard realized he could now see a reflection of the window in his small eyes. 'Still am, in a way. So he wouldn't risk causing me conflicted loyalties by telling me things. But, yes, I heard on the grapevine, and I didn't like it one bit. I don't know really what happened between them, but I think he was a bloody fool to want to leave her.' Sir Gerald reached into his pocket, produced a monogrammed cotton handkerchief and trumpeted a blast, which he wiped away vigorously.

'He wanted to leave her?'

'That's what I heard. And run off with that feminist harridan. What's her name?'

'Natalie Krugman?'

'Yes. Martin's life has always been littered with unexploded emotional ordnance, but Ms Krugman... Well, I met her at one of Martin and Liz's parties at Oxford. A one-woman minefield. Sexy as hell, but absolutely bloody lethal.'

As Craig left, and drove away down the long, sweeping drive, he reflected that for all his wealth and power, Cunliffe had something in common with him. A big Liz-shaped hole in his life.

Mulholland looked up as Gillard walked back into the incident room. 'Our Mr Horvat is a naughty boy,' she said. 'Nothing on the

PNC as Aleksander Horvat, but Timon A. Horvat, a taxi driver in Hull in 2007, was cautioned about inappropriate behaviour with a 14-year-old girl. He's on the child protection register.'

'Let's look at the mugshot,' Gillard said. Mulholland pulled it onto the screen and maximized it. The beard and moustache failed to hide the characteristic miserable expression. 'That's him. Let's pull him in for questioning. I'll get Townsend to make a request to Ljubljana to see if he's got previous over there. What about DNA?'

'We're still waiting for the results.'

'It would be good if it was his DNA that turned up as the sixth person in the Knights' house.'

'You mean the glass?' Mulholland asked. 'It had lipstick on.'

Gillard shrugged. 'You never know these days, do you?'

Mulholland smiled. 'You know, walking round the house on Saturday, with Oliver and Chloe, I got to thinking about timings. The professor may not have meant to kill Liz, and may have been in a panic. So he covers her absence by telling everybody that she is in Dungeness for the weekend. He must have hidden her body somewhere in the house, and then realized he had to get it out once everybody started phoning up wondering where she is.'

'Having a garage attached to the house helps, doesn't it?' Gillard said.

'Yes. He could carry her body out of the house, wrapped first in the rug, then a bin bag, through the kitchen side door, and stow her in the boot without any danger of anyone in the houses opposite seeing what he is doing.'

'So then he drives her down to Dungeness, a much more remote house, where he can set to work dismembering the body so she will be easier to dispose of,' Gillard said.

'Exactly,' Mulholland said. 'But why did he wait from Friday morning to Tuesday afternoon to do it? There's the danger of visitors to the house, Oliver or Chloe or someone else, and the deterioration in the body to think about.'

'Ah, but he needs a reason to be seen heading down to Dungeness,' Gillard said. 'We gave him that when I spoke to him on the train, and he said that's where she would be. Any other trip to Dungeness, say in the middle of the night, would have left him with a car journey to explain. But this way, he was actually appearing to be helping us, when in fact he was using it as a cover to dispose of the body. The fact that he answered the phone there when I rang gives him a kind of alibi. He was exactly where he was supposed to be.'

Mulholland nodded. 'If he'd had the nerve to reappear on Tuesday, drive back to Coulsdon and so on, I don't think we'd have even been looking at CSI, at least not yet. Liz Knight is a non-vulnerable adult, not a missing child. With her background of depression we might just have assumed that she'd decided to leave him.' She shrugged. 'Instead, he panicked. Instead of taking his time to cover his tracks a bit better, he just bolted for it. Almost amateur!'

'Not that amateur,' Gillard said. 'We still don't have a clue where he is.'

Chapter Eighteen

Monday, 24 October

It was Chloe Knight's 19th birthday, and liaison officer Gabby Underwood was spending the morning with her at Oliver's house while she cried intermittently. Oliver, signed off from work with stress, alternated between comforting his sister and attempting to extract the latest information on the investigation from Gabby. 'They really don't tell me more than the basics,' Gabby protested. 'It's partly to protect you both.'

'How do you protect us by keeping us in the dark?' Oliver asked, his face ruddy with anger.

'An investigation moves forward, often slowly with various theories advanced and then disproven until we get to the truth. We don't want to make you anxious by letting you know every twist and turn until we're sure,' she said.

Oliver stamped off to his study, where he was composing a magnificently officious letter of complaint to the chief constable. Gabby sighed and was walking back into the kitchen to make coffee when the doorbell rang. Chloe opened it, and a thickset uniformed male constable was standing there with a large cardboard box. 'Post from your parents' house, Miss,' he said. 'Perhaps you would give it to your liaison officer. No parcels or packages. It all appears harmless, but if there is anything offensive we suggest you immediately put it to one side for our perusal.' He smiled and added, 'I gather it may be your birthday, so perhaps I could add my own congratulations. Despite the sad circumstances.'

'Thank you,' she said, and closed the door.

The box contained a huge sheaf of birthday post. Since the publicity over the murder, there had been an unending stream of correspondence to the Knights' home, much of it offering sympathy. Teddy bears and flowers had appeared on the drive, notes and photos had been taped to the lamp post, conspiracy theorists posted on Facebook and Twitter. Only a tiny number of the communications were offensive or accusatory, and Gabby Underwood had succeeded in intercepting most of them. It was less easy to deal with the intermittent stream of gawkers and ghouls who wandered up to the house, some even straying onto the drive for selfies or in search of souvenirs.

Chloe quickly flicked through the post, and gasped at the handwriting on one envelope. She quickly stuffed it down the back of her jeans, only just in time before Gabby came in from the kitchen with mugs of coffee in hand. 'Ah, birthday post,' Gabby said, smiling at Chloe, whose eyes were once again brimming with tears. Gabby smiled wanly at her. 'When you feel ready, we can go through these together. It's best if I take a quick peek before you see them, just in case there's something nasty. But I expect almost everyone will be sending you their very best wishes at a difficult time like this.'

Chloe nodded. 'I'm going to the loo first,' she said, and scampered off to the downstairs toilet. She closed the door behind her, bolted it, and pulled out the envelope from her jeans. It was postmarked France. As she opened the envelope and slid out the card, her chest start to convulse and she had to clamp a hand to her face to muffle her sobs. The handwriting was a complete giveaway.

It was from her father.

She opened the card and began to read.

Gillard had arranged to interview Dr Natalie Krugman at King's College London, where she was a visiting professor. She had made it clear that it had to be brief, as there was only a nine-hour stopover on her flight from New York to Sydney. As part of yesterday's research he had read the first 20 pages of her breakthrough essay 'Rape, Fatherhood and the Male Mythos'. It had posited a mirror-image world in which women had the sexual aggression of men, where perfect male bodies were everywhere in the media, where out-of-shape women stood around in groups to loudly comment on, leer at and grope young and even underage men. For all its exaggeration for effect, Gillard found the gender-reversed vision she conjured powerful, and profoundly unsettling. It made him very nervous about today. This was a woman who, as one reviewer had put it, could probably emasculate simply by telepathy.

Gillard and Mulholland were shown into a small room in King's Department of War Studies, which had been the only private space available at short notice. Krugman stood to greet them. Tall and raven-haired, with a streak of white hair which hung over one ear, she was dressed in a black trouser suit. There was a lean, hawk-like intensity to her which her huge amber-green eyes magnified. Gillard made the introductions, while Krugman offered them seats on the other side of a small desk.

'I am profoundly shocked by this whole business,' she said, playing with her iPad. 'I'm just not sure I can be of much help.'

'Can I ask how long you have known Martin Knight?' he asked.

She leaned back in her chair, letting it swivel slightly from side to side.

'I was an undergraduate when I first met him in Oxford in 1996, I think.'

'So he was already a professor?'

'Yes, he taught at a couple of the lectures on my course.' She smiled, revealing a generous mouth. 'He really liked to shake things up. There was nothing dusty or academic about his teaching.'

'Did you meet him one-on-one at that time?'

'At departmental parties, probably. I don't really recall. I'm not sure what the niceties of Oxford academia in the 1990s have got to do with all this,' she said, turning her hands outwards and stretching her long, talon-like fingers. She was wearing black glossy nail varnish.

'I'll get straight to the point, then,' Gillard said. 'We understand that you and Martin Knight had an affair, is that correct?'

She didn't seem surprised to be asked. 'It was a few years ago, but yes, we did.'

'How long did it last?'

'Exactly? I couldn't tell you. It started in May 2010, but when exactly it ended I couldn't really say. I mean, what is the definition of an affair? We have kept in touch, on and off, for years, and the affair, if you want to call it that, was just a few months. I've been in my own partnership now for a few years so it has definitely been more casual.'

'But it's still sexual?'

'Yes, when it suits me.'

'Did you ever meet Mrs Knight?' Gillard asked.

'Sure. Several times.'

'What did you think of her?'

'Bright woman, I guess, was my first reaction. A bit dowdy. Not quite single-minded enough. But it must have been hard being married to him. There isn't room for too many egos in that marriage, I guess.'

'Did she ever threaten you?'

'Threaten *me*?' Krugman laughed as if the concept was absurd.

'When she discovered the affair, we have heard that she was pretty angry. And we have a witness who claimed she had warned you off.'

Krugman smiled coldly. 'She made some drunken remarks to me at some LSE party we were at, but to be honest, I didn't take it that seriously. My relationship with Martin was already winding down when she found out about it. She seemed more upset that Martin and I had used their holiday home in Dingyville or wherever…'

'Dungeness…?' Mulholland said.

'Somewhere like that. Yeah, it was her family place, a shack on the beach. But she was mad that we'd used her bed.'

'How did she know?' Mulholland asked.

'Martin said she found one of my earrings on the bedroom floor. I must have been careless.'

'What did she say?' Gillard said, aware that he too had made love to Liz in that very same bedroom.

'She said that I had better leave him alone "or else", whatever that means.'

'What was your reaction?'

'I told her she was drunk. Which she was. And I also told her that since I'd finished with him, that she could have him back. Which wasn't strictly true. I guess I was drunk too.'

'Can you remember exactly when that was?'

'No.'

'So, just to be clear, you had finished with Martin Knight, but you still had sex?' Gillard asked.

'Boy, you Brits only think about one thing. Sure. I think I screwed him most times we met. But you have to understand, I didn't want to *own* him. Emotional empire-building isn't my shtick. I didn't want to take him away from her or anything like that. Whatever she might have said.'

'She may have thought otherwise,' Mulholland muttered.

'Mrs Knight's friends did implicate you as the cause of a

series of rows she and her husband had in the last few years,' Gillard said.

Krugman shrugged her shoulders. 'Yeah, Martin told me about the rows. It was up to him to balance his domestic situation with what we had. If he'd wanted to stop seeing me, he would have.'

'Is there anything else you would like to tell us?' Gillard asked.

Krugman stared coolly at them for a long time. 'I can't think of anything.'

'So you don't know where he is?' Mulholland said.

'I haven't the faintest idea,' she responded. 'I live on another continent.'

'When did you last see him?'

'We had dinner in London about two weeks ago.' She prodded and flicked at her iPad for a minute. 'Wednesday, October 12.'

'Where did you have dinner?'

'Someplace in Covent Garden.'

'Do you have the name?'

'No, I don't. White linen, Italian fusion, sexy waiters. He paid, so look it up. You have his credit card records, right?'

Gillard looked at Mulholland, who shook her head. 'He may well have paid cash,' she added.

'Whatever,' Krugman responded.

'But we do have copies of your recent email correspondence,' Gillard said. 'There are certain things that we would like you to clarify.'

Krugman's eyes locked onto Gillard as if peering into his skull and finding something of interest. 'I have absolutely nothing to hide, I can assure you.'

Gillard retrieved a file from his briefcase, then set before her a printout of the email exchanges from April. 'Do you recall sending these messages?' She picked up the sheet and scanned them, saying nothing. 'You talked about seeing him in Spain. And he talked about "dealing" with Liz. Do you know what he meant by that?'

Krugman sighed, and then smiled. 'He meant that he wanted to get a divorce. He was going to discuss it with Liz. And yes, there was a time back in April when I did consider letting him live with me, on a kinda exploratory basis.'

'Where? In Spain?' Mulholland asked.

'Yeah, maybe in Spain. As you know, he'd come into some money, and wanted to buy a luxury place in Spain. He had shown me some property plans when I saw him in... March, I think. The places looked pretty cool, and enormous. But I soon realized it was never going to work and told him.'

'There's nothing in the email traffic to support that assertion,' Mulholland said.

'Honey, I'm not in the habit of offering audit trails of my private relationships,' Krugman growled. 'Especially to the agents of the surveillance state.'

'Ms Krugman, a woman has been murdered,' Mulholland said, her voice steely.

'Not by me. And, I am overwhelmingly convinced, not by Martin either.' She locked eyes with Mulholland. 'Look. We talked it out on the phone. I called him and explained that it wasn't going to work. If he'd have been willing to come to the States, then maybe. I wasn't going to be in London enough, and certainly not in Spain enough, to make it work. If it could have worked at all.'

'But you were aware of how much money Martin had come into?' Gillard asked.

'Sure, but it made no difference. I've got money too.'

'Your email said you had a fight with Thibault, which I take it is Thibault Gregory, your ex-partner, about a house in Los Angeles,' Mulholland said.

'Well, sugar, I see you do your research in the *National Enquirer*, how diligent. But if you read a little wider you would also know that Thibault moved out in June, two months after that email, and I sold the house. So I do have the money. Look, I'm not going to deny that Martin was keener on living together than I was, but he did accept in the end that it wasn't going to work.'

'Do you have evidence of that? It might help your case,' Gillard said.

'I don't need any damn evidence. There is no case. I'm an innocent party.'

'That remains to be seen,' Gillard said. 'To go back to last Wednesday, after the meal did you go back to Knight's home with him?'

'No I did not. I've never been to his home, I mean the home in Surrey.'

'But you have been to the holiday home?' Mulholland asked.

'Sure, I told you. Just the once, and not since 2012.'

Mulholland turned to her briefcase and removed her DNA swab kit. 'As we explained, we need to take a DNA sample for elimination purposes...'

Krugman leaned over, grabbed a Q-tip and quickly swabbed the inside of her own cheek. 'There you go,' she said, offering the object back before Mulholland had even donned her latex gloves.

'So where did you stay that night?' Gillard said.

'At the Kensington Place Hotel.'

'Did Martin Knight stay with you?'

'For a few hours. And yes, before you ask, as I know you will, we had sex. In fact I screwed him so hard and so long I had trouble waking him up to go home to his frigid little mouse of a wife. There, is that enough detail for you?'

It was at that precise moment that Gillard knew he hated this woman.

Gillard and Mulholland had a coffee at the King's refectory, finally finding a table away from the throng of students. 'So what did you think?' Mulholland said.

'She appeared to have nothing to hide. And she couldn't easily be implicated, if the details of her movements are correct. She hadn't been in the country for two months, then she was in for two days, Tuesday and Wednesday, and flew out at a time when Liz Knight was still alive. I'll get Rob Townsend to confirm the details with American Airlines.'

'I could easily imagine her as inspiration for murder, couldn't you?' Mulholland asked. 'She radiates a kind of predatory self-confidence that most women can't match, and would find intimidating.' She scrutinized Gillard expectantly as she blew on her coffee.

'You're asking if I find her attractive?' Gillard let his gaze drift to the high ceiling and the mezzanine floor, where a group of female students were looking over the edge, files and papers shielding their chests. 'She's got a striking face and a good figure along with a sort of exotic allure, but I think most men would simply find her terrifying.' The thing that stuck most deeply with Gillard was that Krugman hadn't merely been factual about the nature of her 'screwing' Knight, she had used the verb transitively, the male being the passive recipient of her attentions.

'She could tell that we didn't like her,' Claire said.

'She pressed some buttons for Martin, though,' Gillard said. 'I'd love to put her at the murder scene, but I doubt we can do it.'

A call from Kent Police's CSI chief broke into the conversation. 'Go ahead, Nigel,' Gillard said.

'We've got confirmation on the human bone and flesh fragments in the waste pipe and the soakaway trap. The DNA belongs to Liz Knight.'

'No room for error?'

'No, there was a considerable presence of her DNA. We're 100 per cent sure. The rest turned out to be chicken fat and fish, a normal result for a kitchen waste pipe. There were also a few red woollen fibres. We've matched them up against those found in the Knights' home in Coulsdon, and the rug in the boot of his car. The blood, torn fingernail and hair on that rug are hers too. A few of the hairs match those from Professor Knight's LSE office chair and his comb.'

Gillard thanked him and hung up. Mulholland nodded as he passed on the news. She looked like she had something to say. 'Come on, spit it out,' he said.

'Okay. When Krugman said Liz was a frigid mouse, you looked like you were going to punch her.'

Gillard shrugged. 'It was pretty rude, wasn't it?'

'Craig, it's so obvious that you are still in love with Liz Knight. But however much you want to protect her, or her reputation, you can't. No one can help her now. Because she's dead.'

Monday's next interview was with Vuk Panić, Martin Knight's colleague at LSE's Mannheim centre. Gillard wanted to get a lot more insight into Knight's secret life, and this man, seemingly a good friend for a number of years, had known enough to drop the hint about Dr Natalie Krugman. Gillard and Mulholland had been late getting back from King's to Caterham police station, and Panić was already there. The desk sergeant had shown him into the interview suite.

Gillard glanced at the CCTV monitor before going in. Panić was sprawled across the sofa reading a hardback, for all the world like he was at home. When Gillard came in, he sat up slowly, pausing to finish the paragraph before standing up. Gillard introduced Claire Mulholland to him, and then noticed the title of the book: *Condemned from Birth: Essays in Class, Crime and Offending*.

'Another of Martin Knight's tomes?' Gillard asked.

'Yes, a series of brilliant monographs. You should read the

one about Surrey Police and the Deepcut Barracks suicides. It's very incisive.'

'Why do you assume I haven't?' Gillard asked.

'Touché, detective chief inspector. Yes, we all have prejudices.'

'I want to ask you in more detail about Knight's past. The friends he had, the places he worked, whom he may have visited.'

'I have prepared,' smiled Panić, lifting a hefty briefcase onto his lap and bringing out a sheaf of documents, pamphlets and journals. For the next hour, Gillard and Mulholland heard a detailed story of the seemingly inexorable rise of Martin Knight. Panić was hazier over the earlier years, but seemingly had a good memory for the last ten, when Martin's academic star was already in the ascendant. There was plenty of detail, and the detectives struggled to keep up with the names of journals, honours, awards and fellow academics.

'Okay,' said Gillard. 'A couple of specific areas I want to home in on. We've heard about the affairs – with the Brazilian postgrad student and Natalie Krugman. Were there any others, to your knowledge, especially recently?'

Panić pursed his lips. 'I never met the Brazilian woman, so can't help you there. Martin was actually quite discreet, and I really only know about the affair with Natalie because she was so open about it. If he had any affairs more recently I don't think I would have known.'

'No students he fancied? No likely postgrad students on his one-on-one tutorials?'

Panić smiled indulgently, glancing across to Mulholland. 'It is no secret that Martin has an eye for the ladies. But things in academia have changed in the last decade or two. I mean, once upon a time, affairs with students were seen by some lecturers as almost a perk, and were overlooked by the university. But now it is a much more high-risk experience, and the female student body is so much more, let us say, assertive about abuse of power. Which isn't to say it doesn't happen.' He shrugged. 'If he did, he never told me.'

'All right,' Gillard said. 'In Martin's academic experience and training, would he ever had covered forensics or had to examine and dissect bodies?'

Panić looked surprised by the question. 'I'm sure he would have had the opportunity for some theoretical forensic work. It's very fashionable now, of course. It probably wouldn't have been when he was an undergraduate. But practical work on cadavers? Not so likely.'

'Did he visit prisons and spend time with prisoners?'

'He must have done. Look at the extent of his work on incarceration, youth justice and so on. Why are you asking this?'

Gillard paused to consider how to phrase the answer: 'You might be aware that we have found only parts of Mrs Knight's body. We want to know who might have had the stomach to dismember her. If the professor hadn't any experience, as you suggest, of dealing with cadavers, then perhaps he had a contact inside the prison system. Someone he might have met, and who owed the professor a favour.'

Panić's eyes widened as he considered this apparently shocking idea.

Not getting a reply, Mulholland interjected: 'Mr Panić, did

Martin Knight meet any murderers? Someone who might for a fee have been willing to do his dirty work?'

He paused and then seemed to have a light bulb moment. 'Well, I did once meet Jimmy Bartram at one of Martin's parties, in perhaps 2007 or 2008. A fascinating individual.'

Mulholland looked quizzically at Craig. He returned her gaze, and asked: 'You've really never heard of the Shoreditch crane murder?'

She shook her head.

'Nasty,' Craig said. 'Bartram got 20 years, went down in 1981. Got a Ph.D. inside, wrote a bestselling crime novel under a pseudonym which was made into a film, and is now a fashionable poet-cum-advocate of prison reform, and distinctly trendy. He's all over the *Guardian*. Opinion pieces, book reviews, you name it.'

The two detectives thanked Panić for his time, and ended the interview. After he had gone, Mulholland asked: 'So do you think this Bartram bloke could have cut up Mrs Knight?'

'Well, let's put it this way. In 1975 Bartram used a blowtorch to kill a drug addict called Colin Ian Anderson who owed him money, and disposed of his body in 12 parts in plastic bags. These were cast inside a concrete counterweight, which was substituted by his building trade mates for one in a tower crane being used for the construction of a city high rise. Because of the recession, and the bankruptcy of the contractor, Anderson's corpse was up there for six years before the crane came down. Sadly for Bartram, the concrete had cracked and the body parts were found.'

'So he's easily capable, then,' Mulholland said.

'Was, at least. He's pushing 60 now, and claims to be a different man. And there isn't a molecule of his DNA anywhere in any of the three crime scenes. But if it wasn't him, then he would have the contacts for someone who would happily do it now, for a fee.'

'Let's get him in.'

'Don't expect it to be a pushover,' Gillard warned. 'He's always been tough, but now he's got money and clout too.'

His reflections were interrupted by a call over the radio. It was Rob Townsend. 'Go ahead, Rob,' he said.

'You'll like this. We now know who the mystery sixth person is whose DNA was in the Knights' home.' His breathy voice seemed excited.

'Don't keep me in suspense,' Craig said.

'Dr Natalie Krugman.'

'Fantastic.' He felt like punching a fist into the air with delight. Rob was right, he did enjoy it. But not just because it was progress in the case. It was a much more vindictive pleasure than that.

Chapter Nineteen

My arm is still sprained and sore where Martin forced it up my back yesterday evening. His fierce hand pressed my tearful face to the implacable cold quarry tiles. A woman squashed to the kitchen floor, her right and proper place, how appropriate. My fingers fought on, even with his knee in my back, as I prostrated myself to some hopeless Mecca. But my Sabatier eventually dropped, brittle as a shattered dream, with not yet a drop of blood to whet its keening blade.

Liz's diary, October 2014

Things turned out to be less simple than expected. By late Monday afternoon, Rob Townsend had verified all Krugman's flights with American Airlines, and they squared with the account she gave. She had left the UK for New York at 13.50 on Thursday, 13 October. That would mean that while Krugman must have visited the house, she couldn't have been there at the time of Liz Knight's death. The cleaner's last sighting of Liz was only a half-hour before that flight left. The blood fluorescence timings, though approximate, also ruled out Krugman's involvement.

'Okay, everyone,' Gillard called into the incident room. 'Ten-minute brainstorm.'

He set up the laptop and projector screen. On the whiteboards, he squeaked out some notes with a marker pen. 'Okay, here's where we are,' he said, tapping his way down the points on the whiteboard. We've got a large amount of forensic evidence linking Professor Knight to the death of his wife. There is her blood in his car, lots of her blood in her bedroom, and her blood, some teeth, and other human remains in their holiday home. So far, there is no other suspicious DNA from anyone outside the family in any of those places, except that of Natalie Krugman. And she has a rock-solid alibi for the time of death. Any dissent?'

Gillard looked around at his team: Claire Mulholland, Rob Townsend, Carl Hoskins, Colin Hodges and Michelle Tsu; all nodded their agreement. The only one not there was financial specialist Shireen Corey-Williams, still working with Oliver Knight through the family's assets and property.

'That seems to be overwhelming circumstantial evidence,' he said. 'What we don't have is the body or remaining body parts, and the murder weapon, or weapons. A number of different tools may have been used to dispose of the body. However, we are now in a better position to lay out what we think may have happened, starting from Wednesday evening. Want to have a go, Claire?'

Mulholland walked up to the whiteboard and wrote down some timings. 'Okay. At 5.15 p.m. on Wednesday, 12 October, Liz

Knight is seen to leave school by multiple witnesses, and gets into her car. At six she joins Helen Jennings at Bacchus wine bar in South Croydon, where she stays until approximately 7.15. That is corroborated by a text to her phone at 7.40 p.m. near her home. She may have been driving. Meanwhile, Martin Knight is having dinner, we believe, with Dr Natalie Krugman. According to Krugman's statement, Martin Knight leaves the Kensington Place Hotel…'

'Well shagged and smug with it,' muttered Hodges.

'Thank you, Colin… leaves the Kensington Place Hotel at, let's say, 11 p.m. He gets the last train home. We know this because a text he sent to Krugman pinged a tower in Clapham Junction at roughly the right time. At some point he deletes that text, presumably to stop Liz finding it, but I've recovered and read it. Just an innocuous expression of thanks. We assume he arrives home at, let's say, half past midnight. Now we've got a gap.' She pointed to the whiteboard. 'From now until about ten next day, Thursday morning, when we have a sighting of Professor Knight walking from home to Coulsdon South. There is a final sighting of Liz Knight, according to the cleaner, at around 1 p.m., which pretty much coincides with a 1-minute-40-second call to Martin Knight's mobile from the home landline.'

'Was a message left?' asked Michelle Tsu.

'No. Unfortunately, we have no idea what was said on that call,' Mulholland said. 'To continue, Liz Knight was never seen again. She didn't answer any calls to the house landline, of which there were two. Martin takes the train home at his usual time, as we know from the cell site analysis. But whether he came straight home, and what happened there when he did, is unknown. We can place him in his home office at 10 p.m. for the Skype call, and in the small hours from his use of the laptop. Everything else is in the realm of conjecture,' she said, putting down the pen.

'Okay. Let's suppose that Liz Knight had found out that her husband was once again sleeping with Natalie Krugman. Her first real chance to tackle him about it, without the cleaner there, is when he comes home that Thursday evening. She is in her bedroom. They have a row. Perhaps he just stabs her. Either way there is a huge amount of blood.' The next picture was of a horribly blood-stained red rug, mostly now black with dried blood. 'This we think is where she died. There isn't any real evidence of a struggle.' The next picture was of a wheat-coloured carpet bleached almost white over an area roughly the size of a washbasin. 'The blood soaked through the Moroccan rug, which has no backing, and onto the bedroom carpet. CSI say that there is no evidence of arterial squirting, which would have produced spray on walls, and certainly over a wider floor area than this. The blood penetrated the carpet underlay, and pooled in the ceiling cavity.' She showed another image, of the almost black blood pool, confined by floor joists. 'The murderer was very diligent in cleaning the carpet, and covered up the bleach stain with a fresh rug.'

'But what about the text Liz sent to her friend?' Michelle Tsu asked. 'That was in the evening, wasn't it?'

'Yes. That was at 7.16 p.m. A friend, Margaret Appledyke, received a text from Liz's phone, excusing herself from her birthday meal on the grounds of illness.'

'So she's still alive as late as that?' Michelle asked.

'Not necessarily,' Claire said. 'I interviewed Mrs Appledyke several days ago, and there is an oddity. It is the use of the term Maggie to address her in the text. While most of her friends know her by that name, Liz unfailingly called her Magsy.'

'So Professor Knight sent that text from his wife's phone?' Colin Hodges asked.

'We can't be sure,' said Gillard. 'But pretending to be Liz ill in bed and not taking calls would certainly buy him some time.'

'Or, just possibly, an upset Liz did go to bed, not feeling up to a birthday party,' Claire said. 'Either way the timings to the nearest hour are not crucial anyway. There are no more sightings of Mrs Knight, while from all the mobile signals we have of Professor Knight he carried on his usual commuting routine.'

The door opened and Detective Superintendent Paddy Kincaid came in, tie askew, his face ruddy. Everyone looked at him expectantly. 'Don't mind me,' he said. 'Carry on.'

Mulholland continued: 'That evening Martin Knight did a great deal of googling about the disposal of bodies from home on a laptop that remains in his possession,' Mulholland said. 'It's pretty conclusive evidence, if not of murder, then at least of intent to dispose of a body, and it corroborates everything we've seen so far. So, at some point, Martin Knight did several things. He stored the body somewhere wrapped in the Moroccan rug, while he cleaned and bleached the carpet, and found a new rug to hide the stain.'

'He's really not very clever, is he?' asked Kincaid. 'It might have started as the perfect murder on paper, but that's the problem with academics. Once it got messy and gory, it started to go tits up. Apologies ladies, I meant breasts skywards.' He permitted himself a small smile. 'Then he started to panic. In theory he would be forensically aware, and that text subterfuge was clever too, but he's made a lot of mistakes.'

'We shouldn't underestimate him,' Gillard said. 'He's managed to go to ground pretty effectively. The e-fits, with and without beard and glasses, have generated plenty of sightings, but none that stand up. We've got his car, so he may well have another vehicle. His known mobile hasn't been used, so he's probably got a disposable. The laptop's not been connected to the Internet since the night of the murder so, once again, perhaps he's bought another. His passport's not been used. Perhaps he's got a false one. His bank cards haven't been used, and we're hoping to find out from Shireen very soon if he has alternatives we don't know about. If the actual murder smacks of panic, the preparations for murder and for getting away unnoticed certainly don't. They were organized and careful.'

'Someone's been helping him. I'd put money on that American feminist,' Kincaid said, rubbing his hands together with a glee that indicated that it wasn't just money he'd put on her.

Mulholland interrupted: 'Dr Krugman's really not in any position to help him go into hiding, at least in this country. She has no home in the UK, and no family here. Her flight details check out, and there's proof she was in New York giving a lecture the next day. She's only spent a total of nine days in the UK in the last year and a half. Though some of the email correspondence we have between her and Knight hints that they were planning to live together if he left his wife, there is no hint that she had any kind of bolthole locally that he could use. It was only the Spanish place that was talked about.'

'Can you review for me the measures you put in place to find Knight?' Kincaid asked.

Gillard moved across to a whiteboard which was covered with marker pen notes, and turned it so that Kincaid could see it more clearly. 'Here's the timeline since I spoke to him,' he said, indicating a vertical line down the board. 'Anyone trying to disappear in our modern world will leave a trace, as you know, yet there has not been a single one on bank cards, passport, phone or laptop. We've got a European arrest warrant in place, his picture is out to Europol in 28 countries, and his card and phone details have been disseminated. He must have used a vehicle to get away from the Kent coast, and there is no decent public transport anywhere near the place his own car was abandoned. Colin and Carl have called in the CCTV on railway stations and in trains, and British Transport Police are helping out. It will take another week or two to be sure, but it does seem unlikely that he travelled by train, not least because his face is all over the papers.'

'So what is your own favourite theory?' Kincaid asked.

'Going abroad, with the help of an accomplice. The proximity to the Continent is an obvious temptation, with half a dozen ferry routes within two hours' drive, as well as Eurostar and Le Shuttle. On the way out, an accomplice could have smuggled him in the back of a van or an estate car. Someone could have given him a lift from Dungeness to Dover or Folkestone, or possibly right through to Calais or Boulogne, tucked in a boot or the back of a van. It's often been done.'

'Only in one direction. You couldn't get back into the UK like that,' Michelle Tsu said.

'How did you get in, then, love?' Kincaid muttered, exchanging smirks with Hodges.

The room went silent and everyone looked at Michelle's stony face. 'I was *born* here,' she said. 'And so were my parents.' Michelle looked at Claire and rolled her eyes, earning a smile of solidarity in return.

'Look, it was just a joke,' Kincaid said. 'Anyway Knight probably doesn't want to come back. He's jetting away to the sun aided by a hot bit of fluff. The full Ronnie Biggs.'

'I think it's unlikely he's left by air,' Gillard said. 'A booking requires a credit card as well as a passport number, and he'd have to show his passport at the check-in desk even if not at the outward border control. There's also a vast amount of CCTV coverage.'

'What about smaller airports?' Hoskins asked.

'We've already checked Lydd airport, which has plenty of light aircraft movements. They are adamant that Knight hasn't been through there. A ferry is far simpler, especially if he stays hidden in the vehicle. What about his contacts, Claire?'

'Michelle and myself have gone right through his LSE call log, his and Liz's home address books, his email contact lists and the contact list on his phone. Not one of those contacts claims to have heard from him since he disappeared. Someone might be lying, but it's not obvious who. We've tried to find the accomplice by seeing which of his friends and contacts isn't currently where he or she normally would be,' Claire Mulholland continued. 'But it's a big job.'

Kincaid stared at Claire: 'You can halve the work by just concentrating on the women. The accomplice is a bird, trust me. Some bit of stuff we haven't managed to track down. Just look at the extramarital leg-over he's done. Our professor is a bit of a fanny magnet.'

Mulholland's face tightened. Kincaid delighted in ruffling female feathers, particularly if he could see the effect, and he was on fine form today. Female officers did all they could not to react. But for all of Gillard's distaste for Kincaid, underneath it all was a decent detective nose. And on this occasion Gillard reckoned he wasn't far wrong.

Warming to his theme, Kincaid continued: 'Knight has got to eat. He's got to have somewhere to sleep. He's got to get some cash, unless he's got a great wodge of readies with him. He's been invisible for a week, but he can't stay that way for ever.'

'He can if he's dead,' muttered Michelle Tsu. 'He could have committed suicide, and that's why we can't find him.'

There was a general nodding among the assembled detectives, some of whom hadn't considered this possibility. Gillard shook his head. 'I don't buy it. Even if we ignore the planned nature of the murder of Liz Knight, this doesn't fit the pattern. Most suicides in cases like this are committed at home, or somewhere near where the car is driven: a quarry, a lake, big cliffs like Beachy Head, something like that. Suicides usually want to be found, because they've got something to say.'

Kincaid chuckled. 'Craig's right. Could you really imagine a windbag like Professor Knight topping himself without leaving a suicide note as long as an election manifesto? Believe me, he's not killed himself. No way.'

'Or you'll eat your desk, sir?' Claire asked.

'Too right I will. With mustard.' Kincaid folded his arms. 'And bloody onion rings.'

Professor Martin Knight's card said simply:

To My Darling Chloe

I'm so sorry I can't be with you at this difficult time, and know you must be very upset. I'll get back as soon as I can, and then we can talk. I know it's hard, but try to have a happy birthday.

All my love
Dad xx

'Why didn't you tell me about this?' Oliver said. 'I have a right to know too.' He was sitting at home with his sister, looking at the birthday card that Chloe had kept hidden from him all day.

'If I show it, the police will just take it away,' she said. But I want to keep it. It's all I've got of Dad. He said he would see us. It's up to us to persuade him to come back and answer all the questions, isn't it?'

'Chloe,' Oliver said, gripping her arms. 'You can't keep this hidden. It's interfering with the investigation. You'll get into so much trouble.'

'I know, I know. But it's just so awful. There has got to be some explanation. I told him that he has to.'

'You *told* him?'

'I emailed him to thank him for the card.'

'Well that's it, then. The police are monitoring all activity on his mobile. They'll know about the card.' He paused. 'Did Dad reply?'

'Not yet. But at least I know now that he's all right, whatever happened to Mum.'

Oliver rubbed his chin and said nothing.

Tuesday, 25 October

Croydon police station looks like a cross between a crematorium and a multi-storey car park, a contender for the most miserable of Britain's many soulless public buildings. For DS Claire Mulholland, summoned for a Girl F meeting with DCI Brian 'Radar' Dobbs first thing on a rainy Tuesday, it looked its depressing worst.

Dobbs was waiting for her in a borrowed office, surrounded by paperwork, every inch the bespectacled 1950s door-to-door insurance salesman. Tall and moustachioed, Radar had been a Hong Kong policeman and before that an RAF police officer. He was considered diligent if unimaginative, but had a good record in re-examining failed investigations, which is why Rigby had appointed him to head the Girl F cold case review.

'Why is he called Radar?' Claire had asked Kincaid earlier that day.

Kincaid had smiled and just pulled his own ears out. 'He's part of Britain's early warning system,' he said.

Now, in the flesh, Claire could see Kincaid wasn't exaggerating about the huge ears. But what he hadn't mentioned was Dobbs's ridiculous thin beige moustache clinging to his top lip, a runaway eyebrow come down for a drink.

'Claire, thank you for making yourself available,' he said, without quite making eye contact. He pointed to a seat, and she sat. 'I'll get to the point. I think Harry Smith is the man who abused Girl F. I need someone of your calibre to get him to admit it, and quickly. We have to release him by tomorrow night.' He turned his myopic gaze upon her.

'Okay,' she said. 'I spent last night reading up on the case. How is the CSI coming on?'

'Well, he's clever. That much is clear already. The computers we seized had been cleansed of presumably incriminating data by the time we got there, using professional software. Given we were there within half an hour of the attack, that was going some. We found cameras, video recording gear and a portable studio at the house, all of which fits his claim that he's a professional photographer. Nothing on the camera data cards is incriminating. Likewise, the house is spotless too. Every surface lined with disposable cling film. The man's beyond forensically aware, he's got OCD. I have to say that given the number of years since Girl F could have been here, we'll be very lucky indeed to get a speck of forensic evidence. But there may have been other, more recent, victims. I'm getting the Met to comb their records of unsolved abuse allegations, and I want you to do the same for Surrey. Requests are out for Sussex and Kent, likewise.'

'Has he said anything so far?'

'Not a thing. We've had two teams of detectives asking him the same questions over and over again, and he's just ignored them. Seems completely impervious. He knows he'll go down for the attack on the PCSO, but he seems to know that we've got nothing on him for Girl F.'

Chapter Twenty

The gruesome sight was enough to sicken even hardened detectives. It was a sunny summer day at Romney Marsh in Kent, when officers discovered a murder so savage and bestial it would leave the stolid residents of the Garden of England in shock. A young woman's body in the marsh. Cut into pieces.

(*Daily Express*, 23 June 1954)

Wednesday, 26 October

The search of Walland Marsh went on for days. Many interesting items were found. A rusting Webley revolver turned out to be of Second World War origin, and there were fragments of anti-aircraft shells, a discarded machine gun belt and a piece of a Hurricane cockpit discarded during a bail-out, all of the same vintage. Rusted parts of agricultural machinery were also found, along with some 1970s car parts still in their sealed packets. But of the missing body parts of Mrs Elizabeth Knight there was no sign whatever.

First thing on Wednesday morning, Mulholland and Gillard came down to join the search and to finally meet Harpy Singh. There was still a bit of mist across the marsh when Gillard pulled the Ford Focus into the gravel car park of the old boat yard a mile north of Dungeness on the road to Lydd. There were five other Kent Police vehicles there. At the centre of a huddle of five anoraked officers and four in wet suits stood a svelte woman with a mane of dark hair that she was in the process of twisting into a bun. At Gillard's approach she turned around and smiled. Dark commanding eyebrows and huge brown eyes made this more of a Bollywood face than one suited for sifting swamps for rotting corpses.

'DCS Harpy Singh,' she said, extending an arm. Gillard shook her hand and introduced Claire Mulholland. 'Get your wellies and latex gloves on, chaps,' Singh said. 'Got something you may find interesting.'

A big Yorkshire sergeant in a wet suit whose name Gillard didn't catch led them over to the point where the discovery had been made. The thick, glutinous mud clung to his boots, sucking and sapping each step towards what he was sure would be a grisly find.

'It's bits of bone,' said the sergeant. 'In a taped-up bin bag.'

'Human?' Gillard asked.

'Mebbe.' The officer lifted his gloved hands to show him. The wet bin bag had been wrapped to the rough size of a fruit juice carton, but had come undone when the tape lost adhesion. He laid the package on a plastic sheet, where it sagged and fell open revealing nine gristle-covered vertebrae, three of them still connected, all coated in a silty residue. 'Fancy a plate of oxtail stew?' asked the sergeant. He seemed pleased when Claire Mulholland grimaced. He was clearly a soulmate for Kincaid.

Gillard watched an officer taking photos of the find with a big camera. As she readjusted the position of the plastic sheet, the vertebrae slid and revealed what looked like a scrap of fabric. 'I don't want anyone touching this. We're already disturbing the evidence, and I think we need help.'

It was time to take the forensic work to the next level. The CSI teams from Kent and Surrey had done a fine job, but he really needed more authority, and more certainty. That meant getting a Home Office forensic pathologist on-site. The one he wanted was Dr David Delahaye. Gillard had worked with him before, and trusted his judgment completely. And as Gillard recalled, the doctor lived in Rye, just a few miles away. He slid out his phone and called him.

It was less than an hour when a sleek black Tesla pulled onto the gravel apron by the marsh. Admiring glances from the male officers brought all work to a stop. Dr Delahaye, a tall, slight figure with a domed bald head and metal-framed glasses emerged from the driver side door, eating an apple, and shook hands with Gillard and Harpy Singh. The doctor was in mustard-coloured corduroys, a waxed jacket and wellingtons. On the other side of the car a pony-tailed girl of perhaps 12 in a pink anorak slid out of the passenger side, inquisitiveness scribbled all over her face.

'You were lucky. Just caught me on my way back from picking up Cordelia,' Delahaye said, eating the core of the apple, stalk included, in two crisp bites. 'Got another case in Canterbury at 11. I can give you 15 minutes. Where's your find?'

The detectives walked over with him to the plastic sheet, where he knelt and stared. 'Where did you find this?' he asked, and was shown the section of marsh 20 metres away. Gillard noticed Delahaye's daughter crouching between him and the pathologist, her neck straining for a better view. 'Urggh. Is that from a person, Daddy?'

'It was once, Cordelia. Part of a female of childbearing age, from the anterior tilt in these remaining connected lumbar vertebrae.' He pointed to the gristle which still surrounded parts of the bones, and the fragment of fabric. 'Delighted to see this. Textile analysis could provide valuable corroboration.' He looked up. 'Freshwater marsh, yes?'

'That's right,' the Yorkshire sergeant said.

'Good. If the supposed victim's been dead, what, two weeks, is it?'

'Nine days,' Gillard said.

'Excellent. Not too long. Then there's a good chance we can get a little DNA and maybe, if we are really lucky, some mitochondrial too. Not with salt water though. Corrodes the cells too quickly, even in bone.'

'So you can find out who this lady was?' the girl asked.

'If we are lucky, Cordelia.' He turned to her. 'You remember I described to you a process called polymerase chain reaction?'

'To make enough cells for measuring?' she asked.

'Yes, to amplify the unique codes in cells by copying them to a measurable size for our tests. Our biggest worry is hydrolysis, which is the severing of chemical bonds within the cells. That happens because water reacts with those organic cells. In bone the main damage is through the loss of hydroxyapatite protection through the dissolution of the inorganic element of the bone.'

The child nodded, sagely. She had obviously heard it before.

'How old is she?' Harpy Singh asked Delahaye.

'I'm 12 on Boxing Day,' the girl said proudly.

'What's this?' said Delahaye, looking at one of the shovelled piles of silt.

'It's the surrounding muck, just in case there's owt small in there for yer to look at,' the wet-suited sergeant said.

'Yes, well done. And here's why. There's another section of bone in there, see?' He pointed to what had at first appeared to be a vaguely conical pebble in the gloop. 'Coccyx – that's a tail bone, Cordelia. If I'm not mistaken, there are some clumps of hair here clinging to the fabric.' He stood up. 'Well, I'm feeling quite optimistic about this. I'll know for sure once I've had a chance for a proper look. Three to four days after you send it to me.' He reached out his hand to his daughter and led her away. Cordelia looked over her shoulder for the last glimpse of the human remains.

'I hope she understands all that,' said the Yorkshire sergeant. 'Then mebbe she can explain it to me one day.'

Wednesday afternoon found DS Claire Mulholland waiting impatiently for the full results from the CSI at Harry Smith's house. She had three hours left before he had to be charged or released, but she needed to maximize the leverage against him. At a quarter to four, the results arrived, and they weren't up to much: no trace of Girl F, no youthful fingerprints or footprints. Only two DNA profiles had been found in the house. One was Smith's, from his toothbrush and hairs in his bed. The other was from a fragment of discarded tissue found down the back of a settee, and which was found to contain semen. It wasn't Smith's, but there was a match from the national database.

It was Timon Horvat, aka Aleksander Horvat. The Knights' tenant.

'Well, well,' muttered Claire to herself as she speed-read the lab document. Dots in her head were being gradually connected.

'What have you got, Claire?' asked Paddy Kincaid as he walked past.

'We've got a weird connection between the hunt for Professor Knight and the Girl F case. One of Knight's tenants, Timon Horvat, has been having sex in Smith's house.'

Kincaid seemed taken aback. 'Maybe it was with Harry Smith himself?'

'Maybe, but with a record for approaching underage girls I would think his tastes fall in more predictable areas,' she said.

'Did you see the message for you from the Slovenian cops?' Michelle Tsu called across from the opposite desk.

'No, I didn't,' she answered.

'They say Horvat has no history of sexual offences back home. But they added something quite interesting. He was charged in

Ljubljana in 2002 with being an accessory to murder, but was acquitted because of a lack of evidence.'

'In what way was he an accessory?' Tsu had Mulholland's full attention now.

'I put the printout in your in-tray, but basically he was accused of helping dispose of a body after a gangland killing. He has all the requisite skills. He worked in an abattoir for a decade.'

Mulholland's jaw hung open. When she closed it again, there were three words in her mind: Bring him in.

'I've got to drive up to Croydon and interview Harry Smith now, sir,' she said. 'Can I ask you to get Horvat arrested?'

'Consider it done,' Kincaid said.

Harry Smith was seemingly asleep in the custody suite when Mulholland arrived. 'Wakey-wakey,' she said, as Sergeant Connolly let her in.

'Come to let me out?' Smith said, stretching his arms and yawning. His right cheek and nose were still swollen, and a purple bruise spread below a dressing up to his brow.

'No, I'm here to ask you some questions.'

He looked up at the wall clock. 'Not for long, lassie.'

'We've got 40 minutes,' she said.

'Where's my brief?' Smith cracked his knuckles methodically, one finger at a time. Something about it really irritated Claire.

'He's here,' she said, as the door opened. The duty solicitor, a pale young man in a grey suit, came into the room, followed by DCI Craig Gillard. Claire had asked Craig to come along, seeing as there was now a connection with Timon Horvat.

'Where's my own solicitor?'

'Stuck in traffic, and we don't have time to wait for her,' Mulholland said. She assembled her papers, waited for Gillard to sit down and, after the formalities for the tape, said: 'Have you ever taken an underage girl to your home?'

He smirked and closed his eyes, and said: 'Tick-tock, tick-tock, tick-tock.'

'Have you ever met a girl called Francine Cole?'

'Tick-tock, tick-tock...'

The charade continued, every question met with the same response.

Gillard got up and wandered around behind Smith with his hands in his pocket. He then leaned down and whispered in his ear. 'We know you like to take dirty pictures, Harry. We know exactly what you are.'

For a moment he was silent, his pale eyelids hidden behind pale gingery eyebrows. Then: 'Tick-tock, tick-tock.'

'Tell me about your friend Aleksander Horvat,' Mulholland asked.

Smith stopped ticking.

'Looks like you need winding up,' Gillard whispered into his ear. 'Or maybe you're just retarded.'

'You're not as tidy as you think,' Mulholland said. 'We found Horvat's semen in your house.'

For the first time, Smith began to look uncomfortable.

'Tell us what you know, and we can make your last half-hour here comfortable,' Gillard said. 'Come on, start from the beginning, give us some names.'

'Albert, Alan, Alastair, Adrian, Archie...'

Mulholland and Gillard exchanged expressions of frustration. 'I promise you, we will nail you, if it takes us ten years,' Gillard said.

'And by that clock you haven't got more than ten minutes,' he replied. 'Tick-tock, tick-tock. It's also three hours since I've had any refreshments, so you can get me a coffee. Milky, with two demerara sugars.'

'You can wait until we've finished,' Mulholland said.

At the end of the session, the duty solicitor announced that Smith had now to be charged or released. Mulholland shrugged; they would have to let him go. As she and Gillard walked out, frustrated, they heard Smith shout: 'I still want that coffee.'

Thursday, 27 October

The new day arrived like a wave of misery for Gillard. Having foolishly trusted the forecast, he had decided to cycle into Caterham, and it had unexpectedly poured with rain. A large and filthy quarry lorry had almost knocked him off when turning left in front of him without signalling, and he was in too much of a hurry to chase and get the registration number. When he did arrive at the Caterham incident room, it was to discover Claire Mulholland was waiting for him with DC Colin Hodges.

'Craig, I'd hoped to give you some good news this morning,' she said, her face taut.

'What's happened?' Gillard had heard about the DNA link between Horvat and the Girl F case. With the Slovenian's slaughterhouse background, it had the makings of a breakthrough.

'Horvat's vanished,' she said.

'Me and Carl were down there at five this morning, with the operations team and a ram and everything,' Hodges said. 'But there was no one in. He'd buggered off in a hurry, I should say. No note to say goodbye, nothing. Place in a complete mess.'

'We got straight on to ports, airports, Chunnel with his passport details by 7 a.m.,' Mulholland said. 'But he might already be away. The duty inspector has got the European arrest warrant paperwork underway. For some reason we don't have details of his vehicle, but we've got on to his employer.'

Hodges added: 'We've taped off the flat and secured the door. Carl rang CSI, thinking that he might have left some dabs or something. Wasn't sure what you wanted, but we got his computer, which is now being examined by the anoraks.'

Gillard tried not to express his profound surprise at this level of professionalism from Tweedledee and Tweedledum. 'That's great work.'

Hodges paused, then asked something that had clearly been exercising his brain. 'So if Horvat is a slaughterman, do you think he could have chopped up Mrs Knight?'

'It's quite possible.'

Craig needed a lunch break. When he was at Mount Browne, it was easy. Fifteen minutes sitting on a bench with a sandwich in the extensive leafy campus, looking over the rooftops of Guildford. Always helped to clear the mind. Anything was better than sitting munching away in front of a PC, dropping bits of bread and tomato into the keyboard. In Caterham's crowded incident room, since the Knight inquiry began it had been difficult even to find time. So when a spare midday hour appeared, his mind turned to a Mexican takeaway in South Croydon that had been recommended to him. As he was emerging from the incident room, he ran into PCSO Sam Phillips.

'Hi, Sam. Your first day back, isn't it? Are you fully recovered from your tussle with Smith? And how's the leg?'

'All much improved, thanks.' They exchanged a few guarded pleasantries before he asked casually. 'Fancy a bite of lunch?'

'I can't,' she said. 'I'm not due a break until three.'

'Wait a mo,' he said, and took out his phone to make a call to her boss 'This is DCI Craig Gillard. I'm borrowing PCSO Sam Phillips for an hour or so, for an operational matter. Is that okay?' He laughed. 'Yes, I'll return her unharmed.' He turned back to her. 'Your sergeant is fine with it.'

Sam had her hands on her hips. 'Excuse me. I'm a woman. Not a piece of kit to be borrowed, signed out, used and returned. I get a say, don't I?'

Gillard laughed as he shepherded her to the unmarked Ford. 'Sam, I'm not making this up. I'm on my way to one of the rental flats in Thornton Heath that the Knights owned. A suspect in the Knight case has done a runner and I need someone to watch my back while I root around. Yes, on the way back I'm going to buy a bite to eat and tap your brain about Harry Smith.' He leaned into the back seat and pulled over a grey fleece jacket. 'No need to be in uniform though. Slip this on.'

'Okay, so I'm being officially abducted.' She tossed her PCSO hat on the back seat, and exchanged her equipment vest for the fleece. As they got into his car she said: 'Thank you for the kind message, by the way.'

Craig shook his head as he drove off. 'Christ, Sam, I've been worried about you. Not only about Harry Smith, but that crazy ex of yours. Still, it's clear now you know how to defend yourself.'

She laughed. 'I'll never live it down, I suppose. Beating him up.'

Craig chuckled. 'You have achieved in legitimate self-defence what many, many officers would love to have done to Smith, but of course they can't. He'll go down for the attack on you at least, but if Claire Mulholland has her way, for a lot more besides.'

As Craig weaved skilfully through the lunch hour traffic to Thornton Heath, he filled her in on Timon Horvat's relevance to the Knight case and how his DNA had also been found in Harry Smith's home. They turned down a street, and parked by a slightly tired-looking terraced house. The front door was locked, and she watched as Craig used Oliver Knight's keys to let them both in, past a heap of local newspapers, post and pizza flyers. They went upstairs and saw the door to Horvat's flat, covered in police tape and badly smashed by the ram. A temporary police padlock and hasp had been put on it. Craig unlocked it and, after donning a pair of blue latex gloves, let himself in. He asked Sam to stay behind at the doorway.

'I don't think there's been any CSI done in here,' he said. 'Tweedledum and Tweedledee were on the hurry-up, and only took his computer, so I'm going to see what else I can find.'

Half an hour later he emerged, holding a data stick in his hand. 'This is going to be important,' he said.

'How do you know?'

'Because it was hidden so well, in a pleat of the bedroom curtains, under the pelmet.'

'That's the last place anyone would think to look.'

'Exactly. I was lucky. I started with electrical-linked places, fuse boxes, cooker hood, that kind of thing, because he's an electrician and he's familiar with those spaces. But when I was standing on his bed looking at a light socket, I noticed a strange deformity in the curtain tape.'

'Well done Sherlock!'

He gave her a look. 'Now for that sandwich. I'm starving.'

They no longer had time for a Mexican, but sat in a quiet side street between a tyre place and a Jamaican hairdresser's, each eating an overfilled chicken salad bap they had bought from a Greek shop round the corner. Sam looked at Craig, his mouth bulging, mayonnaise dripping down his chin. She started to giggle. He pointed to the mirror, and to her. You're just as bad, was the message. Unvoiced laughter, basic food, the dull beat of hip-hop from the hairdresser's mixed in with the huff and whine of the tyre joint: as a date, it wasn't exactly a trip to the Ritz. But in his own, unvoiced way, Craig seemed to be saying sorry to her, carving out time to be with her in a busy day and showing his concern for the latest chapter of her accident-prone life. She deliberately brushed the crumbs on her lap onto the floor of the car, knowing it would earn her a mute rebuke. Mouth full, he glared at her in mock anger, and she felt a smear of warmth butter her face. Actually, this is all right. I can handle this. This is a life, with evidence he cares. Unspoken perhaps, but obvious. It's more than I've had for years, and right now, it's enough.

Craig finished his bap, wiped his mouth with the balled-up bag it came in, and flicked it at her. 'You untidy little bugger,' he said, leaning across to look at her. 'I'm going to ferry you back to your boss now, with good reviews: "The Phillips model is reliable, if a bit basic. Easy to use, starts first time, perhaps a little heavy on fuel."' He nodded at the crumb-coated footwell.

'A bit bloody basic!' She hit him playfully on the shoulder and pulled him into an embrace. They kissed gently for a couple of minutes, and as they emerged realized that two dreadlocked punters at the hair salon were laughing at them. 'Well,' she said. 'Ethnic minorities making a mockery of the law again!'

'Luckily they don't know we're the law. That would make them much more nervous.' Craig started the engine, and as they pulled away, exchanged thumbs-up greetings with a good half-dozen salon staff and customers peering from their window.

As they reached Caterham police station he let her out. She leaned back in through the window and said: 'Detective Chief Inspector, thank you for a very nice "operational matter".'

'The pleasure was all mine. Now, I'm going to see what it was on that data stick that Horvat didn't want anyone else to see.'

On his return to Caterham, Gillard found Research Intelligence Officer Rob Townsend and showed him the data stick. 'Can we take a quick look at this now on your machine?' Rob's PC was a standalone set up to handle any malware that computer evidence may contain. 'I need a second pair of eyes too.'

They inserted the stick, which listed hundreds of image and video files. The very first video they chose, at random, showed such a sickening act of abuse that Rob turned away from the screen. 'I've got daughters of that age, Craig. I can't look.'

'Just stay one minute,' Gillard said. The video looked quite professional, properly lit, taken in a white, featureless room. He set fast-forward at maximum speed, and then halted it. 'Rob, look at this. Do you recognize anything?'

The officer had a quick glimpse at the screen, which showed a naked teenage girl kneeling in front of a partially clothed man. His face was pixelated out, but it was clearly neither Horvat nor Smith. The girl's long hair was bunched in his tattooed fist, pulled in towards him, and her eyes were screwed shut against the act she was forced to perform. 'The man or the girl, sir?'

'Neither. Look behind her, here. You can just see into the corridor.' He pointed at the screen.

'You're interested in the wallpaper, sir?'

'Red fleurs-de-lis on a cream background.'

'Very nice. B&Q probably have it, sir. I can check if you want to order some.'

Craig looked balefully at him. 'Stop being a dimwit, Rob. This is the wallpaper in Harry Smith's hallway. And there's the reflected sheen of the plastic film he puts everywhere. Even if Smith didn't take part in any of these acts, the fact they took place in his home means we've got him.' Craig stopped the video and turned to Townsend with a smile. 'Rob, I've got a meeting now, can you book this evidence in for me? Let Claire and the others know the good news.'

'Okay.'

'I expect Radar Dobbs will be able to dig up the manpower to examine all the images. Claire will want stills of the most incriminating stuff. And make sure it's all backed up.'

'Righto, sir,' Townsend said.

Finding Horvat was now a priority because it could unlock not just one but two major inquiries. Gillard scanned through the notes that DS Mulholland had made until he came to the details of Horvat's employer, RCL Electrical Contractors (Redhill) Ltd. He picked up the phone, punched in the number and waited to be passed to the managing director.

'Roger Carlton speaking.'

Craig was suddenly lost for words. This familiar voice was his old schoolmate, the boy who had gone crumpet-hunting at the girls' school on that fateful night in 1986. 'Roger, it's Craig Gillard. Long time, no see, mate.'

Roger soon overcame his surprise and they spent a good few minutes catching up on 30 years, Roger's marriage and four kids, Craig's career, marriage and divorce. It was ten minutes later when he was able to get to the reason he had called.

'The reason I'm calling is about Alex Horvat. Has he been in contact in the last day or two?'

'No, as I told the female officer, he's buggered off with one of our vans with three grand's worth of copper cable and tools in it, and I'd very much like to get it back.'

Gillard double-checked the registration number, which was exactly as Claire had recorded it. He switched to the Police National Computer. There had been an ANPR match in north London this morning, and another a half-hour later in Hertfordshire. It seemed not to have been shared with other forces, so he made a note to do so. 'Any ideas where Horvat would go?'

'Maybe Hull. He had connections there,' Roger said.

'He was a taxi driver there, wasn't he? Back in 2007.'

'I think so.' Finally, Roger said: 'Saw you on the telly the other day about that Elizabeth Knight murder. That wasn't the girl you were nuts over at school, was it?'

'No, someone different.'

There was a long pause. 'But she was a Liz, wasn't she? Such a gorgeous girl. I was jealous as hell. Parents lived at Marlpit Close, as I remember.'

'Did they?' Craig realized his fiction was beginning to unravel under the accuracy of Roger's memory.

'Go on, course you do. You spent enough time mooning about there. In fact you were a complete pain about the whole thing. Told me once you couldn't live without her, remember?'

Craig forced a laugh. 'Well, that's all a very long time ago.'

'So what did happen to her, Craig?' He was beginning to be very persistent.

'She fell in love with someone else.' *Who then screwed other women, murdered her, cut up her body in a sink, dumped it in a marsh and ran off abroad.*

'Oh well, win some, lose some, eh?'

'That's it.' Gillard said his goodbyes, then hung up. He

slumped in his chair and rubbed his face. It was five minutes before he could force himself to pick up the phone. He called Claire Mulholland and asked her: 'When are you planning to get Harold Smith back in for interview?'

'First thing tomorrow,' she replied. 'Now you've finally got enough mud to make it stick.'

'Good, let's throw some muddy questions at him together.'

Gillard headed off to the incident room, just in time to hold open the door for the diminutive figure of DC Shireen Corey-Williams who was struggling with three big boxes. She looked exhausted. Her frizzy black hair, normally a bouncy halo round her brown face, was tied back with a scarf. 'I need coffee, and I need it now,' she groaned, as she sat down on a typist's chair. 'I've had four solid days going through acres of paperwork with two lawyers and the dullest forensic accountant in the world and still didn't get a breakthrough.'

'So what did you learn?' Gillard asked, gesturing for DC Colin Hodges to get some coffee.

'The first thing you asked me to do was to test whether Oliver could have killed his parents. Well, there is nothing in his financials to support that hypothesis. They think pretty well of him at his firm, but I also get the impression that they think he lacks imagination and drive.'

Gillard laughed. 'Seeing what he stands to inherit, I can fully appreciate it might undermine any career drive.'

'Exactly. We did a search at Companies House. He's not a director of any companies. Neither could we locate any hidden bank accounts, offshore funds, trusts or tax-exempt foreign hidey-holes on his computer or laptop. All paperwork at his house seems legit.'

'Did you check his girlfriend?'

'Yes. Sophie James, junior chiropractor. Clean as a whistle, no debts. Oliver hasn't been married, or lived with anyone before. The usual places to hide money haven't cropped up. Oliver and Sophie were at the theatre with friends at the time of his mother's death. The alibi checks out.'

'Okay, so Oliver Knight is in the clear. What more did you learn about the Knights' finances?' Gillard asked.

'Everything looks above board. There are none of the tell-tale signs of a man about to become a fugitive from justice. No unusually large cash withdrawals, no juggling between accounts, except for the purchase of this villa in Spain. However, given that most of the legwork was done by Mrs Knight, and none of the others speak Spanish, it can hardly be a property conspiracy *against* her. Nevertheless, as it was the bulk of their wealth, that was what I spent most of my time on.'

She offered Gillard a pile of documents, including the brochure he'd already seen. 'It seems this property venture was Liz's idea, to build half a dozen more villas on the land, with the aim of doubling their money in five years. I've looked through Oliver's documents. There's a notarized copy of the registration document from the Colegio de Registradores, the Spanish land registry, which matches the deed drawn up by the Spanish notary and checked by Oliver. The seller looks to be a Spanish limited company. Seems to be a bona fide transaction.'

'Except that from what we've seen of Professor Knight's emails to Natalie Krugman, he wanted to move with her to Spain.'

'That's right,' Shireen said.

Gillard rubbed his chin and grimaced. 'It still seems pretty hare-brained for him to buy the place at all. Why not keep the money and do a flit? Then he could join Natalie Krugman somewhere that works for her. Buying property just ties him down.'

'Maybe he was outvoted by the rest of the family,' Shireen said. 'Anyway, once we catch him we can ask him.'

Gillard nodded glumly. There had been a *Daily Mail* article about Martin Knight two days ago headlined 'Why Haven't They Caught Him?' Worse still, a sidebar piece catalogued the failings of Surrey Police from the Deepcut Barracks suicides through the Milly Dowler murder and the Girl F case. Though it wasn't credited, the analysis leaned heavily on Professor Knight's own critique of the force. Fortunately for Gillard, the only officer named was Alison Rigby, described as 'a powerful new broom' to bring the force into the 21st century. As if to emphasize the point his phone rang. It was her.

'Yes, ma'am.'

'You're probably aware that Lord Justice Cunliffe's report on Girl F is being published tomorrow.'

'Yes. Detective Superintendent Kincaid told me.'

'Ah, of course he did.' Rigby giggled. She had a surprisingly girlish laugh. 'He's not looking forward to it. The thing is, Craig, there is a press conference in London tomorrow afternoon at three o'clock at which the judge will be releasing his findings. It would look really good if we could find Martin Knight by then. I don't like the way the headlines are drifting. That way we shift the focus to the positive for the force, rather than dwelling on mistakes of the past. Think you can do that for me?'

'We've got some leads, but to actually nab him by tomorrow… That's quite a tall order, ma'am.'

'Craig, I'm six-one, all my orders are tall. But I have every confidence in you.' She hung up.

Chapter Twenty-One

Friday, 28 October

It is my conclusion that the handling of the Girl F case and its aftermath are perhaps the most consistent and protracted policing failures in modern times. Not only on the policy issues of the girl's vulnerability, the racial and social stereotyping exhibited by members of the force, but bungled evidence handling, inept statement logging, poor supervisory oversight and numerous other matters betray a lamentable lack of professionalism. There is some evidence that lessons have been learned and managerial oversight of officers improved since the original report, and the IPCC interim findings, but the fact remains no one has been convicted fully eight years after the death of this unfortunate teenager.

(Executive summary of the Cunliffe Report, 2016)

Harry Smith was back at Croydon police station. His solicitor, a tiny but intense middle-aged Asian woman called Samira Jindal, was sitting with him in the custody suite, radiating enough anger for both of them. The moment Gillard arrived with Connolly, the custody sergeant, Jindal launched into them. 'My client has very kindly agreed to be interviewed for one more hour despite only two days ago being released from 48 hours confinement on the very same matter.'

'He's on police bail,' Gillard said. 'We can bring him in when we want.'

'No. Not without persuading a magistrate—'

'Ah, but we have new evidence we want to put to him,' he said. 'DS Mulholland is bringing it any time now.'

Jindal paused, then flicked through some of the pile of documents in front of her. 'My client is not well, and the stress of these groundless accusations is damaging to him. He needs frequent breaks for medication, which he has not been given. He also says that when he was in custody he wasn't given the kosher food he requested.'

'Och, he's not a Jew,' Connolly said.

'Sergeant, it is not your job to decide—'

'Lassie,' he retorted. 'Two days ago he asked me for halal food and to be allowed out for prayer and ritual ablutions. Is he claiming he's converted from Church of Scotland to Islam and now Judaism in the course of a week? Or is he just taking the piss?'

There was no reply from Jindal, and from Smith just the same sardonic smile that had played across his face in earlier interviews. The colourless eyes, the pale eyelashes and the smirking lips seemed designed to enrage every officer who saw him.

'Let's get on,' Gillard said, making the preparations for the tape recording, and then turning to Smith. 'All right, Harry. Do you know where Aleksander Horvat has gone?'

'I don't know anyone of that name.'

'Also known as Timon Horvat,' Gillard added.

Smith squinted out of the narrow window in the interview room. 'May rain today,' he said. 'Been a wee bit threatening, hasn't it?'

'We found Horvat's van and a load of copper cable by Immingham docks yesterday. Do you know where he's going?'

'There's a warm front coming in, the forecaster said. So I'm glad I packed an umbrella.' Smith seemed to have an extraordinary ability to tune out everything that was said to him.

'Horvat had in his possession—'

'That isn't new evidence,' Jindal said. 'You asked him all this before.'

'Horvat doing a runner is a new development. Besides we *do* have new evidence,' he said. His phone vibrated, and he looked at it. 'This will be it now,' he said, stepping into the corridor and closing the door before taking the call. It was Mulholland. And it was very bad news.

'Sorry not to be there, but the data stick has gone missing,' she said. 'Dobbs is going batshit.'

'What do you mean, gone?'

'Disappeared. Vanished. Mislaid.'

'We've got the data back-up though, surely.'

'No. Hadn't been done yet. Rob Townsend had signed the evidence bag out at noon. It was on his desk for two hours unattended while he was in a meeting. He had been intending to get technical services to back it up this afternoon, ready for Dobbs's arrival. But the evidence bag was empty when he returned.'

'For fuck's sake!' Gillard yelled. 'That evidence was vital.'

'I know. We're going to have to let Harry Smith go.'

'That's the least of it,' he said. 'Smith's got a crooked ally at Mount Browne. Someone with the freedom and authority to walk into the detective block, and to know exactly where to find what he was looking for. And the balls to take it.'

'It's shocking,' said Mulholland.

Gillard hung up, wondering who on earth at Mount Browne could be working with a suspected child abuser like Harry Smith. If he really had an ally in the police, it would change everything. No wonder no progress had been made on the Girl F case for years.

He sighed heavily, then called Connolly out. Through the custody suite window, Smith could be seen radiating a smug grin and leaning back in his chair, his arms behind his head. Connolly shook his head in disbelief at the news, then shepherded Gillard back to the interview room.

'Okay, Harry,' Connolly said. 'You're free to go.' They watched him walk out towards the car park with Jindal by his side and a huge grin on his face. It was raining hard now, just as Smith had predicted. He opened up a large golfing umbrella to cover them both. That was when Gillard realized he didn't even have a raincoat with him.

The Jimmy Bartram sitting in the Waldorf Hotel in London's Aldwych didn't look at all like the haunted 22-year-old scarecrow captured in the 1981 newspaper archive photos. Gillard spotted him reading the *Financial Times* at a secluded table, well away from the pre-lunchtime groups. A surprisingly slight figure in an expensive dark green suit, flowery mauve open-necked shirt and cowboy boots, he peered over the paper and nodded at him and Mulholland. He had collar-length grey hair, mauve-tinted spectacles and a single crucifix earring. Only the heavily-lined face, white scrubby beard and the blue-green gargoyle tattoo that arched from his chest like a satanic stowaway spoke of his former existence.

Gillard, suited up in a forgettable grey M&S three piece, and Mulholland, in black trouser suit and white blouse, looked short on panache by comparison. Bartram offered them a seat and ordered coffee and cakes for three from a waitress who seemed to know him. Gillard knew this was going to be hard work. Bartram had stipulated the time and the place, and limited the discussion in advance to 15 minutes. 'I'm flying to New York this evening, and I need to spend a little time with my publicist before the limo comes at five,' he had explained over the phone, in a still-broad London accent. 'I'm happy to cooperate but don't you waste my *facking* time, oright? I've had enough police interviews to last me a lifetime.'

'Look,' Bartram said, pointing at the *FT*'s editorial on Cunliffe's Girl F report. 'You're famous. "Surrey Police displayed a high-handed indifference to the fate of a vulnerable young girl, and their subsequent investigations over five years were as limited in their scope and resource as they were self-serving in their conclusions. Institutionalized failings by unimaginative officers—"'

'Have you finished?' Gillard asked. 'We don't want to waste your valuable time.'

'Oright,' he said with a grin. 'Fire away.'

Once Gillard began with the questions, Bartram turned out to be a model of reasonableness. 'Yeah, I met Martin Knight a couple of times. Great bloke,' he said with a grin. 'And I don't buy this shit about him murdering Liz.'

'Why not?'

'No motive and no means. I mean, I can't see him with a hacksaw and an apron.' He turned to Mulholland and winked at her. 'Believe me, darling, I know what's involved in butchering and rendering a human body. I've seen every bone, sinew, tendon and organ, from the stink when you rip open the stomach to the ooze of shit from the large intestine, I know what that's like.' He lifted a plate towards her. 'Fancy a cupcake?'

'That's why we thought you might have helped him out, Jimmy,' Mulholland said, clearly needled. 'He needed a man of your skills.'

Bartram laughed, revealing bad teeth held together with lots of metal. 'Just like I guessed. Every time something happens, even now, nearly 40 years on, it's "Well, fuck me, it must be down to Jimmy." I mean you plods have no imagination, do you? Think about it. I'm a success story from the penal system, ain't I? Did my time, behaved nice, studied hard, no reoffending, got a job. Got some respect.' He looked up at them, all trace of humour gone. 'Except from you lot. In the plod book, there's only story. Once a con, always a con, right?'

'It's just a question, Jimmy, that's all,' Gillard said.

'With a ready-supplied answer preloaded in your head, like Windows facking Ten on my home computer.'

More cake and coffee arrived. Hostilities were suspended while the waitress poured. Bartram held his cup with his little finger cocked, as if he was a duchess. Suddenly his face lit up.

'Hi, Jimmy, darling.' A tall and shapely 20-something blonde with a skimpy black dress and calf-length roman sandals arrived at the table. She had huge green eyes and a wide smile. When she kissed Bartram it looked like she really meant it.

'This is Grace, my publicist.'

'And girlfriend,' Grace said, finally noticing the others. 'Delighted to meet you.' Her voice was as smooth and educated as his was rough and ready, and she reserved every word for the centre of her universe, Jimmy Bartram, convicted dismemberer of the human body. 'Come on, Jimmy, I've packed your bag, but you promised me a few minutes' cuddle upstairs before we leave.' Gillard felt an immense pulse of envy, surely the only reason Bartram had concocted this hotel set-up.

Bartram caught his expression and gave him a what-can-I-do kind of shrug, before turning back to Grace. 'Okay, honey. Run along. I'll be up in a couple of minutes.' He turned back to

Gillard and Mulholland. 'Look. For the record… One, Knight never asked me to do anything. Two, I haven't spoken to him for over two years. Three, everyone knows I'm strictly legit in all things. Four, I'm sure I've got a great alibi for any time, any day or any week you care to mention.' His eyes flicked to Grace's disappearing rear. 'Five, I can afford very, very good barristers these days who believe attack is the best form of defence.'

The two fuming detectives watched him walk away. 'What a sanctimonious prick,' Mulholland said.

'Totally bulletproof, unfortunately. He knows that if we had a single shred of DNA evidence against him, we'd just have arrested him.'

'So is he super smart, or is he innocent?' Mulholland asked.

'I just don't know,' Gillard said.

The belated discovery of Martin Knight's card to his daughter came as a bombshell to the investigative team. Gillard, wearing plastic gloves, turned over the envelope with tweezers. He and DS Mulholland were sitting in the evidence room at Caterham police station, surrounded by shelves along which paper evidence bags were carefully indexed. Among those bags were samples of clothing, carpet, hairbrushes, computers and other objects from the two Knight homes. In the freezer was a section of bloodstained ceiling from the house in Coulsdon, and a tube of mainly human flesh from the overflow pipe of the kitchen in Dungeness.

As expected, forensics had found little on the envelope itself, just a confusing mass of fingerprints from postal staff. It was postmarked Chartres, south-west of Paris, but a postmark could not isolate which postbox had been used in the district. There was no saliva DNA on the envelope seal either, one of their biggest hopes.

The card itself was more productive. There was a clear thumbprint from Martin Knight, and the handwriting was definitely his, according to both Oliver and Chloe.

'So he's happy enough for us to know that he's in France,' Gillard said.

'It's not quite the behaviour of a boastful perpetrator, though. It just seems that he really wanted to tell his daughter that he was thinking of her,' Mulholland said.

'And she was prepared to hide it from us, and to email him back,' Gillard said. It was only yesterday evening that Oliver Knight had handed the card in to Gabby Underwood, with a note of apology written by Chloe. 'Still, it means he's outfoxed us by crossing the Channel without being spotted.'

'Maybe. Another appeal for him to turn himself in might be useful,' Mulholland said.

'I doubt it, somehow.' Gillard held the card up to the light. It was a standard British greetings card, made by Hallmark. 'He must have taken it with him in advance, intending to send it,' said Gillard. 'There's a certain amount of planning, considering everything else he must have been thinking about, wouldn't you say?'

'It doesn't fit with the idea of panic,' she said.

'No. What we need now is for him to use a cash or credit card. He can't go for ever without using one. He's got to stay at a hotel, or with a friend, he's got to have a vehicle,' Gillard said. 'His French is supposedly okay. Enough to get by with, but it would be quite obvious he was an Englishman.'

Gillard looked around the room at the accumulated evidence of the death of Liz Knight. 'The coroner wants to wait for the result of the DNA tests on the vertebrae before releasing an interim death certificate for Liz. You can't live without a spine, after all.'

'Oh, I don't know, Graham Coldrick manages well enough.' Claire had always had a low opinion of the chief constable.

Gillard smiled. 'Oliver Knight has been on at me about getting permission for the funeral, and as I didn't have anything to tell him, they have already arranged for a private memorial service, next Friday. I shall be going, of course.'

Claire Mulholland looked at him. 'It will be your opportunity to let Liz go too, won't it?'

She watched Craig Gillard shrug the comment off with something inaudible. It had hit home, though. She was sure of that.

A week later

The night before the memorial service Craig took the opportunity to go swimming. He was running over in his mind those who could shed further light on what happened. Kathy Parkinson, the woman who knew Liz best; Helen Jennings, who had travelled with Liz for six weeks to help refugees earlier in the year; Jimmy Bartram, a former murderer who was quite capable of doing Martin Knight's dirty work; and

Dr Natalie Krugman, Knight's inspiration for murder. Only the first two would be at the memorial service. Gillard turned these possibilities over in his mind as he completed relentless fast lengths of front crawl. At 6.45 p.m. he emerged, and after a shower went to his locker. Just as he unlocked it, his phone vibrated.

It was Rob Townsend, and he sounded beside himself with excitement. 'Professor Knight's still around near Paris, sir. He's made a withdrawal of 500 euros on his cash card at a place called Gretz-Armainvilliers.'

'At last!' Gillard said, towelling his body. 'Find out if there's any CCTV. Make sure our French counterparts have got all the European arrest warrant paperwork they need.' After he hung up he considered what this development now told him. Knight must have run out of ready cash, or perhaps the accomplice could no longer supply him. The noose was tightening, Gillard was sure of it. Right around the professor's neck.

At just before nine the next morning Gillard was at home looking in the mirror, doing up his black tie and checking his formal police uniform, ready for the memorial service. A call from Townsend made him jump. The research intelligence officer had spent the last hour on the phone to French police and relayed the disappointing news.

'There's no CCTV on that cash machine, nor anywhere nearby. The gendarmes told me Gretz-Armainvilliers is a fairly ordinary town, just a few minutes' drive off the main N4 route, south-east of Paris. Knight used a cash machine outside a Crédit Agricole branch at half past eleven in the evening, according to his bank. A lot of them don't seem to have CCTV. The gendarmes are checking every hotel within an hour's drive.'

'Any luck finding the data stick?'

'I'm afraid not.'

'Whatever you do, keep it from Alison Rigby.'

'Too late, sir. DCI Dobbs complained to her already. I got a right roasting. But as I said to her, we should be able to leave evidence in our own offices for an hour or so, shouldn't we?'

'Any luck tracing who it might have been?'

'Could be any one of a hundred people with access to the building. There's CCTV at the entrance, but nothing inside.'

Gillard hung up, and swore quietly. The idea of Harry Smith getting away with abuse made his blood boil.

A few minutes later Gillard drove over to pick up Claire Mulholland. He wondered how much cash Knight would get through. If he needed more, say, once a week, then he really was going to get caught fairly quickly. All they needed was a little bit of CCTV, a little glimpse of his vehicle, and a little bit of luck. Feeling cheered by this turn of events, Gillard forgot his nerves until he arrived with Mulholland at the leafy parish church of St John's, just a few minutes' drive from the Knights' home. There was a significant uniformed police presence, a gaggle of reporters and a couple of media satellite trucks. Gillard was greeted rather coldly by Oliver Knight. Another man handed him an order of service. Reading it he saw that the ceremony was intended to celebrate the life and achievements of Elizabeth Knight. Being an official presence at these kind of events always made Gillard feel uncomfortable and conspicuous. He was the man who was supposed to be offering answers to a bereaved family, and had so far failed to do so. He was the man who was tasked with finding Martin Knight and again had failed to do so. Everyone who looked at him on his way in seemed to be asking questions, raising expectations, demanding answers. It was giving him a headache.

Liz's parents, looking very frail, were deep in conversation with Claire Mulholland, and as Gillard entered the gloom of the church Kathy Parkinson introduced herself. She was wearing a lot of dark eye make-up which with her blue chiffon scarf and dark trouser suit made her look like an upmarket travel agent. She steered him away from the throng towards one of the many huge displays of flowers which filled the transept and nave. 'I'm glad to finally talk to you, Craig,' she said. 'This is such a terrible business, isn't it?' She leaned forward to inhale the scent of a spray of lilies.

'It must be particularly awful for Oliver and Chloe,' Craig said. 'I know that Gabby Underwood has had her work cut out keeping Chloe's spirits up, particularly.'

'And how are your spirits?' Kathy said.

Craig looked at her. 'What do you mean?' he asked.

'Well, you were once in love with her, weren't you?' She smiled indulgently at him.

'That was a long time ago.' He looked around the church, happy to look anywhere except into this woman's overly sympathetic face.

'You and I met a few times, you know. Back in 1986.' Kathy smiled again.

'Did we?' Craig risked a glance at her.

'Yes. It was at The Bell on a couple of occasions, one of them when Martin was down from Cambridge. I was one of Liz's friends even then. You don't remember me, but I remember you.'

Gillard was feeling quite uneasy now. 'I'm sorry. It was quite a long time ago.' But he did recall seeing Martin. The smug, moneyed boy who had stolen his beloved woman away.

'I could certainly see what Liz saw in you.' Seeing the look of surprise on Gillard's face, she continued. 'You were quite a physical presence, and I don't mean in any sporting way. Liz up until that time had been immersed in intellect. At home, at school, music, chess, literature. All those expectations. And of course she was very cerebral, more so than the rest of us. But you were this rather well put-together young man, quietly strong and self-possessed.'

Gillard directed his gaze upwards to the delicately repaired ceiling of the church. The pale plaster cherubim and seraphim under the wooden beams, their slender trumpets spreading the secrets of the wounded heart. 'You really have me at a disadvantage, Kathy. You observed all this about me, and I don't recall you at all. It makes me feel quite awkward.'

'Don't feel awkward about it. It's the kind of thing that inevitably happens. Everyone could see you only had eyes for her, more's the pity. I used to see you, sitting on your motorbike at the end of her street, in the weeks after your relationship with her ended. You looked so sad, and rather adorable.'

'I was a bit sorry for myself, that's for sure,' Gillard said, scanning the gathering congregation, seeking someone who would rescue him from this emotional interrogation. He spied Helen Jennings, wearing a tight black jacket and a broad-brimmed bolero hat at a rakish angle. She waved at them, and her long shapely legs carved a path through the throng towards them. On her arm was a tall and very handsome Mediterranean-looking man with swept back hair and designer stubble. 'This is Juan,' she said, introducing her beau. 'Juan, this is Detective Chief Inspector Gillard, and my old friend Kathy Parkinson.'

The conversation soon returned to small talk, and Gillard was able to slip away to where Claire Mulholland was talking to Alison Rigby. The assistant chief constable radiated authority, not only from the silver epaulettes and collar insignia on the tightly fitting uniform, but her sheer height and bearing.

'Learn anything?' Rigby asked.

'Not so far, ma'am.' His eye was drawn to the latest arrivals. Sir Gerald Cunliffe and his wife, who walked up the aisle and were shown to a row near the front. Sir Gerald stopped to exchange brief words and a perfunctory smile with Alison Rigby: two worthy adversaries from the Girl F circus, in circumspect acknowledgment.

The service was very tasteful, with music by Bach, Telemann and Schubert. A solo Ave Maria was sung exquisitely by a young niece of Liz's. It was only during this song, when Claire looked up at him in concern and offered him a tissue, that Craig realized that tears were running freely down his face. This slight flurry of activity caught Alison Rigby's attention too. The flash of ice-blue eyes showed something like shock at seeing the crumpled mask that his face had become.

Craig switched off as best he could during the readings. He saw ahead of him a trembling Chloe Knight, her brother's arm around her shoulder. She was just about holding it together. It was a relief when the final hymn had been sung, the final prayer offered, and the congregation filed out into the cool, breezy air through which a watery sun shone. He turned on his phone, and it rang immediately. Rob Townsend again.

'Martin Knight's been withdrawing more cash, sir. This time at a place called Itteville, south-west of Paris. It was a Crédit Agricole again. I've got all the usual requests in to the French police.'

Gillard hung up just as Alison Rigby approached. He told her the news and added: 'He's getting through a fair bit of cash. I think we're going to catch him.'

Rigby, an inch or two above him in her heels, held him with an intense gaze. 'Craig, are you finding this case a bit too much for you? Do you need some time off?'

'No, ma'am.'

A look of alarm must have crossed Gillard's face, because Rigby gave a smile of understanding. 'It's all right, Craig. I know how much it means to you. I know you won't rest until we've got him.'

She walked away, and suddenly Craig Gillard felt that he'd been outmanoeuvred. Did every woman in his professional life somehow know what was going on in his head, without being told? On the spur of the moment, Gillard turned back and caught up with Rigby. 'Ma'am, I think we can catch Knight quite quickly if we move the investigation across to France. I'd like visit my opposite number, and perhaps also to take a look around the Knights' newly acquired holiday home in Spain.'

'I don't see that being a problem,' she said. 'As long as it produces results. But do please think of the media attention. It goes without saying that I don't want to see invoices for four-course *menus dégustation* or luxury hotels. Am I clear?'

'Crystal clear, ma'am.' Kincaid had been spreading a rumour that the ACC kept a jar on her desk which contained the testicles of male underlings who had displeased her. Gillard had no intention of being part of her collection.

After the memorial service, and once Rigby had departed, Gillard walked around the churchyard pondering the life and death of Liz Knight. As he looked up Kathy Parkinson approached. 'This is rather a long shot, I suppose, but a friend's let me down and I've got a spare ticket for *Richard III* at the Globe tomorrow night. Would you like to join me?'

Craig hesitated. Professional entanglement with witnesses were frowned upon, and he had a long-standing grudge against Shakespeare from miserable classes at school. He also had to catch a flight to France the next morning. His face must have betrayed these misgivings, because she sweetened the offer.

'I'll let you into a secret,' she said. 'Something Liz told me which may help you.'

'Can't you tell me now?'

She shook her head and laughed. 'One good turn deserves another.'

She knew exactly how to press his buttons. 'Okay,' he said. 'But I'll have to pay for the ticket. It could be seen as a bribe otherwise.'

'Of course,' she said. 'Then I might have to reluctantly let you pay for dinner as well, on the same principle.' She laughed.

'It had better be something good,' he said, realizing how he had been outmanoeuvred.

'Believe me, it is.' She flicked her scarf at him, catching him across the face. She then turned and walked away, knowing he was watching her.

Richard III was superb, well worth the trip by train to London Bridge and the rainy walk to the theatre. Kathy Parkinson had shared the bill on their quick pre-theatre pasta at Garfunkel's, but as promised let him pay for his theatre ticket. It was during the interval, while squeezed against a red plush curtain in the crowded bar, that Kathy had finally agreed to let Gillard know the secret she had been harbouring.

'It was something that happened in October 2014. Liz told me she had cooked a special romantic candlelit meal, as some form of reconciliation after the end of Martin's affair. They were clearing up together afterwards, having had a few glasses of wine, when he said something extraordinary. Martin said that it was a pity Liz hadn't made more of her academic potential, and been a bit more like Natalie Krugman.'

'Whoa. That's inflammatory,' Craig conceded.

Kathy nodded. 'Liz plucked out a ten-inch Sabatier carving knife from the knife block and went for him. He got some cuts to his arms and hands, but disarmed her.'

'She wouldn't have meant to kill him.'

Kathy laughed at the naiveté. 'My God, Craig, you are blind to how much anger there was buried in Liz. At that moment, I'm sure she would happily have killed him! In fact I just wish she had, before he murdered her.'

Chapter Twenty-Two

It's no good padding about like a caged leopard. The die is cast. I have to think. It's what I always did best. This is a game of chess and I can win. I know I can.

Liz's diary, February 2015

Sunday, 6 November

If Kathy Parkinson had expected a romantic evening using Liz's secrets as a lure, it hadn't worked. The elegant blouse she had worn, her perfume, her explanation of the meaning of the play had registered with Craig, but only vaguely. He instead turned over the revelation in his mind, a picture of Liz with a knife superimposed over everything Kathy was saying. As they'd parted at Upper Warlingham Station, Kathy invited him to call her again. After thanking her for the evening Craig had given a noncommittal response, and saw the slightly disappointed moue on her face. The only emotion Craig felt was a tenderness. Poor Liz, unhappy enough to strike out at her husband with a knife.

By Sunday Gillard had to set such thoughts aside as he prepared to take the search for Martin Knight to France. The reason for ACC Rigby's warning about expenses didn't emerge until Gillard was waiting to check in at Gatwick for the flight to Paris. A bulky figure sidled up to him and pushed his large wheeled suitcase into his knees. 'Don't mind some company?'

Paddy Kincaid. The detective superintendent said that he had pulled rank on Claire Mulholland, who had originally been approved to accompany Gillard. 'Man of your reputation, Craig. Didn't think it was a good idea to send you on an all-expenses paid junket with an attractive female officer. People might talk.' He winked horribly at him.

'You should know that Claire Mulholland and I have a very professional working relationship. She's a happily married woman, and I like her husband.' Gillard left unsaid the thought that Kincaid was happy to participate in the junket himself.

Since the memorial service for Liz Knight, there had been two further cash withdrawals on Martin Knight's cash cards. One was in Houdan, a small town an hour west of Paris, and one a day later in a tiny village called Kirch-en-Bourses, south of Chartres, both at Crédit Agricole branches.

On the same day, and just 30 kilometres away, there had been one sighting of a man matching Martin Knight's description, driving a UK-registered vehicle at a rest stop on a motorway. An arrest was made a few hours later, but it turned out to be the wrong man. That lead having been closed down, the two detectives spent the flight flicking through Knight's financial paperwork. It included all the details of his numerous credit and cash cards, his patterns of previous spending as well as his last logged mobile phone calls.

When they arrived in France, they were met at arrivals by the French detective who had been assigned as liaison in the case. Caspar Glomiquet was a tall, shaven-headed officer with a goatee beard, who spoke excellent English, and Gillard took the opportunity to brief him on the full details of the case. Glomiquet, who was a sergeant from the Service de Coopération Technique Internationale de Police said he had read everything he could about the case. Gillard was impressed that there was little he wasn't already aware of.

'Pretty unusual for a professor to cut his wife up, *non*?' Glomiquet said, as they walked to the French detective's unmarked silver Renault. 'Teeth, blood and bones, all in different places. Are there any practical skills? Is he a hunter or an outdoorsman in his recreation?'

'Not unless you count the occasional weekend mountain biking. I'm not sure that really qualifies,' Gillard said.

'We haven't recovered the tools he did it with either,' Kincaid said. 'There are lots of the victim's body parts missing. Knight must have been pretty cunning about hiding them. We've used ground-penetrating radar in the garden of their home, and dogs to track across the marshes in Kent. Nothing,' he said, looking out of the window as the car slid along the motorway west of Paris.

By now, nearly a week after the first cash withdrawal, it was clear that Martin Knight was being clever. Despite wanted posters put up in town halls and post offices, and despite some coverage on French TV, credible sightings were rare and soon disproved. He was apparently staying clear of modern shopping centres with their profusion of cameras, but instead would go off the main routes to small traditional towns. Post office cash machines and small branches of Crédit Agricole, the traditional lender to the French farmer, were the least likely to have cameras.

Glomiquet said he was taking them to the village of Itteville, in Île-de-France, scene of the second withdrawal. 'Normally, this would be an unusual place to stop for cash, but it fits the pattern we have been seeing. It's a tiny village with narrow streets, and a cash machine right next to the *tabac*.' He stopped the car next to the tiny single-storey bank branch. 'The transaction was timed at a quarter to ten in the morning. There is no CCTV anywhere in the village.'

'Right,' Gillard said. 'Is this machine heavily used? If not, we might be able to lift some fingerprints. I sent you a file copy of Knight's DNA and prints a few days ago.'

The Frenchman blew a sigh. 'I can check. But even an infrequently used machine will still get ten users per day. I don't think we are likely to get a result there, especially as it was three days ago when he used the machine.'

'What about cars?' Kincaid said.' Are there any number-plate recognition systems nearby?'

'Yes,' Glomiquet said. 'Mainly on the *péage*, the toll routes.'

'Well,' chuckled Kincaid. 'I bet he's avoiding them. Every time me and Muriel come to France we always drive an extra 20 miles rather than pay a toll. And Knight's got an even better motivation than simply refusing to give his hard-earned cash to the bloody French government.'

Glomiquet ignored the comment. 'We are already trying to fit any British number plates picked up to the pattern of movement we have seen around Paris with the cash withdrawals. But it's a big task. Many cameras don't have ANPR, and those that do only work on French national plates. Foreign or unrecognized plates are all dumped in a big computer file which can only be sorted by date, and requires manual oversight. Still, the further Professor Knight travels, and the more cash machines he visits, the greater chance a plate will crop up that fits the pattern of travel.'

'What if he's driving a French car?' Gillard asked.

'Then it's easier. They will more easily be able to sort out which vehicles have been in all those places. Of course it would help if we knew exactly what kind of car we were looking for,' Glomiquet said. 'Then it would be easy, yes?' He shrugged expansively.

Gillard felt the sting of reproach. 'We've got Knight's own car still in Britain, and his wife's. There's been no use of his credit cards, so he's not hired a car in Britain or abroad, at least not from one of the big operators. He could have bought one privately and be using it illegally, but that will catch up with him in the end.'

'Okay, Creg,' Glomiquet said. Gillard enjoyed the French version of his name. 'We've circulated the professor's details and pictures to hotels and guesthouses. There are a fair number of petrol stations with private cameras too, and we've asked for their cooperation. The trouble is that if he's travelling using a false name and in an unidentified vehicle, we'll be lucky to catch him.'

The three detectives stopped at a roadside bistro for lunch – seafood soup followed by duck pâté with crusty bread. Glomiquet surprised them by ordering a small *pastis*, which he downed in one. Kincaid and Gillard went back with Glomiquet to visit his office in the suburbs of Paris, but this shed little new light on the investigation, so they headed off early to the motel that Surrey Police HQ had booked them. It turned out to be a shabby place in an anonymous suburb just off the N104 at Évry.

There was no one at reception. Kincaid rang a bell, and a middle-aged woman, stick-thin and caked with make-up, emerged from a back room. She looked up the booking. '*Oui. Une chambre double avec un lit matrimonial. Premier étage.*' She handed Gillard a key.

'*Excuse mois,*' he said. '*Combien lits de cette chambre?*'

The woman winced at Gillard's mangling of her language. '*Un lit, monsieur.*' A sly smile spread across her jaw. '*Voulez-vous en plus, messieurs?*'

Gillard turned to Kincaid. 'There's only one bed, sir.'

Kincaid, looking puzzled, said to Gillard. 'Who booked this bloody room?' I bet it was on Rigby's orders.'

'It was admin at Mount Browne, so perhaps, yes.' Gillard asked the receptionist, who was clearly revelling in their British embarrassment, if there was another single room available, or one with twin beds. The woman made a meal out of consulting her computer, tapping her teeth with a pen and exhaling in a perplexed the-things-I-have-to-do fashion. Eventually she showed them a rather small and old-fashioned box room in a gable next to the laundry, which had no en-suite toilet and a sloping ceiling designed to dent the heads of the unwary.

'He'll take it,' said Kincaid. 'I'll have the original room.'

They met up again an hour later in a pizza place across the way, where they shared a thin-and-crispy family-size dish. While they were eating, Gillard laid out a map of Île-de-France, which had all the places marked on it that they knew Knight had visited: Gretz-Armainvilliers, Itteville, Kirch-en-Bourses and Houdan for cash withdrawals, and somewhere around Chartres for posting the birthday card.

'It's all in a very odd order,' Kincaid said, dropping a lump of sweetcorn on the map. 'Look at Houdan, it's way over to the west. And this Gretz place is in the south-east. It's like there is no rhyme or reason to the cash withdrawals, except perhaps to throw us off the scent.'

'All but two have been from Crédit Agricole,' said Gillard. 'I've got a list of their branches with cash machines, but there are literally thousands. Almost every little town has one.'

Next morning Craig was awakened just after six by a call from Rob Townsend. 'Professor Knight used his credit card last night, for the first time. He got a cash advance from a machine in a suburb of Paris called Neuilly-sur-Seine.'

'Fantastic news.' Gillard knelt on the floor to open his map of greater Paris. 'That's almost in the centre of the city. There's bound to be CCTV, surely.'

Two hours later the two British detectives arrived with Glomiquet at the shopping precinct on the western edge of Neuilly. Crowded around and above the two-storey mall were a number of tower blocks which boasted the names of several large international corporations. The cash machine belonged to BNP Paribas, and was one of five machines in a 24-hour foyer attached to the bank. The foyer seemed to be in constant use by a well-dressed clientele from the surrounding offices.

Glomiquet went into the bank to talk to the female manager, a middle-aged woman with spectacles dangling on a chain. She came out with a male security guard who prevented any new customers entering the foyer, instead directing them to other machines in the main body of the bank. The manager escorted the detectives into the foyer, and after the last customer had left, locked the door.

'Here,' she said, in excellent English, pointing to a small hole in the ceiling from which a couple of wires trailed. 'This is the CCTV fitting. We have been waiting a week for it to be upgraded. So we have no footage of yesterday's transactions.'

'Are there other cameras nearby?' Gillard asked.

'Yes, several. There is one across the road, and another on the bank opposite,' she said, pointing.

Glomiquet spoke to her rapidly in French and then turned to the others. 'We can't spare any resources, so the banks will courier the recordings directly to you in Britain,' he said. 'If you need further liaison, I can of course always help.'

Gillard got his own bank card out and went to one of the machines. 'Time me, would you, Paddy?' He went through the various menus, and made a small advance on his credit card. He rejoined the others. 'How long?'

'Forty-eight seconds,' Kincaid said.

'So we should add that delay into the CCTV timings when we see people emerge.'

Gillard and Kincaid thanked the bank manager, and left with Glomiquet. 'I think the professor's made a major mistake,' Kincaid said. 'We're going to get proof positive of him being here, maybe even a vehicle registration number. He can't stay hidden for ever.'

Gillard flew back to the UK leaving Kincaid behind to keep an eye out for any fresh cash withdrawals in France. The CCTV discs were already waiting on his desk at Caterham, but no one else had thought to take a look. The recordings covered a half-hour each side of the 9.33 p.m. transaction. A Post-it from Glomiquet on the sleeve carried a brief message: *Malheureusement, il pleuvait.* What he meant was soon clear when they played the disc. The intense shower not only blurred the images, but many pedestrians were using umbrellas, which not only obscured them from the high cameras, but also blocked out others. They had to work with very brief glimpses of faces and features.

'You've got all these people going in and out of the foyer door, sir,' said Hoskins, fast-forwarding through the disc. 'But we can't see who goes to which machine, and so can't exactly match each person to their transaction nor the time of it.'

The first quick run-through had shown half a dozen men who looked vaguely like Knight, at least if Knight had tried to disguise himself. One was a bearded fellow with a rough head of hair wearing a bulky raincoat. If anything he looked a little broader than Knight, and wore glasses when the professor didn't. Still, he was the best prospect, and better still he had emerged from a car which was illegally parked right outside the bank. It should be possible to identify the number plate, especially when the make and model was matched with other cameras on that road. There was also a man in a hoodie, again thickset, but probably a little too tall. He moved like a younger man, with some vigour in the shoulders. He had spent a long time in the foyer, as had two other younger men, African-looking, who could be disregarded. Finally there was a man in a suit with a large umbrella about whom nothing could be determined except his relatively skinny build. If none of them was Knight, as seemed likely, then they at least would have seen him. Dispersed amongst these male possibilities were a number of young female customers, and a few of both sexes who were clearly elderly.

Hoskins went back to the start of the disc, and with Gillard at his side homed in on the three most likely men. The bearded man, the fellow with the hoodie and umbrella man. He let it run through at normal speed, to watch their gait. 'What do you reckon, sir?' Hoskins asked.

'The guy with the hoodie isn't Knight. Let's have a look at the fellow with the beard and raincoat, just one more time.'

Hoskins ran it through. The view on the way in was good, just for a second. The man held open the door to a tattooed woman unseasonably dressed in a strapless blue dress and carrying a large pink frilly umbrella, who was going into the foyer. The man gave her a lingering look as she went in, and the camera caught his smile. Gillard strained to discern more, but the definition wasn't good enough.

'It could be Knight, I suppose. Can we get this image enhanced, Carl? To get the glare off?'

'Let's see what the tech lab can do,' Hoskins said. 'Of course there's always a chance that Knight's been robbed, and one of these other blokes has the card.'

'Or that he's given the card to an accomplice,' Gillard added, 'who could be female.'

'Christ, if he did that we're really screwed,' Hoskins said. 'We'd have no idea who to look for.'

The summons to Mount Browne came on the afternoon of Gillard's return to the UK. It was already the end of November, nearly two months after Liz Knight's murder, and Craig knew that Alison Rigby was going to want some answers.

He knocked on the door of her office and received the curt command, 'Come.'

Opening the door, he stepped in. The ACC's office was a large one, bigger than the chief constable's, but with a view over an estate of 1960s police housing. Rigby was clearly buried in paperwork. Her desk was piled high, and she was signing and passing across papers to an out-tray at a rate of knots, while dictating a letter into a tape recorder. She ignored him totally for a full two minutes while she continued her multi-tasking. Finally she looked up. She was wearing reading glasses, and her icy eyes were even more glacial than normal.

She finished the letter with a 'Yours et cetera', turned off the recorder, beckoned him over, and pointed to a low chair by a coffee table. He looked at it, and she nodded. *Sit.* She didn't actually say that word, but she clicked her fingers and pointed again. Like the good dog that he was, he sat.

She stood up and walked around the front of her desk to lean on it, arms folded, looking down at Craig. Bar her white blouse, she was dressed in black from head to foot: trouser suit, patent leather shoes, square earrings of some no doubt expensive mineral, but which looked to him like small Lego bricks. 'Things aren't really going terribly well, are they, Craig?'

'Ma'am.'

'We've not found Professor Knight at all, and only a small portion of Mrs Knight. We seem to be no closer to a conclusion, do we?' She leaned forward, and her blouse gaped slightly, revealing a crescent curve of freckled breast in a lacy bra. Black, naturally. He forced his eyes back up to her face, and banished as best he could the image of what it would be like to make love with her. She would be on top, naturally.

'Well, ma'am, we are—'

'Rhetorical question, Craig. I only ask questions where I already know the answers.'

Then why have you got me here? Gillard thought. He looked at her desk. With shock, he realized there actually *was* an opaque glass jar there, twice the size of a jam jar, with a screw-on plastic lid. An emasculatory vision flitted through his imagination.

'So, is our professor on the CCTV footage from Paris that arrived yesterday?'

'It's too early to be sure, ma'am. We're having it enhanced—'

'Too early! Seven weeks since the murder, Detective Chief Inspector. This isn't some elusive billionaire drug lord with a network of criminal associates, safe houses and bogus bank accounts – he's a bearded overweight academic from suburbia. We should be able to pull him in on a piece of string, and the fact we have failed to do so is making Surrey Police a laughing stock. More particularly it is making me a laughing stock.'

'Ma'am, if I may explain. It seems increasingly likely Martin Knight has an associate. Someone who drove him through to France on a ferry, someone who speaks fluent French, maybe even has a home in France, near Paris. There has to be, because nobody seems to have seen him. There are no credible sightings, despite an extensive publicity drive in the French press and on TV. If it wasn't for the cash withdrawals and his letter to the daughter, we'd have nothing to go on.'

Rigby's gaze was so intense it was giving Craig a headache. 'I was before the Home Affairs select committee last week on the subject of Girl F.'

'I watched you, ma'am, on Parliament TV. Impressive.'

'No, I wasn't. It was a humiliating experience, because I don't have answers. Cunliffe's report ripped us to shreds.' She folded her arms. 'By the way, Craig, if I want my arse kissing I'll ask Kincaid to do it. At his evolutionary stage he's more comfortable on all fours. For you, with your track record, I had higher hopes. Now go away and solve your case.'

Craig Gillard returned to Caterham to look again at the CCTV discs. He was just getting ready to let Hoskins head off home for the evening when the email from the lab came with the enhanced images attached. As soon as they sat down together, Hoskins already bundled up in his coat, it was clear that the bearded man wasn't Martin Knight. The shape of the face was wrong. 'Oh, well. So much for that,' said Hoskins, standing up. 'Shall I get you a coffee on my way out, sir?'

Craig held up a hand. 'Look at this,' he said. 'Not the bloke, but the woman in front.'

'Always happy to look at a fit woman, sir,' Hoskins said, sitting down.

Even with enhancement there was nothing of her face to be seen beneath the pink umbrella, but she had dyed green hair neatly tied in a ponytail. She looked to be in her 30s. Her strapless blue dress revealed a swirling tattoo on her tanned and rain-spattered back and another, smaller and darker, on her right upper arm.

'Kincaid would like her,' Hoskins said, pursing his lips with approval. 'Good legs and high heels. Looks like she's going on a night out.'

'We haven't got the enhanced version of her coming out of the foyer, have we?'

'No, that wasn't on the segment we chose.'

'Pity, let's look at the original.' Craig inserted the original disc and fast-forwarded through. The CCTV showed the woman emerging with her umbrella already up, but still no view of her face. Craig looked at the timing on the bottom of the screen. 'She was out the door 53 seconds after the transaction time stamp. That's about right, if she didn't hang about.'

'There's a purse still in her hand,' Hoskins said. It was a distinctive embroidered bag, with sequins that caught the light. 'Maybe she was in a hurry.'

'Let's go back to the enhanced image.' Gillard switched tab, then pulled up the enlargement. The arm tattoo was perhaps the size of a packet of cigarettes. 'What do you reckon to that tattoo on her arm, Carl?'

'Is it a dog's head, sir?'

'I thought that at first, but it's actually a horse's head. Stylized, from the side. Do you play chess?'

'No, sir, too brainy for me. Draughts I can do.'

'Well, what she's got is a chess piece tattooed on her shoulder. A knight.'

'As in Martin Knight, sir?'

'Precisely.' The hairs on the back of his neck stood up. Was this the woman? An accomplice and lover to help Knight escape. No wonder there had been no credible sightings of Knight himself. But who was she? And where was Knight?

Chapter Twenty-Three

The press seized on the CCTV image with huge enthusiasm, the tabloids carrying it on front pages under the headline 'Who Is This Woman?' Many reprinted the knight tattoo. Tattoo parlours on both sides of the Channel were asked if they had recently been commissioned for such an image. Gillard finally felt optimistic that they would quickly catch Martin Knight, and his girlfriend, besotted enough to have his symbol slowly and uncomfortably injected into her skin.

The French police had done their bit, and after several days' delay had got the bank to contact every customer who had used the bank foyer during the crucial half-hour. They had interviewed about half, had images of a couple more, and only six were being elusive. The Martin Knight lookalike, who turned out to be a Swiss architect, was one of the first to come forward, and had volunteered a description of the woman.

Gillard had asked research intelligence officer Rob Townsend to scour his academic and private sector contacts to get some further analysis of the French images. He wanted to know the woman's height, weight and approximate age. All that would help narrow down who it could be. But it was the tattoo that intrigued him most.

'The knight's piece in chess,' remarked Kincaid, in one of his more reflective moments, can jump, can't it?'

'Yes,' said Gillard. 'In this case, even across the Channel.'

'My dad taught me the moves. The knight, I think, was one square straight, and one diagonal.'

'That's it,' said Gillard. 'Very hard to envisage where it can go, a move or two ahead.' Kincaid looked at him and nodded sagely. 'That's him, then, the elusive bugger.'

The phone lines buzzed with reports of women with horse-shaped tattoos, which turned out to be dragons, or dogs or, in one case, a pet rabbit. The LSE staff, shown pictures of the woman from the cashpoint, were unable to offer any help, nor were Knight family members or friends. After another week with no fresh useful leads, and without further cash withdrawal transactions, Gillard once again began to get pressure from above – daily phone calls from Rigby, chasing progress. But next morning there was progress from a different direction: Dungeness.

Chapter Twenty-Four

Gillard was running late. He had a flight booked back to Paris in three hours, and still had to get to Gatwick. Knight had seemingly made a new cash withdrawal, and Kincaid reckoned he had a plan to catch him red-handed for the next one. So when his desk phone rang he was tempted to let it go to voicemail. But something made him pick it up.

It was Dr David Delahaye. 'Craig, it's about the bones in the marsh. I've just got the results back and emailed them to you. But just to confirm, we had three connected human lumbar vertebrae, two disconnected thoracic vertebrae and a coccyx, all in unexpectedly poor condition given the assumed duration of immersion. There was too little DNA in the bone and remaining flesh for PCR. There was contamination with salt residues, which might explain some of the problem. However, we have had the benefit of corroboration. The scrap of fabric, displaying a lacy edging, appears to be part of a woman's underwear, within which were trapped a number of pubic hairs. Now I expect the dismemberment scene was fairly bloody, but sadly blood seems to have dissolved from the material due to the prolonged exposure to cold water. But luckily not from the hairs. They absorbed blood cells along with some of the insoluble human fat, presumably during dismemberment, and that fat protected them from aqueous damage. So we were able to extract some DNA in the end.'

'And?'

'And all that DNA belongs to Mrs Knight.'

'Are you certain?'

'Well, not *completely*. There is a 0.03 per cent margin of error.'

'That's pretty certain in my book.'

'Mine too,' Delahaye responded. 'I'm sure the coroner will be satisfied. We're still waiting for a technical opinion on the origin of the textile. The bones seem in my experience an appropriate match for a woman of her age. Some of the vertebrae bear abrasions indicating a serrated knife or saw blade had been used on them. Our Professor Knight is a brutal fellow, isn't he?'

Kincaid met Gillard at the airport, looking very pleased with himself. 'I've cracked it. Just a bit of brainpower, that's what was required.' The detective superintendent tapped his temple.

'Oh yes?' responded Gillard, far from convinced. 'What have you found?'

'I'll tell you in the car. Don't want anyone overhearing.'

As they were driving back to Paris, Kincaid said: 'Name all the places where Knight has withdrawn money.'

Gillard sighed, and closed his eyes. 'Let's see. Neuilly-sur-Seine, Itteville, er, Houdan…'

'Yes, that's an N, an I and an H. Any more?'

'Gretz-Armainvilliers, the first one. And Kirch.'

'Yes, Kirch-en-Bourses, so that's a K, what does all that spell?'

It was a moment before Gillard responded. 'K, N, I, G and H. Ah, I see what you're up to.'

Kincaid nodded smugly. 'Guess where yesterday's withdrawal was?'

'I've no idea. Troyes?'

'Nope. A hamlet called Saint-Martin-en-Forêt, an hour and a half south of Paris.' He looked at Gillard and enunciated the word: 'Martin.'

'So once we get a T we have Martin Knight.' Gillard looked out of the window. 'He's playing with us. Have you called Glomiquet?'

'Yes. He's unwilling to commit the surveillance required to cover every place beginning with T within 100 clicks of Paris.'

'I see his point. So we'll have to be ready ourselves.' Gillard was unconvinced this approach would work, but in the absence of other live leads he would give it a go.

For the next three days there were no new cash withdrawals, and no shortlist of number plates from ANPR that matched Professor Knight's curious crab-like journeys backwards and forwards across Île-de-France. Later Glomiquet escorted the two British detectives to the French regional ANPR control room. Though it was interesting to see the set-up, Gillard felt they were killing time with a bit of official tourism. Glomiquet disappeared on other duties, leaving Gillard and Kincaid at a loose end, with Kincaid having spent 90 minutes over coffee in the refectory scoring the passing female officers marks out of ten for 'shagability'. By breakfast time on day four, Gillard called a halt.

'I think we can use our time better,' he said, putting down his croissant.

'Fed up with *pain au chocolat* already?' Kincaid replied, his moustache thick with crumbs.

'Not exactly. But I am wondering about the Knights' newly purchased holiday home. It's an obvious place for Martin Knight to use as a refuge.'

'A bit too bloody obvious, surely.'

'Ah, but remember Osama bin Laden, hiding in plain sight? He was virtually next door to the HQ of the Pakistan intelligence service.'

'I don't think Knight would have gone to Pakistan.'

Craig rolled his eyes. 'We can catch a flight to Malaga and be back by tomorrow morning.'

'I suppose I better check in with the dominatrix before we do that,' Kincaid groaned. He lamented how tight a leash Alison Rigby kept him on. He constantly chafed at having a micromanaging female boss, something he never imagined he would have to suffer in what he called the good old days of policing in the 1990s.

Rigby, though, was happy to let them spend a day in Spain. Gillard had already tipped off his Spanish counterparts two weeks ago through the formal channels, but now on the quiet had phoned one or two he'd worked with before on the extradition of Costa Brava-based gangland figures. He was looking forward to seeing just what Knight had spent his inherited millions on.

Chapter Twenty-Five

Friday, 11 November

It was a warm and sunny afternoon when Kincaid and Gillard emerged through customs in Malaga and walked over to the car hire desk. When Kincaid saw the modest economy vehicle that had been booked for them by Mount Browne, he said: 'Bollocks to that. I'm not driving a frigging Micra.'

Gillard stood back as an irate detective superintendent tried to negotiate an upgrade to something he thought appropriately grand. Finally, after lots of gesticulating and poring over papers, Kincaid turned around to him. 'Got us a Seat Leon ST Cupra. Plenty of poke.'

'We're only going a few miles up the road,' Gillard said.

'I need a little respect at my time of life,' Kincaid said, patting Gillard's shoulder.

With Kincaid driving, and Gillard in charge of the satnav, it didn't take long to find the district of Marbella where the Knights' expat palace was. It was on the inland side of the coastal motorway and, as described on the brochure that Gillard kept on his lap, occupied the top of a hillside terrace a few miles inland off the A355. He could see it well enough, but every road they took seemed to go past it. The liaison officer for the Guardia Civil was supposed to meet them outside the nearby Coviran supermarket entrance at five, but Kincaid wanted to find it for himself. Consequently they were a half-hour late. Sargento Primo Irujo from the Policía Nacional criminal investigations department stood in the shade of the supermarket. He looked like a middle-aged male model, with a crisp white shirt, mirror shades, absurdly tight trousers and black, pointy shoes.

After introductions were made, Irujo asked them to follow him, and climbed back into his Land Cruiser. Gillard soon realized why he needed such a vehicle when Irujo turned off, just past a narrow bridge, down into a ravine on a steep concrete track encrusted with sheep droppings. Kincaid's hire car ground out a couple of times as he wrestled it around a tractor-rutted path, and climbed again up a narrow winding track. 'The Micra would have been even worse,' he growled in self-justification.

They continued to wind upwards through a maze of narrow walled lanes overshadowed by stands of prickly pear and aloe vera until five minutes later they ground to a halt outside the grand wrought iron gates of a two-storey stucco house, merely the gatehouse to a more extensive series of whitewashed buildings and palm-tree-lined terraces beyond. 'No wonder we couldn't find it,' Kincaid said. There was a CCTV camera on the wall beyond, and what looked like a video link from the gate.

'This is Casa Alta de Marriego,' Irujo said. 'I came earlier this morning, but there is no one here. It was sold a few months ago, according to the agent, no?'

Gillard dug out the keys. They were old and rather rusty, with a tatty and illegible paper label. They didn't look at all like they were designed for the modern gates, which would probably have a remote control. They pressed the button on the control panel, but nothing happened. 'These must be keys for a side gate,' Gillard said.

'Let's have a look,' Kincaid said. He flicked through the glossy brochure, and then turned to the back where the address was printed. Gillard meanwhile was looking at the legal document from the Spanish land registry. 'It's Alta de Marriego all right.' They all trooped along a narrow path, spattered with sheep droppings, which skirted the right-hand side of the high whitewashed walls of the estate. The land here was rough. Piles of rubbish had been thrown down the slopes: plastic bottles, polythene bags, fruit peel and rusting bed springs had been dumped over many years. There were a few olive trees and some tethered goats, before the land fell away sharply in a series of eroded sandy terraces towards the main road heading inland, at least 200 metres below. Straight ahead was a flat-roofed building with an unpainted wooden gate.

'Maybe this is the way in,' Gillard said. He tried the keys, which worked to unlock the door.

'This is the Casita Alta de Marriego,' said Irujo, tapping an ornate ceramic tile set into the wall by the door.

'Pardon?' said Kincaid.

'It's not the same. It means the small house at the high place of Marriego.'

'Well it must be part of the same estate,' Gillard said. 'The key works.' He looked inside the building. It looked like nothing more than a shepherd's hut, with a wooden table, a small portable TV and some old dark furniture. There were sideboards full of odd crockery, half-finished bottles of various local spirits and an array of spiders and ants. A large and elderly three-piece suite dominated the main room. It certainly looked like no one had come to visit for a few months. They emerged again into the warm sunshine, and inspected the wall beyond the Casita. There didn't appear to be a side gate.

'Can we ring the agent?' Kincaid asked. 'We need to get into the main house.'

'*Mañana*, of course,' said Irujo. 'He is closed this afternoon.'

'Can't we ring him at home?' Craig asked.

Irujo's face turned downwards in disapproval at this rather hasty approach. 'Is it so urgent? You can see the place exists. You have the paperwork, and I think it's very unlikely that your fugitive professor is here. I mean he is not a moron, eh? To hide in his own house.' Irujo permitted himself a laugh which displayed a perfect semicircle of whitened teeth.

'We need to get in today, sonny.' Kincaid's jaw was set, bulldog-fashion. 'Can you see to it?'

Irujo shrugged and turned away to make a phone call.

The agent, Miguel Vila, was there in half an hour, his Pajero jeep revving hard as he came up the hill. He was a short, slightly chubby man with deep-set eyes and a sallow pockmarked face.

He shook hands effusively with each of them. He produced a key fob, which he pressed to open the gates. 'I have telephoned Mr and Mrs Van der Hoeven, but they seem a little confused why the British police need to look around the villa.'

'Who are the Van der Hoevens?' Kincaid asked as they walked inside the courtyard.

'They are the owners.'

Craig exchanged a glance with Paddy Kincaid. 'I think there is some confusion,' Craig said, passing across the brochure from his collection of papers. The agent looked through it, nodding. 'Yes, that is the sale particulars. Casa Alta de Marriego,' he said, pointing to the address printed on the brochure. 'It was prepared by my firm, for the vendors, Desarrollo de Propiedades Costeras Marbella SA.'

'Martin and Elizabeth Knight bought this in June,' Craig said. 'Here are the documents from the Spanish land registry to prove it.' He passed across the English copy of the registration and the transfer documents.

'Have you the Spanish original?' Vila asked. Craig passed across the six-page document written in Spanish.

Miguel glanced at it and said. 'No, this is not correct. The original has a seal on it. This is a photocopy.'

'I don't see what bloody difference it makes,' Kincaid said. 'They've paid the money, they've got the signatures.' He flicked through the document to the final page, and jabbed his finger on the final page of the transfer.

Miguel stared at it, creasing his face at the names. 'This is not correct. These people...'

'Martin and Elizabeth Knight,' Kincaid growled.

'Yes, I know them. They came to look around the *casa*, but they didn't buy it. And the sellers listed here, Desarrollo de la Tierra Costeras Marbella, this company, are not my clients. They could not have sold it.'

'Sounds pretty bloody similar,' said Kincaid.

'Perhaps deliberately,' Miguel responded. 'The property was not theirs to sell. These documents are, I'm afraid to tell you, false.'

'You mean forgeries? Deliberately falsified?' Craig asked.

Miguel shrugged. 'Deliberate, I cannot say. Do not worry. The Colegio de Registradores, the land registry, will not have made this mistake. I will get a certified copy from them. That will clear up what has happened.'

'How long will that take?' Craig said, aware that their flight back was tomorrow.

Miguel blew out his cheeks, and Irujo said something to him in Spanish. After a short conversation Irujo said: 'I can get this pursued through a magistrate's request if you want, but it may take a day or two. There will be expenses, of course.'

Kincaid looked at Gillard. 'Come on, Craig. We don't need to sort this out,' he said. 'It's a civil matter if the Knights have been diddled out of their inheritance. We really only need to know if the fugitive professor is here or not.' He turned back to the agent. 'So perhaps you would be good enough to show us around, Miguel?'

'Certainly, sir,' Miguel said. 'Now the main entrance here leads to the outside jacuzzi and the main swimming pool...'

While Kincaid and Irujo were given the full buyers' tour, Gillard sat in a shady corner, flicking through the bundles of documents. Unlike his boss, he was far from convinced mistakes in the legal technicalities of sale were an irrelevant detail in the murder of Liz Knight. A £4 million investment was an obvious motive for murder. If the money had been siphoned off somehow, that could explain everything. He decided to phone Oliver Knight for help. He was a conveyancing solicitor, after all, and had claimed to have checked the documents.

Oliver's reaction was chilly and defensive. After 15 minutes of trying to read parts of documents to each other, Gillard could see he was getting nowhere. 'Okay, Oliver, we'll obviously have to wait for the originals from the Spanish land registry. But I'll tell you this. The agent who sold the place you *think* you bought says he knows the owners, a Mr and Mrs Van der Hoeven from Utrecht in Holland. It has their furniture and books in, and for much of the year they live here. In the end it may come down to your family having to take civil legal action.'

Craig Gillard was surprised by the furious volley of foul language that Oliver bellowed at him before hanging up. Everyone had their breaking point, and for Oliver Knight hearing that his family, already short of two parents, may have lost most of its wealth could well have been it. Craig rang liaison officer Gabby Underwood and tipped her off that Oliver Knight was likely to be a handful because of this news. Her reaction showed some wisdom.

'If you don't mind me saying, sir, this news should have been given face to face. It's a bereavement too, in a way. And if it makes him feel that he was responsible for any losses, that's even worse.'

Craig was forced to agree. Why was it, though, that every female police officer seemed to make a habit of correcting him?

Kincaid emerged after the full 40-minute tour. 'Bloody lovely place,' he breathed. 'Wine cellar, choice of jacuzzi, sauna. I'd love to live here.'

'So would the Knights, poor sods.' Craig risked a grim smile. 'So any sign of the mad professor?'

'Nope.'

'Any unmade beds? Any recently used crockery or glasses lying around? Any paperwork? Any recent oil stains on the garage floor? Where might we find the best dabs?'

Kincaid looked upwards. 'Okay, so I may have been a bit distracted.'

'I'll take a quick shufti, then, shall I?'

After he had walked around the impressive house, Gillard had to admit that it seemed unlikely that Knight had been there. 'Okay, let's go.'

'About time. Now on to more important matters. I want to find a good place to eat this evening before we go home,' Kincaid said, rubbing his hands together.

Chapter Twenty-Six

Kincaid met Gillard in the reception of their motel at seven, wearing a rather flamboyant open-necked shirt, and some obscenely tight maroon trousers. 'I tell you what, Craig, let's get ourselves a massive seafood feast, paella with lobster on top, and wash it down with a bottle of Rioja, eh? Maybe head on to a nightclub after.'

'Fine, if you're paying,' Craig said. His mobile vibrated, and he picked it up. 'It's Townsend,' he explained. 'Yes, Rob, what have you got?'

Craig listened, and nodded, while Kincaid looked on.

'Paddy, Professor Knight's just used his credit card to get a cash advance. In a town called Reus. He's here in Spain.'

'R for Reus,' Kincaid muttered. 'No, it doesn't begin with a T. We've got K, N, I, G and H. It has to be a T.' He looked crestfallen that his theory had crumbled.

'Never mind that. Townsend says we can get a flight there this evening. He's arranged for a liaison officer to meet us, and go straight there.'

'What? You're bloody kidding me. I want paella, I'm famished.'

Kincaid continued to grumble as he went back upstairs to pack, and again while Gillard drove them back to Malaga airport.

'I've got good news and bad,' Craig said, pleased with the information he had held back.

'What's the bad?' Kincaid asked, his face downcast.

'There's unlikely to be any CCTV, again.'

'Big deal. We already know who we're looking for. And the good news?'

Gillard laughed. 'The good news is that Reus is a suburb of Tarragona. As you're starving, it seems you're going to get your T after all.'

The flight was crowded, and involved a change in Madrid before heading onwards to Barcelona, the nearest sizeable airport. Kincaid, desperate for food, had bought a small but deadly in-flight microwaved snack, a grenade of boiling cheese cunningly wrapped in cool pastry, and had burned his mouth.

It was nearly ten o'clock in the evening when they touched down at Madrid. Gillard and Kincaid wearily trundled their luggage along a busy glassed-in arrivals corridor, looking for the transit desk. Through the big windows to the left, giant aircraft were nosed up to the gates below them, passengers gathered around the desks where final ticket checks were taking place. On the right-hand side the corridor gave a view out over an atrium full of glitzy shops. Kincaid stopped when he saw a snack vending machine and began to fiddle with change in his pocket. He returned with a triangular vacuum pack of sandwiches: thin, barely filled with a sliver of pink, and unappetizing. 'No comparison with a sodding paella,' Kincaid said, leaning on the handrail and staring two floors down into the crowds percolating through the mall on the right.

'Jesus, will you take a look at this,' Kincaid said, through a mouthful of bread. He pointed down to the seating area. A curvaceous woman in her 20s with a mass of dark curly hair was bending over her luggage, revealing a deep and suntanned décolletage. 'Not many of those to the pound, eh, Craig?'

With a weary sigh, Craig glanced at the girl. She soon turned away, and Craig's eyes were drawn to the woman sitting next to her. She was in her 40s, wearing a royal-blue trouser suit and white blouse. Her luxuriant hair was white as snow, held in a French plait that reached down to her shoulders. She had sunglasses perched on the top of her head, which she adjusted with a delicate hand, while she read some hefty hardback. Some level of subterranean recognition seemed to surface in him. Those hands were just like Liz's. The shape of the head was familiar too.

Surely, it couldn't be.

It was. Liz. She was alive.

And she was here.

Chapter Twenty-Seven

Gillard was totally stunned by the vision he had just seen. He needed corroboration to prove he wasn't going mad. 'Look, Paddy. The woman next to Miss Busty.'

'Which woman?'

'There!' Craig pointed impatiently. 'With the plait.'

'Where?'

'She looks just like Liz Knight.'

'Her? You're imagining things, Craig.'

The woman looked up at the flight display screen above her, and Craig got a better look at the side of her face. Then she glanced in his direction. It was just a moment. Their eyes connected and his body turned to ice. She blinked expressionlessly, then turned away.

'Liz,' he shouted and banged on the glass. 'Liz, up here!' The only sound he could make on the double-paned security glass was a soft thrumming noise. Passing passengers in his corridor turned to stare at this madman banging on the glass. Craig paid them no attention. It *was* Liz Knight. New hairdo, new hair colour, lost loads of weight. It was impossible, but she was right *there.* And she had seen *him.* She stood, grabbed her wheeled suitcase and started to walk past Unicaja and Swarovski. She was wearing slight heels, but her walk was utterly distinctive.

'Craig, what the fuck has got into you?' Kincaid was staring at him. 'She's dead. We've got her gnashers in an evidence bag in Surrey, most of her spine is in a chiller with Dr Delahaye, plus at least six pints of her blood, all confirmed by DNA.'

Craig grabbed for his smartphone. He set it for zoom but when he turned back to the glass to look for her, she had gone. 'Paddy, where did she go?'

'She went underneath us,' Kincaid said. 'You might as well give it up. That mall is in international departures. It'll take half an hour to get through security.'

'Paddy, do me a favour. Take a picture of the departures board, I want to know where she might be going to. I'll see if I can find her, get security to get her.' He ran off, pushing his way past the throng of passengers who had just arrived on another domestic flight.

Kincaid watched him go. 'He's got it worse than I ever thought,' he muttered. He sighed, got out his smartphone and took a picture of the departures board. It was 15 minutes later when he caught up with a breathless Craig Gillard in the domestic arrivals hall, where he was entangled in a confusing conversation with two young security officers, one of whom was staring at Craig's police card. 'All going smoothly, then?' Kincaid asked.

Gillard scowled at him. 'Not really. This one doesn't speak English, and the other does, but he's new. They'll only hold departures for an imminent terrorist threat.'

'Quite right, I should have thought. Look. We can put in a request for the CCTV footage when we get home.'

'Paddy, that's too late.' Kincaid had rarely seen Gillard look so animated. 'If I can get an officer to come with me, I've got my passport and there shouldn't be any trouble getting me quickly through security into international departures.'

'And are you just going to visit every bloody gate until you find her? Do you have any idea how many gates that might be?' Kincaid asked.

The new security officer offered an answer. 'One hundred and four from this terminal alone,' he said proudly. He had a wispy moustache and looked like he was too young to leave school, let alone provide security at a major airport. 'Why don't we make a public announcement for this lady?'

Craig shrugged. 'She wouldn't cooperate. I suspect she's travelling under a false name. I need to stop her boarding.'

'Look, Craig. Can you imagine if they did hold the flights for you, the busiest airport in Spain, because you thought you'd seen someone who we, of all people, know to be dead. Can you imagine what Alison Rigby would do to you?'

Craig imagined the jar on her desk. He knew it was no use arguing. 'I don't know, Paddy, maybe Liz and Martin cooked this whole murder thing up together.'

'If you go to the ACC with this cock and bull story, the first thing she is going to ask is whether I corroborate your description of that woman as Liz Knight. And Craig, I'm really sorry. I may not have known her like you did. But I would say it wasn't her. To me she looked nothing much like the pictures

I've seen. So if I was you, I should keep schtum about the whole thing, all right?'

Getting no reply, Kincaid turned to the young security officer. 'Thanks for your help, lads. I think we're all a bit tired, it's been a long day. We'll be in touch later through official channels.' He handed them his business card.

It was midnight when they arrived at Tarragona. The liaison officer, a tired-looking and portly fellow called Gomez briefly showed them the cash machine, a lonely branch of Caja Rural in a desolate and windswept modern plaza. The CCTV lens and much else besides had been covered in spray paint graffiti. He then dropped them at an anonymous modern motel near the E15 motorway. Kincaid said he was off to check some paperwork before bed, and took the official evidence briefcase with him. Gillard sloped off to his own room, along the woodchip wallpaper corridor with its scuffed skirting, passing doors through which snatches of TV soap or sports were amplified. His thoughts turned to Liz Knight. Was he really so smitten that he'd started to see ghosts? Or project her image onto others? Liz was dead, lost, murdered, her family torn asunder, and he had to confront how little progress he had managed to make in finding the culprit. He felt that he'd not only failed himself and Surrey Police, but failed her.

He rang Claire Mulholland at home, probably the only one to whom he could confess his conviction that Liz was alive. He woke her up, but she gave him a sympathetic hearing. 'Craig, it's very easy to make these mistakes. We all do it. The scientific experiments show again and again how we are unreliable witnesses. You're probably just projecting the face you know—'

'But Claire, what if it actually is her?'

She paused. 'Well, if Martin didn't kill her, why has he run away? Anyway, we both know what you suggest is impossible. She's dead and buried everywhere but in your head.' She bade him a gentle goodnight and hung up.

Sleep came with difficulty for Gillard. The night was punctuated with loud conversation in the echoing corridors, and the slamming of doors. He was awakened in the morning before seven by a couple upstairs having noisy sex, a female making demands in breathless Spanish. Annoyed and aroused in equal measure, he levered himself out of bed, lurched into the en suite and showered, keeping the hot water at its thunderous maximum, scouring his skin of doubts and worries, determined to throw himself into the new day. When he emerged, upstairs were still at it, so he dried and dressed rapidly, enthused about the idea of an early meeting to get the show on the road. With one hand over his free ear, he rang Kincaid's mobile, which went straight to messages. Craig padded down the corridor, looking for the motel's inclusive *desayuno*. There was a breakfast room, with stale coffee in a press-pump flask and a single anonymous pastry per person, brought around by an elderly woman. When he'd finished he rang Kincaid's mobile again, which seemed to be switched off. He hauled himself back up to his room to pack, and the neighbours upstairs were *still* at it. Or perhaps this was a new session. He carried his luggage down to the hire car, and then went back to his room. This time he rang Kincaid by dialling the room extension. He distinctly heard the phone ring in the room above him, and the woman, whose previous vocalizations included a repeated joyful '*Si, mas!*' went quiet. There was some male muttering, then the phone was answered. 'Kincaid.'

'Don't mean to spoil your fun, but Gomez will be here at nine. That's in 20 minutes.'

'Fuck.'

'Er, you don't have time, sir. Not for any more.' Gillard heard Kincaid laugh.

It was a very self-satisfied Detective Superintendent Kincaid who eased himself gingerly into the passenger seat of the car at ten past nine, and spent a long time delicately rearranging his groin. 'Ah. Bit tender now. Still, it was worth it, I can tell you.' Kincaid looked like he was girding himself up for giving out the full gory details when Sargento Gomez's car pulled into the car park. As the detectives got out of the car to greet him, a buxom, African-looking woman in a bright green dress, absurdly high heels and enormous matching handbag came clattering out of the motel. She blew a cheery kiss goodbye to the assembled detectives, which Kincaid returned. She then slid herself into a sleek red Porsche Panamera, easily the most expensive vehicle at the motel, roared out of the car park and pipped the horn as she passed them.

'Not on expenses, I trust?' Craig whispered.

Kincaid tutted at him. 'Do I look *that* stupid?'

It was eleven in the morning and Gillard and Kincaid were in the Spanish ANPR control room in Barcelona, looking in vain for any number plate matches to those accumulated around Paris. 'Bollocks to this,' said Kincaid. 'Let's see if there's been any more card activity.'

He rang Rob Townsend, and Gillard saw him take down some details.

'Got anything, have we?' Gillard asked.

'Not much. Professor Knight's been shopping, that's all.'

'Where?'

'Not clear,' Kincaid shrugged. 'It was a cardholder-not-present transaction. Could be anywhere. Doesn't help us much.'

Gillard stared at him. 'What did he buy? At what time? And how much did he spend? Have you got the merchant ID so we can trace it?'

Kincaid shrugged. Gillard reached for the phone, and Kincaid put a heavy hand on his. 'Best let this one lie, Craig.'

Craig stared at him, a look of incredulity forming on his face. 'Paddy. Please tell me that you didn't use Knight's card details to book that hooker last night.'

'Cerise is a high-class escort from a very reputable Barcelona agency,' Kincaid said, his eyes going a little misty. '*Ángeles Oscuros*. Dark angels. It just seemed a terrible shame to waste that pre-approved credit.'

'I don't believe I'm hearing this, Paddy,' Craig said. 'I really don't. Are you crazy?'

'Are you crazy, *sir*, is what you meant to ask. This particular agency is very discreet. It will not cough up the name of the escort, nor the location where the service was provided without a magistrate's order. I know because they were caught up on

314

that city banker case back in 2011. And of course you are not going to apply to a magistrate, Craig, are you? Instead, you're going to come back to Blighty with me, to work out where the fuck Knight really is and who that woman is who is protecting him.'

Craig said nothing, his face tight with anger.

Kincaid then pointed a belligerent finger into Craig's face. 'And you are never, repeat never, to breathe a word of this to Muriel or anyone else. Understand?'

For a few seconds they just stared at each other. For the first time, Craig Gillard began to reconsider some of the unsubstantiated allegations made against Kincaid in the 1990s, when he was a DI. Accusations by a small-time drug dealer that Kincaid had beaten him up in a cell, claims that he had stamped on a detainee's face in the back of a police van, and that when removing a female demonstrator from the fence she was clinging to, he had bent back her fingers so far that they broke. Craig had always assumed the allegations were false. Now he realized that in all likelihood they were true. The man was capable of anything.

Chapter Twenty-Eight

December arrived, with no further sightings of Knight or his supposed girlfriend, nor any fresh cash withdrawals. Craig Gillard was dispirited. He'd had all Liz Knight's body parts retested for DNA by an independent commercial lab, but the results had confirmed everything. Her blood, bones, teeth, hair samples all matched between the Coulsdon home, the Dungeness house and the hair samples recovered from her chair at the school office where she worked.

Gillard was reluctantly drawn back to the original line of inquiry, that Liz was dead and her husband had killed her. The only problem being that the only remaining lead was the property scam that cheated the Knights of most of their wealth. The Spanish Policia Nacional had now emailed to him PDFs of the original document the Knights had signed. To help interpret them, he had arranged a Skype call to Spanish property agent Miguel Vila. With him in the Caterham incident room were Paddy Kincaid, DC Shireen Corey-Williams and DS Claire Mulholland.

'Before we talk to Vila, let's step back,' Craig said. 'Normally this would be a civil matter. And it is certainly complex. But if the Knights have been defrauded of four million quid, we have a strong motive for murder. Would you agree?'

'Isn't there a slight problem?' asked Claire Mulholland. 'I'm coming cold to this part of the investigation, but it seems to me that if they were defrauded, it was back in June, right? Neither Mrs or Mr Knight had disappeared. No one had been murdered. So if whoever it was had already got the money in June, why kill anyone in October?'

There was some nodding of heads, and everybody looked at Craig. 'I agree, it's not obvious. Unless the fraudster was on the verge of being discovered by someone in the family,' he said.

'They should have killed Oliver Knight, then,' said Kincaid. 'He's the legal eagle.'

'It doesn't easily fit with Liz Knight being killed in her own bedroom with no non-family DNA found,' said Claire.

Craig shrugged. 'I can't fault your logic. Okay, let's see where this leads us anyway.' He connected the Skype call to Vila. After greetings, Vila leaned in close to the computer and said. 'I have discovered what has happened.'

'Okay, let us have it.'

'The Knight family have indeed bought a property with seven hectares of land almost exactly at the address on the documents.'

'You cannot have two different seven-hectare properties in exactly the same place, surely,' Gillard said.

'Oh yes you can,' Vila said. 'What the Knights have bought is the Casita Alta de Marriego and the seven hectares to the *south* of the grid markers shown on the ownership documents.' He lifted up a sheaf of papers. 'What they thought they were buying is the Casa Alta de Marriego and its associated land to the *north*. The original deed is clear, but the copies you have are of documents that had been subtly altered in both Spanish and English to substitute '*norte*' for '*sud*' and '*casa*' for '*casita*'. Whoever did it also appended a page with the description of the internal facilities of the *casa*, which of course do not apply to the *casita*.

'So the Knights just own that tumbledown shepherd's house and the rough lands beyond?' Kincaid asked.

'That's right. In fact the southern land which the Casita sits on is of no development value. It is steep, unstable and completely unsuitable for building.'

'So can we assume the vendor perpetuated the fraud?' Craig asked. 'They clearly came out millions of euros ahead.'

'It seems likely. The vendor company bought that land six months previously for 30,000 euros, through a *sociedad limitada* registered in Panama. It's a symptom of secrecy. I'm not a lawyer, but my brother is. We spent a bit of time researching this over the last week. In Panama, directors have to be listed, but they are usually nominees. The true owner's name doesn't appear, and there is no way of finding it out. So that's where it ends. The money, I am sure, is irrecoverable.' He gave a huge shrug that filled the screen.

'What about local taxes, and all the reporting requirements?' asked Shireen. 'Was no one present for the transaction?'

'The notary, a Mrs Sanchez de Piernos, confirmed that everything was in order. The entire transaction was conducted by post, which is not unusual for expatriate purchases.'

Gillard thanked Vila, and hung up. Then he spoke to DC Corey-Williams. 'Shireen, I want you to tap our police resources in Spain and check all this.' He sighed. 'And tomorrow I have to break all this bad news to poor Oliver Knight.'

Craig had agreed to another trip to see a play with Kathy Parkinson. He hadn't enquired too much about it; he just knew it was good to get out a bit more, though he guessed that he was playing with fire. It turned out to be some modern play with a forgettable title and lots of meaningful silences played in some warehouse north of Camden. It had only four actors, one a voluptuous black woman with a commanding voice who spent much of the show effectively naked because of the way her thin white shift was lit from behind. Craig had to be woken by Kathy with a nudge to the ribs halfway through the second act.

'So you didn't find it erotic, then?' she asked as they took the train back. Gillard's response was non-committal, and remained so even as he drove her home from the station at Upper Warlingham. He agreed to go in for a coffee, and was then ambushed on the sofa. Even as she kissed him, he knew that if he didn't do anything he would end up sleeping with her, a key witness. Rigby would kill him. But on the other hand he was now highly aroused, and who would ever know? He extracted himself to go to the bathroom, mainly to make his decision rationally, without her busy hand down his trousers. While in there he heard Kathy on the phone.

'Wrong number,' she said, immediately he emerged. Guiltily.

Craig saw his jacket, previously crumpled beneath them, was now smoothly folded on the back of the sofa. 'Was that my phone?'

Kathy hesitated. 'Yes. I picked it up to turn it off. I didn't want you to be called away. Selfish of me, I suppose. But I inadvertently hit the answer button. Sorry about that.'

He looked at his phone. Last call was from Sam, two minutes ago. Not a missed call either. Kathy and Sam had conversed for a good minute. *Shit, shit, shit.*

'I'm sorry, Craig. It wasn't deliberate.'

The erotic moment had clearly passed. He grabbed his jacket, said a curt goodbye and walked to the door, closing it gently behind him. Once in the car he called Sam back and got voicemail. Left an explanation along the lines of don't get the wrong end of the stick. Kathy and I are just friends. Nothing was happening there.

It wasn't a complete lie. But it wasn't honest either.

Next afternoon

Oliver Knight let the four detectives in and led them to a big conference room on the top floor of Barker Caynes Tipping. Chloe Knight was already sitting there. She offered Craig Gillard, Claire Mulholland, Gabby Underwood and Shireen Corey-Williams some chocolate biscuits, while Oliver went to extract all the document copies he had, and then instructed his secretary that they were not to be disturbed. When they were all settled, Oliver asked. 'So where is our money? You said you knew where it had gone.'

'Panama,' said Gillard. 'To a limited company protected by banking secrecy, I'm sorry to have to tell you.'

'So it's gone. Pretty much everything Chloe and I stood to inherit.' Oliver Knight's head sagged into his hands, and he ran his fingers up into his scalp.

No one said anything for a while. Gabby Underwood, always ready with professional empathy, leaned out to put a comforting arm on Oliver's shoulder. 'We can still follow other clues,' she said. 'We won't give up.'

'That's all very well,' Oliver said. 'The main problem with all this is how it could have happened. I checked all the documents thoroughly when Mum first brought them to me. They were copies, yes. We had a couple of small changes we wanted making. When those had been incorporated by the notary in Spain, we got the final version posted to Mum. She and Dad both signed, and I witnessed.' He clenched and unclenched his fists as he admitted it was the first time he had seen the original document that his parents had signed, which showed that they bought a shepherd's hut and some poor land for five and a half million euros.

'Did you check the originals again at the time of signing?'

'No, not really. I scanned the first paragraphs, and then Mum said it was okay, she'd already compared them line by line. I mean, she spoke fluent Spanish. I don't.' He threw up his hands. 'Are you saying she lied?'

'Not lied. Anyone can make a mistake,' Gabby said, with a smile.

'This is not a mistake my mother would have made, I assure you.' Oliver gestured angrily at the papers. 'She was an absolute stickler for detail.'

'Well, someone has made these changes, and someone pretty professional and proficient too,' Corey-Williams said.

An hour later, having dropped off Chloe and Oliver Knight at his home with liaison officer Gabby Underwood, Gillard drove Claire Mulholland and Shireen Corey-Williams back to the Caterham incident room for a review of progress. They were Gillard's most trusted investigative brains, but the brooding silence in the vehicle betrayed the knot they seemed to be in, trying to connect the murder of Liz Knight and the theft of the family inheritance.

'Someone's lying,' Gillard said. 'Either the notary or Oliver.'

'Perhaps it was Liz Knight who wasn't telling the truth,' Shireen said. 'This whole scam wouldn't work without someone who was in an intermediary position to prepare and present false documents for signing by Martin and Liz, and then get them witnessed by Oliver.

'Liz is the obvious person,' Claire agreed. 'No one else was involved in visiting the Spanish land registry, getting the documents drawn up, reading and checking them in two languages, and presenting them for signature. With her, it's fairly easy; without her I can't see how it could work.'

'Can anyone think of a single reason why she should steal her own money, though?' asked Shireen. 'It just doesn't make sense.'

'Maybe it would do if she thinks her husband is about to divorce her to marry Natalie Krugman,' Gillard said. 'It cuts him out of the cash. But she'd need help setting up the finance deal in Panama, surely.'

Shireen's mobile buzzed, and as she answered it she held up a hand to get the rest of the team to quieten down. After two minutes making some notes, she hung up. 'That was a friend of mine who works in the London Asset Recovery Team. I'd asked him for pointers on how we tackle Panama.'

'Any conclusions?' Gillard asked.

'Not encouraging ones. The Panamanian company which sold the property to the Knights no longer exists. According to an official notice, it was liquidated in September.'

There was a collective sigh. 'All right, everyone, thank you for your help,' Gillard said. 'I want to look at this again from first principles, starting with key witnesses. Starting tomorrow morning.'

'Shireen and I are going for a drink, Craig. Fancy joining us?' Claire asked.

'Thank you, but I have plans,' he replied with a grin.

Sam had seemed to be quite understanding when Craig called her the next morning. She listened to his explanation of why he was at Kathy's flat. 'Just tell me the truth, Craig. That's all I ask. Be honest with me, and I'll be honest with you.'

'So are you still going to come around to sample my cooking tonight?'

'Of course,' she had said. 'I wouldn't miss that for the world.'

Now it was almost half seven. Craig Gillard looked at the assembled herbs on his chopping board. He'd never cooked with lemongrass before, and the kaffir lime leaves looked like something from a compost heap. Fresh chillies, garlic and a tin of coconut milk, plus a little sachet of some ferocious Thai red curry paste he'd got in an Asian shop in Croydon. A tiny sample on the tip of a finger had almost blown his head off. Still, Sam had said she loved Thai food and he was determined to cook it from scratch. What was the point of him doing the cooking otherwise? There was white wine in the fridge, an Austrian Gewürztraminer that the man in the wine shop said was aromatic enough to hold its own against spicy food. He'd bought some candles, selected a little of his favourite Simply Red to play on repeat.

The time came and she hadn't arrived. After half an hour he became a little agitated. So why wasn't she here? At 40 minutes he rang and left a message on her mobile, and turned off the oven. At two hours, with two more messages, he knew she wasn't coming. Craig gave the dinner a stir. He could eat it, watch TV and forget about her. Or he could drive round to see she was okay. Maybe the dreaded Gary Harrison had re-emerged.

Half an hour later, at 10.30, he was sitting in his car outside her darkened flat. Sam's green Renault wasn't there. No one answered the doorbell. Craig sighed, and reclined the seat. He seemed to spend half his life mooning outside the homes of women who had let him down. Enough. He quietly put the car into gear and, after reaching for a CD from his 1980s collection, slid away back to his Thai meal for one.

Okay, he hadn't been fully honest with Sam. She had seen through him. And she had lied to him in turn. She never had any intention of turning up.

The next day's re-interviews included visits to Liz's parents, Chloe Knight, and Knight's academic secretary, Zakira Oglu. To save his embarrassment Gillard had asked Mulholland and Michelle Tsu to interview Kathy Parkinson. But the one person he really thought hadn't told him all she knew was Helen Jennings, for whom he'd saved the day's last appointment. Now, as he watched her on CCTV waiting for him in the Caterham witness suite, he could see the symptoms of her anxiety. She had power-dressed in a houndstooth jacket with padded shoulders, a shortish black skirt and dark tights which showed off her long legs, and medium-high-heeled shoes. She spent a lot of time running her fingers through her already very neat hair, and only sniffed once at the plastic cup of perfectly vile police coffee that the desk sergeant had given her. If clothing and make-up are part of women's armour, Helen Jennings looked fully protected. Gillard waited for DC Shireen Corey-Williams to arrive before going in.

'Thank you for coming in at short notice, Mrs Jennings, and sorry for keeping you waiting,' Gillard said. 'We have a number of questions that we'd like to ask you.'

'That's absolutely fine,' she said, smiling warmly. 'Has there been any breakthrough yet? Do you have any idea where Martin's got to?'

'Actually, we'll be asking the questions, Mrs Jennings,' Corey-

Williams responded. Gillard glanced at the DC, never having witnessed her interview technique before. A tad harsh, he thought.

After going through the verbal formalities for the recording, Craig asked. 'Can I ask you to detail your movements between May and August this year?'

'I think I already emailed you my online diary,' she said, smiling again. 'Is there any particular day you want more details on?'

'Have you been abroad in that time?'

'Yes. I went to Portugal for a fortnight in June. It's in the diary. And I went on a cruise along the fjords of Norway in August. It is absolutely lovely there.' She directed a beguiling smile at Shireen, but if she expected to generate some reflex warmth from her face she would have been disappointed. Shireen was as blank as a slab of Lake District granite, seemingly devoid of any empathic handhold.

Helen switched her gaze back to Gillard. 'If you haven't been there, you should go.' The smile was infectious and clearly practised.

Craig fought not to respond. 'Out of my price league,' he muttered.

'Can I also ask you whether you have been to France or Spain in the last two weeks?' Shireen asked.

'No, I haven't.'

Shireen pushed across the desk a large photograph of the woman entering the French bank. 'This is a blow-up of a CCTV image from Neuilly, a suburb of Paris. You might have seen it on TV or in the papers.' It wasn't a great image, despite enhancement. It was partially dark, it was raining, and the woman's umbrella blocked a view of her head and neck. The knight tattoo looked fuzzy, but the woman's shapely legs came out very well. One of the reasons the tabloids had loved the picture. 'Do you know who this woman is?' Shireen asked.

'Should I?' She picked up the picture and stared at it. There was no sign of nerves now, Craig noted.

'Is it you?' Shireen asked.

'I'm flattered you might think so,' she laughed. 'But no, it isn't. I don't have any tattoos, for a start.'

'That doesn't prove anything. Some tattoos are temporary,' Shireen said.

'What has this woman done?' Helen asked.

'She may have helped Martin Knight to get abroad undetected,' Gillard said.

'Well, I certainly wouldn't have done that. I don't even like him very much, and Liz was my friend.' She looked genuinely shocked at the suggestion. 'Is that the only reason you've got me in here?'

'No,' Gillard said. 'Chloe Knight had mentioned that you and Liz Knight travelled abroad together earlier this year to help refugees. Can you tell me more about it?'

'It was Liz's idea. We all saw the pictures on the TV, all the suffering. And over a bottle of wine one night in January, I think, we decided that we should do something about it. Liz raised a lot of money through her church and at the school, and I managed to get an ex of mine to lend us a long-wheelbase

Transit with a trailer. We bought a hundred tents and loads of blankets and water filters, and emptied the charity shops of teddy bears. Liz researched what it was that they needed, particularly the medical stuff, as she'd done some St John Ambulance volunteering when she was younger. We also had over a thousand pairs of shoes, trainers and wellingtons. Many of the refugees from Syria and Iraq only had sandals. It took us five days to get to Athens, taking turns to drive, and we slept in the van. It was wonderful, like being students again.' She unleashed that radiant smile again, still trying to generate empathy.

'But then it got a bit harder. Once we got near the coast, there was such a confusion. So many different groups trying to help, so many organizations raising money, so many refugees wandering around. We went across to Chios on a ferry with a Dutch group, and the moment we arrived we got stuck in. There was a large group of Syrians just getting seen to by the Red Cross. Two boats had come in that morning but a number of people were missing. It was terrible, some of the families were distraught. One man lifted his two children out of a waterlogged inflatable boat, then turned straight back and tried to wade out to sea to look for his wife who had fallen overboard. It was dark, and hopeless, but he was hysterical.'

At this point even Shireen looked sympathetic. 'Had she died?'

'Yes. Fourteen bodies were picked up that day. Some had been in the water a long time – weeks, months. They were bloated, unrecognizable, and stank worse than rotten meat. I saw a Red

Cross volunteer try to pull a bloated body from the water into a boat. But the arm just came away in his hand. At that point, I'm afraid, I was sick.'

She paused. 'There was a makeshift mortuary, a big tent, just a hundred yards from the beach with a giant portable refrigerator, but it was full. They were supposed to retain the bodies for identification by relatives, but there were just too many arriving. Dozens every day. The Greek authorities put enormous pressure on the Red Cross to get them buried quickly. I remember Liz telling me that in some cases they were buried without a death certificate because there were too few Greek officials to issue them. I have to say the whole process was smelly, chaotic, and quite stomach-turning. Liz had a stronger belly for it than I did, and did more than her fair share in the mortuary and helping with the burials. The first few days I just collected up lifejackets and did laundry. It was all I could face. Pathetic, really. I wish I'd had her strength.' She looked down, and a look of unfathomable sadness crossed her face. 'Poor Liz.'

'You went out on 6th March. When did you get back?' Shireen asked.

'I got back on April 14th. I dropped Liz at Athens airport – she wanted to round off the time away with a week's skiing in Romania.'

'Skiing must be tough if you normally walk with a stick,' Gillard said.

'She didn't have a stick then. The arthritis was quite intermittent at first. It was only when she got back that it became quite chronic. By the way, the skiing was a secret.

Oliver and Chloe apparently love skiing, but Liz just wanted to decompress on her own, and get the refugee experience out of her system.'

'How did she get home?' Gillard asked.

'By train, I think.'

'Mrs Jennings, do you have any legal training?' Shireen asked suddenly.

'No. We didn't need any for the refugee work.'

'Do you speak Spanish?' Craig asked.

'*Un poquito*,' she answered. 'Enough to get round a menu, but that's it. My Portuguese is better; I've got a place in the Algarve.'

'Or property experience? Have you ever been an estate agent?'

'No.' She looked quizzically at them. 'What strange questions you ask! It's almost as if I'd applied for a job selling villas in Spain or something.'

The two detectives didn't say anything.

'It's something to do with the Knights' place in Spain, isn't it?' She leaned forward inquisitively.

'There's nothing we can really say at the moment,' Gillard said. 'Thank you for coming in.' Gillard stopped the recording, wound up the interview, and escorted her out to her car.

'Look, I'm sorry that was a bit full on,' Gillard said.

'Well, I was made to feel I was a suspect, rather than a witness. Perhaps I should have brought a solicitor.'

'That isn't necessary. We just had to check a few things. But if you have any ideas who that woman is, do let us know.'

Gillard waved her off and went back to join Shireen. 'So, what does your intuition tell you?'

She looked up at him and said: 'The first thing was that she was trying to flirt with you, and was having some success. Every time she smiled at you, you smiled back.'

'Did I really?'

'Yes you did. As you asked.'

Gillard shrugged. 'But I don't think she is either the property fraudster or the woman in France,' Gillard said.

'Can't tell either way, really. We've got nothing to nail her with, have we?' Shireen pursed her lips and shrugged. 'So what about Dr Natalie Krugman? Could she be the fraudster?'

Gillard blew a sigh. 'It wouldn't make sense for her to be involved in defrauding Martin Knight of his inheritance when he'd seemingly offered to share it with her anyway.'

'Good point,' Shireen conceded.

Gillard checked his phone, which showed an email from the Visual Analysis Centre in Cambridge. 'Ah, could have done with this an hour ago. Analysis of the CCTV shows the woman with the umbrella is between five-two and five-six, and probably weighs eight to nine stone.'

'Too short for Jennings,' Shireen said. 'How tall is Krugman? Taller than that, surely.'

'Yeah. She was nearly my height,' Gillard said. 'And besides, our American contacts confirm the last time she was anywhere in Europe was when we interviewed her. I'm afraid our ardent American feminist is in the clear.'

Shireen threw up her hands in frustration. 'That means we don't have anyone left, do we? Our tattooed accomplice remains a mystery.'

Chapter Twenty-Nine

February

Claire Mulholland was sitting at her desk in Mount Browne, Guildford, eating a yoghurt when an urgent email flashed onto her screen from Europol. It listed a police number in Vilnius, Lithuania for her to ring regarding a fugitive from Britain. She put her yoghurt aside and picked up the phone. A female officer answered, in a thick east European accent, and after a few minutes checking, said 'We have arrested a Slovenian national known as Timon Aleksander Horvat, whom I believe you are looking for.'

'That's great news. What's the offence?'

'He has been working here as a truck driver, and was involved in a minor accident last night. We checked his papers and the computer showed a Europol warrant outstanding. We can extradite him to you fairly quickly once the paperwork is finalized.'

'That's great, but I think it would be quicker if I came over to interview him immediately.'

Horvat looked just as thin and nervous as Claire remembered. He was sitting across from her at a large table in Vilnius police's surprisingly modern video interview room, with a solidly built and unsmiling female officer and a thin, spiky-haired male translator.

'So, once again, Timon,' Claire said. 'If you cooperate with us, we can put in a good word. So let's run through those questions again.' She paused so the translator could catch up for the sake of the local policewoman. 'Did you know Harry Smith?'

Horvat shook his head.

'Please speak for the tape,' Claire said.

'*Ne*,' said the translator, a faint tang of alcohol on his breath.

'Did you ever visit this address?' Claire showed him a photograph of Smith's home.

Horvat shook his head. '*Ne*,' said the translator.

'Have you ever paid this man, who we know as Harold Smith, to procure you sexual services?'

'*Ne*,' said Horvat, turning to the translator, who then turned to Mulholland and said, 'No.' The Lithuanian policewoman sighed, and turned a pencil over and over in her fingers.

'Did you ever meet this girl, Francine Cole?' She pointed to the photograph on the table between them.

Horvat shook his head. '*Ne*,' said the translator.

'Do you find underage girls attractive, Mr Horvat?' she asked.

Horvat hesitated, and the Lithuanian policewoman said something. 'She thinks he does,' the translator said to Mulholland.

'All right,' said Claire. 'Mr Horvat, the Slovenian police in 2002 charged you with being an accessory to murder, yes?'

Horvat nodded. The translator said '*Taip*,' earning a loud and lengthy rebuke from the policewoman, who then slapped her hand on the table. 'She says I'm an idiot and don't need to translate the obvious,' he said to Claire, who nodded.

'That murder involved the disposal of body parts,' Claire said to Horvat. 'You had experience as a butcher, yes?'

'I was acquitted,' Horvat said.

'Not of being a butcher,' Claire said. 'You worked as a butcher, didn't you?'

'No, I worked in a... a place where they kill animals...' He then looked quizzically at the translator, who leaned towards the local policewoman and said: '*Skerdykla*.'

'An abattoir,' Claire said.

'You speak Lithuanian?' the translator asked, amazed.

'No, I just know that an abattoir is where they kill animals. Mr Horvat, what did you do at the abattoir?'

'Paperwork. I always worked in the office. Ask them. Blood makes me dizzy.'

Mulholland seemed temporarily stumped by the answer and returned to her paperwork. 'Did you ever meet Martin Knight?'

Horvat shook his head. So did the translator.

'Please speak for the tape. He was your landlord, so are you sure?'

'I never met him. Her yes, him no.'

'Did you murder Mrs Elizabeth Knight?'

Horvat shook his head. The translator mimicked him.

'I put it to you that you killed and dismembered Mrs Elizabeth Knight. Is that not correct?'

334

Horvat shook his head and so did the translator.

'Mr Horvat, let's go back to the beginning. I can now disclose to you that we have a tissue with your DNA on it which was recovered from a settee at Harry Smith's house in Croydon. Your DNA, your semen. Can you explain that?' she asked.

'Yes,' said the translator, and began to talk in Lithuanian.

'I meant him,' Claire said, pointing at Horvat. 'And he already speaks English.' She was beginning to lose her patience.

Horvat said nothing, chewing on air.

'Mr Horvat, we can forensically place you at Harry Smith's house sometime in the two weeks leading up to 27 October 2016. We also found in your own home, in the pleats of your curtains, a data stick with videos and images of children being abused. Abuse that we can prove you took part in,' she lied.

Something began to happen behind Horvat's expression, as if he was melting from the inside. His eyes became shiny, and he said. 'I am sorry.'

'Don't say sorry to me, it's those children whose lives you have ruined. Now once again,' she said sliding forward the picture of Harry Smith. 'Do you know this man?'

Horvat reached forward and picked up the picture. 'This man is Scottish Barry. It was him that organized everything.'

Over the next hour, confession poured from Horvat like blood from a slaughtered pig. He confirmed that vulnerable underage girls were picked out by the man he now knew was Harry Smith, taken to Smith's home in his car, given cocktails of drink and drugs, and promised a modelling career and money if they performed on camera. Another man, a thickset bully called McGinley, was the main abuser. There were others who paid Smith for the privilege. Horvat confessed it had occasionally included him, though he was adamant he had never met Girl F. What about Smith? Horvat only ever witnessed him as cameraman and voyeur: fastidious about clean-up and precautions, repulsive and creepy. He didn't think Smith ever had sex with the girls. Smith oversaw the medicinal douches that the girls took afterwards to remove any incriminating male DNA. It was Smith too who took responsibility for the video files, which were his sales tool. Interested men came to watch the videos at his home, the male participants' faces, tattoos and other distinguishing features pixelated out. Those who liked what they saw were told they could have any of the girls for £100. McGinley was the enforcer, making sure everyone paid, and that the punters kept their mouths shut. When Girl F committed suicide, Horvat said, Harry Smith panicked. He deleted all the videos and disposed of the hard drive on which they were stored. From then on, no cameras were used, and the operation was run only occasionally and for only a few live participants.

Claire Mulholland flew back to Stansted with a Vilnius Police video disc of the interview, a comedy of nods and head-shaking, and Horvat's signed statement in English and Lithuanian. Would one incriminating witness be enough to convict Harry Smith? She hoped so. She rang Gillard, and told him the news. Gillard was overjoyed, and convened a meeting to spread the good news. The moment Paddy Kincaid heard, he wanted to be part of it.

'Girl F has been the bane of my bloody life, it's destroyed my career and made people like Knight famous on the back of my misery. If I did things wrong at the start, I'm going to put them right now. So I'm going to be there when we get that bastard,' he said. 'Smith's going to trial in two weeks over the PCSO attack. It'll take a few hours, but I'll get a watertight warrant for first thing tomorrow. We don't want Smith's lawyer whining to a judge that we did it wrong.'

The raid was set for five in the morning.

At half past four on a damp Monday morning DCI Craig Gillard and DS Claire Mulholland were sitting in an unmarked car opposite Harry Smith's Croydon home. It was quiet, and there were no lights visible from within. DCs Carl Hoskins and Colin Hodges, in the back of a white Transit van across the street, had the door ram. On Gillard's signal, Kincaid and DC Aaron Gibson slipped out of a third car, eased open the back gate and went round to cover the rear, to make sure Smith didn't slip out of the French windows and over the fence into the alleyway behind.

Gillard then walked up to the front door, banged on it and gave half a minute for Smith to respond, before he gave Hoskins and Hodges the signal to use the ram. But before they'd even made the first strike, there was the sound of breaking glass and shouting from the rear. Craig told Hodges to hold off on the ram and follow him, leaving Hoskins and Mulholland at the front.

By the time Gillard was in the small overgrown back garden, he could see that Kincaid was already in the house, a broken pane on the French windows showing traces of blood in his torchlight. 'Help me get him down,' Kincaid shouted from inside. Craig stepped into the dining room at the back of the house and saw a male body hanging from the upstairs banister of the open-plan staircase. Kincaid and DC Gibson were already halfway up the stairs manhandling the body, getting the weight off the rope so it could be cut. 'Is he still alive?' yelled Gillard.

'Could be,' said Gibson, but to Gillard's eye the angle of the neck looked fatal. It took five minutes with three of them crowded on the narrow staircase before they were able to get Harry Smith's body down onto the stairs, and even then Kincaid slipped and managed to let Smith's head crack loudly on the newel post, where it left a bloody mark.

'Christ,' said Gillard, as they laid the body on the ubiquitous carpet protectors at the bottom of the stairs. 'If he hadn't already been dead, that would have finished the bugger off.'

'CSI aren't going to be very happy with this,' said Claire Mulholland, from the French windows. 'It's a right mess.'

'We saw him through a gap in the curtains, and thought he was still kicking,' Kincaid said. 'Didn't we, Aaron?'

'That's right, sir,' said Gibson, adding: 'You've got blood all over your hands, sir.'

'Yes, where I broke the window.' Kincaid wiped them on his handkerchief. 'Anyway, CSI will have better things to do than poke around with a nonce's suicide.'

'Yeah, good riddance,' said Hodges from the doorway.

'Well, it won't help us find out if he really did abuse Girl F,' Claire said.

'What more evidence do you need?' Kincaid said angrily. 'The silver car, the extra-strong mints and Horvat's testimony that Harry Smith was Scottish Barry.' There was a general murmuring of agreement. 'Case over, gents,' said Kincaid. 'Girl F is solved. Hoo-bloody-ray.'

Gillard and Mulholland stayed until the 7 a.m. arrival of Yaz Quoroshi and his CSI team. As the morning light began to filter in, it was clear how compromised forensics would be. Bloody handprints on the white woodwork of the staircase, on the rope and on Harry Smith's clothing. As Yaz muttered to himself about the mess, Craig and Claire stared at each other in the garden.

'Are you thinking what I'm thinking?' Craig asked.

'Yes. Why would Harry Smith kill himself now?' Claire asked. 'He had been released from custody. He knew we didn't have anything on him, apart from the assault on Sam Phillips.'

'Of course, we knew about Horvat's testimony, but he wouldn't have,' Gillard added.

'Unless whoever stole the data stick tipped him off.'

'Possibly. It's incriminating, but not enough for such a stubborn little bastard to top himself, is it?'

As they returned to their vehicle they saw DC Gibson, skinny and nervous, taking a crafty drag on a cigarette.

'A quick word, Aaron,' Craig said.

'Sir.' Gibson dropped the fag as if it were poisoned and trod it out.

'When you got round the back, could you see at all?' Gillard asked.

'Yes, sir. I had a torch, and the patio lights went on when we triggered the movement detector.'

'Sounds a bit dazzling. Was there any light inside?'

'No. The curtains were closed, and it was dark. But Detective Superintendent Kincaid put the lights on after he went in.'

'If the curtains were closed, and it was dark, how could you see if the body was moving?'

'I didn't see it properly until I got inside and the light was on. I suppose it could have been moving.'

'But when Kincaid said he thought the body was moving, that was before you'd gone in, wasn't it? Before he'd broken the pane in the French windows. From what he said, and you seemed to agree, it was seeing a body appear to move that was the motivation for breaking in.'

Gibson thought about it for a moment. 'I'm not sure, sir.'

'Was there a gap in the curtains?' Mulholland asked.

'I presume there was where Detective Superintendent Kincaid was standing. I was behind him.'

'So you couldn't actually see a gap in the curtains, or into the room?' Gillard asked.

'Not exactly, but I trust what Detective Superintendent Kincaid says.'

'That may be good politics,' Gillard sighed. 'But it's not good evidence.'

'He's very senior,' Gibson said. 'I didn't think I should disagree with him. And to be honest, I wasn't sure either way.'

Gillard smiled, and patted the young DC on the shoulder. 'It's okay. You did nothing wrong. Best not mention this to anyone though.'

'Yes, sir.'

After the constable had departed, Gillard turned to Mulholland. 'There's something very fishy about this, Claire.' He led Claire back to the damaged French windows, beyond which two CSI technicians were kneeling over the body of Harry Smith. 'Look at these security measures. It's just what you'd expect from someone as obsessive as Smith.' He pointed to a full, window-width, sliding security grille, bolts top and bottom, and a five-lever mortice lock. All seemed to be in working order. There were no fragments of wood, forced screws, or bent bolts.

'There's no sign of anything being forced,' Gillard said. 'Kincaid simply punched a hole in the glass, reached in and depressed the handle to open the door. Not one of these security devices seems to have been set. Why would that be?'

Gillard was about to leave when a young female CSI technician in a Tyvek suit crackled down the stairs from which Smith had hung himself. She called excitedly to Yaz Quoroshi, and waved a small piece of paper. 'He left a suicide note.'

'Read it out, then,' Gillard called out.

'"I am so sorry about the girls, about Francine, and the others. I can't face what I have done any more." He's signed it too.'

'So maybe Kincaid is right – Girl F is solved,' Mulholland said.

'Suspiciously neat, isn't it?' Gillard said. 'I've asked if Dr

David Delahaye can look at the body. If there's even a hint it wasn't suicide, we should know.'

Three days later

Even in death, Harry Smith seemed to be able to smirk. His naked body, waxy and mottled except where it was gouged and empurpled by rope, lay on a stainless steel table in the mortuary at Croydon University Hospital. Despite evidence of a huge blow to the right side of his head, from which grey matter and plenty of blood had dribbled, his face was set in habitual self-satisfaction. Only the blueness of his lips disturbed the expression. Looking down at him, in the harsh light required for *post-mortem* examination, were DCI Gillard, DS Mulholland, forensic consultant Dr David Delahaye and mortuary technician Nick Stevens.

'Where's Mr Dobbs?' Delahaye asked. 'I was led to understand he was in charge of the Girl F investigation.'

'I don't know.' Gillard looked at his watch. It was gone six in the evening, but Radar Dobbs wasn't generally considered a clock-watcher. 'Let's carry on anyway.'

'I've had a good look at Mr Smith, and it seems to me the cause of death is asphyxia, which is consistent with hanging,' Delahaye said. 'The furrows on the neck are the inverted "V" that one expects with a fixed noose, with a gap at the apex, here.' He pointed to a gap in the rope mark. Next he opened one of Smith's eyelids and, with his pen, pointed to the dilated irises. 'This is, again, what one would expect. There is petechial haemorrhage, behind the conjunctiva and cyanosing of the tongue and lips.'

'What about the blow to the head?' Mulholland asked.

Delahaye shook his head. '*Post-mortem* trauma.'

'We did that,' Gillard conceded. 'Getting him down.'

'However, there are other matters which muddy the water somewhat,' Delahaye said. He looked at the two detectives, his glasses glinting coldly in the light.

'Beneath the ligature mark of the rope is another narrower and deeper mark which follows a somewhat different trajectory. Here.' He pointed to a purple crease at about the level of a shirt collar. 'This is consistent with a different and, I think, earlier ligature from that which was found on his neck.'

'I'm sorry, are you saying that he tried a different noose first?' Mulholland asked.

'No, the angle doesn't work for a suspended body,' Delahaye said. 'It's quite difficult to see because of the *post-mortem* fingerprints, third-party blood, dust and other contaminants.' He looked up at them accusingly. 'As we can all agree, this was a somewhat confused and poorly controlled crime scene. However, I think what we have is evidence of prior strangulation. The lack of observable texture on the skin hints that an electrical cable was used.'

'So it wasn't suicide?' Gillard asked.

'In my judgment, no. I think fatal asphyxiation was administered by another person. The hanging was probably only five minutes or so *post-mortem*. It's an attempt to disguise murder as suicide.'

'There would be no end of people with a motive to kill him,' Mulholland said.

'Well, we may even find out who. In cases where there is some suggestion of victim fight back, my first port of call is taking samples from under the nails. Mr Smith's nails were quite short, but on the left index finger I think I have a useful sample which appears to include a little blood. Hopefully we can then find out who it was.'

Gillard left the mortuary at 6.45 p.m., feeling optimistic. That was punctured within a minute of emerging into the car park, when he took an urgent call from Alison Rigby's secretary Jill Collins. She told him he was to come to the ACC's office in Mount Browne immediately, along with everyone else on the Girl F team. Radar Dobbs was already there.

'I'm a good hour or more away,' Gillard said. 'Any clue what it's about?'

'Put it this way,' Jill said, conspiratorially. 'There has been a momentous development on Girl F. Graham Coldrick has just this minute resigned as our chief constable.

Chapter Thirty

Gillard and Mulholland blue-lighted their way to Guildford through the tail end of the evening rush hour. They got there in 50 minutes, and after walking through the largely empty corridors of Mount Browne's main building joined Dobbs in what was effectively the antechamber to Rigby's office. 'She's been on the phone to the IPCC for an hour,' Dobbs said. 'She's had me waiting the whole time.' If the complaints commission was involved, it really could be momentous.

'Have you picked up any signals, Brian?' He realized this turn of phrase for a man known as Radar would not be welcome. 'Was it Smith's suicide?'

'Nothing except rumours.' He rubbed his left ear.

Secretary Jill Collins came out, and led them into Rigby's office where the ACC was on the phone, just saying a terse goodbye to somebody. The atmosphere was distinctly chilly, and the three detectives found themselves standing in a line, eyes front, as if this was a military inspection.

Rigby leaned back and surveyed them. 'Some new evidence has

emerged into the public domain on the Girl F case – damning evidence that compounds the damage caused to this police force from previous errors in the investigation.'

'What evidence, ma'am?' asked Dobbs.

'I'll get to that. The upshot of this is that the chief constable has brought forward his retirement to today. I will be assuming day-to-day control of the force, and I will also be taking an even more active role in damage limitation.' She put on her glasses and looked at a document on her desk. 'Harry Smith left several packages with his solicitor Samira Jindal which were to be posted in the event of his death. Once she heard of the supposed suicide, Ms Jindal rang Coldrick and told him that she had carried out her client's wishes.'

This doesn't sound good, Craig thought.

Rigby stood and came to stand in front of her desk, which caused them all to step back. 'One of those packages went to the IPCC, the other to the *Daily Mail*. They contained data sticks with images of child abuse on them. There were also several photographic enlargements of a few of those images and a covering letter which alleges that they show Girl F actually being abused by a senior serving member of this constabulary.'

'Coldrick, ma'am?' Mulholland gasped.

'No, thank God. Not that senior. The newspaper was kind enough to courier the package to us, though undoubtedly they expect an inside track on the story in exchange. The officer in question has been suspended, his home raided under my instruction, and his computers seized. We are urgently seeking his whereabouts.' She gave them all the glacial blue stare in turn.

'The fallout of this development is going to be enormous. This was an officer whom we trusted, and who, for all his obvious failings as a modern policeman, was still allowed to lead major cases. We have to find him now.'

I know who it is, Craig realized. Of course.

Rigby continued: 'His early involvement in the investigation of the Girl F case will be an enormous embarrassment to this force for many years to come.'

'It's Paddy Kincaid, isn't it?' Craig said.

Rigby glared at him. 'Yes. Just hearing his name makes me want to vomit. Craig, I'm putting you in charge of the pursuit. You know the man better than most. Time to redeem yourself.' She turned back to the others. 'Fortunately, Coldrick falling on his sword may make it a little easier for the rest of us, if we can get Kincaid quickly. This is to remain highly confidential. We won't be able to keep the media at bay for long, but if we can manage a few days we might be able to get Kincaid charged first. Being proactive is vital.'

He may only have had a few hours head start, but Kincaid had well and truly gone to ground. He'd last been seen at lunchtime, leaving Caterham on foot. No police vehicles had been taken, and his own car was parked outside his house. Quick checks showed he wasn't at home, his father's house or with his in-laws. His grown-up sons and daughter drew a blank, as did the rugby club. Gillard reckoned he'd not have a friend left in the force when they knew what he was accused of. Gillard only had a small team: DC Michelle Tsu for the ring-around from the office, and two uniformed constables to do the legwork.

Three hours in, all the really obvious places had been checked. And then Gillard had a brainwave. Where could Kincaid go that he knew he wouldn't be disturbed? Simple and obvious when you think about it.

It was gone 2 a.m. when Craig eased his unmarked Ford down a familiar car-crowded street of terraced houses in Croydon. With him, in plain clothes, were PC Tiana Clore, a tough Barbadian built like Serena Williams, and PC Finlay Skinner, a rangy young male of 19. They carried little of the weighty kit which identifies a copper, just torch and Taser. This was all about speed and surprise. The keys to Harry Smith's house were supposed to have been in the Girl F evidence drawer, but of course they weren't. When Gillard had relayed his suspicions, Rigby had ruled out a fully resourced stake-out, which would attract press attention. 'Slowly, slowly, catchy monkey,' she had said.

As they cruised along, Skinner used the dashboard ANPR camera to check up on the parked cars. 'That Ford Ka belongs to Kincaid's daughter,' he said. It was outside Harry Smith's house, now boarded up with metal security sheets.

Gillard grimaced. 'And we know she's at home in Farnborough.' He had always thought Denise Kincaid was a shifty individual. Covering for her dad while he borrowed her car was perhaps understandable, but she'd go down as an accessory. The difficulty now would be getting in quietly, knowing how many pieces of home security equipment

Smith's home boasted. Fortunately, the previous warrant was still valid.

Parking round the corner, the trio approached on foot: Gillard down the long alleyway that ran behind, the other two on the main street. He peered over the back fence at the familiar patio with its rusting trampoline, sagging at one side, broken plastic kiddie slide and wooden shed. Movement sensors triggered the patio lights, and he quickly withdrew once he had seen the reflection of the security grille locked in place behind the unrepaired French windows. No quick exit here. The whole team could go in from the front. Gillard and Skinner left Tiana Clore as lookout, then slid silently up to Harry Smith's front door. The police padlock which had secured it was gone.

There was no warning shout, no knock at the door. Just Skinner's jemmy levering the already damaged door. Three attempts and they were in. Craig hit the light switch and bounded upstairs, while Skinner raced to the rear lounge. Somewhere a sash window rumbled open. Then came a crashing metallic sound. Craig tore through to a first-floor back bedroom and looked out of an open window to where the patio lights once again blazed. Kincaid, in track suit and trainers, was already in the garden and scrambled over the fence into the back alley. How had he jumped down the dozen feet without injury?

Of course – the trampoline, which had been within ten feet of the back of the house. And he'd tipped it over after him to block pursuit. Gillard wasn't going to attempt that jump, but he had a secret weapon. He ran to the front door and bellowed: 'Tiana, cut him off, right-hand end of the alley.'

Tiana Clore exploded past him, a dark streak thundering up the street and out of view, parallel to Kincaid's rightward sprint along the alley. She had represented Barbados in the heptathlon in the London Olympics, and the 200 metres was her best distance: personal best 21 seconds dead.

Gillard shouted to Skinner, rushed out of the front door, and into the garden. They were just scaling the back fence to the alley when they heard Kincaid's gasping breath. Pulling themselves up over the fence, they saw him sprint along the alley past them, heading left, pursued by a black missile called Tiana. Two seconds before impact, a breathless Kincaid whirled around and pulled out a pistol. Glock, semi-automatic, it looked like.

'He's armed!' Gillard bellowed. But Tiana was faster. 'Taser!' she yelled, and a bright jolt of light arced around Kincaid, followed by his roar of agony as he jerked, the gun spinning away as he dropped. When Gillard got to him, Kincaid was lying face down in a puddle of his own urine. Now conscious, the detective superintendent was emptying his considerable vocabulary of racial and sexual slurs against Tiana while she knelt on his back. She had a little smile on her face as she used a thumb lock grip to force his arm so far up that Gillard feared she might dislocate it.

Alison Rigby had Surrey Police on overdrive. Within an hour of Kincaid's arrest, a terse pre-prepared statement was issued to the press saying that a 53-year-old male from Surrey had been arrested in connection with an allegation of child abuse. No mention of Girl F was made in the statement, nor that the unnamed man arrested was a policeman. As intended, the item was largely ignored in the media, despite the coverage given to speculation that Coldrick's retirement was something to do with the Girl F case. Next day she approached Devon and Cornwall Police to bring in an independent team to examine the allegations, even though the IPCC had yet to officially react to its package of child abuse images.

In the subsequent days the new acting chief constable brought the fear of God to the entire staff at Mount Browne. She strode quietly through the hallowed gothic halls, sitting in randomly on meetings, joining smokers as they gathered behind the communal bins, talking to trainees and receptionists, her transfixing blue stare always framed in dark eyeshadow. She directed the media effort too, crucial now to save the force's reputation. A Channel 4 camera crew sometimes scurried round after her on her rounds, part of a hurriedly arranged documentary to run in the summer.

It took a week for the full story of Kincaid's abuse to break, led by the *Daily Mail*, which also secured an exclusive interview with Rigby on the fight to bring in 21st-century policing. She deflected most questions on Kincaid's arrest on the grounds it was an ongoing investigation, but deftly referred to it as a 'historic case of abuse from someone in a position of trust'. It cleverly made the case sound a lot older than it was.

Faced with the reality of the images, Kincaid confessed. He was the enforcer 'McGinley' that Horvat had mentioned. He admitted to four sample counts of abusing Girl F, to tipping off Horvat that the police raid was coming, and to stealing and destroying evidence from Horvat's data stick. He also admitted the theft of a Glock 19 semi-automatic pistol from the Surrey and Sussex Police Tactical Firearms Unit. Finally, after prolonged and dogged questioning by Radar Dobbs, he confessed that it was he who had gone to visit Harry Smith the night before the police raid, ostensibly to tip him off. When Smith's back was briefly turned, Kincaid strangled the smaller man with a length of electrical cable he'd brought for the purpose. The flex wasn't long enough to hang Smith from the banister, but when rooting around in the house he found a length of rope which was.

Dobbs's thorough interrogation managed to confirm what Gillard had suspected. It was Kincaid who, after killing Smith, had unlocked all the locks and bolts at the rear of the house to facilitate his own entry six hours later. Even the garden gate bolt had been slid back ready. Volunteering to get the warrant late on a Sunday had allowed him to manipulate the timing of the raid, and as the most senior officer he was effortlessly able to allocate tasks that suited him.

As Gillard sat with the newly promoted DI Claire Mulholland in the Mount Browne refectory, he reflected on how cleverly Kincaid had played everyone's expectations: 'His motive for being on the raid was unimpeachable. No one could doubt that his career had been ruined by the failure to properly investigate the Girl F case.'

'When in fact he was deliberately hampering the investigation even prior to 2009,' Mulholland said. 'Losing statements, failing to follow up leads, because to do otherwise would inexorably have led his subordinates to him.'

'Exactly. And being first into Smith's home, deliberately cutting his hand on the glass and getting Aaron Gibson to follow him in, allowed him to mess up the crime scene so comprehensively that any DNA of his from the murder would be put down to later contamination.'

'He didn't allow for Dr Delahaye's skill in disentangling two different types of strangulation,' Mulholland added.

'No, but even then he had a defence,' Gillard said. 'Few would have really blamed Kincaid for killing Smith if his motive was anger at the abuse of Girl F and the destruction of his career. I had suspected that was what was driving him. But I never guessed that Kincaid wanted Smith dead to silence him. The same reason he wanted Horvat abroad. To bury his own involvement as an abuser.'

When Craig walked out of the refectory, intending to drive back to Caterham, he was ambushed by Rigby who was just emerging from a meeting.

'Ah, just the man I want to see. Follow me.'

In her new and tastefully redecorated chief constable's office she leaned against her desk and reached behind her for the large plastic jar. She unscrewed the lid, dipped her fingers in, and popped a brown orb in her mouth, crunching it noisily.

Craig was momentarily frozen in shock. So *that's* what the jar was for.

'Maltesers,' she said. 'A middle-aged vice. Want one?' She offered him the jar.

Craig took one and ate it. 'Thank you.'

'So Craig, the media are being rather kind to us.'

'Ma'am?'

'I feared the suspicion in the press would always be that someone in Surrey Police knew that Kincaid was abusing girls and covered it up.' She crunched another Malteser thoughtfully. 'Instead, they have charitably taken the line I wanted: just one rotten egg in an otherwise decent basket.'

'I think that's true, ma'am.'

'Luckily Professor Knight seems too busy hiding to throw any rotten eggs of his own.'

'Ma'am.' Oh God, here it comes.

'And speaking of which, here we are once again, Detective Chief Inspector Gillard.' She went behind her desk and picked up some papers.

'Ma'am.' He didn't know what else to say. It was clearly another of her rhetorical questions.

'It's been six months, almost. Martin Knight is still out there somewhere, making us look stupid. And next week, so I hear, the funeral of Mrs Knight takes place.'

'Yes, ma'am. The coroner gave his permission. Though he's hanging onto the body parts to match with any others that show up.'

'It would have been a good time to find him, wouldn't it? And ideally, the rest of her. But I think we need a fresh pair of eyes. Or perhaps ears.' She smiled at some little private joke. 'I'm appointing DCI Dobbs to lead the case. You will instead be looking at our backlog of unsolved cases. Here.' She passed over a thick file. Craig looked through them with mounting incredulity. Burglaries, a notorious off-and-on domestic abuse case, a sheaf of criminal damage reports and a stolen motorcycle.

'Think of it as penance for not telling me you dated a murder victim.'

It was a freezing February morning, and Gillard turned up the car heater to maximum. He was parked across the road from St John's parish church in Caterham, watching Liz Knight's funeral cortège arrive. Three black limousines and a line of private cars. This was a private affair, and Gillard had not been invited, but he had called in sick to Mount Browne so he could watch from a distance. Oliver Knight appeared dignified as he helped his sister out of the car, and then Liz's parents Tom and Geraldine Bishopsford. He spotted Helen Jennings, Lord Justice Cunliffe, even the infuriating Jimmy Bartram. The funeral director removed a huge spray of white lilies so that the coffin could be slid easily from the hearse. Somewhere among the many floral tributes would be his own flower selections – a wreath of red roses sent anonymously, as well as a more traditional wreath. 'With deepest condolences, Surrey Police.'

There were only four pall-bearers, but they had no trouble shouldering the casket. After all, there was nothing of Liz in there. Just a collection of her favourite books, a copy of her award-winning Spanish Civil War thesis, her runner-up plaque for BBC Young Musician of the Year 1981, photographs and other mementoes, plus 417 letters penned by the pupils at her school. That is what Kathy Parkinson had told him.

Eventually everyone filed inside, and Gillard was left to his own thoughts for 40 minutes, until the tolling of the church bell awoke him from his reverie. As the congregation moved into the churchyard, Gillard emerged from the car, straightened his black tie and tugged the cuffs on his charcoal-grey jacket. Then he strode off through the bracing cold into the graveyard. He stood behind a Victorian tomb, in the shadow of its moss-softened granite angel, and stared down at the mourners who congregated 30 metres away around the open grave. He watched the opening of the Good Book, with its gilt edges, and the gesticulation of the priest, whose white surplice and snowy hair were ruffled by the freezing easterly. He heard only snatches of the words: 'Therefore commit her body to the ground; earth to earth, ashes to ashes, dust to dust; in sure and certain hope of the Resurrection to eternal life, through our Lord Jesus Christ.'

As the coffin was lowered, Gillard watched Chloe Knight sag between the supporting arms of her brother and grandfather. As he heard her sobs, his own eyes began to smart and fill. He waited until the end of the service. Waited still until the friends had departed; and then the uncles and aunts and nieces and nephews; and after another 15 minutes the priest, the parents; and finally Oliver and Chloe. He waited five more minutes until he was sure everyone had gone. Until he had her to himself, for just a few minutes. He emerged from the shadow of the tomb and walked slowly down to the grave, heaped with flowers, a glistening basalt headstone already in place on the family plot, its epitaph gilded in gold.

Elizabeth Knight, 1968–2016

Beloved mother, wife, daughter, teacher.

Loved by all whose lives she touched.

Thy remembrance shall endure

into all generations

I am the resurrection and the life, saith the Lord: he that believeth in me, though he were dead, yet shall he live: and whosoever liveth and believeth in me shall never die.

John 11: 25–6

Gillard knelt to touch the stone and to say his own private goodbyes. As he stood, he noticed the priest just a few feet away. He smiled and said: 'I baptized her and watched her grow. Such an extraordinary woman.' He turned to the grave. 'She's gone to a better place now.'

Gillard nodded. A vision of Liz slipping out of his sight at Madrid airport flitted through his mind. Then where? The finality of her death weighed upon the memory: a funeral, a grave, a grieving family. A six-month investigation. All the evidence, tested and retested. No glimpse can survive such a crushing reality.

Chapter Thirty-One

A year later

While Surrey Police's new chief constable basked in the solving of the Girl F case, a year passed and the high-profile murder case of Liz Knight slowly went cold, despite all the best efforts of the newly promoted Detective Chief Superintendent Dobbs. No new body parts had been recovered from Walland Marsh. No new cash withdrawals or credit card transactions were made. At the start of the summer the investigation was scaled back and the Caterham incident room closed down.

The only officer remaining on the case was DC Colin Hodges, dogged Tweedledee. Hodges joked that he was still happy to work 'under the Radar' as he put it. But for all his shortcomings, Hodges still retained some loyalty to his old boss Gillard. He passed on every new snippet of information. Sporadic bulletins of sightings of Martin Knight, and evidence reappraisals. All of it showed that the meticulous Radar Dobbs was making no more progress than Gillard had.

Craig continued to think about Liz, and wonder whether it was really her he had seen at Madrid. Otherwise he returned to a hermit life, all work and no play. He solved half a dozen burglaries, put a nasty wife-beater behind bars and found several stolen motorcycles at the yard of a bent dealer. Sam Phillips was still at Caterham, but now as a uniformed PC. She had ignored his occasional emails for reasons that still eluded him.

But then, in February, progress came from a totally unexpected direction.

It was almost 10 p.m. on a Monday night when Kathy Parkinson rang him at home.

'Hello, Craig. It's me.'

He felt that was a slightly overfamiliar greeting. Thirteen months since the awkward goodbye at her place and the phone call with Sam, he was surprised to hear from her at all. But as she made small talk he realized she had been drinking. He decided to wind up the conversation as quickly as possible.

'It's late, Kathy, so what can I do for you?'

'Something rather upsetting has happened. At La Porcherie.'

'Has it fallen down?' Gillard asked, then realized that she wasn't laughing.

'No, Craig. They've found a dead body there, in a car. And I have to go over and answer some questions from the French police.'

'Was it actually at the property?'

'Yes, parked on my land, round the back. I had a call this morning. It seems to have been found a couple of weeks ago, but because I've not been for three years, they took a while to trace me. They think people smugglers may have dumped the car a year or so ago there with a refugee in the boot. Oh, it's so horrible.'

'Is your place close to one of the Channel ports, then?' Craig asked.

'No, that's the weird thing. It's in Normandy, 60 kilometres south of Caen. It's an obscure village, on back roads in the middle of nowhere.'

'Doesn't sound an obvious place to dump a refugee. Why did they say it was a refugee?'

'I don't know. But I have to go over within seven days to make a statement.'

'Well, if you can show that you've not been there you won't have much to worry about. I'd still get yourself a French lawyer, just to be on the safe side.'

'I will, but God knows how much it will cost me.' She paused. 'Craig, I was wondering if you'd come over with me. I trust your judgment.'

'Well...' Craig didn't know how to frame his refusal.

'This isn't a ploy, I promise you. And I'll pay for your travel.'

Craig realized he had Thursday and Friday off. He sighed and rubbed his face. 'I'll think about it, okay? I'll ring you tomorrow.'

'Thank you, Craig, thank you so much! There's nowhere fit for sleeping at La Porcherie, so it will have to be a hotel, mind. I'll pay of course.'

He hung up. She'd been as effusive in her gratitude as if he'd said a definite yes. But he hadn't. Had he?

Next morning Craig rang his French police liaison contact Caspar Glomiquet, explained what had happened and asked for some unofficial help. The French officer looked up the case for him and rang back. 'It's sad, but not anything for her to worry about,' he said. Glomiquet said the body had been in the car for a very long time, judging by its decomposition. The man's name was Mohammed ben Alighassir according to the Syrian papers found with him. He was dressed in Arabic-type clothes and cheap plastic sandals, and had on him some other items including a Koran, worry beads and a small amount in Syrian pounds. The house was some way outside the village, so no one had noticed anything. 'It's a British-registered car. I think they probably just want to know that the car isn't hers, and establish her movements. Just box-ticking, *non*?'

'Is there a cause of death?' Gillard said.

There was at the other end of the line what he imagined to be a Gallic shrug, ending with a blown sigh. 'The body is skeletal; I don't think it's going to be easy.'

Gillard made a note of the registration details, thanked the French officer and hung up. He looked to see if anyone was on duty in Mount Browne that evening who would do some incognito checking on the PNC. He was in luck; Rob Townsend was there. 'If anyone asks, you can say the French requested it,' Gillard said. 'In fact, I wonder why they didn't.'

It seemed a long wait, but Townsend eventually came back on the line. 'Okay. It's a Peugeot 407. Last keeper registered was more than two years ago. A Mrs Pamela Jones at an address in south London. Probably stolen at some stage,' Townsend said.

'Can you do me a favour and get a couple of PCSOs to go see her anyway?' Gillard said. 'I'm already in Rigby's bad books so I can't be seen to do it. And check ANPR. I'd really love to know where that car has been.'

'I just did that. Nothing in the last 12 months. Can't go back any longer unless it's terrorism related, and you need a superintendent's signature too.'

'That's true, I'd forgotten.' Radar Dobbs was too meticulous to sign a request pass without checking. Gillard knew his connection with Kathy Parkinson, however innocent, needed to be kept quiet. It seemed that whatever secrets ANPR had on this Peugeot would disappear when the data was wiped after two years. 'The French didn't find anything either. I assume they have similar limitations. Thanks for trying anyway.' Gillard sighed and hung up. He then rang King's College London. He had Kathy Parkinson hauled out of a lecture, and she sounded quite worried as she answered the phone.

'It's all right, it's just me,' he chuckled.

'My secretary said it was an urgent police matter! I've left 200 students waiting for an introduction to the psychology of fear and stress.'

'Well, you have some personal stress to relate to them. Look, it's good news. The case has piqued my interest, so I will be coming, strictly off-duty. I have some excellent contacts with the French police, so I can certainly make this a bit easier for you. How's your French?' he asked.

'Bit rusty, but I did get first-class honours in it, so I'm sure I'll be okay. How's yours?'

'On a par with my CSE in woodwork, but I have a liaison officer who I can speak to. In the meantime, I've traced the car this end.'

Townsend called Gillard back the following morning. 'I got my brother in law at the Met to send a couple of PCSOs round last night – no reply – and again first thing this morning. There was a young Asian couple in residence, just been there a few months. They didn't know Mrs Jones, but have seen the odd bit of mail for her. An elderly next-door neighbour said Mrs Jones had definitely not lived there for three or so years and had gone back to the Midlands where she's got a sister. She used to work as a hospital cleaner at Croydon University Hospital. I'm chasing that up tomorrow, so I'm confident we can get her.'

'If it's a rental place, get them to find the landlords,' Gillard said. 'It's a long shot after so many years, but they may have a forwarding address for our Mrs Jones. Can you check ports and ferry terminals too for booking references matching that Peugeot number plate? They might keep them for several years, and then we'll get the passport number. It would be nice to know what this Mrs Jones looks like.'

'Let's hope they are indexed by number plate,' Townsend said. 'Otherwise there'll be a lot of Joneses to search through.'

'Come on, Rob. Didn't you always want to keep up with the Joneses?'

It was a fine sunny Thursday when Gillard drove Kathy Parkinson onto the Portsmouth to Caen ferry. They enjoyed the nearly six-hour crossing in fine weather and drove the 15 kilometres south from the port into the city. Kathy had booked a room each for them in an Ibis hotel. The next day, at what to Gillard seemed an obscenely early hour of 8.15, they set off from the hotel and, after leaving the city, wove their way through delightful high-hedged countryside to the village of Pierrefitte-sur-Orne, where the gendarmes would meet them by ten. As they drove they ate slabs of delicious raspberry tart. They had intended merely to have coffee and croissants, or at most *pain au chocolat*, but the lure of the fruit tart was irresistible. They reached Kathy's so-called holiday home with their clothing strewn with crumbs.

La Porcherie was a large single-storey barn at the southern end of the village with an external rusted metal staircase and a lichen-encrusted stucco roof that sagged alarmingly in the middle. There was an overhanging gable with a hoist and rusting chains, and the whole building was overshadowed by a huge horse chestnut tree. Ground-floor shutters displayed only shreds of the royal-blue paint they once sported. The barn sat right alongside a little-used country lane, and adjoined a nettle-and-dock-consumed patch of ground that dipped sharply at the back. Rusting agricultural machinery, some of it pre-war, had been dumped alongside. A single strand of yellow crime tape marked GENDARMERIE NATIONALE – ZONE INTERDITE barred the rough gravel drive that edged the property and disappeared around the back. Gillard parked the car, and they got out of the vehicle.

'Did Keith ever do anything to this place?' asked Gillard as he surveyed what even the most optimistic of DIY fanatics would have called a hopeless project.

'Oh yes. We had water connected, and electricity. We started on the roof on the back building, but then discovered the huge and beautiful timbers that held it up had death-watch beetle galleries all the way through, and would need replacing.'

Gillard had got as far as the crime scene tape, and looking over saw that the land behind fell away sharply to a beautiful valley with pastures full of black and white cattle, edged by more horse chestnuts. As he was admiring the view a police Citroën arrived, and Gillard recognized Caspar Glomiquet emerging from the passenger side. With him was a miserable-looking 50-ish man in a car coat and suede shoes who Gillard imagined must be the regional detective. The man walked straight up to Gillard and launched a voluble oration in French, which Kathy interrupted with her own, seemingly fluent response. Introductions were given, and the detective, who went by the name of Raymond Poulet, started shrugging and gesticulating to Kathy about the location of the car. Kathy passed across various documents including her own passport, driving licence and ownership documents for the property before the conversation clearly turned to a broader subject.

Glomiquet came to Gillard's rescue. 'He's basically saying that this is a routine inquiry. Madame is not under any suspicion. A British car, ready to be taken back across the Channel, a Syrian refugee, desperate to get to the UK, who presumably paid his life savings to be smuggled in. His thinking is that at some point the guy in the boot died, maybe suffocated, who knows, and the trafficker panicked, and found somewhere remote to dump the vehicle.'

Gillard looked quizzically at the French detective, and then back to Glomiquet. 'But presumably a European national, perhaps even British, was on hand to go with the car, to get it across to Britain? And why would the guy be in the boot so far away from the Channel crossing?'

Glomiquet turned to Monsieur Chicken, as Gillard had already started to think of him, and a new, richly gestured, conversation began. Poulet's final shrug told Gillard, even before Glomiquet's translation, that exactly how this poor guy had died wasn't really of much interest to him. 'He says they have so many of these people to deal with,' Glomiquet said, excusing his colleague's apparent indifference. 'He says he would rather concentrate on preventing more coming than worrying about the dead. Especially someone dead for more than a year.'

'But what about his family, they must be missing him,' Kathy asked, then repeated it in French for Monsieur Poulet. There was a volley of French in return.

'He asks whether we have ever had dealings with the Syrian embassy in Paris,' Kathy translated. 'They will try, but it's hopeless. He says the paperwork goes in and never comes out again. The details will also be sent to the refugee agencies operating in Greece and Macedonia, to see if he was registered there, to Lampedusa in Italy in case he arrived from Libya, and to the border forces in those countries. There are also voluntary organizations which have Facebook pages to reconnect family members with each other. But he thinks the chances are that we will not get a result.'

Gillard felt his fists balling and stretching in frustration. 'Caspar, can you ask him if they plan to do an autopsy? And if they have finger-printed him and taken a sample for DNA.'

Glomiquet's conversation with Poulet was quite brief. 'It depends on the coroner. If there is no reason to suspect foul play, he would be surprised if the coroner orders one—'

'Of course there is foul play! This guy was illegally trafficked here—' Gillard exclaimed.

'But according to the *médecin légiste* it was at least a year ago,' Glomiquet said, translating from Poulet. 'That accords with evidence for how long the car was here.'

'What firm evidence could there be?' Gillard asked, exasperated.

Poulet pointed at the tree above them and the windscreen wipers of Kathy's car as Glomiquet translated: 'Beneath the blades and in the windscreen well he found not only dead chestnut leaves from the autumn, but a layer of horse chestnut flowers which would have been deposited the previous May.'

'Fair point,' Gillard conceded.

'As for finger prints, the poor condition of the body precluded it. He is not sure if DNA samples have been taken. He did not order them, but the mortuary may do so for its own records.'

Poulet stared belligerently at Gillard and then said in fractured English. 'You are the man who failed to find the fugitive murderer Knight, *non*? Maybe you should get back to your own work.'

Glomiquet made his own apologies to Gillard as Raymond Poulet strode back to his car. Gillard didn't blame Poulet for being irritated. He was being questioned about a death in France by some off-duty English policeman who didn't even speak French. But every family deserved an answer, and Gillard knew that somewhere a Syrian family would be sick with worry. Gillard thanked Glomiquet, wished him a good journey, and said he would be in contact again soon, if he ever got on the cold-case review.

'Yeah, so, what about that professor, eh? Knew how to give us the slip, didn't he?'

'Yes, he did,' Gillard muttered, but Glomiquet didn't hear. The French inspector had already turned the Citroën around, and the liaison officer had to hurry to get in.

Kathy looked up at Gillard, and saw the dissatisfaction radiating from him. 'There's nothing you can do, Craig,' she said.

'Maybe, maybe not,' he said. Gillard ducked under the crime tape and entered the courtyard. Kathy followed. 'Are we allowed to do this?' she asked.

'Nope.' Gillard looked at the yard, a few dozen square yards of hard-standing which had over the years been fractured by weeds. He could clearly see where a car had been left. All around the yard the nettles and rosebay willowherb were high and lush, except for a car-sized area where brown stems were flattened, and only now were fresh shoots emerging. He looked around for 15 minutes, but could find nothing of interest.

Gillard was back at his desk in Mount Browne on the Monday, and he'd no sooner got a coffee and logged onto his computer before Shireen Corey-Williams tracked him down. 'Good time in France?'

'Yes, a very interesting insight into French investigative priorities,' he said. Gillard knew he would be unwise to let anyone know that he had travelled abroad with a witness in the Knight case. If Rigby found out, he'd be crucified.

'Rob Townsend's been keeping me up to date,' she said. 'First off, he looked for the previous owner of the car before Mrs Jones, but it seems it was bought for cash at an auction in Hampshire. They say they have no idea what the purchaser looked like.'

Gillard grunted. Whoever bought the car knew how to maximize anonymity. 'Anything else?'

'Yes. We got a bit of luck with Eurotunnel. The car was booked through to France by a Mrs Pamela Jones on Wednesday, 19 October 2016 at 9.45 a.m.'

'Less than a week after Liz died. I wonder if Mrs Jones is our accomplice.'

Shireen smiled. 'Maybe. I requested the full file details from the Passport Agency to go with that passport number, and here it is.' She led Gillard to her desk and pulled up the PDFs of the scanned documents.

Pamela Jones had an utterly average name matched by an utterly average face. The passport picture wasn't great, but it showed her as about 50 with fleshy cheeks, a slight double chin, big round purple-framed spectacles and a mass of dense dark curls, held back by an Alice band. Pleasant looking but plain, forgettable in any crowd.

'So here's what we have about her,' Shireen said. 'Born in Stoke-on-Trent in 1964, maiden name Robinson. Widowed. No kids. The passport was applied for in early 2015, and was her first. The only record we have for it being used is on that Le Shuttle departure to France. One way. There is no record that she ever came back.'

Tracing the passport holder's onward travels wouldn't be easy; Gillard knew that from previous experience of tracking criminals who fled the UK. There were normally no checks within Europe's huge Schengen passport-free area, and the only automatic notifications would be of an arrival back into the UK, or of trips to the US, where the Advanced Passenger Information System required a separate notification. Apart from that it would be down to making requests to each and every airline, ferry operator and train company. No easy task, Gillard thought ruefully, even with a dozen officers to call on. If only she weren't called Jones, the second most common name in the UK. More than half a million, probably hundreds of Pamelas among them.

'She doesn't look to me like a refugee smuggler. And I may only be a woman,' she said, looking up at Craig, 'but I don't detect the exotic beauty that might have inspired Martin Knight to commit murder.'

Gillard laughed. 'No, I couldn't agree more. But then passport pictures can make Beyoncé look like Ken Dodd.'

'But not vice versa, sadly,' Shireen said.

Craig smiled at her, then on the screen he flicked through the copies of a neat passport application, and the original photo booth pictures the Passport Agency had sent. He suddenly noticed Shireen inhale and stiffen. A malign presence loomed behind them. He turned around to see Alison Rigby, a mug of coffee in hand.

'What's this about refugee smuggling? Got a new case?'

'No ma'am. An unidentified body has turned up in a car in France, and we were wondering—'

'Whether it was the rest of your ex-girlfriend, I suppose.' She came over to them and the two detectives parted to let the chief constable look at the screen and the pile of documents. She picked up the top sheaf and began to read. 'From my schoolgirl French it seems the body is of a Syrian national. I may be a bit slow, but I don't see the relevance.' Rigby turned and glared at Gillard. 'It's not as if you don't have a full caseload.'

Gillard's Adam's apple slid slowly up then down. 'There may indeed be a connection to the Knight case, ma'am, because the car was found dumped at the holiday home of Mrs Knight's best friend Kathy Parkinson. It's a British-registered vehicle which crossed to France on a date that Martin Knight would have found useful, had he been able to hide in it. And we now know the name of the woman who owned it and drove it abroad.'

'Really.' Rigby tossed the documents back and stood with her hands on her hips.

Craig then summoned all his courage and asked. 'And I was wondering if I could get your permission to briefly visit France again to see the vehicle and the body. Once I've made more progress on the car.'

Rigby gave him a hard and discomforting stare. 'As you are clearly obsessed by the Knight case, it would be obtuse of me not to let you apply your talents formally. Dobbs has had nearly a year and hasn't made any more progress than you did. At least you are coming up with some fresh ideas.'

'Yes, ma'am.'

She scrutinized him thoughtfully for a full minute. 'All right. You can go to France. And I'll let Dobbs know that you are once again leading the investigation. We can reopen the incident room in Caterham too.'

'Thank you, ma'am,' Gillard said, trying to suppress his grin.

With Rigby's backing, the trail of Pamela Jones hotted up. Having a common name was only a slight inconvenience to Gillard in tracking her down. The hospital referred the question of her employment to an agency which confirmed that Mrs Jones had worked for them as a ward cleaner for six years until 2013. The addresses on file matched the one she had moved out of, plus an earlier London address in Streatham. The employment record enabled DC Corey-Williams to access Mrs Jones's National Insurance record, which revealed that she had last worked at an electricity showroom in Wolverhampton in 2016. Two more phone calls, and Shireen had a current address.

Four days after getting hold of Mrs Jones's passport, the woman herself was sitting in an interview room in Wolverhampton's Bilston Street police station opposite DCI Craig Gillard and DC Shireen Corey-Williams. And she looked absolutely terrified.

'The reason we've asked you to be here today is to help us in connection with the death of a Syrian man, Mr Mohammed ben Alighassir,' Gillard said.

'Death? I don't know what you're talking about.'

He passed across a photocopy of her passport and a sheaf of paperwork. 'Mrs Jones, we know that on Wednesday, 19 October 2016 at 9.45 a.m. you took your Peugeot 407 on Le Shuttle at Ashford International station to Calais. We don't know exactly where you went after that, or how you got back without using your passport, but we'd very much like to.'

Mrs Jones was speechless. 'I haven't got a car any more. Nor a passport.'

Gillard had to admit that Mrs Jones gave an absolutely brilliant rendition of shocked and innocent helplessness. He pointed to the photocopy. 'This is you, yes? Your photograph?'

She nodded. 'But I've not been abroad since I was a girl. I did have a temporary passport once, but I got seasick on the ferry to Ireland. I never applied for this one. Honest.'

Shireen held up two sheets of paper. Impatience was scribbled all over her face. 'We got all the details from the passport office. Your application form, signed. Your submitted photograph. The details of your address. The utility bills and credit card statements you sent in, with your name on, all tied to this address.'

'But I didn't apply for it. I didn't send any photos, or bills. You've got the wrong person. You must be mistaken. Jones is a very popular name.'

Shireen laughed incredulously. 'Look here, Mrs Jones,' she said pointing at the passport photocopy. 'It's not just a random

Jones, is it? This is your own face, you would agree with that? How did anyone else get these photos of you? Did they push you in a booth at gunpoint? Now it's not unheard of for someone to pinch someone else's identity to get a passport. But they would usually put their own photograph in if they intend to use it, wouldn't they?'

'I don't know. I'm sorry, but I don't know.' She was twisting a wedding ring on her finger. Tears were not far away.

'Okay, Mrs Jones, let's start with the basics,' Craig said in a gentle voice. He shuffled through the papers and selected a water bill, which he pushed across to her. 'Okay, have you ever lived there?' He tapped his finger on the address portion.

She read the address out: '146B Manor Road, Thornton Heath. Yes. From 2013 to 2014.' She actually smiled, as if this was the first piece of good news she had received all day.

Gillard snatched back the statement and looked at it, his brain racing. Why hadn't he checked this before? 'Would you excuse us a minute?' He then guided Shireen outside into the corridor.

'What is it?' she said. 'What's the matter?'

'Two things,' he said. 'One, from the first moment we sat down, it was absolutely obvious to me that this is not the Mrs Jones we are looking for. She has no idea what we're on about, and she's clearly not the sharpest knife in the block. But the second thing which I bloody should have noticed is the address.'

'What about it?'

'It's only when she read it out I knew. 146B Manor Road in Thornton Heath is one of Liz Knight's rental properties. I've been there. It's upstairs from Horvat's flat. Oliver Knight showed me around it.'

'That's a coincidence, though, isn't it?'

'No,' said Craig. 'That is no coincidence.'

Chapter Thirty-Two

It took an intervention by the chief constable with her opposite number in Caen to get permission for Craig Gillard to be allowed to view the body found in the boot of the Peugeot. It was already Thursday, and he didn't want to wait until the following week in case the French decided to give up waiting for the Syrian embassy and cremate the poor man. He booked a last-minute flight late on Friday morning, hired a car and drove straight to the main police station in Caen to meet the duty liaison officer.

A female uniformed officer in her 40s wearing the tightest skirt he'd ever seen was waiting for him. She repeated her enormously long hyphenated name for him three times, but all he caught was her first name: Liliane. After some pro forma security checks, she drove him to a secure car pound nearby where the Peugeot 407 was parked, along with dozens of other seized vehicles.

'It is good you came today. On Monday it will be gone,' she said, handing him the keys.

Craig looked across at her. 'Why?'

'The case is closed.' She handed him a document. 'A charity in Greece managed to trace Mrs ben Alighassir, the man's wife, who lives in a hostel in Berlin. She came over yesterday and identified the body.'

'How? It's a skeleton!'

'What is the problem? It's all in here,' she said, waving the document. 'She got separated from her husband when a refugee boat capsized, and now she has found him. So no case.'

'No DNA test?'

'Why spend 400 euros of taxpayer money to confirm what we already know?'

Gillard looked heavenward. 'But I have traced the owner of the car in the UK, as I mentioned on the phone.'

'The deadline for claiming the vehicle back is past.' She looked at him blankly.

'Well, let's see.' Craig donned a pair of latex gloves and walked round the vehicle. It was a 2009 model, in poor condition, with two hub caps missing. The windscreen was still choked with dead leaves and twigs that had presumably fallen on it over the year it was parked at La Porcherie. They were indeed horse chestnuts. The battery was flat, so the automatic unlocks didn't work. Craig used the key to open the driver-side door. It was tidy. There was nothing in the side pockets or the glove compartment. The back seat area offered no insights either. Finally he opened the boot which, appropriately enough, smelled as if someone had died in there.

'I presume forensics have been all through this?' Craig asked.

Liliane drew deeply on the cigarette that Gillard hadn't notice her light. 'I have no idea.' The smoke curled slowly from each nostril. Craig decided that she wasn't anywhere near as attractive as he first thought. He said a perfunctory goodbye to Liliane, realizing that he had better get a move on to visit another corpse.

The Caen mortuary was a newly constructed and anonymous building on an industrial estate, wedged between a manufacturer of garden furniture and a tractor dealership. Gillard's was the only car in its car park, and the office door appeared to be locked, the blind half lowered. Well, it was France, and it was 2.45 p.m. on a Friday. Gillard, who had let the mortuary manager know he was coming, stood impatiently for 15 minutes before a white Toyota van drove into the car park. A dark-haired young man, perhaps 25, in jeans, sunglasses and Guns N' Roses T-shirt emerged and waved a hand in which he held a burger, its paper shiny with grease. A piece of onion sat on the edge of his chin, contemplating further descent.

'I'm Christophe,' he said, his mouth half full, offering a large meaty paw.

Gillard shook it and introduced himself. 'Are you the manager?'

'No, just a technician,' he said, as he consumed the last half in a single anaconda bite, balled the paper and tossed it into the badly managed flower borders. He slid his fingers down his jeans, from the look of them his habitual degreasing routine. 'Who is it you want to meet?' He made it sound like a visit to some home for the elderly. Gillard read out the case number he had been given.

'Ah, him.' Christophe unlocked the door, powered up his PC and fiddled about with various other items at the desk. He leaned over his chair, bashed various numbers into the keyboard with clumsy but practised fingers, and called up a record. Gillard could make out many lines of writing in the reflection on Christophe's glasses.

'Has an autopsy been requested?' Gillard said.

Christophe shook his head. 'The only reason he's not been cremated yet is because the coroner hasn't yet countersigned the identity confirmation signed by his wife.'

'What do you have down as the cause of death?'

Christophe scanned the screen. 'NNS.'

'What's that mean?'

'Natural, non-specific. The text says that because of the decomposition it wasn't possible—'

'Okay, I get it,' Gillard said. He knew a 'get out of jail free' when he saw one. 'Can I see him?'

Christophe nodded, and rummaged in his desk before finally discovering the keys to the door behind him. He led Gillard into a bare corridor which had various metal doors going off to either side. Industrial-sized cartons of what could have been bleach or disinfectant were stacked along one wall, and their taint added an edge to the cool air. At the end Christophe unlocked a hospital-style set of double doors. The room beyond was large, the same size as an exhaust-fitting centre, but bare of everything but a series of giant filing cabinets against one wall. The disinfectant tang did not completely hide the odour of death and decomposition, something that Gillard thought he would never get used to. Christophe grabbed a gurney which lay next to a wall and rode it across the room like a kid riding shotgun on a supermarket trolley. Just before it crashed into the cabinets he jumped off and trod on the footbrake. He then manoeuvred the gurney against a cabinet door, pulled the door open, and slid out a surprisingly diminutive body bag.

'*Voilà*. Mohammed ben Alighassir. Do you really want me to open it?'

'Yes, please.' The bag was inflated with gases, so he knew this wasn't going to be pleasant. Christophe went and fetched two plastic aprons, face masks and plastic gloves.

Even with all that, Gillard was unprepared for the stench that gusted from the bag when he opened it just a few inches. The corpse was curled up on its side like a huge foetus, still dressed in what had once been a loose long shirt and dark trousers. The body was mostly skeletal, but waxy strips of dried flesh still clung to one side of the ribcage to the clothing, and the underneath of the skull. Rust-brown skin, delicate as parchment, scrolled around stick-thin limbs.

'The body must have been tightly sealed against the air in the boot, so the anaerobic digesters in the gut just got to work. Good job we didn't find him after three months. He'd just have been a big bag of goop,' Christophe said.

'Definitely male?' Gillard asked

'Sure,' Christophe shrugged.

In places the body appeared to be glued by the remaining flesh to a section of a plasticized canvas, in which were dried, porridge-like lumps. 'What's that?' Gillard asked.

'He was found in a builder's bag, and had to be cut out of it to get him in the body bag. Whoever had found him had dumped him in the bag with a box load of absorbent pellets, probably cat litter, to minimize the smell. In fact, a lot of the pellets just absorbed him.'

'May I take a few samples?' Gillard said.

'Sure, help yourself,' said Christophe. He handed him a pair of plastic tweezers and some sample vials. Gingerly Gillard looked at the leathery remains in the bag and picked out four flesh fragments, each of which he sealed in separate screw-top vials. Once sealed, he put them in a plastic evidence bag, and then doubled sealed it in another.

'What do you want all these for?' asked Christophe.

'Just testing a little theory.'

'Well, take all you want. The cremation is down for next week.'

On the flight on the way home, Gillard's thoughts circled like a stacked airliner, whining and turning without ever seeming to get closer to the firm ground of certainty. Pamela Jones was utterly convincing as the framed innocent. Her DNA appeared nowhere in any aspect of the Knight case. Yet it was her picture on a passport applied for in her name. Who could have got those pictures without her knowledge? Nobody. A fellow tenant or the landlord could have got most of the details – copies of utility bills and so forth. The Slovenian child abuser, Horvat, had some opportunity. So could Martin, Oliver or Liz Knight. As landlords they might have required utility bills. Could Martin really have prepared a false passport for his accomplice? It was a lot of trouble to go to, and probably unnecessary. After all, if his accomplice, the tattooed girl, wasn't known in his usual circle of friends, she could have travelled on her own passport.

Ignoring the 'fasten seatbelts' sign, Gillard made his apologies, extracted himself from his window seat and clambered out to the aisle. He pulled down the heavy briefcase from the overhead locker and squeezed back into his slot. Among the documents he noticed a pro forma letter from Oliver Knight's employer, Barker Caynes Tipping in response to the inquiry from the PCSOs. It merely recorded the dates of Mrs Jones's tenancy, enclosed a copy of the receipt for return of deposit and was p.p.'ed with just the merest peremptory dash of ballpoint.

Gillard's brows furrowed as he looked at the date of the end of the tenancy. Strange. It was three months before the date of the passport application, and a year and a half before the registration of the purchase of the Peugeot. If Mrs Jones had left as stated, it was simply not possible for her to have dealt with the paperwork for the passport or car.

As soon as he arrived at Gatwick he rang Oliver Knight, who was quite grumpy about being rung at a quarter to nine in the evening. Gillard asked him about Pamela Jones. Could there be some error in the tenancy record?

Oliver Knight blew a sigh. 'I really don't have that type of information here. I can get Wendy at the office to look it up. I hardly remember the woman at all, except that she was late with the rent on a few occasions. In the end I think that's why Mum gave her notice.' Everything in his manner proclaimed how beneath him such queries were.

'It seems she left in November 2014,' Gillard continued. 'But then she applied for a passport in February 2015, and a vehicle was registered to the address in May 2016.'

'Well, quite possibly. How can I help?'

'Mr Knight, she wouldn't have been there to receive the documents. Someone else seemed to have rifled through her correspondence and papers sufficiently to get all the documents for a passport application. Including photographs.'

'I'm sorry, officer, but to me that stretches the limits of credulity.' Oliver Knight had returned to his habitual officious tone.

'What documents do you require for a tenancy?'

'My mother simply required proof of earnings, a personal reference, and two proofs of ID—'

'And a passport?'

'Not necessarily. Some of her tenants didn't have passports. We were happy to take a driving licence or an electoral register entry, plus a utility bill or bank statement less than three months old. Look, couldn't this wait until office hours, it would be much easier to check?'

'Did you sign the back of Mrs Jones's passport photographs to verify it was her?'

'I really don't recall.' There was a great rumbling harrumph. 'Detective Chief Inspector, I hope it won't have entirely escaped your notice that in the last 18 months my mother has been murdered and cut to pieces, my father has disappeared, and we've been swindled out of a multimillion-pound family fortune. My sister tried to cut her wrists last week, and is being treated for depression. So I hope you'll forgive me forgetting whether or not I signed a tiny photograph for an old tenant a couple of years ago. Goodnight.' The line went dead.

The next morning Gillard decided to approach the problem from the other direction. He rang Pamela Jones to ask her opinion of her landlords, the Knight family, and more particularly Liz Knight. She was more than happy to give her impressions. 'She was all right face to face,' Jones said. 'But behind me back she was a bitch. She chucked me out just before Christmas!'

'But you were apparently behind with the rent,' Gillard said.

'No! I never was. I never owed a penny, not in any place I ever rented. She said she needed to give me notice because a member of her family was moving in, which was allowed under the lease agreement.'

'Can I ask what kind of paperwork you had to supply for the tenancy agreement?'

'Well, it was ridiculous what she asked for. Utility bills and bank statements, okay, but there were loads more documents too. Birth certificate an' all. I had to get photographs done because the solicitors needed them, apparently. But I'd never been asked before, not anywhere.'

Gillard thanked her and hung up. It was beginning to look more and more like Liz and Martin Knight had cooked this bogus passport application up together. But why? He'd just learned something that shocked him to the core. Liz had been capable of lying. She'd told Oliver one reason for evicting Pamela Jones and used another to the woman herself. He just couldn't square it with the Liz he had loved. Gillard's next call was to financial specialist DC Corey-Williams.

'Shireen, I've got a priority job for you. I want you to find me every single document that links a Mrs Pamela Jones to 146B Manor Road in Thornton Heath, south London.'

'So do we have Mrs Jones in the frame?' Shireen asked.

'Not her, but the identity thief. I want every utility bill, every insurance policy, and especially every bank account. We've got one credit card number because it was used to purchase a ticket on Le Shuttle, so you can start with getting a full list of transactions with that.'

'That will take a while.'

'I know, but I'll probably be able to help. I'm going to the address to check any post that's been accumulating there, and on to the landlord's office at Barker Caynes Tipping in Croydon where some of it may have been forwarded.' Seeing another call coming in from Rob Townsend, Gillard said a hurried goodbye and hung up.

'Rob. What's up?'

'I thought you'd like to hear the news, sir.' Townsend sounded almost beside himself with excitement. 'We've found Professor Martin Knight.'

'Go on, don't keep me in suspense.'

'He's dead. The Syrian wasn't a Syrian. It was him. It was Martin Knight.'

Chapter Thirty-Three

Gillard was absolutely staggered. He just couldn't work it out, and he didn't have time. He had been ordered to go back to Mount Browne immediately to brief the Chief Constable. Alison Rigby was waiting for him in her office, surrounded by paperwork. If she was pleased to have discovered where Professor Knight had been hiding from justice, she didn't show it.

'DC Townsend copied me in on the test results, but I'm baffled. Perhaps you would be good enough to summarize where this takes us.' She rested her elbows on the desk holding a pencil between her fingertips.

'The DNA test showed it was Martin Knight in that Peugeot boot, ma'am,' Gillard said. 'It seems he'd been there for up to 18 months.'

'So Professor Knight was dressed as a Syrian refugee, right down to the cheap plastic sandals and worry beads. The passport was for a genuine Syrian man. Why would anyone want to disguise him as an Arab?'

'The only reason I can think of is to minimise the chance a DNA test would be undertaken, to avoid any chance of the French police discovering that for all the time that Professor Knight was seemingly leading us on a wild-goose chase around Paris, he was actually already dead.'

'So who killed him?'

'I don't know. There were no other DNA markers or fingerprints on the car.'

'Jimmy Bartram? It would be nice to take him down a peg or two,' Rigby said. 'He's taken on a bit of the mantle of Knight as tormentor in chief of the British constabulary, if you've seen his latest *Guardian* articles.'

'I have. But unfortunately, ma'am, Jimmy's in the clear. No forensics, and watertight alibis.'

'Horvat?'

'Possibly, but the only time he went abroad was to save his own skin over Girl F.'

'But he would have been able to create a false identity using Mrs Jones's documents, wouldn't he? Seeing as he was living in the same house.'

'Well, partly. But some of the more valuable documents, like her birth certificate for example, were given directly to either Mrs Knight or her son.'

Rigby sighed and took off her reading glasses, giving Gillard the full benefit of the paralysing blue stare. 'Whoever killed Knight presumably wanted us to believe that he was still alive,' Rigby said. 'To sustain as long as possible the idea that it was Knight who killed his wife.'

'That's right, ma'am,' Gillard said. 'Whoever killed Professor Knight presumably did so in Dungeness, shortly after killing and dismembering his wife. They then chucked him in a builder's bag in the boot of the Peugeot. Someone masquerading as Pamela Jones then took the car across to France and dumped it at the holiday home of Kathy Parkinson.'

'Hmm. Kathy Parkinson.' The chief constable's faced adopted a faraway look. 'Was it her we saw using the cash machine in France on CCTV?' she asked. 'Did she lead us on the wild-goose chase?'

'No, ma'am. She was here in the UK at the time. And the woman we're looking for is younger and of a more petite build than Ms Parkinson.'

'But you said it was her holiday home. That's a bit of a coincidence, isn't it?'

'Yes, and it does indicate someone within the Knights' friends or family who would know that Ms Parkinson's holiday home was rarely visited and thus a suitable place to abandon a car. But I think we can be sure a man was involved. Martin Knight would have weighed around 200 pounds. Getting him in the boot of the car wouldn't have been easy.'

'So you're sure that the Pamela Jones in whose name all these documents were isn't the person we saw on CCTV footage?'

'Absolutely sure. The real Pamela Jones is a much bigger build, older and, to be quite frank, not smart enough to have done this.

'So it's not Ms Parkinson or… what is the other one's name?'

'Helen Jennings. No, like Ms Parkinson, Ms Jennings has

multiple colleagues who saw her in the UK on the same days that someone was in France pretending to be Martin Knight.'

'And Natalie Krugman was in the US at that time, wasn't she?'

'Yes, ma'am. Her alibis are rock solid too.'

'It's a curious case,' Rigby said. 'The family inheritance is gone, via Panama. Mr and Mrs Knight are both dead, and we have no credible suspects. You can just imagine what the press is going to say, can't you, Gillard?'

'Yes, ma'am.'

'I've already briefed Christina McCafferty. We'll release only the minimum information about Knight's death, even to the family. They'll know that their father is dead, found in a car boot in France. Nothing more. Make sure your team understand, okay? Keep the family liaison officer away from the latest details. I don't want any leaks.'

Like a bad dream, the grey-stained concrete of Croydon University Hospital seemed to keep reappearing in Gillard's investigation. As he drove his Ford Focus into the packed car park on a damp Thursday morning, he gazed around at the tired-looking buildings. This was where Mrs Jones had worked as a cleaner. Only ten minutes away on foot in Thornton Heath was her former home, the rental flat owned by Liz Knight, and it was 20 minutes to Oliver Knight's office at Barker Caynes Tipping. The mortuary here was also where the smirking corpse of Harry Smith had been examined by Dr David Delahaye, and the marks of strangulation had been found.

Gillard had once again arranged to meet the forensic

consultant to examine some human remains. Those of Liz Knight. And so the nightmare loop continued.

Delahaye was already there with mortuary technician Nick Stevens when Gillard was shown through the rubber-lined double doors into the mortuary. Greetings were exchanged.

'I was fascinated by your hypothesis, Craig,' Delahaye said. 'No one has ever asked me anything like this before.' He went over to a laboratory table on which the mortal remains of Liz Knight were already on display, under a dazzling light, labelled like exhibits from the British museum. There were five teeth, a piece of dental bridgework, two surgical screws and, at the centre, a collection of vertebrae.

'I have to admit that something about the vertebrae had already been bothering me,' Delahaye said, tapping one of them with a plastic scalpel. 'As you recall we were able to extract DNA from the blood in the pubic hairs and hair roots which were trapped in the underwear. But there was a complete lack of confirming DNA in any of the bones or the gristle surrounding them. There were indications of saltwater contamination in the bones, which might have suggested the body had at first been recovered from the sea, or a saltwater rather than freshwater marsh. But if that was so, I would not have expected so much DNA to have survived in the hairs. They too are eventually damaged by salt water. In cases like this I always follow *lex parsimoniae*.'

'What?'

'The simplest plausible explanation, Craig. Also known as Occam's razor. So I assumed this disparity of pathological journey merely told us something about the process of dismemberment, in which the hairs and fabric were perhaps a later and inadvertent contaminant.'

'So what would the less plausible alternative be?'

'That, by design or error, we have two bodies mixed up together.'

'So back to my original idea, David. Given that we have about three litres of Mrs Knight's blood, lots of her flesh, teeth and a metal pin from her leg, could our supposed murder victim still be alive? Could she have faked her own death?'

Delahaye sucked his teeth for a long time. 'Theoretically, and assuming she was forensically very well trained, had plenty of time and access to certain resources,' he said. 'It's not impossible. So long as the vertebrae are not hers.'

'So what other skills and resources would be required to make it possible?'

'Well, I'm not sure. Give me a day or two to think about it and I'll give you a definitive answer.'

Family liaison officer Gabby Underwood was already there when Craig arrived at Oliver Knight's house to break the news of his father's death. Chloe was there too, ghostly pale, and nails bitten to the quick. Before a word was said, they seemed to know. Chloe's reaction was to fold inwardly, knees tucked up, head down, like a damaged doll expecting to be consigned to the toy box. It was quite possible to perceive what this traumatized 20-year-old would look like on her deathbed. Oliver by contrast seemed to have shed age and experience. No longer the smug solicitor, but a confused puppyish schoolboy in an ill-fitting suit, unpolished black shoes, a red rash of some kind now visible at the hairline, a knee jostling to some unheard rhythm.

'This is all impossible,' Oliver said. 'Stuffed in a car boot, in France. Where in France?'

'In a rural part of Normandy,' Craig said.

'And you don't know how he died?'

'The cause of death could not be determined after so long.'

Gabby's sympathetic smile stretched across her face, a mask against infectious grief. She slid away silently, as if on castors, to make the umpteenth cup of coffee that morning. She had earlier warned Craig that Chloe had now dropped out of university and was receiving counselling after a suicide attempt. And that was before the latest news.

'So could he have killed himself?' Oliver asked. 'Was anything found with him? Like a note.'

'Nothing was found.' Gillard paused, feeling unequal to the task of concealing the full circumstances of their father's death. 'I'm really sorry we cannot provide answers. However, the coroner is likely to order a full post-mortem, as the French procedure was rather inconclusive. So I'm afraid the body of your father is unlikely to be released for a funeral for quite some time.'

Oliver nodded. Chloe said nothing, her head slumped on her chest. Craig and Gabby exchanged glances. There was nothing more to be done, but Gabby had already indicated she would keep up regular contact with Chloe, whose vulnerability was now palpable. The inevitable social work of policing once again taking as much time as preventing and detecting crime.

The discovery of Martin Knight's body reignited press interest in what was now assumed to be a double murder. Chief Constable Alison Rigby was happy to have the previous large investigative team restored. The only detective held back from the original team was Detective Inspector Claire Mulholland, the apple of Rigby's eye, who was working with Radar Dobbs, tying up the last loose ends of the Girl F case.

For Gillard, his first full investigative team meeting was going to be important.

On the day of the meeting, a delightfully bright April Monday, he'd got up at five, cycled 20 miles, showered and headed off to the Caterham incident room for seven, where he sat down with a fruit yoghurt and a banana to take a last look at the evidence he was going to put before his team.

For Gillard, a hunch about the case had been growing inside him since talking to Delahaye. A series of emails late last night from Shireen Corey-Williams had turned that hunch into something more certain. The emails included statements for two credit cards in the name of Mrs Pamela Jones. One card they had known about for a year; it had been used to buy the Peugeot in which Martin Knight was found dead in France, and to buy the Le Shuttle ticket which had taken Mrs Jones and her car to France. The second, whose existence Shireen had only just uncovered, was used to buy a series of one-night stays in hotel rooms around Paris at the same time that Martin Knight had been making his cash withdrawals there. It was also used in a tanning salon in Chartres, and in Neuilly at a woman's hairdresser's, just half an hour before the woman with the knight tattoo went to the cashpoint. Finally, that second card had been used to buy a one-way business class air ticket from Paris to Bogotá, via Madrid.

Madrid.

Gillard checked the date, but his gut already knew. The flight left Madrid an hour after Gillard had been at the airport with Kincaid. When he had been transfixed by the woman in the duty-free shopping area, who looked so much like Liz. Kincaid, who also saw her, had persuaded him that it wasn't really her, could *not* be her. All the evidence backed Kincaid's view, but the image had just kept coming back. Now Craig knew he hadn't been imagining things. She really was alive. And she had gone to Colombia. Since the date of that flight, neither credit card had not been used at all. In all probability Liz Knight, newly enriched by her murdered husband's inheritance, had discarded the identity of Pamela Jones and found another.

She had fooled them all. Brilliantly.

Craig Gillard walked into the Caterham incident room and smiled at the team gathered there. DCs Shireen Corey-Williams, Michelle Tsu, Rob Townsend, Carl Hoskins and Colin Hodges had been told to expect a momentous announcement about the case, and following the news of the discovery of Professor Knight's body, they assumed it would be mainly about that. They were wrong. Claire Mulholland, sitting in, was the only officer whom Craig had already briefed.

'Glad to see you are all here on time,' Gillard said. 'The news I've got may be quite surprising to many of you, especially as inevitably we get used to certain ways of thinking. Now we have to go right back to the beginning.'

'Someone killed them both, that's what I've always thought,' Hodges said triumphantly, then turned to Hoskins. 'It was Jimmy Bartram, I told you weeks ago. You'll owe me a tenner.'

'Sorry, Colin, if that's what you thought you're going to be down by a tenner,' Gillard said. 'It's something much more fundamental. Everybody, this began as the investigation of a murder, of Mrs Elizabeth Knight, by her husband Martin.' He paused for effect. 'It is now the investigation of the murder of Professor Martin Knight by his wife Elizabeth. And I believe she is still alive, living abroad, probably in Colombia, with the proceeds of her husband's inheritance.'

There was a stunned silence for a moment. 'How can that be?' asked Michelle Tsu. 'We've got all the DNA confirmed on her body parts.'

Gillard smiled. 'Yes, that fooled us all for a long time. But there is nothing we have that she can't live without.'

'The vertebrae, surely,' said Shireen.

'And a lot of blood,' said Hodges.

'First off, those bones are almost certainly not hers. I don't know how she got hold of them, but it's not impossible for someone who had been helping in a makeshift mortuary in the Aegean.' He relayed what Delahaye had told him about the incompatible levels of salt-induced deterioration between the hair and the bones. 'The next question is the huge amount of blood. We know that Liz Knight had done some time with St John Ambulance, and we found a phlebotomy certificate from 2002 in her office.'

'Phlebwot?' asked Hoskins.

'She had trained to be able to take blood samples. As Delahaye described it, it would be quite possible for someone to gradually extract, store and freeze several litres of their own blood over the course of a week or two. Once thawed, you could easily give the impression of a massive fatal bleed.'

'But CSI found some of her teeth, and the pin from her leg in the holiday cottage waste pipe. How did that work?' Hodges asked.

Gillard shrugged. 'We don't know for sure. But it's quite possible to travel abroad for dental work, say implants, and to request to keep the teeth that are removed. I checked with her British dentist yesterday, and it seemed Liz Knight was a year or more overdue for an appointment at the time of her death. This was uncharacteristic, as she had needed quite a lot of treatment over the years since her road accident, and may indicate that she was getting treatment elsewhere. The leg pin likewise could have been replaced after surgery abroad. This is something we are actively investigating.'

'What did Delahaye say about the pipe full of human fat at the cottage?' Michelle Tsu asked.

'He couldn't be sure, but you can use oxygen bleach, commercial stain-remover products like Vanish, to remove DNA from organic material, rinse it with lots of water to get rid of all the bleach and then flush through some blood, which would adhere to the fat and flesh with a new DNA marker. The effect would be to substitute her DNA for whatever was there before, making it seem to be her flesh. It may previously have been chicken, pork or even fish.'

There were some very sceptical looks from around the room.

'I can see what you are thinking: that this is a long shot. But remember, we are dealing with an extremely intelligent and resourceful woman. She has had plenty of time to plan this like the expert chess player she was, or should I say, is. And if you accept this thesis then everything else that we struggled over for many months falls neatly into place. For example, it was Liz Knight who used a laptop purchased by her on her husband's credit card to research body disposal, knowing we were likely to uncover that search history. Martin Knight probably never knew the laptop existed. The property scam in Spain, in which she appeared to be the victim, was in fact only really possible with her connivance, and it enabled her to cut her husband out of his own inheritance.'

'We kept coming to that point, but dismissing it because she was dead,' said Shireen.

'Exactly. Being dead is incredibly convenient, because it makes her invisible. Yet she was able to recreate an electronic life for her dead husband through cash withdrawals and so on.'

'What about the card from France?' Michelle Tsu asked. 'It was in his handwriting. I had it checked by experts as well as the Knight kids. Ninety-nine per cent certainty it was his, they said.'

'I don't know. Maybe she forced him to write it before she killed him.'

Tsu snorted in disbelief.

'So how did she actually kill him?' said Hodges, arms folded in scepticism. 'And how did she get a big bloke like that into the car. She's only a little thing, ain't she?'

'Five-three,' said Hoskins. 'Walks with a stick. She must have had help.'

'Bartram, like I said,' Hodges muttered, through the side of his mouth towards Hoskins. 'For a half share in the lolly.'

'These are all good questions, and the answer is: I don't know,' Gillard said. 'She might have been able to drug him and take him abroad before killing him there. But what I can tell you is that Liz Knight was the only one in a perfect position to create a new identity around Pamela Jones. The real Mrs Jones is a woman who had barely travelled abroad, yet now apparently with passport, driving licence, insurance, two credit cards, bank account, you name it – all applied for well after she ceased to live at the address that Liz Knight owned. I have to hand it to her, it's a flawless way to become another person.'

'But Liz Knight can't still be using Pam Jones's ID can she?' Shireen said. 'Now we've got her bank details. None of the accounts we found have been used for over a year.'

'No. She may have something set up in Colombia, if that was her final destination. Anyone looking at a map would know Colombia is the next-door country to Panama, where the inheritance money went. With the kind of money she has access to, and fluent Spanish of course, I don't think a new identity is going to be a problem. I'm pretty sure she's living comfortably somewhere in the Spanish-speaking world.'

'So was she the tattooed woman we saw in high heels in the bank CCTV?' asked Michelle Tsu.

'I believe so,' Gillard said. 'Which if so means she was previously faking the need for a walking stick.'

'Aw, come on,' said Hodges. 'I spent hours looking at the CCTV. That was a tasty-looking piece with a slim figure and lovely legs. Nothing like the worn-out middle-aged woman with a double chin. With or without a walking stick, it can't be the same person.'

'Never underestimate what high heels do to a woman's legs,' said Michelle Tsu, who when off duty had a penchant for stilettos.

'And a crash diet, probably,' added Gillard. 'It was cleverly done, no doubt about it. I believe she may have taken some drugs that made her put on weight in the months prior to the murder, so she looked different for the pictures we put out to the press. Both the Knight children had remarked on the change in her appearance, which they put down to the prescriptions she was on for arthritis. But from the medical records I've seen there actually is no diagnosis to confirm arthritis. It's an ongoing line of inquiry with her GP.'

A buzz of whispers went around the room.

Hodges put his hand up. 'I may just be a dim plod, but if Martin Knight was last known to be alive on the Tuesday evening when you spoke to him, then she either killed him there and somehow got him in the boot of that Peugeot, or she persuaded him to travel with her to France. But the Le Shuttle ticket was only for one person – Mrs Jones, right?'

'Yes.'

'So the professor was already in the boot, either dead or alive.'

'That's a reasonable supposition.'

'And his wife got him to dress up like an Arab before killing him, because as we all know, dressing a corpse is almost impossible,' Hodges added.

Gillard shrugged. 'I know it sounds implausible. But it's the best theory so far.'

'So what's your next step?' Claire Mulholland asked.

'We've got two areas of inquiry. I'm seeing Liz Knight's GP this afternoon, and Michelle, I'd like you to contact the clinic in Brasov, Romania which Pamela Jones's credit card records she visited during her so-called skiing trip in April 2016. I think we'll find that she didn't spend much time on the slopes.'

'But she's got away with it, hasn't she?' Claire asked. 'In South America, untraceable and loaded.'

Gillard nodded. 'But she'll make a mistake. Everyone does. And then we'll get her.' Though heads nodded around the room, he himself was far less sure.

It was almost 7 p.m. and the surgery was closed for the evening when a tired-looking and apologetic Dr Ranveer Jethani was able to see Gillard. They had met once before, briefly, and the detective briefed him on their line of inquiry.

'What I need you to do is to check whether anything prescribed here could have been used to change Elizabeth Knight's appearance in the months before her disappearance. From what her family said she gained a great deal of weight, especially around the face and neck, ankles and so on. She'd also begun to walk with a stick.'

'Really? Well, looking at her records, she hadn't actually visited the surgery since late 2015.' The doctor pulled up the screen and read down through the notes. 'Yes, we have various prescriptions related to her road accident in 2007, and some regular antidepressants.' He looked across at Gillard quizzically.

'We know about that,' Gillard said. 'Was there anything for arthritis? She'd told her family that she had been diagnosed with it.'

'That's actually not true, as I told you on the phone. She had tested negative on the blood tests so far, though that's not conclusive, as arthritis is a complex set of conditions. No, the only thing that could conceivably have caused any weight gain is Prednisol, which was prescribed for IBS in November 2015.'

'IBS?'

'Irritable bowel syndrome. Prednisol is the standard treatment, because it is a corticosteroid. But it is most unlikely the dosage she was on would have caused the symptoms you describe.'

'What could have happened at higher dosage?'

'Well, let me see.' He took a textbook from his shelf and leafed through. 'Yes. It can produce a "moon face" type swelling, weight gain and redistribution of fat deposits, including to the back of the neck, which is particularly ageing to look at.'

Gillard opened his laptop and selected a video on the desktop to show the doctor. 'This is Mrs Knight at the time

401

of her birthday party in August 2016. Would you say she was exhibiting the side effects you described?' He clicked play.

The doctor nodded his head. 'That certainly looks right. But with such a low dose—'

'I suspect she got more of the drug from another source. Mrs Knight travelled to Romania in April of 2016, where, as I understand it, prescription medicines can be bought over the counter.'

'That's entirely possible, then,' the doctor said. 'And the side effects are entirely reversible when the patient ceases to take the medicine. So it would have been ideal for her.'

Gillard checked his phone on leaving the surgery, and saw he'd missed a call from Michelle Tsu.

He rang her number, and when she picked up asked her how she'd got on with the clinic.

'They wouldn't say a thing until I got the Romanian police liaison officer to call them from Bucharest. Eventually they rang me back and confirmed that they did have a patient called Pamela Jones in April 2016, and that she had an operation on her leg in which several pins and screws were replaced. They weren't able to tell me if Mrs Jones kept the old pins.'

'That's great news. If they have email or phone contact details for Pamela Jones we want them.'

'Okay, I'll get them.'

As soon as he hung up, a call came in from Gabby Underwood.

'Bad news, sir. Chloe Knight is in intensive care in Redhill. She's taken an overdose.'

'Oh, Christ. Poor thing. How is she?'

'Not good. She's unconscious and has kidney problems. I don't think they know what she took.'

'Thanks for letting me know,' Gillard said, and hung up. For some reason he felt guilty, as if the problems of the Knight family were of his making. It was an unseasonably warm evening and he drove straight to the leisure centre, did his usual couple of kilometres in the pool. After his shower, he decided to take a half-hour in the steam room. It was entirely deserted, and as the scalding heat flushed sweat from every pore it suddenly occurred to him that Chloe might through her own grief and misery make it possible to bring this case to a close. Liz had been very close to her daughter, and if there was one thing that might entice her back to the UK, however briefly, it was the knowledge that her daughter might die without ever seeing her again. A plan gradually began to form in his head. It would need permission from the Chief Constable, but it might just work.

Next day

'You must tell the Knights' children,' Rigby said, when Gillard went to see her the next morning. 'If you have evidence that Mrs Knight is alive, you cannot justify withholding that from the family.'

'Ma'am, with respect,' Gillard responded. 'They've only just got used to the idea their father is dead. And we don't yet have any material evidence that she's alive; it's just that everything makes more sense if she is. Besides, if we tell them that we're assuming this as a faked death, there is a good chance that Mrs Knight will get to hear about it.'

'How?'

'Well, I wouldn't be surprised if Kathy Parkinson or Helen Jennings were in contact with Liz. She would need her eyes and ears in Britain, and someone's bound to be keeping her up to date on the state of play of the investigation. We'd frighten her off returning.'

Rigby gave him the blue stare of death, glasses off, for a good half-minute. 'All right, I see your point. We'll assume the faked death is just one line of investigation.' Rigby stuck her glasses back on and returned to her paperwork. Gillard assumed the meeting was over and began to leave.

'Gillard?'

'Yes, ma'am.'

'Let's hope Chloe Knight pulls through. This case is tragic enough as it is.'

Gillard tried to put himself in Liz Knight's shoes. She'd eased herself out of a loveless marriage, kept a multimillion pound inheritance and disappeared into a country where she spoke the language, and where almost anything can be bought. Anything, that is, except the love of her children and the comforts of the settled life, friends and career she'd left behind. Liz Knight was a very self-contained individual, but Chloe's illness would be a powerful draw. He was certain she would come back.

Gillard had already alerted the UK Border Agency about Pamela Jones's false passport. He also asked the British consulate in Bogota to forward a list of every Colombian female applying for a visa to the UK, with a copy of all identity documents. That produced a much longer list than he expected. Tweedledum and Tweedledee did the donkey work, sifting through it, and found nothing. Of course there was no guarantee that Liz would already have a Colombian passport. There were all sorts of other possibilities.

Days passed, and there was no news. Chloe regained consciousness, was sitting up in bed and was transferred to a hospital at Caterham Dene, much closer to home. Gillard had Gabby Underwood pop in from time to time. He had taken the risk of briefing her on his theory that Liz was alive, and asked her to watch out for any signs that Chloe had been contacted.

'Such as?' Gabby asked.

'Well, changes in mood for a start.'

'I haven't noticed anything.'

Gillard hung up. He had to consider the possibility that Liz Knight hadn't made contact, didn't intend to come, and was actually a little bit more cold-blooded than he had assumed.

It was ten o'clock that evening when Gillard was called at home. 'Hi, it's me.'

He recognized Sam's voice. 'Hello, stranger.' They exchanged small talk for a few minutes, then Craig said: 'I've still got your Thai curry in the fridge.'

'I hope that's not true.' She sighed. 'Look, you weren't honest with me, so—'

'I was. Nothing happened. I told you. We went to two plays, that's all.'

'Well, she felt she could answer your phone and demand to know who I was. That, to me, is an established girlfriend exercising her property rights.'

'Or an arrogant bitch trying it on,' Gillard replied. 'So what did you tell her?'

'I said I was a friend. I still regard myself as one, despite everything. Anyway, that's not why I rang,' she said. 'I was asked to help Gabby Underwood babysit Chloe Knight when she was recovering from her overdose. I looked up her profile on Facebook, because it might give some clues about her state of mind which I could tell Gabby, but of course it was private. So I made a friend request, in my personal windsurfing instructor profile, and a couple of days later, when Chloe was well enough to get back on social media, she accepted.'

'You're not supposed to do that.'

'I know. And you're not supposed to date witnesses. Anyway, one of Chloe's new friends is from Colombia, one Allessandra de Cortijo. Cat picture only, unfortunately. I was able to see she is already a friend of both Kathy Parkinson and Helen Jennings. I didn't dare make a friend request to either of them, as they don't seem to share much publicly.'

'So you've been doing a little bit of investigating on your own, Sam. Without telling me.'

'Craig, to be honest it didn't start out as investigating. I was trying to help Gabby get an early warning of Chloe's state of mind. But then I spoke to Shireen, who told me about the

Colombian connection and that you now think Liz Knight may be alive.'

Gillard paused. 'Sam, what you've done is a brilliant, if illicit, piece of investigative work. I'd wager that Chloe and this woman Alessandra have been exchanging private Facebook messages.'

'I'd lay money on it. And they may be planning to meet very soon.'

'What makes you say that?'

'Chloe has just posted about going to spend the Easter weekend in Portugal.'

'What, this weekend?'

'Yep. Flying out on tomorrow morning to Faro. To stay at Helen Jennings's place in Albufeira.'

Craig gasped. That coven of Liz's cronies all seemed to be in on it. And he'd only 12 hours to organize a way to catch her. Good Friday, a nightmare day for any security operation at a busy airport.

Gillard got hold of Rob Townsend at home, and the two of them worked the phones all night to get everything in place. Rob's checked with all airlines serving Faro, and found a booking for Ms Allessandra de Cortijo from Bogota via Madrid. After changing planes from Avianca to TAP, she would arrive in Faro on Friday morning at eleven. Craig rang Rigby's home number, and with her backing arranged police liaison teams in both Faro and in Madrid, and a Europol warrant in the Colombian name, as well as updating the existing one for Elizabeth

Knight. He woke up DC Shireen Cory-Williams to go to Faro immediately and then follow Chloe herself when she arrived from London. The most protracted effort during the small hours was getting the warrant to Facebook's London security team to allow them to break into the private online messages shared between Chloe and her Colombian friend Allessandra. Craig had waited as long as he dared for the content of those messages to be released, but in the end had to give up and catch the 7.15 train to Gatwick.

As he arrived at South Terminal he saw his flight was delayed 90 minutes, putting his own arrival in Madrid half an hour behind the Colombian flight. However, just before boarding he rang his old Spanish police colleague Sargento Primo Irujo, who was already in place at Madrid airport. Irujo told him local security officials were ready to pick up the woman at the arrival gate.

On arrival in Madrid, Gillard rang Irujo the moment the aircraft engines were turned off. The Spanish officer was slow to answer, and when he did he said the Avianca jet was already disembarking. There was no one on board answering to the name Alessandra de Cortijo.

'Search for her. Check all documents. She must be there,' Gillard yelled.

'No. The seat booked in Ms de Cortijo's name was unoccupied, although given that the flight wasn't full, she could have sat in a number of seats.' There was a lot of noise in the background, passengers protesting in Spanish, presumably about the delay, and continuous public announcements.

'Keep them there until I arrive!' Gillard said. His jet was stuck at a remote stand, waiting for steps and a bus to take them to the terminal.

'It's all right, I'm on the air bridge now, and the security staff are requiring each passenger to show their passport as they leave the aircraft. So far there is no Allessandra de Cortijo and no Elizabeth Knight. But Craig, it would have helped if we had a reliable image of the woman.'

'Yes, I know, but she's changed her appearance. And I thought I'd be there to check. So are most passengers off the jet?'

'Yes.'

'And the onboard toilets searched?'

'Of course.'

'Damn!' Craig was perhaps the only person in Spain who would recognize Liz Knight in any guise, but he was currently trapped in a window seat, blocked in by ungainly passengers removing luggage from overhead lockers. The doors had yet to open. 'Primo, hold the flight to Faro. Her booking for that leg is also in the de Cortijo name – if she tries to board it, she'll be caught.'

Even as he said it, Craig realized that Liz would never do anything that stupid. She always seemed to be a step ahead. Then suddenly he realized. 'One thing, Primo: you did also check the other identity Rob gave you, didn't you?'

'What other identity?'

'Mrs Pamela Jones.'

'I know nothing of this Jones. Hold on.' There was a volley of Spanish, back and forth. 'There was no Jones booked on the flight, Craig.'

'Of course not. She's got another fucking passport. Didn't Rob tell you?' The call was suddenly cut off, and Craig yelled in frustration. 'Damn the bitch to hell.' He just hoped that Rob had spoken to passport control and that they at least would be looking for her under all three possible passport names.

It was 15 minutes before Gillard managed to get into the arrivals hall, to be met by an exasperated Sargento Irujo and two enormous security men in sunglasses and with the usual symbol of authority: trousers tucked into their boots.

'Any luck?' Craig asked, but could already see from their faces that there wasn't. He was ushered through a security door into a car which took them from Terminal One to Terminal Four, where the Avianca jet stood connected to an air bridge.

'We have confirmation from Bogota that a woman boarded under the name and passport Alessandra de Cortijo, and we now have a picture from that passport,' Irujo muttered, as they left the car and climbed the security stairs into the busy terminal. His demeanour clearly showed he was offended from Craig's earlier shouting at him. 'Here. Is that her?' He showed Craig his smartphone, on which was a faint image showing a blonde with big hair, heavy pink eye make-up and blue eyes.

'Maybe,' Craig responded. 'With coloured contact lenses.' There was a vague resemblance to Liz in the shape of the face, but it was a pretty good disguise. 'What about her checked-in luggage? Did you stop that being checked through to Faro?'

'Yes.' Irujo spoke to one of the security men, who lumbered off to an office near to the baggage claims. Five minutes later, he returned with a modest-sized turquoise wheeled suitcase. Irujo nodded, and the guard levered it open with a screwdriver. Craig knelt to look through. It was packed with women's clothing, plus two wigs: one blonde, one mid-brown. And there was a diary.

'This could be vital, once we've got her.' He scanned the crowded hall but couldn't see Liz anywhere. His gaze lifted again to the balcony, a walkway above them which was part of the transit area, and gave a view over all the carousels. He had a feeling he was being watched.

'I'm sure she's here somewhere,' he said.

'Well, if so we need something to give the CCTV people,' Irujo said. 'Some image of her apart from this.' He waved his smartphone. 'They can find her wherever she is in the airport.'

'Okay.' Craig brandished his smartphone and showed them three pictures: Liz as she was at her 48th birthday party, tired and double-chinned, plus an earlier picture of her with a hat and ice cream at the beach, which was the only one that Oliver Knight had been able to lay hands on at short notice. Finally there was the passport picture of Pamela Jones.

'*Mierda!* It's not the same woman.'

'I told you the pictures wouldn't help as much as you think,' Craig said. 'But I'll email them wherever you need them.' As he was taking down the details, Irujo took a call on his radio.

'They've held a Mrs P. Jones at passport control!' Irujo looked triumphant. 'Upstairs.' He started to move off towards the escalator.

'Hold your horses. What's the forename? And does the passport number match?'

Irujo spent the next two minutes in a heated conversation by radio, before turning back to Craig. 'It's Paula V. Jones. Travelling in a party of six. The number doesn't match.'

Gillard sighed. 'It's almost certainly not her, but detain her.' He finalized the email and hit send, transmitting the pictures to the CCTV control room and the other security officials.

No sooner had Irujo signed off than his radio again crackled into life again. After listening for a moment he said: 'A Mrs S. P. Jones has been held from an easyJet flight. Terminal One.'

'I can't see how she would have been able to get there. She'd have to have gone via passport control,' Gillard said.

'Craig, tell me: do they hold her or not?'

'Yes. For now.'

The next call for Irujo came on his smartphone. He answered and listened carefully, before turning to Gillard. 'A Mrs P. W. Jones has just paid cash for a ticket at the TAP counter in the transit lounge. *Joder!* Are they breeding these Joneses?'

'It's a very common British name. And it's Easter, this place is heaving with Brits,' he said. 'Where's this one going to?'

'Lisbon. Quarter past eleven.'

'That could be it.' From Lisbon, with a rental car, Liz could be in Albufeira in a couple of hours. 'Which gate?' Gillard squinted up at the departure screen above his head and answered his own question: Gate 102. 'It says the flight is closed. Can you hold it?'

'Yes. But it's a long way to 102.'

Craig grabbed one of the security guards and they both set off at a run.

Forty minutes later found DCI Craig Gillard leaning over the balcony, breathless, looking down at a seething mass of people crowding the baggage area of the arrivals hall. He had run a good half-mile to Gate 102, and then jogged back. Mrs Jones, whoever she was, had not boarded, and had checked in no luggage. The milling and restive crowd at the gate, wondering why their flight had been called and was then delayed, did not include anyone who looked like Liz Knight. While he was there, photographs of two detained and rather irate Mrs Joneses had been emailed to him from different parts of the airport. Craig had quickly confirmed that neither of them was Liz Knight. Primo Irujo had gone down to the gate for the Faro flight, but had rung Craig to tell him that no one there matched any of the pictures on his smartphone.

Now, still a little out of breath and feeling humiliated, he was waiting for the female booking agent at the TAP counter to come back to him so he could get a description of whoever had booked the last-minute ticket to Lisbon. Liz was running rings around them, once again.

His phone rang.

'Hello, Craig, it's Liz.'

Chapter Thirty-Four

Gillard could feel beads of sweat on his palm where he was holding the phone. His head was swimming, trying to figure out where she could be.

'How did you get my number?'

She laughed. 'I have my sources.'

'It's time to give it up, Liz. You can't escape.' He could hear airport announcements at her end as well as his own. She must be close by.

'That's why I'm calling. But don't try to look for me. I can see you, and if you try to get help, the deal's off. Just listen, come alone, and I'll guide you to me. I've something to say, then I'll give myself up. Agreed?'

'Yes.' Craig couldn't help himself; he looked left and right, but all he could see were crowds of passengers moving along the walkways.

'Turn right along the walkway, keep your eyes to the ground.'

'You can't hide from this for ever, Liz.' Craig walked briskly, and took a last glance down to baggage reclaim, where Primo

Irujo was briefing more security guys. The view was lost as he emerged into the transit lounge proper.

'Go to the VIP lounge,' she said.

Craig saw the lounge, and went in. He explained who he was to the receptionist, and then looked across the crowded room towards the windows. Liz was sitting alone at a small table, reading a magazine, with a glass of wine and an orange juice. Her hair was long, wavy and dark. Not at all like the permed blonde Allessandra de Cortijo. She was wearing a dark blue business suit, a multicoloured silk scarf, and had sunglasses perched on her hair. On seeing him, she waved him over with a smile, as if they were merely two old friends who had run into each other by chance, rather than a harried policeman and a fugitive murderess.

A call came through to Craig from Primo Irujo, but he turned off the phone and slid it into the pocket of his suit. This was now something he could do alone. As he approached, she stood up to greet him. Her eyes were green, not brown.

'I know you're going to arrest me, but you can still give me a peck on the cheek.'

Craig did so, then looked at his watch. 'You've got ten minutes of freedom left.'

Liz made a moue of disappointment. 'But I've so much to say. And you, Craig, looking well and keeping yourself in good shape, I see.'

'Well, you've certainly been busy and active too. And Martin's body. That's an impressive bit of weightlifting…'

She laughed – the same infectious chuckle he had always

loved. 'I've got you an orange juice. I thought you'd be hot after all that running about I made you do.'

Craig hesitated to pick up the glass, and Liz laughed 'It's all right, I'm not going to poison you! I just bought it at the bar. Do you want me to drink some first?' She reached towards it.

'It's all right.' He took a small sip. It tasted fine. 'We eventually figured out how you did it,' Craig said. 'The forensic misdirection, the clever trail that made us think you were Martin in France. And, of course, pirating the identity of Pamela Jones.'

Liz smiled. 'That was the key. I spent months offering the Thornton Heath flat cheaply, and got hundreds of tenants applying. I whittled them down to single or widowed women of roughly my age, no kids. The hardest thing was to find someone who didn't already have a passport, and whose looks I could impersonate.'

'You look a lot different than the real Pamela Jones,' Gillard said.

'I do *now*. And I look very different from the Liz Knight who was "murdered".'

'Absolutely, you are utterly...rejuvenated. That was Prednisol, wasn't it? Obtained in Romania.' He took a big pull on the juice.

'Full marks for research,' she said, approvingly. 'I made sure there were lots of pictures taken at my birthday party, when I was at my worst,' she said. 'I deleted a lot of other recent pictures of me on our family computers that showed me in a better, slimmer form.'

'So whose vertebrae were those in the marsh?'

'Some poor migrant woman from a capsized vessel near Chios who washed up late one evening. She'd obviously been at sea for weeks, and was little more than a skeleton held together by her clothing.'

'Helen had talked about that.'

'That night, I was rostered for mortuary duty with a German woman, Inge. Poor Inge kept dozing off, so I sent her back to her tent and said I would finish the shift alone. That gave me the chance to look into the coffin. I used a pocket knife to separate the spine, which was harder work than I expected, and took 15 minutes. I put the bones into a large plastic food box, packed in salt to destroy the DNA, and hid it amongst my gear. No one checked the body the next day before it was buried. When I got home, I spent weeks marinating the bones in salt water to ensure that no original DNA had survived. I couldn't afford to take any chances.'

'What about the birthday card to Chloe? Did you forge that?'

'No forgery involved! It was a birthday card Martin wrote two years ago when Chloe had just broken up with a boyfriend. I had reminded him to write it because he would still be away in Finland on the day, but he forgot to post it and I discovered it in his luggage on his return. I thought the message fitted very well. "Sorry I can't be with you at this difficult time".'

Craig shook his head at her ingenuity. 'Martin's a hefty fellow. Who helped you carry the body?'

'That part was quite simple. Martin got in the boot himself!' She laughed. 'You see I was waiting for Martin in Great Wickings on the Tuesday night, knowing he would come there. He knew that the only reason I would go off in a huff was because I had discovered him and Natalie Krugman rekindling their affair. That's why he didn't want to report me missing. He knew where I'd be. It's where I'd gone the first time, so it stood to reason.'

Gillard said nothing, just watched her face. She didn't look at him, but gazed around her.

'In chess, you have to anticipate the moves of the other player. Martin was a decent chess player, but he didn't know he was *in* a game. It was easy to predict what he would do, because I was following a path that I had taken before. I had seen what he did then, and knew he would think that it was me who was being predictable. So on the Tuesday night in Dungeness, I knew he'd come in, get himself a Scotch, top up the glass from the tap – leaving fingerprints – then sit down to wait for me. I was hiding in the pantry. I had already added Rohypnol liquid to his Glenmorangie.'

'They don't make it any more. There's a blue taint to stop date rape.'

'Ah, I got some generic Indian-made flunitrazepam at the same pharmacy in Brasov.'

Craig held up his orange juice in mock scrutiny, and she laughed. He found himself laughing too. It gave him a warm feeling.

'You see, Craig, all I had to do was wait. Once you'd exchanged calls with Martin – yes, that was a tricky, unplanned moment for me – he went back to his Glenmorangie, as I knew he would. He expected I would come back and he was ready for a row. By the time I slipped out of the larder he was already under the influence the drug. I told him that I was going to make his fantasies come true. Being so suggestible, thanks to the drug, he was more than happy to slip into some Arabic clothing for a game of "Guantanamo Bay mistress punishment", or whatever I called it. Once dressed, I tied his hands and gagged him, then went to fetch my Peugeot, the one you found at La Porcherie.'

'I suppose you picked up the clothing from some poor refugee?'

'And the documents, worry beads, a cheap Arabic watch. At Chios we were handing out clean dry clothes to new arrivals, and the old stuff was intended to be burned. Lots of refugees threw their ID away, as advised by people smugglers. I had a lot of stuff to choose from.'

'All that blood, Liz. All yours. It must have taken you a while.'

'Two weeks, that's all. I stored it in the freezer. Did you find the stab marks in the carpet?'

'Yes, very clever. What about dumping Martin's car? Who helped you with that?'

Liz smiled. 'No one. I worked entirely alone, and everything I did was carefully planned, some of it more than two years in advance. None of my friends knew I was still alive until two months ago. On the night Martin arrived, my Peugeot was parked on the shingle near an unoccupied holiday home down the road from Great Wickings. Once I had tied Martin up, I left him for two minutes at around eleven while I went to get the Peugeot, and reversed it up to the car port, past his BMW. I'd already put a builder's bag in the boot, and I got him to shuffle out to the car. Once he'd sat on the boot edge, it was quite easy to get him to lean back, then I helped him in, and helped him curl up in the boot. He was quite happy, I can assure you, and almost unconscious. I gave him an injection of ketamine to be on the safe side, another drug easily available from our helpful Romanian pharmacy. That gave me many hours. I then changed into male clothing, loaded the bloodied rug into the boot of his BMW, and drove it to the new housing development, stopping off en route to deposit a package of bones in the marsh.'

'It suppose it had to be from his car in case we got tyre prints,' Gillard conceded.

'Exactly. In the boot was a teenager's BMX bike I bought on eBay. I put on a hoody, big gloves and baseball cap and cycled back to Great Wickings. It was only about eight miles. I make a convincing teenage boy, when I want to.'

'Helen told me you were the understudy for the Artful Dodger in *Oliver* on one occasion.' Gillard shook his head. 'When did you actually kill Martin?'

'Pretty much as soon as I got back from dumping his car. The actual *coup de grâce* was a four-inch needle, which I pressed up under the lobe of his ear into the brain. He was already unconscious and wouldn't have felt a thing. It's also undetectable *post mortem*. The wonders of the Internet, you know – finding out how professional assassins work.'

Craig felt relaxed enough for the big question now. 'Why kill him? You could have just divorced him.'

Liz gave a great sigh and looked out through the window. 'When I first met Martin I thought everything was going to be wonderful. I willingly gave up everything for him.'

Craig's face tightened. He was one of those discarded things.

'It's what you do when you are in love, isn't it? Giving up the bursary... well, I never forgave him for tricking me into that. He was nice at first, but so competitive. He didn't seem to want me to do as well as he did. He hated playing chess with me, even bridge. He was always a very sore loser. Then the accident. I'd told him I would drive, but he thought he was sober enough. He couldn't bear the idea of losing his licence, so it was me who got the criminal conviction, as well as damaging my teeth and breaking my ankle.' She thought for a while. 'The affairs were such a cruelty. The Brazilian girl first, then Krugman. They even had sex in my bed in Great Wickings, did you know?'

'Yes, Krugman told me.'

'I wasn't having it. I warned him, and I warned her. Do you know, she even laughed into my face? I knew this inheritance was coming up, and I predicted Martin would be off as soon as he could get his hands on it. Then when I found out they were seeing each other again—'

'How did you know?'

'I installed a key logger on his PC, so I knew his passwords. I read all his emails.' She said it so matter-of-factly. The jealous wife – a part of Liz he could never have imagined.

'So if you knew his passwords, why didn't you just take the money from his account? Why go to the trouble of this complex fraud?'

'If I had simply taken the cash, even if I had got away with it, then Martin was the victim and I was a thief. My children would hate me. But by faking my own death to hide the theft,

I would bask in their unending love, a legacy burnished by my victimhood. And I would get a new and wealthy life.'

'But even if it worked you would never see them again.'

'I could watch them from afar, just as I already have with Chloe on Facebook. That's a lot better than being an embittered ex-spouse stuck in a flat somewhere while a younger woman takes my family over.'

'So you'd rather destroy your family than lose it?'

She shrugged. 'The kids would recover eventually, but with the murder against his name, Martin is destroyed in life and legacy.'

'But he wasn't a murderer. And you are. And very soon the world will know that.'

She sighed in acknowledgment. 'I actually enjoyed killing him. Do you know that? I felt he deserved it. All that credit he got, the huge write-ups, the accolades, the warrior for justice whose wife was less than a footnote. I had ambitions, I had dreams.'

Craig didn't say anything. He watched her play with her drink, and then look at him again.

'I know I broke your heart, Craig, all those years ago.' The eyes seemed to hold him, radiating intelligence. He suddenly felt a bit woozy, as if he'd had a fast pint or two on an empty stomach.

'You did,' Craig said. 'I loved you so much, Liz. You were everything to me.' Even as he said it, he knew that he shouldn't be so frank with her. It was way past ten minutes now. Time for the arrest.

She nodded, and leaned closer, laying her hand on his. 'You could have me again, Craig, I want you to know. For ever. Help me escape this trap, let me get back to Bogota. I'll wait for you there. I promise you. Kathy has told me all about your loneliness, your obsession, your unhappiness. It doesn't have to be a life of empty yearning. Just think, I can be yours for ever, with all the money we'd ever need.' Her eyes widened as she brought her face close to his and kissed him slowly, deliciously. 'Craig. I promise that if you do this for me, we can start a new life together.'

Craig felt like he was hearing her words from above, as if he was lying at the bottom of a swimming pool. He looked at the empty glass of orange juice and realized. Drugged, despite her protestations. He thought about standing up, but it all seemed a tremendous effort. He could vaguely hear his name being repeatedly called in an airport announcement.

Liz seized both his hands in hers. 'Craig. Trust me, I'll look after you. Don't pay any attention to the PA. You'll be much safer if you sit here and wait for me, won't you?'

Craig felt his head nod. The warmth of the trust he felt in her was very reassuring, and he was so relaxed and happy with the world. He felt 18 again. With his lovely Liz.

'I'm just popping to the loo,' she said, standing up. 'I'll be back in a minute or two. I'll get two more tickets and then we can go back to Colombia together, can't we?'

Craig felt a sense of panic that she would leave him. But also some deeper imperative that he could not let her go. He seized her hand, held it as tightly as he could.

'Let go now, Craig. I'll only be a minute or two.'

At that point she jerked her hand back, tipping a glass over, but failing to break his grip on her wrist which was now a tug of war over the table. She then called out loudly something in Spanish, some urgent call for help and, judging by the emphasis, some insult. She slapped his face hard with the other hand. There were gasps around the room, faces horrified by the unfolding scene. Craig yelled for Liz to sit down, but his words just stalled in his mouth, a sibilant sludge he was unable to mould into words. He was too woozy to stand and his free hand, fishing for his detective ID, couldn't even locate his jacket pocket. Some part of him, deep below the dulled consciousness, remained resolute, determined to hold on. From the glares and shouts of others, it seemed Liz had quickly depicted him as a drunken English holidaymaker, trying his luck and unable to take 'no' for an answer. Everyone was instantly on her side for this all-too-plausible scenario.

A bulky middle-aged Spaniard from the next table dragged Craig to the floor, tipping over the table, cuffing him about the head, but also dragging Liz to her knees. In this tiny arena, between the overturned table and chairs, she remained manacled by the strength of Craig's grip, despite the Spaniard's attempt to uncurl his fingers. A crowd was above him, shouting. The shame, the embarrassment he knew would come later. He absolutely could not let Liz escape. It had become the one certainty of his life. Trying to fend off the Spaniard with his free arm, Craig saw past him where Liz was delving into her shoulder bag with her free hand. Saw her pass a disposable cigarette lighter to her captive hand. Watched her extract an Estée Lauder perfume atomizer from the duty free plastic bag.

Liz, you wouldn't.

Saw her pull off the cap with her teeth.

Liz, you can't.

Aim the can at his face. And smile.

Liz, no!

Press the button. The searing cold spirit stung his eyes, his nose, his mouth.

No!

He heard the click of the lighter. Expected the agony of the impromptu flamethrower, but it didn't come. A second click. 'Come *on*,' he heard her say. Then he heard a commanding voice, saw the blurred crowd part behind her. Someone grabbed the lighter from Liz's hand. The familiar face of Primo Irujo leaned above him. Thank God, Craig thought. And he finally let go, falling into oblivion.

Gillard came round in an ambulance, a medic at either side, and beyond the open doors it was beginning to get dark. He was asked to count fingers in front of his face. His eyes still stung and his vision was blurred. It was a good hour before he even knew it was the same day, and that he was still at Madrid airport. Only once the medics were satisfied he was not in danger did they allow Sargento Primo Irujo to come in to see him. The Spanish officer stared at Craig as if he was an idiot, and waved a hand in front of his nose. 'You stink like a Moroccan rent boy.'

'It's not the first time I've been told that.'

'We've got her safely locked up. How are you feeling? Do you remember anything?'

'A bit,' Craig said. 'Was it Rohypnol?'

'Who knows?' Irujo shrugged. 'She'd done a good job on the crowd. There was almost a riot when we arrested her instead of you.' He and the medics shared sly smiles and a sentence of two in Spanish. 'But never accept drinks from strange women, eh?'

Craig knew he would never be able to explain to Irujo Liz's hold over him. The hold that she exploited to very nearly escape him altogether. She had known exactly what cards to play.

Chapter Thirty-Five

The newspapers went wild over the discovery that Liz Knight wasn't a murder victim, but a murderer. The story of her life was now played out in extended coverage on TV and radio, and Surrey Police was constantly receiving requests for interviews, most of which were deftly handled by Alison Rigby. Craig returned to a hero's welcome at Mount Browne, even though he was destined to endure a lifetime's ribbing about falling for a spiked drink. Rigby gave him a commendation for the Queen's Police Medal, though after the awards panel examined the full circumstances, it was never awarded.

Elizabeth Knight denied murder, but pleaded guilty to manslaughter on the grounds of diminished responsibility. The Old Bailey jury, told of the huge amount of premeditation that had gone into the killing, had little difficulty in finding her guilty of murder. She was sentenced to 18 years, and transferred to the high-security wing at HMP Bronzefield in Kent, where she was allocated the cell that serial killer Rosemary West had once inhabited. During the trial, the story of her Colombian life since the murder emerged. She lived in the high-altitude university city of Medellin, and had moved in with a history academic, Professor Juan Rodrigo Jimenez, who was completely unaware of her past. She had built a convincing story around the name Pam Jones, and the need to start a new life after her divorce from a violent partner. She spent most of her time studying for professional qualifications that would allow her to build a new academic life at the local university.

Oliver Knight soldiered on as a solicitor, never quite recovering from the ordeal of losing both parents, then getting one back. He never visited his mother. Liz's parents were traumatized by the jailing of their daughter, never accepting that she could have committed the crime of which she was convicted. Her father died within a year of her conviction, and her mother two years after that. Chloe Knight never went back to university. She eventually became a probation officer. Once close to her mother, she never visited her.

But Craig Gillard did.

Just once.

At the prisoner's request, a year into her sentence.

Shown into the interview room, he at first thought she wasn't there. There were only a dozen or so greying middle-aged women, none of them petite or attractive. Finally he saw her, arms folded on a scuffed plastic table, in washed-out jeans and a grey sweatshirt. She was fidgety and her once full head of chestnut-brown hair was lank and streaked with grey. Her face was pasty and lined. She was well on the way to becoming the Pamela Jones she had once impersonated. Only the quick bright eyes were the same.

'Craig, I'm so glad you've come. It's nice to see your face.'

He smiled. He wasn't falling for that one again. It was a face she'd been prepared to set fire to, after all. 'You said you had something to tell me.'

'I want to confess something. A secret I've been carrying with me.'

'I'm not a priest. I can't give absolution.'

'No.' She reached forward for his hand, and he pulled it away. 'I want to confess to another murder.'

Chapter Thirty-Six

Craig Gillard looked around the room to steady himself. There were three female custody officers, all big women untroubled by doubt. 'We could do this in a proper interview suite, on the record?'

She shook her head. 'I just want to tell you. Not anyone else.'

'Okay, then.'

She looked away. 'My parents loved me. That was the first thing I was ever sure of. They doted on me until I was four and my brother Andrew was born. Did you know I had a little brother?'

'I did hear during the course of the investigation. But didn't he die during a road accident?'

She nodded. 'Andrew was what they call a bonny baby. Curly blond hair and blue eyes. Quite adorable. Never cried, like I had. Suddenly it was like I had never existed. I hated him.'

'Childhood jealously isn't unusual,' Craig said.

'I pinched him to make him cry. Isn't that horrible?'

Craig shrugged.

'I pulled the ears off his rabbit. Spat in his food—'

'I'm not here to play shrink to your childhood reminiscences,' Craig said.

Liz smiled. 'Every Wednesday we walked to the library. My mother pushing Andrew, who was just a year old. This day we were early, just returning books, so she left me outside with him in his pushchair. Just for five minutes.'

Craig folded his arms, but said nothing.

'A Land-Rover with a trailer from the Downs had pulled up, at the tail end of a traffic queue. The trailer was full of logs and branches that they had been cutting up on Farthing Downs. The pavement sloped a little towards the kerb, and I released the pushchair brake and gave Andrew just a gentle push. The pushchair ran down to the kerb, tipped and fell between the Land-Rover and the trailer. He cried, but no one could see. The Land-Rover pulled away and my brother was crushed to death by the trailer.'

'You did it? Really?'

'Yes. I immediately ran inside, crying, my usual refuge, and said that Andrew had released the brake. There was a terrible fuss, but I got hugged so hard and so often afterwards that it all seemed a good thing. I was back in the centre of their adoration, more precious than ever. And the idea of killing started to give me a warm feeling. I never had any moral resistance to it. Death was something useful.' She laughed bitterly. 'The papers claim I'm a psychopath. The shrink here said I scored quite highly on the Levenson Psychopathy Scale. But it isn't true.'

'You were just a child,' Gillard said.

'Ah, but the child is mother to the woman, to misquote Wordsworth.'

'You *were* loved, Liz. By your parents, by your kids, even by Martin. And by me. Each of those loves you have thrown away. It was never enough, was it?'

Liz looked at him anxiously, scanning his face.

'It's not true,' she said quietly. 'Think about it. I had accomplished the perfect crime, and was safely abroad. But I came back for Chloe, just as you hoped I would. I risked it all for love.'

'That's true.'

'So I'm not a terrible mother, am I?'

'I don't know, Liz. I don't know.' He got up to leave, and she felt for his hand.

'I love you, Craig,' she said.

'No, you don't. It's taken me a lifetime to come to terms with, but no, you don't love me. You never did.'

He got up from the table, and walked away.

He didn't look back as he passed through one security door after another, finally emerging into the car park. There, on time and waiting for him, was an old green Renault. 'It's done, Sam. It's finished,' he said, as he slid into the passenger seat beside his wife of three months.

Sam Phillips smiled, and kissed him. 'Good. Now, finally there'll only be the two of us.'

DCI Craig Gillard never saw Liz again. But he did return to HMP Bronzefield once more. It was two days after news of

Liz's suicide. She had stolen a DVD from the recreation room, smuggled it back into her room, snapped it, and used the sharp edges to slash her wrists. She had known how to do it effectively: deep parallel strokes along the inside of each arm, not across the wrist. She was found dead on the morning of her daughter's 21st birthday.

The prison governor showed Craig the neat and tidy room that Liz had inhabited. On the wall were two fading cuttings from *The Times*. The first was from the day after she had been sentenced.

Wife Sentenced Over Top Criminologist's Murder

Thwarted academic Elizabeth Knight was yesterday sentenced by an Old Bailey judge to 18 years for the premeditated and calculated killing of her criminologist husband Professor Martin Knight. Mr Justice Kemp described Knight as one of the most 'malevolent and cunning' individuals to come before him, having faked her own death so well that the police and forensic services had been 'completely taken in'. The jury heard how she cheated the entire family out of a multimillion-pound inheritance before fleeing abroad, intending to start a new life having framed her wholly innocent husband for her supposed murder. Professor Knight, an academic star who advised several UK governments, was found dead in a car boot in France in February. (See p.2 for more details: 'Best criminologist of his generation'; Obituary p.10.)

The second cutting was from the day when her death had first been erroneously announced back in 2016.

Mrs Elizabeth Knight

Elizabeth Knight always seemed destined for great things, but her life was overshadowed by her brutal and still unsolved murder in October 2016, when she was 48. Born Elizabeth Bishopsford in 1968, she was already a promising pianist at the age of nine, a runner-up in the BBC Young Musician of the Year aged 13, and a chess prodigy who represented England Girls in the 1984 Budapest Olympiad. She made her way to Cambridge where, by the age of 20, she had established herself as a notable historian of the Spanish Civil War. Her interviews with the last remaining Republican survivors of Franco's jails, later published as Enemies of God, won the 1988 A. J. P. Taylor prize for undergraduate European history, and she was offered an Eleanor Roosevelt bursary and research fellowship at Harvard. Married the following year, she decided to remain at Cambridge with her husband, the noted criminologist Martin Knight. Hugely popular at university, one of her contemporaries, Gerald (later Lord Justice) Cunliffe said: 'Everybody adored her. Always the smartest person in the room, her brains were always tempered with a self-deprecating wit that men found irresistible.' A lectureship at Oxford followed, though ill health hindered her academic progress. She went on to become head of history at King Edward VII school in Surrey and later deputy head. Her disappearance and murder led to one of the biggest manhunts that Surrey Police had ever run. She is survived by a son and daughter.

Crocodile Tears

I hope you have enjoyed *The Body in the Marsh*. If you would like to visit my website **www.nicklouth.com** you can also download a free, previously unpublished short story called *Crocodile Tears*:

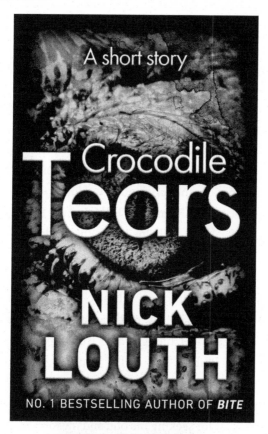

Acknowledgements

A great deal of research goes into a police procedural thriller. I would like to thank Greg Miles and his colleagues at Surrey Police, and particularly retired detective inspector Kim Booth, and his former colleagues in Lincolnshire Police for their considerable help. LSE Professor of Criminology Jenny Brown, and LSE visiting fellow Marianne Colbran steered me on policing policy and criminology. Home Office forensic consultant Dr Stuart Hamilton, DNA expert Hazel Mitchell and Dr Jennifer Ward all helped with the 'body', while Shane Jones of Kent Wildlife Trust and Owen Leyshon of The Romney Marsh Countryside Partnership were invaluable with the 'marsh.' Any remaining mistakes I claim for myself.

I am also indebted to my readers panel, particularly Sara Wescott and Cheryl Cullingford. I would particularly like to thank Sam Phillips and Helen Jennings, who asked to have characters named after them. I hope they are not too displeased with the outcome! Particular thanks to Canelo's Michael Bhaskar for seeking me out, and my former agent Alex

Christofi for recommending me. I would like to thank everyone at Canelo for their energy and enthusiasm in production and promotion, and Séan Costello for copy editing. Above all, I would like to thank my wife Louise, who helped me hatch the plot while on a very long car journey down to southern Spain in 2016, and who took care of everything else while I gradually knocked it into shape over the following year.

Lightning Source UK Ltd.
Milton Keynes UK
UKOW04f0606281117
313454UK00003B/226/P